RESISING JAX

A DARK REVERSE HAREM

CALIA QUINN

AUTHOR CW

Resisting Jax is a reverse harem romance that is only suitable for adults age 18+ due to the adult themes in the content, even though this book does have strong themes, it does have a HEA.

Even though as the author I would much prefer you to go into this book blind. I do however understand that everyone's tastes are different and I would not want to be the cause of any underlying triggers for you the reader.

Due to the sensitive content in this book, a list of CW is posted below.

WARNING:

Breath play; kidnapping; violence; strong sexual themes; trauma; close proximity; close impact play; grief; psychological trauma, dub-con, non-con, torture, knife-play, grief.

While there are many CW there are also some very sweet scenes in this book but sweet doesn't need a CW but there's balance (wink wink)

The non-con in resisting Jax has nothing to do with any of the MMC and is an integral part of the storyline.
Happy reading!
I have no doubt that the Kane brothers will not only heat up your panties but they will melt your heart

Calia Quinn xoxo

AUTHOR NOTE

Are you still here?

Of course you are, you naughty girl.

Sit down, relax

And turn that page like a....

GOOD GIRL.

THE KANE BROTHERS ARE WAITING...

Part I
Jackson Kane

Could beauty tame the beast?
I'm no good for her.
I know I'm no good for her but I
want her anyway.
I want her before I crawl back
into the darkness.
I know it's wrong.
She's like a butterfly.
She's calling me home.
Can you really step into the light,
when you've lived in the dark for
so long?

Jax is also known as Jackson Kane. I just preferred to refer to him as Mr. Grumpy Pants. I'm not sure when his apparent distaste for me started. All I know is that each time he sees me, that smile instantly slips, and it's like he's sucking on sour grapes.

"Oh, hottie alert, hottie alert." Essie squeals excitedly.

"You say the same thing every day." I roll my eyes while the rest of the office erupts into girlish laughter.

I had thought about leaving numerous times, but after working here for seven years, the girls were more like family than colleagues, and the thought of starting over again just gave me a nauseous feeling. So what if my boss hated me? It's not like I had to put up with him for 12 hours a day, I think, with a grimace.

"So you're telling me if Jax walked up to you looking like sin, looking deep into your eyes challenging you to leap, you wouldn't grab that man with both hands and finally taste heaven?" Samantha challenges.

Samantha was always risque of our little group. Her bright blue eyes twinkle at me, challenging me to respond, and her wavy, sun-kissed blond hair waves around while she cackles with the other girls.

"I wouldn't piss on Jax if he was on fire." I spit out.

The sounds of laughter that had spread across the office instantly died down. You would have thought someone had died.

It was deathly silent.

My comment can't have shaken them to silence.

It was just another day in the office.

Spinning my chair around, I'm met with a steely grey gaze that freezes me to the spot.

"Cara, my office now." Jax growls, never taking that stone-cold glare off of me until I rise from my seat and slowly follow him towards his office.

"You done it now, girl." I hear Essie whisper as I pass by the shocked group of women.

The walk to his office takes forever, and all I can hear is the click-clack of my red heels as they hit the stone floor.

He doesn't look back, not once, to make sure I'm still following him, but why would he? Nobody says no to Jackson Kane.

Walking into his office, the air felt stiff somehow, or maybe that is just how I felt because even though I hated working with the grump, I didn't want to lose my job over some girlish banter.

What was I supposed to say when Samantha challenged me? Even though he was the grumpiest bastard I had ever met, I often thought about what his large, calloused hands would feel between my legs. *Shit, no, don't think of that now, the heat travels up my face, and I can feel the sting from the burn on my face.*

He sits, pushing those fat fingers across his plump lips, his gaze still steely, looking at me curiously. I half expect him to tear me a new one, but he stares back at me as I sit at his desk.

Neither one of us says a word.

I'm mesmerised by the slow movement his finger makes across that lip. I can't peel my eyes away from him. Taking my bottom lip gently between my teeth, I wonder how heavenly the grump tastes.

"Wouldn't piss on me if I was on fire." He raises a curious brow.

"I didn't mean that. It's just—you know what it's like out there."

"I'm afraid I don't, Cara. Why don't you enlighten me." I'm sure I see the faint hint of a smirk as he moves his fingers across the dusted stubble that adorns his face.

"Jax—."

"See, you speak to me like you don't hate me, yet you wouldn't piss on me if I were on fire." Once more, that bloody eyebrow raises. I would love to walk around this desk and shave that bloody eyebrow from his face, but then he couldn't raise that bloody thing in my direction.

"It was just—." And I've lost words. There are no words that are coming out of my mouth. Why today, of all days, does my vocabulary decide to have a meltdown? I sit there with my mouth gaping open like I'm surprised. Well, I am surprised. I'm surprised I can't make a coherent fucking sentence.

"Relax, I wouldn't piss on you if you were on fire either."

Charming.

"That is not why I called you in here."

"It's not?"

"Cute, that you'd think I give a shit about your nonsensical office babble, but no."

"Then, what was that?"

"Fun?"

"Fun? So, that's how you get your kicks, Mr. Kane, by making women squirm in your office."

His once steely gaze holds something else. I almost think I see a flash of darkness, but as quickly as it comes, it's gone.

"I need you to accompany me in London. I have a few important meetings and will need an assistant. Do you think you can handle that?"

"Me? You're asking someone who wouldn't piss on you if you were on fire."

"Yes, well, Cara, that's part of the charm. None of those women can string a sentence together when I ask them a question, so you seem like the lesser evil."

"I—I would be honoured, Mr Kane."

"You can call me Jax again, Cara; you're not in trouble." A smirk finally appears on his lips. I'm glad I can amuse the grump.

He stands and walks to the front of the desk, leaning across the mahogany desk with his arms folded. His dark hair falls across his eyes but doesn't disguise the steely gaze he gives me. The conversation is over. He's probably waiting for me to leave.

Standing, I rock on my heels and can feel the impending doom of my face splatting on the ground, but as my shaky legs wobble, it's so much worse. I topple forward and crash into Jax's hard body, and sweet baby Jesus, does he smell like the darkest sin? His hands wrap around my arms with little to no effort; he plants me firmly on my feet, looking up at him. That steely gaze bores into mine.

"I sure hope you can put one foot in front of the other in London." He seemed annoyed, but I couldn't blame him. I had just crash-landed into his body. Nervous laughter falls from my throat. "Monday then, Miss Roberts, a car will pick you up." I nod because I have nothing else to contribute, and his scent makes my head whirl.

How was I supposed to survive three days with my sinful grumpy boss?

Turning, I shoot out of his office and finally collapse against the door. A gulp of air enters my lungs, and I can finally breathe. Had I been holding my breath the entire time? It sure felt like it.

"He has that effect on most women." Sarah smiles.

"He leaves an impression," I utter.

"I have emailed you the itinerary for your trip. Everything is in there."

"Thank you," I smile," you're a lifesaver."

"Just doing my job."

"You coming out tonight?" I ask Sarah.

"You're still going out?"

"After that, I think I need a stiff drink, plus it's Friday; what else would I do," I smirk.

"You know who they invited, don't you?" Her large brown eyes twinkle against her dark skin. Her midnight black hair swishes on the head of her shoulders against her midnight blue pantsuit.

"They didn't?" I open my mouth in horror.

"Oh, they did." She laughs.

"Why? He never comes."

"God loves a trier, babe."

"Probably best he stays away anyway. The grump would probably kill the mood." I walk away with Sarah's laughter echoing behind me and sit back in my chair, ready to crush some numbers. I feel eyes burning a hole through my back.

"You're still here?" Essie asks.

"Where else would I be?" I smirk.

Suddenly, I'm surrounded by a group of vultures hovering over me. I groaned; they would never let me get back to work until I divulged what they deemed office gossip, but I knew once I told them that the chatter would never cease, and I would never hear the end of it.

"Spill." Samantha grins.

"There isn't much to tell." I try to act nonchalant.

"Don't give me that."

"If I tell you, will you let me get back to work?" They all nodded their agreement, but somehow, that didn't seem possible. "He offered me to go to London on Monday as his assistant."

"You and Jax...alone," Essie utters, trying to hide her disappointment, but it was evident on her face.

"Well, I'm guessing there will be other people there, and it sounds boring, but as I had just insulted him, I thought the best thing to do was to agree." They all nod their agreement.

"Guess you aren't coming tonight?" Samantha pouts.

"Three days with that great grump, of course, I'm coming."

"You know who else might be coming." Essie excitedly announces.

"Oh, babe, you invite him every week, and he's a no-show every week. Plus, can you imagine Jax on a night out," I roll my eyes, "he would probably complain the entire night and glare at everyone in sight. Best the boss stays a no-show, uh."

"One day, he might surprise you." Essie offers.

"Well, hopefully, that isn't tonight." I wink.

The chatter dies down, but I can still hear their hushed whispers as I pound my fingers on the keyboard, trying to focus on the job, but I can't.

It's almost impossible.

The only thing I can think of is how heavenly his body felt pressed against mine, the warmth of his hands on my arms spread across my body nearly instantly, and the scent of Jax is something I will never get used to. I can still feel the tingling between my legs at the proximity of being near Jax.

I try to push all those sinful thoughts out of my head, but my head is swirling. The ticking of the clock is like the death of time. Tick-tock, the sound pummels my eardrums, and it feels like the day will never end.

Looking over the itinerary of our three-day trip, I suddenly wished I had refused his offer of being his assistant. I had to spend all of my time with Jax. How was I going to handle that? I barely lasted 10 minutes in his office.

I thought back to when I first started at Jackson Realty. I was qualified; I had spent five years at University studying business management but hadn't quite managed to rank up to my expertise level. It was my dream to work in corporate. I loved numbers, and I was very competitive, and as a fast-paced company, it was exactly what I had been searching for.

I was repeatedly told my talents were wasted here. A rival of Jax's company had headhunted me a few years back, but I had kindly refused. It was better pay, better company benefits and on paper, it was perfect, but you didn't see many companies run the way this one was. It was like we were all a family. Nobody had left when I was here, and everyone who came here felt right at home. I had a sneaky suspicion that they didn't leave because of Jax.

I, of course, understood where they were coming from. I wasn't immune to Jax's charms. Although it appeared, he had no charm on the surface. A man like that didn't need to. It was just something about him. His aura may be addicting and sinful, like carbs. Yes, Jax was like carbs, bad for you but oh so fucking delicious. You knew you'd regret eating them but needed to eat them anyway.

"Earth to Cara." I blink, still lost in my thoughts. "Meet you at THE STARLIGHT at 8 pm?"

"Sure, sorry I was miles away."

"Oh yeah, thinking of the many positions Jax will put you in." Samantha winks.

What an idea, I think with a grin.

"More like what a headache he's going to be."

"One day, you might admit what we all know."

"Oh yeah, what might that be?"

"And spoil the surprise," She winks, "but I will tell you this, your little I hate Jax doesn't fool anyone in this office, least of all Jax."

I clutch at my heart, "I'm positively offended." I slur.

"Sure you are." She laughs as she walks away.

I was the last to leave, as usual. Walking into the cold night air, I feel the biting cold pinch at my cheeks. It made no sense even to me. I always stated how I couldn't wait until the day was over, and yet, I would stay back well over the hours I was paid.

"Are you looking for a raise?" His deep growl sounds behind me. Quickly spinning on my heel, I turn to see that steely grey gaze. "You stay here too long, Cara. Don't you have a home to go to?" He raises those damn eyebrows again, and I fight the urge not to let the annoyance display across my face.

"Funny, Jax." It is the only thing that falls from my lips.

"Seriously though, why do you stay so late?"

"Why do you?" Stupid, stupid Cara. Naturally, he doesn't dignify my comment with a response. "I heard they offered you to come out again." I almost want to slap my hand across my mouth. He grunts at me anyway. "Well, you know what they say, Jax."

"No, but I'm sure you'll offer your pearls of wisdom."

"All work and no play makes Jax a dull boy." I wink and watch his face twist into confusion. That's it, Cara. Keep antagonising the grump, I think with a shake of my head.

I don't wait for a response. I turn on my heels and quickly get into my car. I was looking back at him one last time before I drove home. My interactions with Jax were getting stranger by the day. I'm unsure why he tolerated my insults, but I think it amused him.

Chapter Two

Girls Night Out

Cara

We came to **THE STARLIGHT** every Friday night. Often, it got pretty wild. It was a great way to break up the working week. Walking into the bar, I'm reminded why I need this every week, especially tonight, more than any other Friday.

Walking through the double glass doors, my body instantly relaxes. The smell of sweat and alcohol attacks my senses, and finally, I smile. The work attire and grime from my body are now replaced with a tight black bodycon dress that hugs my curves. The clack of my black heels can barely be heard as I step across the sticky floor. Scanning the area, I find the booth where we sit every week. There were my girls, the source of my sanity. A feeling I had often come to realise as—home.

Samantha

Samantha sits there; her sunlight-golden blond hair falls to her shoulders in loose waves. A red dress that sits on her thighs and red heels. Her blue eyes glisten as she throws her head back and laughs.

Samantha was older than the rest of us, but not by much. The type of women that worked for Jax were all young. I had asked him once why that was, but he had just grunted like it wasn't a concern.

At 33, Samantha was the wisest yet took risks like a teenager. Every night we came here, she would find some outrageous plan that usually involved me making a complete idiot of myself, but God loved her. Did that woman know how to have a good time?

Essie

Essie was more reserved than any of the other girls. Her mousey brown hair is cut into a pixie cut, framing her small face. Her deep brown eyes always made me think of all the secrets she hid within them. Looking at her attire, she wears a long black maxi dress that falls over down to her ankles and black pumps. I'm not sure how she got in here every week with those, but she claimed she would rather stay home than kill herself in 6-inch heels. She was so sweet; you were urged to wrap her in a blanket and cuddle her.

She was the youngest, and it showed. She was only 21 years old and had the biggest crush on Jax. It was heartbreaking because the grump wouldn't give her the time of day. It was probably just as well that all he did was grunt because her crush had grown over the last year since she had been with us.

Her story was sad. Her mother had been put into rehab when she was a baby, and with no father, she had been shipped off to live with her strict grandmother. She had lived a sheltered life but made sure she made it to our girl's night every week. Little by little, she had started coming out of her shell. I smile as I look across at her. Seeing her blossoming into the beautiful woman I saw today was beautiful—a far cry from that timid young thing hidden under baggy sweaters and jeans.

She looks around the room as if she's searching for something. I shook my head. I knew exactly who she was searching for, but she wouldn't find him here. When would she realise that Jax wasn't the same man she envisioned in her head?

Sophie

As usual, Sophie is crammed between them, looking like a movie star. Sophie married young and, by all accounts, didn't need to work, but she said, how else would she get life experience? Her Liam agreed and said gaining independence would be suitable for her. Of course, we all joked that he was her sugar daddy, but I had often had lunch with both of them and even with the age difference, you could see the love between them. Hell, I was almost jealous. Love just hadn't found me; maybe I was too aggressive for love, plus I was married to my job anyway. What did I need a man for?

Sophie has her silvery blond hair pinned up in rolls that fall across her porcelain face, deep, plump red lips and a beauty spot on her cheek. Her blue eyes scan the room. She reminds me of a young Marilyn Monroe, and she certainly dressed the part. I think she couldn't also be looking for the mystery of Jax, rolling my eyes.

Sophie was a different breed, and while I thought she probably appreciated our boss's dashing looks, she did it to get a rise out of Essie, which was mean. Still, she scowled at anyone who held his attention because she had never gotten it.

I never got the vibe that Sophie was purposefully mean to Essie and that she wanted her to get over her apparent obsession with our boss. She would trail her long, manicured finger up Jax's arm, hoping it would get a rise out of her while purring in his ear, but Jax never helped the situation. He would raise that bloody brow and ask how her husband was while the rest of the office cackled while he walked away.

Sarah

Then there was Sarah. She was like the sister I never had. She has such a beautiful personality and an even prettier face. She had been Jax's secretary for as long as I had been there. Sarah was the only one I hadn't seen get all gooey over Jax. She reminded me of a young Halle Berry.

There, she sat as confident as she did at the office. A beautiful silk dress that clung to her slender frame was held only by two thin straps on her slender shoulders. Her dark skin glistened under the low lights of the club.

I wasn't sure what Sarah's story was, not for want of trying. She always looked so happy, but then there were those fleeting moments when a flash of sadness would cross her eyes, but it was only fleeting. Even if she dealt with something dark, I knew she would never let it be known.

She was always a smiling, happy girl in public, but Sarah was a very private person. She was only twenty-three, but she reminded me of a mother hen. Always trying to fix everyone's problems, but I often thought: who was there to fix hers?

The music plays in the background, growing louder and louder as I approach the girls. The smiles instantly rise on their faces as they turn and look at me. Quickly scooting over so I can take a seat in the booth.

"At last, I thought you'd bailed," Samantha screams over the music.

"As if I would miss this."

"Got you a drink, babe." Sarah put the garnished margarita with lime on the table before me.

"Ah, did I ever tell you, Sarah, you are my guardian angel?"

"Not sure they ply you with alcohol." She smirks.

"Why the hell not? How else am I going to make bad life choices?" I grin while taking a sip of my drink.

"If she's your guardian angel, you're my bloody spirit animal." Sophie clinks her glass against mine before we both take another sip.

The chatter finally dies down, and they all dance on the dance floor, keeping them entertained for the next few hours. I finally catch my breath, thinking I'm alone, until I look to the side and see Sarah smiling back at me.

"Didn't feel like dancing either?" I ask.

"No, not tonight." She smiles.

"Are you okay?" I ask.

"I'm just fine, doll, enjoying the ambience before I head home."

"What is home like for you?"

"It's...well, I wouldn't want to depress you with my tales of woe." She takes another sip of her drink.

"Ah, Sarah, you can tell me anything...you know if you're in trouble—."

"It's not that."

"If you're uncomfortable talking about it, it's okay. I just wanted you to know, as your friend, I'm here."

"I don't want to ruin your night." She smiles.

"Ah, what sort of friend would I be if I didn't listen to your woes? Now, none of this talk about ruining nights, spill." I smile.

I felt like I was turning a corner with Sarah. She never openly spoke about her life with anyone. Well, anyone except Jax. I'm sure he had secrets about everyone in the office, not that you'd know because the grump just stomped around like a dinosaur with a sore head. I was unsure if she would tell me anything because the way she nervously bit on her lip seemed like she was pondering if it was a good idea.

"It's nothing really." She sighs, "It's just hard looking after my mother. You know she's sick, right?" I shook my head because I had no idea. Sarah had never broken face. In fact, everyone in the office seemed to think her life was perfect and well put together...I guess you never really do know what battles someone is facing alone.

"I had no idea." I smiled, trying to comfort her, but I knew it wouldn't help. "Is it serious?" I manage to squeeze out, just barely a whisper.

"She is terminal," she sighs.

"Oh, I'm so sorry." Tears fill my eyes, and I rush to wrap my arms around her, and something surprising happens...she welcomes my embrace and quietly sobs. I'm not sure how long we stay like this, but it's the closest I have felt to anyone in a long time.

"I understand." I finally utter the words that I had denied myself for years.

"You do?" I nod, feeling the fresh sting burn behind my eyes and cloud my vision."

"My mother has been in a home for the last few years. I applaud you for keeping down a job and look-ing after yours; I can't imagine how hard it must be for you. I just—." The words get caught in my throat, "I didn't think I could do her justice, the dementia had got progressively worse…" I take a sip of my drink.

"I'm sure she is in a better place. At least you know she's well taken care of." Sarah pats my hand in a motherly way.

"I just feel…"

"Guilty?" She asks, nodding she smiles, "Me too."

"Look at us, bonding and shit." I laughed, but it was much more than that. The conversation and words that had never wanted to leave my throat. Had finally crawled out and found a likely ally.

There were no more words that needed saying; we just sat in knowing silence, understanding each oth-er's pain, and for now, that was all we needed. It wasn't long before the girls ruined our peace.

"Hey, party poopers." We both laugh at Samantha. "Are you ready for the main event?" She winks while directing her words at me.

Well, this didn't sound good.

Anything that Samantha started always spelt disaster for me, but when in Rome.

"Sure, why not." I smile, not really understanding what I have just agreed to.

"You know what time it is." Samantha wiggles her brows in my direction.

"What are you looking at me for?"

"You're tonight's volunteer."

"Funny that, I don't remember volunteering."

"It was a unanimous decision."

"You all volunteered me...to do what?"

"Well," Essie starts, "you won't be here."

"I will only be gone for three days and back before the next night out."

"Yes, well, we volunteered you anyway." Sophie smiles.

"Take one for the team, babe." Sarah slurs.

"Oh, not you, too." I roll my eyes but can't help but grin as I look upon their eager faces.

"Sorry," She shrugs her shoulders with no remorse.

"Okay, fine, want to let me in on your dastardly plan?"

"Double dares." They all scream in unison.

"Oh no."

"What?" Samantha asks innocently.

"Not after last time."

"Hey, how was I to know he had a wife?"

"The funniest part was when she asked if they wanted to do a three-way." Essie throws her head back while laughing maniacally.

"That was not funny." I pout.

"No, the funniest part was when the wife threw that bloody mary in her face." Sophie cackles.

"Yeah, hilarious; never did get that bloody stain out of that dress."

"Teach you to wear white." Sarah laughs.

"Touche."

"Anyway, there should be no wife on this occasion. You're completely safe."

"Safe? With you lot, I highly doubt that."

"Come on, it will be fun." Essie bounces up and down with glee.

"Fine, what do I have to do?"

"Simple, just walk up to the next man that walks through that door and kiss him," Samantha announces.

"That's it? Kiss a stranger?"

"That's it."

"What's the catch?"

"What do you mean?"

"Well, it seems too simple for one of your dares, so what's the catch?"

"There is no catch, but if you happen...to make a connection, well, bonus." Samantha beams.

"Is this a dare or a date?" I raise a quizzical brow.

"It's whatever you want it to be."

"Sam," I groan.

"Honestly, it is just a little bit of fun, but in all the time I've known you, which is what five years now," I nod, "I've never seen you show interest in any man," she pats my hand, "I want to see you happy." They all nod their agreement.

"Well, nobody but Jax." Sophie winks, and I watch Essie's face fall to the floor.

"I am not interested in Jax." I protest.

"Every woman is interested in Jax," Samantha states.

"Well, maybe I'm the exception to the rule."

"Okay, okay, Jax is off the table."

Oh God, I wish she hadn't said that. How many times had I imagined Jax spreading me across his desk, too many times to count, and now all I could envision was being spread wide, feeling his hard body...no, stop. I chide myself.

The heat has crawled to my face and other parts of my body. The heat burning between my legs, not from the excitement of kissing a stranger but from thoughts of Jax that still lingered in my mind. I throw my drink back, ready to meet the stranger who I would devour with my mouth.

"What the hell? You only live once, right?"

"Actually, the Bible says...."

"Ah, babe, I love you, but please, no God in our house of sin tonight." I wink.

I watch as Essie smirks while sporting a lovely shade of red across her face. I knew it was her upbringing, but tonight had nothing to do with her religion. If a man was upstairs watching me right now, I'm not sure he would look on with admiration, more disgust.

Essie was brought up to be a good Christian girl. Had we corrupted her pure mind? I liked to think so, I think with a wicked grin, but in all seriousness, her grandmother had pounded her religion into that poor girl and shoved her Bible verses so far down her throat that when we had first met her, she was terrified of saying or doing anything. If that was the godly way, I would happily burn in hell.

Women had been repressed for centuries; what happened to being independent and taking your power back? I would never tell her what she should and shouldn't believe in. I respected her decision and found it humbling that someone of her young age had seen a higher power to believe in, but there was no place for the holy spirit on these nights out. Any other day, I would happily talk about her beliefs, but not here, not with alcohol running through my system. She deserved a night off, and I definitely needed it.

"What about you?" I ask Essie.

"What about me?"

"See anyone that takes your fancy?"

"Well...I'm saving myself."

"Not for Jax?"

"Of course not." She laughs, but it's not a genuine laugh; it's more like a nervous laugh.

"Can I ask you a question?"

"Sure, Cara."

"If it was possible between you and Jax, what are your expectations?"

"Well, hypothetically, I guess married, children, the white picket fence."

"Oh, babe," I pat her hand like a mother would, "I don't think Jax is the marrying kind."

"What do you mean?"

"Well, in all the time I've worked there, I've never seen him entertain a woman, let alone get serious with one. I just don't think Jax is who you think he is."

"Who do you think he is?"

"A grumpy—."

"Okay, enough of the boss talk." Samantha chimes in.

"But I want to hear what Cara thinks." Essie wails.

"Trust me, honey, nobody wants to hear what Cara thinks."

"Gee, thanks, Sam."

"Stop stalling and go catch you, a man." She winks.

Oh, of course, go embarrass myself by throwing myself at the first stranger who walks through that door. I secretly hoped that she had forgotten about the stupid dare. Still, it seemed even drunk Samantha remembered her evil plan.

"I don't think I'm drunk enough for that yet," I smirk.

"Hey, what happened to you only live once?" Sophie cheekily smirks.

"Who's side are you on?"

"I'm on the side of you walking your fine ass across that room and planting one on the next lucky guy that walks through those doors."

"Fine, but someone else is volunteering next week."

"It's a deal." She smiles.

Standing up, ready to brace myself to walk across the room. A loud thump hits my ass. "Ouch," I cry out.

"Go get him, tiger." Samantha winks, and the sneaky trio laugh right along with her.

Walking away from the girls who put me in an uncomfortable position once more, the adrenaline courses through my veins. I see a guy who doesn't look too bad in this light. Determined, I reach my target, ready to complete my dare and get on with the rest of the night.

Maybe Sam was right; I could make a connection and finally forget about my off-limits boss.

Now, wouldn't that be something?

I saw her.

Dark hair fell across her slender body.

Cara was all fucking legs.

Christ, I had never seen such long, slim-toned legs in all my life. If she had sexy legs, that meant her ass...shit, no, I can't think about her ass, but it's too late. I'm fucking throbbing as I see those long legs striding towards me, but it's not me she has her eye on. It's the douche in front of me.

I can't let her flirt with some douche who couldn't give a shit about her existence. They did some stupid shit on these weekly night outs but never anything like this. And how did I know this? Because unknown to them, I did turn up every week. I felt like a fucking stalker.

They never knew I was here. I would tell myself I was protecting my staff, but that was a lie. She was why I skulked in the shadows. I'm not sure why, but I made it a ritual to watch her every week. God, I couldn't wait to get her alone.

She's so close now. I need to time this—just right.

I can smell her. Just a few more steps. Her scent envelopes me. Sweetness and desire cloud my vision. Quickly moving the guy aside, I thought he might as well be a rag doll the way I forcefully pushed him to the side. He doesn't know it, but he was just about to taste the sweetness of life, and he would have if I hadn't been here.

Her eyes are closed.

Interesting.

My hands fall across her tiny waist. Lifting her body from the ground, I pull her into a secluded corner, gently pushing her against the wall. God, she fits against my body like she's always belonged there. I can hear the gasps of her anticipation, but god damn it, her eyes are still shut.

I shouldn't be doing this.

I know I shouldn't be doing this.

She's my employer, a great one at that. I couldn't afford to lose her. She's as important as Sarah is. She could have left years ago, but she had stayed; why? I didn't know. I was just thankful she had. I tell myself it would have been easier if she had left. How she taunted me and looked at me turned my body into fucking mush. Nobody affected me like Cara did, not that I would ever tell her that.

She had bewitched me the moment she had fallen into my office. She was on the floor, but it felt like I had taken a tumble. Looking up at me with those icy-blue eyes shimmering with innocence, her long dark hair strewn across my floor, I didn't think I had ever seen anything more beautiful.

What were the odds that a woman would turn my head?

Still, she was about to be an employee, so I had to lock down any feelings or desires I felt for this surprise that had stumbled into my life, and that's what I had done. Kept her at arm's length. Kept the conversation short, straight to the point and only about business.

For 7 fucking years, I had done this, but little by little, she had crawled under my skin, and it was becoming increasingly more and more difficult to deny the fact that under it all.

I wanted Cara Roberts.

So here I am in a darkened corner of a nightclub, about to break a pact I made long ago.

My hands haven't left her waist. My body presses harder against hers. I want her to know what she's done to me. I want her to know how she makes me feel. I can't say it in words, but my body can show her how she makes me feel.

A slow gasp leaves her throat when my body touches hers, and I almost lose the will to live.

Pushing my body even closer to hers. I want to climb inside of her. Finally, submit to every dirty fucking thought I've had about her since I first saw her, but I know I can't do that. My face comes close to hers, my laboured breathing whipping against the perfect creamy skin on her face; she sighs.

I'm about to lose control. Allow the beast that has lain dormant within me for all these years to play, give in to the madness and devour her like I always dreamed of. Her long lashes flutter like she's about to open her eyes until they are still.

The stubble on my jawline dusts against her smooth skin; gently brushing my lips against her cheek, I feel her shudder against me. Slowly moving my lips up her face, gently pressing them against her cheek before my lips hit her ear. A long, slow moan releases from the back of her throat.

"You're much too beautiful for a monster like me," I whisper into her ear.

"Jax." I hear her gasp.

Quickly releasing her, I slip away back into the shadows. Right where I belong. Away from something as pure and ripe as Cara. I would ruin her. Destroy the light and bring her into darkness, but I could still taste light on my lips, and it was a delicacy I had been denied for far too long.

I watch her step back out into the crowd. She's looking around. Was she looking for me? Her eyes dart through every corner of the club, but I'm hidden out of plain sight. She wouldn't see me, no matter how hard she tried.

She was supposed to be drunk.

She wasn't supposed to recognise my voice, but she had.

Then she does something that melts my cold, dead heart. She lifts that little hand and thumbs her cheek where I had kissed her. Closing her eyes, she smiles. She fucking smiles, and something inside of me explodes. Shit, I need to get out of here.

I want to stay and watch her. It's what I usually do, but her fucking scent is all over me, driving me insane. I had her, I fucking had her where I wanted her, and I bottled. I shouldn't have spoken to her; now she knew it was me.

God, this was going to be fucking awkward.

Finally, out in the cold night air, I relax. I could finally breathe, but the tension still crawled up and down my spine.

"Jax." I hear my name has been called. With my chest tightness and body stiffening, I knew I shouldn't turn around. I should keep walking, go home and jack off to the memory of her like I did most nights. It was just a fantasy in my head, and that's where it needed to stay.

"Jax." She calls again, and even now, her sweet voice trails straight to my throbbing cock. "Jax, I swear if I have to call your name again—." Her voice drifts off, but her words still linger in the air, and I find a smirk rising on my lips.

Turning, I race towards her. Her long hair wrapped around her shoulders. Her plump mouth pouted as she bit on her bottom lip. I often wondered what entered her mind anytime she did that; probably nothing I needed to hear, not now, not here, not while I was in this state.

"Yeah, Cara," my head moves closer to hers, my mouth hitting her ear once more, "tell me, what you are planning on doing about it?" I whisper in her ear.

"Jax." She gasps, and once again, I'm losing fucking control. I want to hear how pretty she sings while I'm eating her sweet pussy.

"Go back inside like a good girl," I growl.

Shit, she was going to be the death of me, and I would take damnation in hell to see her on her knees being my good fucking girl, just for one night.

This is easy. Just walk away. Walk away and forget this night ever happened. Yeah, right, her body image will forever be imprinted in my mind. A sign of my own torture because underneath my tough exterior, she fucking terrifies me. I know I'm a coward, but I can't go down this dangerous path with Cara; I need distance. I need to go back to when I glanced at her secretly. I'm too close now, too fucking close.

Just go back inside, I silently beg.

"Go back inside, Cara." My jaw clenches because she's still too fucking close, and her scent clouds my thoughts. If she knew every fucking dirty thought I had about her, she would do well to just run, run as fast as she could away from me, but she's so fucking stubborn; she's still standing here looking up at me with those bright blue doe eyes.

Her hand rests on my arm, and the heat from her hand burns my body. I try to keep a poker face, not letting her know how much she affects me. "Jax, come inside. I know Essie will be happy you came...."

"I'm not fucking here for Essie." I spit back at her.

Her eyes widen, and I feel the tremors in her body. Fear? Excitement? I wasn't sure, but I was playing with fire by breathing the same fucking air as her.

"Why are you here then?" She utters.

I'm here for you. I want to scream. It's always fucking been you.

"I don't know."

Her hand moves up my arm and travels up my back. Her fingers lightly trail the back of my neck, and I have to swallow down a gasp that is dying to fall out. Quickly grabbing her hand and pushing my face closer to hers, I sniff her hair, smelling the sweet scent of vanilla and coconut attack my senses. I close my eyes and wish that things could be different, that I could be different.

"Good night, Cara," I whisper in her ear one last time before looking at her face and seeing nothing but disappointment.

Shit, the pain instantly attacks my chest, but it's the fuel I need to finally turn and walk away from her.

One more day.

One more day until my trip with Jax.

I wouldn't have been counting down the days at any other time.

Samantha had unwillingly entered me into a dangerous game that night when she played double dares. The stakes were higher. I knew that. I had wanted to be wild and free just like she was, even if it was just for a night.

Kiss the next stranger that walks through that door.

Easy.

I wasn't that drunk. I knew that I would remember kissing a stranger. It would just be a funny story to laugh over with the girls.

I strode to him with my head held high, flutters spinning in my stomach. The nervous feeling of doing something I shouldn't shot up my spine. I closed my eyes.

Why did I close my eyes? I'm not sure, excitement, fear. I couldn't really understand my motives. He smelt....fuck, he smelt good. With my eyes closed, everything was heightened, and the alcohol running through my bloodstream, I had never been more excited in my life. I swear I had to squeeze my legs together when I felt my body lifted from the ground and pressed against the wall. Okay, now we were talking, he had taken the initiative, and I was only too happy to let him lead.

The realisation hit me. The way the stubble on his face teased my skin had shivers crawling up and down my body. I thought I was going to melt right there. Until he spoke, his voice decadent like dark cream in your coffee on a Sunday morning. I would recognise that voice anywhere, even in my hazy, lustful state.

"Jax," I finally open my eyes, but he's gone.

I should have let him leave, but I wasn't thinking clearly…shit, I wasn't thinking at all. I called him, but he refused to turn and look at me. I wish he had just kept walking because the swimming desire once again crawled across my body when we met. Once again, he had left me alone in the dark, letting me watch him walk away.

It was for the best.

I knew I should have gone in there and enjoyed the rest of the night, but I wasn't sure I could look at any of them without spilling my guts over the man I had repeatedly claimed to hate.

They would just think I went home with a sexy stranger.

It's best that way.

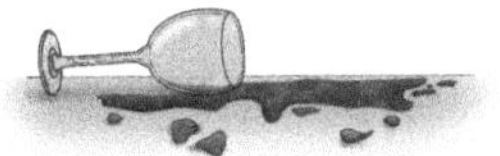

When I arrive at TAVERN 29, the girls are already seated at their usual spot. Laughing and chatting, looking down at the darkened oak table, they've already ordered me a Sangria. Usually, it would take some convincing to get me to drink so early in the day.

Still, a Sangria was a welcome delicacy after my run-in with Jax last night.

Just another day in uptown New York, enjoying their last day before work starts again. The ambience here is what I loved the most. Everyone was already eating and happily chatting away, not a sad face in sight. Soft music plays in the background, instantly calming my body, which felt like it was jolted by electricity. I had repeatedly replayed the events in my head, trying to make sense of Jax's actions, but I hit a wall each time I tried.

It didn't make any sense.

"Well?" Samantha raises her brows with a wicked grin on her face. I knew what she wanted but couldn't give it to her. "Come on, Cara, stop holding out on us."

"I'm not sure I know what you mean." I smile sweetly.

"So, you didn't go home with that tall, dark stranger you locked lips with?"

"Oh, that funny story." I nervously laughed because the story was a lie, but what was I supposed to say? The stranger was Jax, who melted my panties in five seconds. I shake my head. "I didn't end up kissing anyone." Well, it wasn't a complete lie.

"What? Why not?" Sophie screams, alerting everyone in the restaurant to our table because I needed more eyes on me for this conversation.

"Oh," I shuffle my feet beneath the table, my cheeks burning from the lie that is about to pour from my lips. "He was waiting for his wife. I didn't want to ruin another dress." I nervously laugh, hoping that my little white lie would surpass as a decent excuse for why I didn't kiss the stranger.

"Then why didn't you come back and tell us that?" Sophie quizzes me.

"Oh, I don't know...." I sipped my drink, hoping a black hole would open in the restaurant and swallow me up. "Embarrassment, I guess."

"You were embarrassed?" Samantha snorts.

"Yes, well, anyway, I just went home."

"Oh girl, we thought you got lucky." Samantha looks at me with pity.

"Afraid not," I smile, "where's Essie?"

"You know she doesn't come to brunch." Sophie slurs, already well on her way to being merry.

"Of course," I nod, "did I miss anything?"

"Oh yes," Sarah laughs, raising her brows and a glint in her eye, "you missed Essie declaring her love for Jax.

You'll be glad you went home." My brows furrowed, and her obsession with Jax was getting...strange.

But why did I care? Jax wasn't my problem.

He was just my boss, that's all.

"Don't you think somebody should..." The words get lost on my tongue.

"What?" Sarah quizzes me once more.

"You know..." Once again, I shuffle my feet nervously beneath the table. If I'm not careful, I will scuff my heels. "Put an end to her little fantasy." Samantha's brows raise, "I just mean... it's not healthy...you know...for...why are you looking at me like that?" I knew damn well why she was looking at me like that.

"Since when did you care about Essie's obsession with Jax?" Once again, a slight smirk appears on her lips.

"I don't... it's just..."

"Unhealthy, yes, you said that already."

"Well, she's young and impressionable and...."

"You don't want her making moves on your man." Sophie winks.

"My man?" I nervously laugh, but it comes out a little too loud to even sound genuine to a stranger's ears. "Don't be ridiculous, me and Jax," I laugh again, "yeah, when hell freezes over."

"Well, I've heard the temperatures are rising." Sarah raised her glass, and all I could do was groan.

My temperature was definitely rising. My anxiety grew by the second, knowing there was only one more day before I had to face Jax after our run-in at the club. We hadn't done anything, but the way his body had fit so close to mine had my mind going to places it didn't need to. I was instantly reminded of what had happened after I left Jax and got home.

Walking into my apartment, I crash against the door, finally allowing the breath to enter my lungs. How long had I been holding my breath? It felt like I hadn't been breathing while I was with him.

But that couldn't be true.

I would be dead.

It felt like my soul had floated up and out of my body.

I patted my body down to check if I was still alive.

Oh, this was ridiculous; of course, I was alive. So, why did it feel like I had been transported to an alternate reality?

Walking across my apartment, I listen to the clang of my keys as I throw them down onto the white marble countertop in the kitchen. Still in a daze from the night, I walk over to the fridge, popping the cork from my bottle of red wine and watching the crimson liquid slide into the glass.

Finally taking a sip, I kick off my heels and slump onto the plush cream couch. Silence is all around me, back in my domain. Samantha seemed to pity my existence, but I was never sure why? I had everything I wanted: a job that I loved, friends that brought me so much joy, and a beautiful apartment that overlooked the city. What more was there?

I wasn't built for a relationship. A man would just annoy me, and I couldn't imagine having to share my peaceful life with a man. Children? I had never wanted them; they were noisy and messy and needed far more attention than I could ever give them. Could you imagine what they would do to my pretty little couch? I shake my head; no, it would never survive a child.

I was perfectly happy.

So, why did it feel like something was missing?

Perhaps I was overthinking it.

This was Jax's fault; I'm not sure how, but it was. I had never felt anything was missing until I had that tall, dark and sinful man pressed against my body. Maybe that's what was missing. I couldn't recall the last time I had a cock between my legs. Yeah, that must be it; I was just drunk and horny, and yet again, I had gone home alone, but this time, desire had followed me.

Taking a sip of my wine, I can feel my head spin, but it's not from the alcohol, or maybe it was? The images of him replay in my head as if he's stuck on repeat. I can't get his husky voice out of my head; the way his body sends tremors up and down my spine. All the dark and beautiful things I had wanted him to do to me in that darkened corner of the club.

I would have knelt and worshipped his cock if he had asked me to. The way he had touched me and yet not had sent my senses into overdrive. The man nearly had me cumming from his scent alone, but when he spoke, oh God! A song that was ebbed right into my soul. It was like his sinful voice sang a prayer to my pussy.

The heat in my body is rising, lifting that glass to my lips once more and feeling the thick, silky-red liquid slide down my throat as my hand shakes. Quickly placing it on the glass table in front of me, the tremors of excitement crawl up my spine.

My fingers trail down the soft skin of my neck. Closing my eyes, I see him; it's not my finger; it's his. He's in my head, and I can only touch myself just...like...this.

My hand moves slowly down my body until I trail the curve of my breasts that now raise and fall with every anticipated pant that crawls from my throat. He's in my head; every thought of him drives my fingers to move across my supple skin.

He's my dirty little secret.

Teasing my nipples through the thin material of the dress that clings to my body causes excitement. My nipples have already peaked into hardened buds, the desire crawls between my legs, and I'm growing more desperate to touch myself with his name hanging on my tongue.

Sliding my legs apart, I can feel my damp panties press against my pussy, causing a pulsing of desire between my legs. A slow, desperate whimper crawls out of my throat.

I'm so desperate.

So needy.

The desire rips through my soul like a demon trying to claw out of my body. I finally give in, allowing my head to fall back once I've peeled the damp thong that was the only thing between my fingers and my now bare pussy.

My fingers dance across my belly, slowly moving to the crevice between my thighs; with my eyes closed, I hear his dark sultry voice in my head: be a good girl for me, Cara, touch yourself, feel how badly your pussy wants my thick cock to be buried within her.

My fingers lightly graze my wet lips, and a current of desire shoots through my body, pulsing and pressing me to continue the exploration of my soaking pussy.

Dipping a finger into my pussy, my back arches and a loud cry that I felt I had been holding in all day finally falls from my lips.

I'm two fingers in now, and the tremors shoot up and down my thighs; I'm so fucking close. Twirling my fingers, imagining it's him between my legs, I manage to push a third finger in, it's so fucking tight, but it feels so fucking good. Faster and faster, my fingers curl within my drip-ping hole.

The sheen of sweat pierces my body; the faster I push, the more my legs shake.

Cries of desire fall from my lips, and my body is shaking from the impending explosion of passion that threatens to hit my body at any moment.

One more push of my fingers and the words are finally screamed into the empty room as the explosion of my desire covers my fingers.

"Jax," I scream as I ride through the most explosive orgasm of my life.

"Babe, are you okay?" Samantha looks at me with concern in her eyes.

"I'm fine." I try to reassure her. Not wanting to tell her that my little trip down memory lane has me again burning with desire.

"So, are you in?"

Were they speaking this entire time?

What had I missed?

They were all looking at me like I had just landed from outer space, best put on my best smile and feign ignorance.

"Of course I am." I smile, trying to hide that I hadn't a clue what I had just agreed to...once again.

"Great," Samantha clapped her hands, "although I thought you would put up more of a fight."

Uh oh, that didn't sound good.

"So, you want to go first?" Sophie asks.

"Go first?"

"Yes, silly goose, write the dirtiest email first and send it to us all, and we will rate you on it."

"Now?"

"That is what you just agreed to." Sarah laughs.

"But..."

"This is your forfeit." Samantha reminds me.

"Hey, last night wasn't my fault."

"Sure, babe, now get to writing."

This was fine; I could do this. Besides, it's not like anyone else would read this away from this table. I could use him as my muse; after all, unknown to him, he had made me very happy last night.

She slides her body across the bed, arching her back desperately as the sheet's cotton teases her skin; her ass pushes out. She slivers up and down, grinding her hips into the sheets, unaware that you are behind her...

Watching with desperation.

One more move of her ass, and you silently take off that belt.

Wrapping it around her throat, fear and excitement climb through her body.

Pulling her body further towards you, yanking that belt harder around her slim throat, she's gasping for air.

She's soaking; she wants this, you tell yourself. As you ram your thick throbbing cock deep inside her,

feeling her clench tightly around you, you moan your excitement into her ears.

The only thoughts in her head:

AND WHAT WE'RE DOING IS SICK, BUT NO ONE ELSE TOUCHES ME LIKE YOU.

And send.

I'm feeling oddly pleased with myself, grinning like the cat that has got the cream until I look at the faces that eye me with curiosity.

"Well?" Samantha asks.

"I just sent it to you, and it's super hot if I do say so myself." I smile.

"I didn't receive anything."

Impossible.

"Very funny, Sam; I just sent it."

"I'm telling you I didn't get anything, you know if you didn't want to do it...." I put my finger up to pause her as I scan my sent emails and see why it hasn't been sent, but to my surprise, it has; it just didn't go where it was supposed to.

My head is about to explode.

No, no, no, no, no. I silently scream.

But there it is, in my sent folder.

Sent to: Jackson Kane.

There is no such thing as a good Monday.

Ask anyone, and they will tell you.

Of course, nobody had royally fucked up a Monday in such a spectacular style as I had.

Oh, Monday. You sneaky, duplicitous son of a bitch.

How had my day gone so spectacularly wrong? Well, breathing was one thing, and then there was another thing I had done.

Write out a sexy email and send it to the girls.

Another one of Samantha's spectacularly ridiculous ideas. Honestly, I wasn't sure why I joined in on her antics. It always landed me in hot water. It would have been so perfect if they had received it, but no.

No, they hadn't.

I had only sent the sauciest email to my grumpy boss.

My boss, who I had to see in a little over an hour.

Fucking Monday.

The ride over to the company plane is agonising. The awkwardness of him reading line for line what I wanted him to do to me. He had to have opened it by now, and yet, I'm secretly hoping he hasn't.

Of course, it never mentioned his name, but it sat in his inbox like a little cock tease just begging to be opened and read; I was sure he would have read it by now; Jax was meticulous like that. I had thought about backing out, but I couldn't not commit to a job I agreed to do just because I had unknowingly tried to seduce my boss through email.

God, the embarrassment of having to face him.

I board the plane, and he's sat there punching away at his laptop as if he didn't just receive the most embarrassing email. I stand there staring at him, trying to gauge a reaction, but he doesn't even look at me.

"Are you going to continue to stare at me, or are you planning on taking a seat before we take off?"

"I wasn't staring…I was—." My words trail off as I slump into the first available cream leather seat as far away from my irresistible boss as I can.

"Now that you're done staring…"

"I wasn't." I try to protest.

"Once we land in London, we will check in and have a light dinner with some business associates before we retire for the night." I nod, "Cara, I'm going to need you to use your big girl voice; I need you to communicate with me." He sounds stern.

"Sorry, Jax, I'm present; I'm here; that sounds fine."

He doesn't nod or respond; he just returns to his computer. He hasn't even looked at me since I boarded.

Yes, I was right; this was awkward.

"What are you doing?"

"Sitting down," I smirk.

"What was wrong with the seat you were in?" His goddamn eyebrow raises.

Leaning over, I'm so close now, the seductive scent of Jax makes its way around my body, "would you believe me if I said I was lonely." I whisper into his ear.

"No." His answer is firm and direct and, as usual, holds no emotion.

"You know," I trail a fingernail up his bare, tanned arm, his blue shirt sleeve rolled up, allowing the muscles beneath to pop, "if you let your hair down once in a while," my finger stops at his sleeve, "I bet you'd be fun."

My hand is quickly removed from his arm, "we are not here for fun,"

"Of course not," I roll my eyes, "wouldn't want you to combust into flames, now would we." I roll my eyes as I settle back into my seat and close my eyes.

I half expect the grump to retort with a sly comment like I'm used to, but there is nothing. Nothing but the irritating sound of silence that fills the air.

You would think after the panic attack over that email I had accidentally sent, I would cease my moronic teasing with my boss. I wanted to act like an ordinary employee and stop antagonising him. However, my hormones went into overdrive whenever I was near him. I acted like a silly schoolgirl with a crush.

What happened to hating him?

Yeah, what happened to that?

I try to sleep, but sleep evades me; I'm sure I almost sleep, but I hear his silky voice in my ear, smell his sweet scent, and my panties are damp again; my eyes shoot open, and I stare into his steely gaze.

"Were you watching me sleep?" I accuse.

"What? No, I—." A roar of laughter emits from my throat.

"Oh, relax, I'm teasing you," I wink, "unless you were, in fact, watching me sleep," I look at him, trying to gauge a reaction, but once more, I'm met with Mr Serious, "Well, good, that's just creepy."

"Are you okay, Cara?"

"Do I not look okay?"

"You're acting...."

"Yes?" I squint my eyes at him, awaiting the insult.

"Strange,"

"As opposed to when." I nervously laugh.

"Well, stranger than usual."

"Jet lag." I offer.

"I need you on top form. These meetings will be busy, and I need to know that your head is in the game; I can't afford any hiccups."

"Of course, sir, I promise I will be professional." Once again, that dark gaze crawls across his face momentarily before disappearing as if it never came.

I often wondered what caused that. I only ever witnessed it spread across his face when we were alone, and it was only when I decided to be nice because I quickly remembered this was my boss and not some plaything I was trying to fuck.

The image of straddling Jax, what I imagined his thick cock would feel like buried inside my tight wet hole, biting down on my lip, a slight smirk forms.

"Something amusing?" I hear his voice in my ear, and if I don't, I very nearly moan with desire just from that husky voice in my ear. "I asked you a question; you respond when someone asks you something." He once again whispers.

"I..."

"Oh, I never thought I would see the day; you, speechless." He growls, and a tiny moan crawls out of my throat.

"Prepare to land, Mr Kane," the flight attendant interrupts.

"Saved by the bell." He whispers.

Saved by the bell, indeed.

Wait.

What did he mean by that?

Part II
Seduced By
The Devil

They say that even the devil was once
an angel.
That you wouldn't even know
that you were dancing with danger.
How many women had often thought
they were
flirting with destiny but later would
be consumed
by the flames that bound them?
There's a fine line between desire and
danger
And I think I'm about to walk
through the flames of hell,
just to see how pretty those flames
dance around my soul.

"What do you mean they mixed up the reservation?"

"Let's go to the room, and I will explain." His calm voice sounds in my ear.

This man can wet my panties with just the most simple words. I hoped there was a solution to this problem because being this close to Jax made my body do things I couldn't control. Isn't that why I had packed this pink rabbit, to tend to my needs?

We don't speak the entire time in the elevator, but the tension between us feels thicker than usual.

He still hadn't mentioned the email I accidentally sent, but maybe he hadn't got it.

I knew he would definitely have something to say about it if he had. I was very descriptive; it was supposed to make the girls blush, but all it had done was give me an aneurysm.

Walking into the room, it's beautiful. Jax certainly had spared no expense, but in the middle of the room, I saw our problem. Scanning my eyes across the room, it's the only one.

Only one bed.

I was not sharing a bed with Jackson fucking Kane.

"Wait, stop what you are doing right now." He gives me that look that has often irritated me over the years. "Jax,"

"I know it's not ideal.."

"Not ideal? Jax, I can't share a bed with you." I almost scream.

"Cara, it's not the end of the world." A laugh falls from my throat.

"You're funny. You will have to find another room."

"Yeah, that might be a little hard."

"Oh yeah, why is that?"

"There are no other rooms; they are fully booked, but once one becomes available, you are welcome to move rooms."

"I'm welcome to move rooms?"

"Yes, it was your room that they gave away, so, in that respect, I'm doing you a favour by letting you share mine."

My mouth drops open. I can barely believe what I'm hearing. It was like all my fantasies coming true. Sharing a bed with Jax, how many times had I closed my eyes and allowed my toy to bring me to release thinking of Jax in my bed and now it was a reality panic pierced my chest.

"Fine, you can sleep on the floor."

"I'm not paying £3000 a night to sleep on the floor."

"Come on, Jax," I wail.

"Cara, it's not that big of a deal."

"Sharing a bed with my boss."

"I won't tell if you don't." He winks.

"Jax, it's not funny."

"Look, the bathroom is through there. We've both had a long journey; why don't you freshen up, and I will take you for some food."

"Fine, but I'm still not sharing your bed." I pout before taking my suitcase and storming into the bathroom.

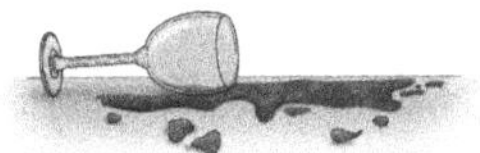

Once the door closes, I finally let out a long, slow breath. The tremors in my body reach all the way up to my chest. This was every woman's dream, especially Essie's. Sharing a bed with Jax, but for me, it was dangerous. I had teased him over the years and pushed the boundaries of our working relationship, intending to get a rise out of him. Still, this situation only left me hot and bothered.

How had the day gone so wrong?

Walking into the hotel, relief washed across my body. I could finally relax, go to my own room, in my own space, away from that sinful man, but it appeared the universe had other plans, and what had my sinful boss done? Laughed it off like it was nothing.

Walking into the bathroom alone doesn't ease the tension trailing through my body. My heart is beating so fast I'm pretty sure it's getting ready to jump ship out of my body, slide across the floor and find a willing body that isn't at this very moment about to have a heart attack with her boss in the next room.

Okay, you can do this. All those inspirational videos lied because no matter how often I recite those words back to myself, I'm not convinced I can. I repeat in the mirror, but the reflection isn't convinced.

I should just go out there and tell Jax that I'm going home, that he will have to find someone else, but we are already here; who would he find on such short notice?

This is silly.

You can do this.

I internally scream because if I screamed out loud, I'm not sure he wouldn't have me carted off to the looney bin; he already thought I was acting strangely. He probably regrets asking me to accompany him on this business trip.

"Cara, are you okay in there?" I hear his muffled voice through the door, but god damn him, he still sounds sexy as hell.

"I'm fine, just getting ready," I call back, maybe a little too enthusiastic. Still, I think it worked because I hear his footsteps move away from the door until I'm once again shrouded in silence, with only the thoughts in my head shouting at me.

Think.

Think, Cara, think.

I can't call Samantha; she would...well, not be helpful.

The other girls would act like Samantha and Essie; I'm sure she would stamp her feet in a jealous rage.

SOS

I texted the only person I could think would be remotely helpful.

Sarah: Hey, what's up? Aren't you with Jax?

I pace up and down, thinking about how I could approach this.

Me: Sarah, oh my God, thank god you answered.

Sarah: Okay, now you're worrying me; what's up?

I'm unsure how to respond; in all my years, words have never failed me, but how do you tell your friend that you're hiding in the bathroom from your boss?

Sarah: Should I call?

Alert him to the madness in here, no way.

Me: No, no, don't do that.

Sarah: Then tell me what's going on.

Me: I guess I'm just freaking out....

The buzz in my hand alerts me to the incoming call from Sarah.

Why would she call?

Didn't I already state that I didn't want that? The buzzing continued vibrating through my hand; I knew she wouldn't stop until I picked up.

"Hey," I whisper.

"Hey, why are we whispering?"

"Jax is in the next room."

"Oh, I thought you would be at the hotel by now, anyway; why are you freaking out? I'm not ungrateful, but I wouldn't have thought I would be your first choice for an SOS call, so what's going on?"

She sounded worried, but why wouldn't she? I had made out that my very life was in danger.

"So, here's the thing: they mixed up the rooms."

"Okay, so just go to your new room; what's the problem?"

"I don't think you understand..."

"That is because you're not making any sense, hun."

"Okay, the short version is I have to share a room with Jax...." I don't think I'm breathing; I knew the situation, but once the words poured out of my mouth, my stomach dropped, my hands became sweaty, and once again, my heart threatened to pound right out of my chest.

"Well, that's not ideal..."

"I'm not done," I wait for a response, but there is silence on the phone, "there's only one bed," I gasp.

"Oh, I see...."

"That's it?" I very nearly screamed, "How is that help-ful?"

"What did Jax say?"

"He laughed it off, said it wasn't a big deal, but it is, it is a big deal."

"Look, Jax is right,"

"Say what now?" I could barely believe what she was saying; my ears were bleeding from her words.

"You are both adults; I know it's not ideal, but..."

"But?"

"You will just have to suck it up, hun."

"Sarah..."

"Look, calm down, make yourself look amazing for tonight's dinner meeting and if it makes you uncomfortable sharing a bed...."

"Yes?"

"Just divide it."

"Divide the bed? That could work."

"Of course it could, hun; now get your butt ready and wow them all with your brilliant mind."

"Thank you, Sarah; I don't know what I would do without you." The tears start welling in my eyes as the tension falls from my body.

"Anytime, hun."

I can do this.

I look in the mirror, and the confidence slowly slips from my face.

I can't do this; I wail at my reflection.

"Cara, have you fallen into the abyss?" I almost chuckle.

"You can't rush perfection," I call back.

Perfection? I was perfectly having a meltdown, and he probably thought I was making him wait on purpose due to the glaring fuck up of our room situation.

Turning the shower on, I know I have been hiding in the bathroom longer than necessary. Any other boss would have sent me home by now, but not Jax; he was patient, even as neurotic as I had been acting. I had to be grateful for that, at least.

The water falls down my body, but the tension never leaves.

Maybe Sarah was right.

It wasn't the end of the world that I had to share a bed with my sinful boss.

This was fine; it was going to be fine.

Jax wasn't interested in me like that anyway; if my ovaries didn't jump every time he was near me, this wouldn't even be an issue.

I could control myself for one night.

I'm sure the room situation would be solved by dawn, and I could build a pillow fort, just like when I was a child, except this time it wouldn't be cosy. It would be keeping someone out, like the monsters we were scared would get our feet as a child.

Yes, this is fine as I blow out a breath and open the door, ready to see what awaits me in the next room.

"Your numbers are excellent this quarter, Jax." Stephen beams.

"Did you expect anything else?" Jax was cocky as usual, but with good reason.

"I'm curious, how did you land the Del Ray property?" Lana asks.

"Ah, you'll have to ask Cara. I take no credit for that one." I instantly blush. Jax giving credit to someone else was like seeing a unicorn farting rainbows. His hand lands on my thigh, but he's still looking across at his associates. His fingers gently move in circles, causing shivers to rise up and down my body.

What the fuck.

"You know, I do believe your blushing, Miss Roberts." He whispers in my ear.

"Jax, what are you doing?" I manage to grit back.

"If you want me to stop...all you have to do...is reach your hand down," his breathing is rapid, and the way his warm breath hits my ear is exhilarating, "near your sweet pussy...." I gasp, "and remove my hand from your leg."

His hand still moves in a circle across my thigh, flattening his palm against my skin, "however, you don't want that, do you?" the blood pumps straight to my head, "you want me to touch you...just like...this." He squeezes my thigh, and I swear I very nearly cum. "I wonder if I reached just a little further...if I would feel how fucking wet you are for me."

"Jax...please." I gasp.

"Shhh, you don't want to alert the table to just how fucking naughty you are for me."

"Jax,"

"You don't know how badly I wish we were alone now." He gasps in my ear.

This wasn't real.

This couldn't be real.

Not Jax, this Jax was daring, sexy and downright fucking filthy. This wasn't the Jax I knew, yet I loved every dirty word that poured out of his mouth and into my ear.

Maybe he had read that email, after all.

"Cara, Cara, did you hear what I said?" Lana asks me, and I softly shake my head, trying to get the mist of desire to disperse.

"I'm sorry," I smile, "I must have been miles away."

"I said how did you manage to secure that property?"

I'm about to respond to her when Jax tightly grips my thigh. "I do believe you are distracted, darling." His deep growl crawls through my ear.

The slippery wetness of my desire coats my thighs. Jumping up, they all look at me. The only person who doesn't seem shocked at my swift movement is the man who caused my body to react this way, and he's currently sporting a knowing smirk.

"If you'll excuse me, I just...need to use the restroom, and I will happily answer your questions." They all nod their agreement, and I don't waste more time at that damn table.

My legs are wobbly, but I finally reach the lady's room. Leaning into the sink with my head down, I hear the door swing open and the click of a lock. Footsteps approach me, and I look down; they are fancy leather black men's shoes.

Men's shoes in the ladies' bathroom?

My head shoots up, and my heartbeat quickens when my eyes finally fall on that steely grey gaze.

"Jax, are you lost?"

"I don't think so." He smirks.

"You do know that this is the lady's bathroom."

"I do."

"Look, I don't know what's gotten into you today, but—."

"You really are oblivious, aren't you." He smirks, and his hands fall down my body.

"Jax, I think...." His hands move over the curve of my ass, and he lets out a long slow growl before moving down my legs. "But...you hate me." I gasp, looking down. He's on his knees, and sweet fucking Jesus, the thoughts running through my mind are definitely sending me to hell.

His hands crawl up my thighs, hooking his finger under the band of my thong, "what gave you that idea." He smirks while raising that goddamn eyebrow. In my haste, I don't even realise that he's removed my thong, and I'm now bare, his fingers sliding up my inner thighs closer to my aching pussy.

"What are you doing, Jax?"

His fingers dance closer, "I told you, I want to see how fucking wet you are for me." A small gasp crawls out of my throat.

"Jax, I'm not sure if you're having a mid-life crisis or an aneurysm, but—." His fingers slide into the crevice between my thighs, and the tremors of excitement pierce my body, "I'm not what you want—." His fingers hit my aching pussy, and my hands land on his shoulders, throwing my head back as small gasps fall out of my mouth.

"Fuck, you're fucking soaked." I hear him gasp while he slides a finger up my slippery wetness. He hasn't even entered me; my body is ready to combust.

He stands, and I'm left disappointed. Did I want him to push his fingers inside of me and finally give me the release I deserved? Yes, yes, I did. I can feel the heat in my cheeks at my own realisation.

"You know, when you blush like that for me, it makes me so fucking hard." He whispers.

"Jax," he turns to walk away, "aren't you forgetting something?"

"Not that I'm aware of."

I hold my hand out, "underwear."

"Oh, these?" He balances my black lacy thong across his finger and allows them to twirl around in the air, "these are mine now." He smiles while placing them in his pocket.

"Very funny." I hear him unlock the door, and he swings it open.

"Don't be too long in here; we still have a business meeting to finish."

"Jax," I scream while rushing forward, running out of the bathroom and colliding with his body. He presses my body against the wall, "Well, I wouldn't have run if I'd known you were just out here waiting for me." I roll my eyes.

He presses his hard body against mine and takes the breath from my body, "Let's get this meeting over with."

"I want my underwear back," I state, no longer noticing that his hard cock is throbbing against my leg.

"Yeah, and I want to spread you wide and devour your fucking pussy that I still smell on my fingers and listen to how fucking pretty you purr for me, but I have to go sit and have boring conversations about a business that is thriving." My eyes widen, "see, we don't always get what we want." He whispers and nibbles on my ear.

"Jax," I moan.

"Mmmm, you do sound fucking pretty when you purr," he runs his tongue across his lips.

"I want—."

"You're going to sit there bare and fucking soaking for me, knowing that any moment I could slip my fingers inside of you, the anticipation of when it will happen will drive you wild."

"Jax," I gasp once more.

"Be a good girl for me, Cara, and before the nights out, you'll be screaming your release into my mouth." He whispers before pulling away and walking back to the table, and I just let him because, well, shit, there are no words.

Jax acts like he didn't just make me walk through the restaurant to sit and talk business with the associates, knowing I'm dripping and exposed.

Honestly, he said the anticipation of not knowing would drive me wild, and he wasn't wrong, but what the hell were we doing? Was I just a passing fling because we were on English soil? I wasn't sure. I wasn't sure about anything.

The only thing I was certain of was Jax was not who I had thought he was. He was dangerous, like fire, and I would get burnt.

I sit there through dinner, and it almost seems agonising; my only saving grace was the wine that kept coming to the table.

Although I was acutely aware of Jax's apparent personality change, I sipped it like a lady for the first time. Being drunk in bed next to Jax was not a good idea.

"Can I steal her? She's brilliant." Stephen jokes.

"No, she's mine." Jax glares at Stephen, and I gently kick Jax under the table.

"Did you just kick me?" Now that glare is on me.

"You're being rude."

"That wasn't rude, darling. It was a fact."

"My underwear is yours, not me."

"Same thing," He smirks.

"That's not…you know what, I'm not doing this with you again." I grit back.

"Doing what?" I feel his hand glide up my thigh, and the sensitivity of his touch shoots straight to my aching pussy. I fight to not cry out. "Doesn't it turn you on knowing you are completely fucking bare for me?" He whispers.

"Jax, I think we are going to call it a night," Lana announces.

"Great," Jax smiles.

"We will see you both at the property conference tomorrow."

Jax says his goodbyes but never gets up from the table. Relief washes across my body because now that they have gone, this little game of his will cease, and while the pang of disappointment hits my chest, I know it's for the best.

"At last, kitten, I thought they would never leave." He gasps into my ear. "Now, where were we?" His hand moved slowly up my leg, dancing so close to where I ached to be touched. "Can you be quiet?" I shake my head, "well, I guess we better be leaving too.

"The dinner is over?"

"Unless you want me to make you scream right here, we can stay."

"But, I thought...."

"What? That was for their benefit?" I nod, "Cara, I wouldn't touch you if you didn't drive me fucking crazy. Do you think I wanted to get hard sitting here at this lunch," my eyes widen, "all I could think about was your fucking pussy, and how much I wanted to spread you across this table and see how pretty you look when you open up for me, I want my kitten purring."

"Jax, I—."

"Come on, it's time to leave."

I wanted to stall. I wanted to say no because while this was the most exciting business dinner I had attended, the stakes were much higher when we were finally alone.

Jax was like a crazed beast, and I wasn't sure who had released the beast from his cage.

His final words are just that—final.

After all, nobody says no to Jackson Kane.

How did I flip a switch so quickly?

I know she's confused, after all the only conversations we had ever had related to the company. It was all work. That night at the club had changed everything. Her scent had embedded its way into my mind. I could fucking smell her on me days later. She had crawled into every part of me, even the dark parts and embedded herself into my soul.

Her overreaction to our sleeping arrangements made me laugh; I tried so hard to keep a straight face while she had her mini meltdown. I was going to try to revert to keeping it all business, but she came out of that bathroom, and something snapped inside me.

The little moans she had let slip from those cock sucking lips had nearly had me bending her over that sink and fucking her into oblivion. Still, she was already suspicious of how I had changed my view of her.

I hadn't.

I had always wanted to devour her.

She just didn't know it.

I watch her as we climb into the elevator, and she's fucking trembling. I could have easily taken her in that damn elevator, but where's the fun in that?

She thinks I have forgotten how she smells, purrs and turns my cock to stone just by looking at her. I will allow her a moment to collect herself. I'm not a complete bastard, but once I walk out of that bathroom, all bets are off.

A smirk forms on my lips when I walk out of the bathroom and look at her propped up in bed. She's only created a pillow barricade between us.

Like that could stop me.

"Well, goodnight." She quickly announces.

"What's this?" I ask, pointing at her lame attempt at a barricade.

"It's called dividing the bed."

"And we need to divide the bed because...."

"Jax, after the way you were behaving downstairs, this seemed like the smart option."

"And you think this barricade will protect you?" I raise a brow.

"I think it exerts a boundary you can't cross." She states that she is clearly pleased with herself.

"A boundary?"

"Yes, a boundary is—."

"I'm familiar with what a boundary is...but tonight, you won't need one," I whisper.

"I tend to disagree, and stop looking at me like that."

"Like what?"

"Like you want to eat me." She slaps her hand across her mouth, "I mean...I didn't mean that."

"Was that an invitation?" I ask with a wicked grin.

"No."

"Ah, just as well; I don't need one."

"Jax, don't you think this is..." She runs her fingernail across those plump pink lips, and I can't wait to see what they will look like, all bruised and puffy.

"Unprofessional." She gasps.

A growl falls from my throat. Even something as simple as running her finger across her lips has me throbbing. In a haze, I throw those damn pillows across the room that stop me from getting to her.

"What are you doing? Do you have any idea how long it took me to arrange those? You are the most—."My lips crash against hers, and I'm instantly swallowed by the desire that consumes me. Her lips press harder against mine with a feverish need, and just when I think it couldn't get any better, she finally does it; her gasps of desire fall into my mouth.

My hands fall down her body, parting her legs to bury myself within them. My lips crash harder against hers, but how she sings for me drives me to insanity. Sliding my hand into her tiny silk shorts, I find her bare.

Oh, what a good girl she is.

My fingers hit her hot pussy, and shit, she's fucking soaking...again. Her head falls back, and I finally release her mouth just in time to hear that long, slow moan fall from her lips.

"See how pretty you purr for me, baby." Her gasps come harsher.

"Please...Jax." She begs with desperation.

"I don't know, kitten...wouldn't that be...unprofessional," I smirk.

"Please." She begs once more.

No turning back now.

My fingers finally enter her, feeling the slush of her desire coat my fingers; her moans are like the sweetest song my ears have ever heard. The deeper my fingers go, the sweeter my bird sings for me. Her body is trembling; she's so close. Sliding my fingers out of her sweet pussy, I bring them to my face and suckle on them like the sweetest dessert I've ever tasted, "Mmmmm, delicious." I utter.

"Why did you stop?" She wails.

"Oh, you thought your release would be that easy?" I cock a brow, "if you want it, Cara, you'll work for it."

Her eyes widen, but still, she says nothing. Removing those tiny shorts, I can see the sheen of her desire on her bare clean shaven pussy, so fucking tidy and delicious with only a strip of hair that stops at her clit.

She looks fucking delicious.

Sliding my hands up her body slowly before I get the urge to dig my face into that sweet pussy, pushing the silk vest up and over her head, I watch with admiration as her large pert breasts bounce. Taking the pink bud of her nipple between my teeth, I allow my tongue to gently stroke her.

"Oh fuck," she cries out. Moving my lips across the bud, I gently kiss it before moving away from her and laying back on the bed with my hands behind my head.

"Is that it?" She asks.

"I told you, kitten, you have to work for it. Now crawl to me."

"You can't be serious." She laughs.

"How badly do you want to cum?" A little purr falls from her lips, "crawl."

She looks like she's contemplating my request. She looks so shy and innocent, and if that look alone doesn't make my cock throb. The anticipation nearly kills me, and then she perches that sexy ass in the air and starts crawling around the bed.

Opening my legs to allow her room to crawl up to my body just as I intended, she stops. Sitting on her knees, pouting.

"What's wrong, little bird?"

"No fair, you still have clothes on." That was a slight exaggeration, all I was wearing was grey sweats, and if she would just crawl and peel them away, she would see how fucking hard she makes me.

"Do you need instructions?" I cock a brow, "fucking crawl." I growl.

A moan falls from her lips before she assumes her position crawling in between my legs, and I want to just ram my fucking cock inside of her, watching her slowly crawl up my body. She's even more perfect than what I had envisioned in my head.

Her hands crawl down my chest, her lips softly kissing my neck, and an explosion of emotions erupts deep within my soul.

"Oh fuck, kitten." I gasp.

Her head moves down my body as she softly leaves kisses down my body; my body is on fucking fire. I'm trembling with desire. Me? I've never trembled at anything, but she's brought me to my fucking knees. She doesn't even know how sexy she looks right now. Still, if I could bottle this memory to revisit anytime I felt sad, I would forever be happy, lost in this moment.

Her plump supple lips press against my skin, sending shivers straight to my cock. If she kept this up, I would cum before she even got to remove my sweats from my body. Her nails hook under the band of my sweats, and she looks into my eyes as she slowly peels them from my body, never breaking eye contact. A slight smirk appears on my lips. She was the fucking devil.

"Come here, kitten." I wave my finger suggestively to get her to come towards me.

"Jax," I raise a brow, "I don't think that's...." Her eyes widen while she looks down at my hard cock, "going to fit." She gulps.

"Ah, don't worry, kitten," she crawls up my body, laying her head on my chest, and it feels close to what I would assume home feels like. "We'll make it fit," I whisper into her hair.

Her hands press on my chest to aid her in sitting up. She has her body raised above my cock. I can feel her body trembling; she's probably excited at finally getting the release I promised her.

"Only the tip."

"What?"

"You did so good, kitten, but you've only earned the tip."

"Jax, you can't be serious," I smirk.

"Mmmm, let's see how wet you get, and then ask me if I'm serious." Her cheeks blush with embarrassment. If she thought this was only torturing her, she didn't know how badly she affected me.

Gripping hold of her hips, I slowly lowered her onto my cock.

Fuck, she was so fucking tight.

Moving my hips, I encircle her hot wet hole, trying to gain entry until I finally push the tip through her wet pussy. "Oh, fuck." I cry out.

"Now move, kitten, but don't push down, only the tip, remember." She nods and slowly moves her hips in circles; the gasps and moans fall from her lips. The grip I have on her hips tightens.

"Oh, Jax," she cries out, moving faster with each groan that falls from her lips.

The way she fucking purrs hits me in places I've never felt before. She circles my cock like she's starved for it. Each fast movement against her dripping pussy brings the beast out in me.

"Kitten, fuck, that feels so good. You're fucking soaking." I manage to grit out. The grip on her hips is tighter, leaving my mark on her body and claiming her as mine before I can take no more.

Thrusting my cock deep inside of her, a piercing scream falls out of her throat. "Pleeease fuck me.... harder...Jax, oh fuck," she cries.

Fuck, she feels good. Too fucking good.

My hands slide up her back, feeling her velvety soft skin against my rough palm; desire shocks pierce my body. In one manoeuvre, I tighten my grip on her neck, listening to the gasps still falling from her lips. Flipping her beneath me, her eyes widen with shock. A slight smirk appears on my lips.

"Was I—."

"You were perfect," I brush her silky dark hair away from her eyes, "that's better; now I can see you looking at me while I fuck you." My cock twitches inside of her as soon as the words leave my mouth, and a small moan climbs out of her throat.

Her eyes flutter close, "no kitten," her eyes quickly open, "watch me...while...I...fuck you." Her eyes widen once more; gripping her legs, I throw them over my shoulders; her breath seems stuck in her throat, "breathe, kitten,"

"Jax...I...its..."

Thrusting slowly inside her, the screams fall from her body, "it's too much, fuck, it's too much," she cries through her screams of pleasure.

I'm so fucking deep; her pussy is clenching hard around my cock like I'm stuck in a fucking vice. The jolt of desire runs up and down my cock with every slow thrust I make inside her, and the screams fall from her body, "it's too much, fuck, it's too much," she cries through her screams of pleasure.

"Fuck, kitten, you're so...fucking...tight...."

"Jax...I...oh fuck," I twirl my hips, sinking my cock deeper inside her dripping pussy; with every thrust, I'm losing my goddamn fucking mind, but she feels so fucking good, I don't want to stop.

"Please...oh god," she cries as I thrust harder inside her, "Jax...it...hurts...oh fuck," she moans.

"Oh kitten, you feel...so...fucking....good," I gasp through my own mounting pleasure coursing through my body at an alarming rate.

Flipping her legs around my waist, I see the relief cross her face, her arms linger across my back, and her touch causes the beast to once again crawl from my body and into this moment.

"I want you sore kitten, I want you so fucking sore," I growl as I press my hips hard against hers; a piercing scream crawls out of her throat, "I want you to feel fucking empty and desperate to once again feel my thick cock inside of you,"

I don't want to hurt her...well, not much, I think with a grin; I want to brand her with my cock like she branded my thoughts in an all-consuming obsessive manner; every time she walks, she will remember why it hurts, and she will beg for me to do it again.

I feel her nails dip into my skin, and the piercing pain sends a shockwave of excitement through my spine; gripping tight on her hips, I roll my body hard against hers; the moans that fall from her throat are incoherent, and my cock is soaked with her juices, my other hand reaches for her mouth, pressing my hand firmly across her mouth and nose, she struggles, her pussy tightening around my cock, I'm so fucking close to exploding.

She shakes her head, fears in her eyes; the little line of tears that crawl out of the corners of her pretty blue eyes does nothing for her; every little tiny drip of water that crawls down her cheek makes my dick harder.

Pushing deeper inside of her, I feel her body still. "Don't worry, kitten, relax; I won't let anything happen to you, relax," I whisper into her ear, "let go...." Her body relaxes beneath my touch, pressing my hand harder against her mouth; a glazed-over look overcomes her, pushing faster and faster; my grunts crawl out in an animalistic growl until I finally release, pouring all of my hot cum deep inside of her, hot willing pussy.

"Who's my good little cock warmer," I whisper before finally releasing my hand and watching as she finally sucks in the air that was previously restricted.

"Jesus Christ, Jax," she gasps, "you're a fucking animal," she smiles.

"Oh, kitten, you haven't seen anything yet,"

I feel soft kisses between my legs. The sensation caused my body to stir in my sleep-induced state.

I must be dreaming.

The pleasure climbs through my body, and the skin against skin never leaves; a sliver of ecstasy crawls up my spine as I feel something warm and wet hit my aching pussy.

My eyes flutter open, and I look down to see a head of dark hair nestled between my thighs, "Jax," I gasp.

His head rises until I stare into his grey gaze, "Good morning, kitten."

"Uh, what...what are you...oh god," my back arches as I watch his long, pink dexterous tongue flick out against my clit.

"I'm afraid I didn't keep good on my promise last night," I look at him curiously, "I promised you'd scream your release into my mouth, but I got carried away," he smirks.

"You don't have to..."

"Oh, I know, kitten, but I fucking want to, and I never make a promise I can't keep."

"Jax..."

"Lie back, kitten, you'll enjoy this," I once again look at him curiously, "I promise," he whispers before his head is once again nestled between my thighs.

What was that saying?

Lie back and think of England...why the hell not.

My head flops back onto the silk pillow supporting my head. I wait with bated breath for the desire to once again crawl through my body, but nothing happens.

Why did this man repeatedly choose to torture me?

Looking down, he's been waiting for me to look at him; he had the patience of steel. His eyes find mine, and the naughtiest grin I've ever seen quickly spreads across his face.

He pushes his lips together, and a tiny whisp of air hits my pussy, causing my body to writhe with desire; once again, he pushes air through his lips, hitting my pussy, "Oh, fuck," I cry out.

"Are you sore, kitten?" He asks me while still blowing his hot breath against my pussy.

"Yes," I gasped.

"Better kiss you better than, kitten,"

Oh god, this man was going to destroy me.

Last night still felt like something I had dreamed up.

Jax was like a machine; I could still feel the twinges of pain between my legs from where he had roughly pounded his thick cock into my aching pussy. He was relentless; I had cried out in pain, hoping for some relief and yet wishing the night would never end. Still, as the tears had fallen down, this seemed to have only spurred him on to fuck me into oblivion.

I hadn't even expected him to be still here in the morning. Didn't men fuck and run?

But there he was, between my legs.

My little beast.

I hadn't been with a man since my last tragic relationship if you could even call it that. Carter was that toxic you'd swear off men for life, and I had, until last night.

Carter was perfect when we met, or maybe I just couldn't see him for what he was….a narcissistic prick who only enjoyed hurting others; if you were miserable, he was happy.

I had never thought I would recover from the mental slavery he had bound me in.

Being stuck in a prison of the mind is a fate worse than death.

I almost lost my fight, but I managed to claw my way back into society and never looked at another man again. Well, not until….Jax.

"Hey," I raise my head and see his eyes fill with concern as he gazes at me.

"Hey," I smile.

"We can stop…." I shake my head, "Cara…"

"Don't you dare stop," I smile, finally admitting to myself that I might actually want this; I might actually want him.

I lay back again, awaiting the pleasure that I know will course through my body. However, once again, the anticipation dies, and nothing happens; I'm just laid there with an empty space between my legs, looking down. There is no head of thick dark hair between my legs. A crease of confusion crosses my brow until my body is pulled across the bed and laid on his chest.

What was I supposed to do now?

I just lay there at a loss for words, listening to his heartbeat against my head; as soothing as it feels, the confusion never leaves. His hand softly strokes my hair, and against my better judgment, my eyes flutter close, and I finally...exhale.

"Jax?" I softly call out to him.

"Yes, kitten."

"Why did you stop?" I feel my body once more being moved; looking into his grey eyes, I notice a softness to them that I hadn't previously seen.

"Sometimes it's not pleasure someone needs; it's comfort."

"That's what you think I need?" I gasp.

"I'm not sure what you need, kitten, but I wanted to comfort you so that you'd know that if you ever decided to open up and tell me what you needed, you'd know that it was safe to do so."

He reaches down and kisses the middle of my forehead ever so gently. As his lips softly press against my head, it's the most intimate gesture I have ever experienced.

Once again, I close my eyes and just allow my body to get lost in the moment.

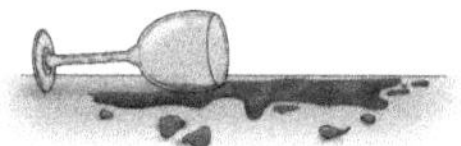

Standing in the boutique, I'm oddly aware of my own reservations. How had I not prepared for this? I knew that this getaway would take me by surprise, and when Jax had asked me if I had packed a gown, I almost laughed, thinking he was joking.

It turned out, on this occasion, he wasn't.

"You didn't need to come with me," I say for the millionth time this morning.

"Cara, I know you like to control everything around you, but on this occasion, you will just have to accept that I need you to look the part."

"You need me to wear a gown to a property conference?"

"Yes." He states sternly. "Now go try on your dresses."

"Well, what are you here for then?"

"A second pair of eyes," he smirks.

I don't even dignify that with a response as I walk away from him to the changing room that houses all the dresses he deems suitable for the event. Walking into the room, it's larger than I expected. I wasn't sure what I expected, but it wasn't...this.

It is wall-to-wall cream...with plush futons and floor-length mirrors. My eyes widen as I scan the area. I had expected a tiny cubicle with one mirror and a curtain door, but this had an actual door you could close and everything!

The dresses were set up on little gold hangers. Ball gowns. I inwardly groan. I hoped that was Jax's sense of humour, which I still didn't understand. When he was sarcastic, I could never define it as when he was being serious. In fact, I was pretty positive the man didn't understand the concept of sarcasm.

The first dress I see isn't so much as a ball gown. It reminds me of a ballerina dress, pale pink, that puffs out and sits above the knee. It is pretty; the skirt flows out, shimmers, and glitters under the light. As I sway, I oddly feel all girlish. All I need now is some little glass slippers. I find myself smirking at my ridiculous thought in the mirror.

"Something funny, kitten?" His voice jolts my body against the mirror, causing my back to crash against it; looking into his grey eyes, I wonder how long he has been standing there.

"Jesus, Jax, are you trying to give me a heart attack." I held my heart in case my dramatics weren't enough to show him that he startled me.

He looks me up and down, "It's pretty, but I don't think it will work for tonight."

"No, I suppose not." I smile.

"I didn't think this would be your first choice. This was put in here for something..." he places his thumb across his lips, "different."

"Something different?"

"Yes, kitten," he moves towards me, but I have nowhere else to go. I'm already backed into the mirror. "Don't worry, you're not staying like this."

"I don't understand Jax." I feel my body being picked up and laid across the fluffy cream futon that faces the mirror.

His hands move up my legs slowly, leaving pimples of excitement in their wake, "you see, kitten, I want you in a princess dress so I can make a fucking mess of you, so you can look like a fucking sweet and ripe little princess who gets embarrassed about making a mess of her pretty dress."

"Jax," I gasp.

"You will lie there and watch yourself in that mirror while I fuck you. You're going to see every dirty little face you make, every fucking blush until you're in such a fucking state.... you're going to scream for me, kitten and show me just what a dirty princess does."

His hands clasp my thong, dragging it down my legs, "Hmmm, just how I like you, bare and fucking soaking...are you excited, kitten." A moan slips out of my throat as he bunches the skirt to my waist, spreading my legs wide, "that's right, kitten, you open wide for me."

"Jax, we can't...somebody might hear." I can feel the heat rushing to my face. Everything about this man had me feeling naughty, and it caused me to blush with each dirty act he had put me in.

"Good kitten, then they'll know who you belong to."

God, what a thought.

"Every..." his lips hit my thighs as I slowly feel his kisses, "single..." moans fall from my lips the closer his lips get to my aching centre, "inch of you..." his tongue slivers out, causing my body to writhe with desire, "is mine."

His kisses move to my aching pussy, I have never been into voyeurism, but this man had me melting beneath his touch. The moment his sweet lips hit my pussy, I'm in a daze, completely taken over by the climbing desire that rushes through my body, and I no longer care who hears.

When his delectable tongue slides up my lips, my body is overwhelmed with desire, and I see stars. The moans fall out of my mouth like bolts of electricity. His tongue slowly glides up and down, flicking harder with each stroke, "oh god, Jax," I scream into the room.

"God...you taste fucking sinful, kitten." I look down and see his eyes staring into mine; the heat creeps into my cheeks. I want to look away but try as I might, I can't bear to tear my eyes away from his.

The naughty little smirk his face holds is enough to make my body tremble, "god, I love how your body reacts to me, kitten, now let me hear you fucking purr."

His head dips back down to the crevice between my legs, and the light brushing of his hair against my skin causes goosebumps to crawl through my body. His lips clamp down around my clit. I can hear the slurping from his mouth as he flicks his tongue across my clit, devouring me with his delectable mouth, pushing me deeper and deeper over the edge. I cry out my desire, my back arches, and my hands plummet into his hair, pushing him deeper into my pussy.

"Oh god, Jax...fuck...just like that...oh fuck.." I scream into the room.

His tongue travels up and down my pussy, and my legs shake with his feverish action. I'm so close, I can feel the building pleasure plummet through me like it's bursting through my veins...then he finally enters me, and it's like seeing colours for the first time.

Jax is relentless with every lick of my pussy, and my legs shake with anticipation. My climax is stronger than I had anticipated. The orgasm erupts through my body like a flash flood; waterfalls of pleasure immediately drench me. I can't even analyse what is happening to me. I'm just breathing and moaning, clawing at his head, with the sensations rippling through my body.

"Oh...fuck...just like that...fuck...please, don't stop." I'm so breathless, and I just can't stop the words tumbling out of my mouth.

Jax plunges his fingers into me, and my body can't handle any anymore as my walls constrict around his fingers. My body is entirely encompassed by pleasure.

The instant I feel his tongue lick up my juices, I still tremble with my orgasmic release. Jax pulls me in for a cuddle, but I can't even think straight.

My heart is hammering in my chest, my body is numb, and my head is swollen from the euphoric feeling that has taken over my senses.

Jax kisses my head, "you are fucking gorgeous, Cara." He whispers into my ear.

He settles in behind me, pulling my body towards his. I'm breathless. I still can't move. The tremors penetrate my body. Looking into the mirror, I see my flushed face, my hair falls around my body in a tangled mess, my lips are puffy and bruised, and my cheeks adorn a flush of pink.

God damn him, he was right.

I'm a mess.

His hand crawls around my throat, pushing my head up to stare at my own reflection, "Look how pretty you look, kitten, my dirty little princess in her princess dress," his head moves close to mine, "Look how fucking delicious you look when you get fucked." He whispers.

"Jax," I gasp.

"So fucking pretty, kitten."

Most people would assume that a property conference would just be suits standing around chatting, but as I walk into the ballroom. Yes really. A bloody ballroom dripping in gold.

The scent of expensive cologne and champagne attacks my senses as soon as we enter the room. Men are dressed smartly in suits, and the women are hanging on their arms in their pretty gowns.

My chest tightens with a single thought: I don't belong here. I stop walking and stand like a living doll, letting my eyes roam across the scene before me. I knew this would be a fancy affair, but I had never expected this grandeur.

"Kitten, are you going to stand there all night." Jax gives me an amused smirk.

"I don't belong here," I whisper.

He grabs my hand, pulling me back out of the room; his hands fall across my waist, pulling my body against the wall; every touch ignites a fire deep within my soul.

This man can ease my mind with just the simplest of touches, and I'm afraid I'm about to fall if I'm not careful.

His scent moves across my body, and I silently breathe him in, intoxicated by his scent alone, "kitten, if anyone belongs here, it's you." I shake my head, "come with me," he sternly commands while grabbing my hand and walking me down a slim, well-lit corridor.

"You see that." He points to yet another floor-length mirror.

"Jax, as good as the boutique show was...I don't think..."

"Look." He commands once more.

"Jax, this is stupid." I feel his firm grip on my chin, forcing my eyes to meet my reflection in the mirror before us.

"What do you see?" He whispers in my ear.

"I...I don't know."

"When you look at yourself, what do you see?"

I wasn't sure what the point of his little exercise was, but I didn't see anything I hadn't seen any other day. I looked in the mirror. Was I supposed to be seeing something different because he had put me in a fancy dress?

"Jax, we are going to be late...."

"Let me tell you what I see, kitten." His hands move up my body; I watch as he moves my hair away from my neck. His fingers trail my neck, and I shudder beneath his touch.

"I see a beautiful," his lips fall across my exposed neck, "woman with the most magical eyes I've ever seen," his lips once again caress my skin. His tongue gently glides across my skin, causing little whimpers to fall out. "Every part of you is perfect, kitten," his hands move down my body, "You're so fucking sinful, kitten; I want to fucking bury myself within you all the time."

"You would say that," I gasped.

He quickly spins me around, pushing my body into the wall; I feel his body press hard against mine, "fuck, kitten, don't you see how fucking amazing you are?"

He's staring into my eyes like he's staring into my soul, "I...fuck, Cara, you belong, you fucking belong." He gasps, pressing his head against mine.

"If I say I belong, can we go back?"

"Only if you mean what you say."

"Jax, I feel out of place in there...."

"I just wish..." my eyes widen, waiting to hear what he wishes, but his head charges forward, his lips brush against mine, covering my mouth with his; tingles rise up and down my body when his tongue flicks out, searching mine, and once his tongue hits mine a surge of desire shoots through my body.

Heat and electricity dance together with want and desire. "I wish you could see yourself the way I see you; then you'd never doubt that you belonged." He whispers against my mouth.

His words crawl into my heart in moments, and I'm pounded with a fear I never thought I would feel.

It was fine lusting after my boss, but I couldn't have feelings for him; I was just getting lost in the moment. I couldn't allow myself to feel something for him; this was only temporary, but the threads of passion inter-twining around my soul would last a lifetime.

"Are you ready to go back inside with the confidence that you belong?" I just nod because, try as I might, every moment with Jax made me fall; this was never supposed to happen. I couldn't fall for Jackson Kane.

"Hey," his fingers brush against my cheek, "are you okay?"

I smile, "I'm fine, feeling better." His brow creases, "Honestly, I'm okay; let's get this over with."

I know he's dubious of my confession, and deep down, I'm not okay; I'm not okay at all. A storm breeds inside of me, but I can't break face. Whatever the situation with Jax, I need to paint a smile on my face and do my job.

After all, the show must go on.

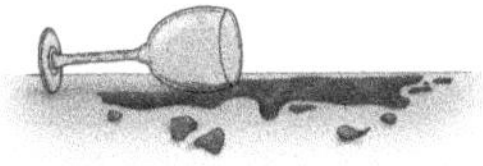

Walking back into the ballroom, I feel a certain ease. The terror pounding in my chest had nearly dissipat-ed, and the feeling that everyone was looking at me like I was the missing link had been removed from my thoughts.

I guess inspirational pep talks did work, after all; that or it was the warm hand clasped in mine that I hadn't noticed until now.

"Jax, you can let go now...you don't want people to think...."

"Now, kitten, why would you assume I give a shit about what people think." He raises that damn eyebrow while he caresses my face with his other hand.

"Jax..."

"I would spread you wide right here and taste every part of your delicious body just so everyone in this goddamn room knew that you were fucking mine."

"Well," I blush, "that sure would be an event they never would forget."

"Come on, let's get you a drink."

I walk through the room; every person we pass doesn't look at me with disgust or bitterness as I had expected; they greet me with smiles and warm greetings.

The moment the champagne passes my lips, I feel the bubbling delicacy slide down my throat and instantly relax. At the same time, an explosion of flavours erupts inside my mouth.

Taking the garnished strawberry from the tall glass, balancing it between my fingers and wrapping my lips around the ripened fruit, squeezing my lips together, I bite down and taste the sweetness of the fruit and close my eyes.

"Jax," I hear a deep, silky voice behind me.

"Elijah," I hear the surprise in his voice, "I didn't know you were coming to this; I thought you hated these conventions."

"Oh, I do, but I thought something interesting might happen."

"Like what?"

"Well, you never can tell... aren't you going to introduce me to your...friend?"

I open my eyes and swing around.

I come face to face with the man behind the voice.

Deep amber eyes that swim with glitters of gold, tanned, dark hair cut short and, my god, a face that must have been carved by the gods. I gulp down the last strawberry as I gaze into his enchanting eyes of gold.

"This is...Cara." Jax grunts.

"Oh...this...is...Cara." He smiles.

"You've heard of me?" I ask, puzzled.

"Jax might have mentioned you before."

"Funny, he never mentioned you." The heat blows my face, "I'm sorry that was rude...I just meant..."

"I'm Elijah." He holds his sizeable, tanned hand out towards me, and I look at it like it will bite me. "Well, don't leave me hanging, darling." Slowly, I take his hand in mine, and he does something surprising; he lifts my hand and places his lips across my hand, placing the sweetest kiss.

My eyes widen, and the tender touch causes a swelling of desire to crawl through my body.

"Well, aren't you charming?" I gasp. "It's a pleasure to meet you," my eyes meet his, "Elijah."

He pulls me closer, his lips hitting my ear, "The pleasure was all mine, darling." He whispers.

"Elijah," Jax sternly warns his friend while pulling me back beside him.

"I was just being...nice."

"Since when did you do nice?"

I could see them sizing each other up. Jax was scowling at the stranger who had shown up out of nowhere, and Elijah was smirking at him like he was enjoying taunting him. I didn't want to be in the middle of whatever this was.

"Well, I'm going to mingle, and you two can do whatever you are doing right now."

"Cara..."

"You seem to have something to discuss that doesn't involve me."

"We don't." They both scream in unison.

I shake my head at them both, "Jax, I will just be mingling. That's why you brought me, isn't it?" He frowns, "Elijah, nice to meet you," I nod.

"Until next time, darling." I just nod as I turn and walk away from them; turning my head, I see them both watching me as I walk away.

I wasn't sure why he thought there would be a next time. I wasn't even sure who the mysterious guest was, let alone why there would be a next time, but his presence had made Jax tense, which....intrigued me.

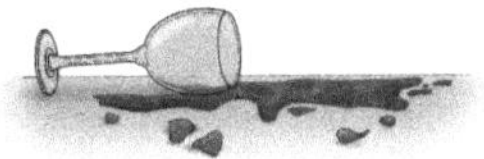

I pick up another flute of champagne on my way to the circle of women and men who are happily chattering away. I spot a familiar face among the crowd, slipping into the bodies as if I belonged there. I sip champagne and listen to the gossip that ensues.

"Did you hear the Oak Haven Mansion has been put up for sale?" I hear Lara announce.

"Nobody will sell that." The small bald man next to her shakes his head.

"Is it a good investment?" I ask.

"Oh yes, but it doesn't come without...issues," Lara responds.

"Issues?"

"Well, they say it's haunted." She whispers to the group.

"Oh, don't fill her head with such nonsense; everyone knows the only reason that house is still on the market is the deaths." The short man gasps.

"Deaths?" I ask.

"Everyone knows about the....accident."

"It wasn't an accident, and you know it," Lara argues, "everyone who occupies that property...well, you know." She moves a finger across her throat, making a gurgling noise.

"So nobody attempts to sell a valuable property because of an urban legend?" I ask; the group erupts with laughter.

"Well, if you're interested...." Lara winks.

"I might be...of course, I would have to get the go-ahead from Jax first."

"Good luck with that; he calls it a dead investment."

"Do you know the owner?"

"Not personally, but I heard he is here tonight."

"He is?" My eyes pique with interest.

"Yes, he's around here...somewhere, names...."

"What did I miss?" I hear his dark and sultry voice behind me.

"Oh, I was just going to give Cara the name of the gentleman selling Oak Haven Mansion."

"And why would she need that." Jax spits at Lara.

"She thinks it's a good investment."

"Oh, she does; as this is my company, I tend to disagree."

"Jax..."

"No, Cara, you stay away from that house and that owner, do you understand?"

"I just thought..."

"Well, next time you brainstorm, make sure you come to me first; you can't sign off on properties, or did you forget that?"

The crowd quickly disperses, and there is just a dark cloud where Jax and I stand.

"Is it the deaths? Because you know there are ways to get around..."

"It's not up for discussion; you stay away from that property. I'm not playing, Cara."

"You can't think it's haunted, too, surely?" I snicker.

"What? Don't be ridiculous."

"Then, why?"

"Why can't you just drop it, I am not buying that fucking house, and I want you nowhere near it; it should be fucking torn down," Jax screams.

"Maybe I should go...." I turn to walk away and feel him grab hold of my hand, pulling my body towards his.

"Shit, I'm sorry... it's not you." He whispers into my hair.

Pushing my head up, I meet his gaze, "Promise me you won't go digging into that house, Cara."

"If that's what you want."

"That is what I want,"

"I promise." I smile.

"Good girl." He whispers while pulling me into his embrace and kissing me softly on the head.

The night had taken a strange turn. While Jax always seemed grumpy in the office, nothing had prepared me for his reaction over a property investment.

While I had promised I wouldn't look into this particular house, there was just something gnawing at me: there was more to the story than just a house.

I wanted to ask. I was dying to know the mystery surrounding Oak Haven, but I would be lying if I didn't say that Jax's reaction hadn't terrified me a little.

I wasn't sure if it was sinister, but I had no place poking my nose into a house I knew we would never accrue. From an investment point of view, it seemed like an excellent investment for his company, so why did his head nearly pop off his shoulders when the house was mentioned?

Jax was quieter than usual, and every time I asked if he was okay, he would just nod. The clients would come, and Jax would potter off, never taking his eyes off me. I'm not sure what he thought I was going to do. Go in search of the mystery owner of the house that had soured his mood.

That is an exciting thought, but I didn't have a death wish.

I am sitting down because I had had enough of this evening, and it started so well. The worst thought I had when I walked through those doors was that I wouldn't fit in, and when I tried, look what happened.

I sigh as I twirl the strawberry around the champagne flute, not intending to drink it.

"Hello again, darling." I look up and see those enchanting amber eyes swirling with mischief. "Mind if I join you?"

"Be my guest," I mutter while placing my hand beneath my chin, staring back into the glass and watching the strawberry swarm around in the beige bubbles.

I'm so lost in my deep thoughts that I don't notice his presence. He would see me sooner than I thought, but I no longer cared.

He was just a face in a crowded room.

That was until...I feel his hand touch mine; the prickling sensation sends a bolt of electricity shooting through my body.

Instantly shocking me.

My hand flips the glass on its side, and my eyes widen as I see where the mess has been directed.

My eyes finally meet his.

His eyes dance with amusement, but his face holds a stern expression.

"Oh, shit." I curse out loud, quickly picking up a fresh set of napkins from the table and kneeling before him.

"I'm so sorry," I mutter, dabbing at his thigh with the napkin, "I don't know why I did that." My hands move up his legs, stroking away the mess I've made. My eyes meet him, and his amber eyes swirl with pools of gold.

He places his hand across mine, letting slip a small groan. if you keep doing that, darling, we will have...a different situation." My eyes lower to his thigh, and it is only now that I feel something pulsing beneath my hand.

"Oh....shit," I whisper. "I'm sorry..." My hands still dabbing at his soaked thigh.

"You know, darling, if you wanted my cock...all you had to do was ask." A smirk plays on his lips, but I'm horrified as soon as the words leave his mouth.

"What..." My mouth gapes open, "but I don't...I mean....it was an accident." I gasp.

"And yet you're still stroking me," he cocks a brow, and as I look down, damn it, he's right. My hand stills and I quickly move away from him.

"Cara..." He reaches out, placing his hand across my wrist.

Can he feel my pulse quicken?

Does he know how excited he's made me?

The twinkle in his eyes shows amusement; I'm not fooling anyone here, least of all myself.

"Please accept my apologies, Elijah. I don't usually make a habit of feeling up associates..." his eyes widen. My self-respect dies, "I would appreciate it if you didn't mention what happened here...."

"Sure, darling, it can be our little secret." He winks, and the swelling desire courses through my body; flinging my hand away from his; I stand, trying to regain composure.

"Good evening, Elijah." I tip my head.

"Until we meet again, darling." He gives me a smile that would start a waterfall party within my panties. Those dimples piercing his cheeks with that seductive smile almost have me swooning...almost.

There were those words again: until we meet again, but this time, I was hoping it wasn't so soon. In fact, I wasn't sure we would meet again at all. He was just here for the conference, and once we were back in New York, London would be a distant memory.

I thought this trip would be arduous, what with being so close to Jax, but that was the least of my problems.

Then, I met Elijah.

How he looks at me makes my belly swell with desire, and I feel guilty. I shouldn't be feeling this way. Not with another stranger, Jax was enough, yet how he looked at me with dark desire made my legs shake. I have to ask myself: what is wrong with me?

Then I remember I'm single, and we will soon return to New York. Our little rendezvous will quickly be over, and Jax will return to giving me the silent treatment and me? Well, I will go back to pretending I hate him.

Jax must have left early because I find the space beside me empty once my eyes open. Just as well, the mention of that house had put him in a bitch of a mood, I heard him come in later in the night, but for the first time since we had arrived, he hadn't disturbed me.

I should see this for what it was...a holiday fling because I couldn't see him pursuing it once we returned home. Honestly, I was as bad as Essie; what did I think would happen? That I would ride into the sunset with my boss. And this is why you don't shit where you eat because it complicates things.

Elijah was a strange surprise; what were the odds that two men would turn my head? I promised myself a long time ago that I wouldn't ever put myself in a position to get a broken heart—never again.

I think back to where my distrust of men stems from, and even though he's long gone from my life, he still haunts my memories, and that is a cold realisation that I know I will never be free from him.

Carter was the love of my life....or so I thought.

Carter was that guy you met right out of high school, the one sweet, gentle, kind, the type that would offer you the world and look at you like you hold all the answers to the universe.

He was perfect.

We were perfect.

Until I decided to move in with him, I had my reservations. I enjoyed my own space, and I wasn't sure I was ready to share that with another person. Still, against my better judgement, as I looked into his blue eyes, shimmering with hope, I had agreed to live with him. I told myself that if it all went south, I could just move out.

Things had been going well. It was like living with your best friend, who you got to fuck at the end of the day. I just didn't realise he was luring me into a trap. It started small. He would criticise me for the most mundane things and pass it off as if he were just looking out for me. I would feel like shit, and he would look happy.

I felt for sure I was going insane. Still, each day, I grew increasingly wary of how this relationship benefited me, if at all and when I sat down to assess if I was happy, truly happy, not the lies I told myself, the answer was clear as day.

No, I wasn't, and I need to find a way out.

The day I sat Carter down was the day my torment started. I had unknowingly locked myself into a nightmare I couldn't escape. I convinced myself each time was the last time. That I deserved everything he gave me. I would daydream of a life that didn't involve him, and that was the only place I felt safe...in my head, alone with my thoughts. It was the only place he couldn't hurt me, but he soon corrupted those too.

I hadn't even realised how much my trip down memory lane had affected me until I felt the fresh tears falling down my face and the tightening in my now dry throat.

Even now, even after all this time—he haunted me.

He can't hurt you anymore.

You're free.

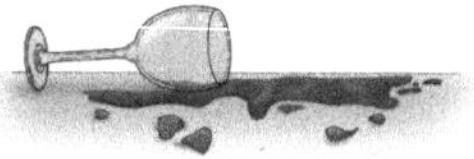

"Oh my God, Cara, what happened?" I'm alerted to the concern in Jax's voice as he races across the room to come to my aid. It was funny; I didn't even hear him come in, but what was funnier still was he wanted to protect me. Who was he protecting me from? Myself.

If the most expensive shrinks in the city couldn't fix me, I wasn't sure what he thought he could do for my already damaged heart.

"Nothing." I smile through the misty, tear-stained eyes. God, I probably looked a right sight, sitting on the bed with my knees tucked into my chest, silently crying alone.

"Kitten..." his hand strokes my hair as I feel him sit beside me, but I dare not look into his eyes to see the dormant pity. "I'm sorry about last night..."

"You don't need to apologise, Jax, it's not you..."

"Oh, please don't say it's not you; it's me."

"But it is me." I sniffle.

"What happened last night..."

"God damn it, Jax, this isn't about that."

He's looking at me like I've lost the plot. Maybe I had. I had thought I was ready to take a leap and have fun with a man again, but this...experience had dipped into the dark corners of my mind, and now I wasn't too sure.

Maybe it was guilt.

I felt guilt over my desires for Elijah; this wasn't me.

"This was..." his hand covers mine, and I think I die just a little inside. "A mistake," I mumble. I quickly move away from him, slowly walking towards the door; I never reach the handle. Jax turns my body, and my back is again pressed against a hard surface.

"Kitten..." I lower my head because I can't bear to look him in the eyes; I'm scared he will see the lies in my eyes. "Kitten, look at me." He commands; I shake my head. "You want to leave?" I nod, and his hand raises my head, "Look...at...me."

Slowly, my eyes raise, and I see the steely grey gaze burning into my eyes, "if you walk out that door...go now and don't ever look back," the stabbing in my chest hit me like a ton of bricks; his fingers gently dance beneath my chin tipping my head. "But if you decide to stay...right now...this will not be a repeat performance," my mouth gapes open; I know what I want to say, but no words come out. "If you stay...I won't let you just walk away from me, kitten."

"Jax, isn't it best to admit what this is?"

"And what is it that you think this is?"

"I..."

"Well... I'm waiting." His stern voice brings me back to reality.

"A holiday fling?" I ask because I'm not quite sure what this was, but I was confident about one thing, this was going to fuck me up in the most delicious way possible...unless I did what he said and walked away, I should walk away, but I just stood there looking into his grey eyes, waiting for him to finally let me go.

"A fling?" His eyes widen, and shock pierces his face, "you think I brought you here for a fucking fling? Could I not have done that in New York?" He grits.

"Well...yes...but..." my lip quivers, "maybe you wanted it to be...a secret." I gasp.

"Now, kitten, why would I want to hide what's already mine?" He cocks a brow.

I'm looking at him, waiting for the punchline, but one doesn't come. His head slowly moves towards mine, and I know I will crumble once he sinks his lips into mine. I will lose what little bottle I have left to just walk away, and I won't stop falling until I plummet to the ground, falling into deep despair when it all comes crashing down.

How did I know it would come crashing down? Because, as such is life, that's what always happens. This wasn't a fairytale, and I was no princess.

His lips touch mine gently, and the piercing fear climbs through my body like a lightning bolt. "I'm not what you want, not really," I whisper against his lips.

"Kitten, you're all I've wanted for seven fucking years and if you walk away from me now... I would wait for seven more. No amount of time could pass that I wouldn't want you...want this...want us."

He takes the breath out of my body with his sweet confession, but that couldn't be true, could it? That would mean I couldn't allow my thoughts to go there; I couldn't fall.

Hadn't I been here before? Look what that had got me.

But he wasn't Carter; he was so much worse. He was making me feel things I had no place in feeling.

"Cara, say something." I look at him, but I still say nothing, "Say anything." I want to respond to him, but I can't find the words to express how he makes me feel. "Tell me you want to walk away...tell me now." He growls.

My eyes widen, and he's challenging me to walk away. I hear him blow out a breath; I should say something. I should say anything. "Last chance, kitten." His mouth upturns; he knows I'm not going to say it. I should just walk away to dint his ego; a smirk plays on my lips. "Too late," he whispers.

His lips are tempting me to delve into his. His in-toxicating scent swarms across me in waves. The heat burns a fire within my soul. He feels so damn good-pressed against me. My body remembers pre-cisely how he makes me feel; all I need to do is take a leap, but I can't do it. The tremor of desire and fear paralyses my body. I know he notices the sudden change; he knits his brows together and steps away from me.

"I'm sorry," I mutter as I turn and walk out the door.

Away from him.

Away from the only excitement in my life.

But as I stand outside the closed door, knowing he's on the other side. I can't do it. I can't move. Why is this so hard? The pain pounds in my chest every time I think of walking away from him, walking away from him for good.

I had thought he would come racing after me.

Is that what I really wanted?

But he doesn't. I just stand there staring at a closed door I walked through. The only thing between us is a door I should have never walked through. I know why I did; he terrifies me.

He scares me how much he makes me feel with barely any effort. Most of all, he terrifies me because he gives me hope that this is real and that I deserve this, but I don't. I was happy working my job and having fun with my girls, and he had to...complicate everything. But didn't I ask for this? Isn't this what I fantasised about all those nights alone in my apartment, and what was I doing now? Running.

Why?

Because I was terrified, I was terrified that Jax would destroy what was left of my heart. I would be lost to this world forever, but I also knew if I didn't walk back through that door, I would always wonder—what if.

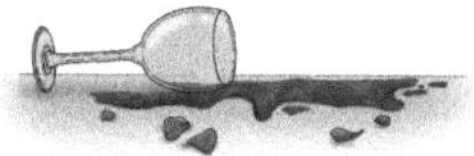

Sucking all the air, I can muster into my lungs, my hand reaches for the door handle, slowly pulling it down and opening it. I step through to see a very tense Jax staring back at me. He hadn't moved. He must have just been waiting for me to come back.

His body leans across mine, his arm raised in the air. His palm is flat against the door; he pushes it with such force that the loud crash makes me jump. His scent invades my space, my head spinning with his dark and musky scent as I let it wrap me in its dark embrace.

His deep, penetrative gaze burns a fire within my soul, silently pulling me in. Enchanting me with every pull of his dark look. He wraps his strong arms around my waist, pulling my body off the ground and crushing my body against his; I let out a breath.

His lips crush against mine in a feverish need of all the things he hasn't said, crashing over me in waves; the intensity of his kiss marks me with a desire that crawls through my body at an alarming speed. Breathless as our lips part, "Don't...ever...fucking...do...that...again." He warns.

I feel my body has moved further into the room, and he sets me down before the bed. That dark look never left his face. Quickly removing my clothes, he doesn't even acknowledge the confusion I know is clearly displayed on my face. "Jax, shouldn't we talk..." He ignores my request and removes my underwear from my body, leaving nothing but my black heels on. "Jax, what are you doing?"

He spins my body around so I face the bed, "All fours, now."

"Jax.."

My body is pushed onto the bed, "you can do it, kitten, or I can do it for you." He growls in my ear.

"Jax, I don't understand; what are you doing?" I whisper.

"Giving you what you asked for." He whispers in my ear, "Now crawl on all fours and move your body against the bed; I want to see how fucking needy you are."

What I asked for? Had he lost his goddamn mind? I hadn't asked him for anything; I was moments away from ending this madness.

His hand moves across the curve of my ass slowly, sliding up and down, sending shivers up my spine. His finger dips into my pussy, my back arches, and a slip of a moan crawls from my throat. "Crawl...for...me." His silky voice vibrates in my ear.

Lifting my legs onto the bed, I crawl into the middle just like he asked, on all fours like a pet awaiting its treat for obeying its master and being a good little soldier. My ass is pushed out, and my back arched; I don't look back even though the anticipation is killing me.

"Lay flat, kitten, spread your legs and grind your hips into the bed." He commands.

Well, that was a strange request.

Laying on my stomach with my legs spread wide, I push my hips into the covers on the bed and feel the tingling sensation hit my pussy at the friction of the cotton against my exposed pussy. Once more, I move my hips but with more force and cry out when the cotton once again rubs against my sensitive pussy.

"Good girl," I hear him gasp.

Grinding my hips into the bed, gasping as the pleasure courses through my body, fucking my bare, exposed, dripping cunt against the sheets. The excitement slides across me and then moves straight to my centre. "Oh, god," I gasped, excited at fucking myself against the cotton.

His hand moves across my ass, gently massaging my bare ass, "all fours, kitten," he rasps. Pushing my ass up and resuming my earlier position, my body jolts as I feel the sting of his palm against my ass.

I hear the sound of his belt opening and being removed; the excitement crawls through me. My head is swimming with desire. MY BODY STILLS AND STIFFENS until I feel that belt wrap around my throat, and panic sets in. I can feel his cock press against my centre, but the only thing I can think about is the thick leather belt wrapped around my throat.

His cock pushes through, and the scream that tears through my throat almost sounds inhuman. He starts rocking his hips harder and harder; the screams move through me like an explosion has erupted from deep within.

The pull on that belt has me gasping for air; arching my back, he pushes deeper into my soaking pussy. "This...is...what...you...wanted," he breathes in my ear. I try to respond, but I'm afraid I may pass out due to lack of oxygen.

My head is pumping, and all thoughts fall out of my head; the only thing I feel is how much his thick cock fills me up, and with every thrust of his hips, the pleasure moves through me like a hurricane. "When I read that email," he tightens his grip on that belt, forcing himself even deeper inside me. "I knew...that's what I fucking wanted too," he moans in my ear, "fuck, you feel so...fucking...good." He gasps.

The belt tightens around my throat, and a dizzying feeling overcomes me. The way he ferociously pounds his cock inside my pussy is both exhilarating and terrifying at once. My muffled cries fall around our bodies. I want to cry out how good he feels, but I'm gasping for breath.

I feel his other hand grip my hip and push even deeper inside me; the burning sensation of pain and pleasure crashes over my body in a frenzy. My legs shudder beneath him as I cry out my release, but the pressure of his cock widening me and filling me up never stops.

The belt wraps even tighter around my throat, which I didn't even think was possible. The air I had been gasping is disintegrated into nothingness; my silent cries only exist in my head, but as the pleasure mounts, it's the only thing that keeps me conscious. "God...you...are...so...fucking....beautiful." He gasps, His cock pulsing deep within my core, "Now, you're fucking mine, kitten." He moans while I feel him filling me up once more with his hot cum, and even though I'm moments away from blacking out, the feeling of his hot cum splashing my walls is the most euphoric feeling.

I want to be filled with his seed.

I want him to fill me up.

We collapse in a heap on the bed, and he finally releases my throat; sharp gasps fall out of my throat, and I just lay there utterly amazed at how wonderful it felt to just let go.

To be able to not think.

To just enjoy the moment and allow my body to be taken over by the pleasure with no thoughts in my head.

Just empty.

Free.

"You know, kitten, you might be my favourite obsession." He whispers.

You might be mine, too.

Part III
The Kane Brothers

It felt like I was living a dream with
Jax,
I didn't know there was more....
I always thought he was a pretty
puzzle,
A loner....
That was until I met....
THEM....

God. She was...perfection.

Jax said he was obsessed, but what was new? He had a new obsession every year. This one seemed different, though, and I wanted to know why? Had he finally done it, had he found a woman who could tame the Kane brothers, which seemed doubtful. Still, she had definitely piqued my interest, amongst other things.

Watching her glide into the room like a fucking angel, my eyes roam across every delicious inch of her.

My body reacted to how she moved; that dark hair Jax had swooned about repeatedly over lunch shone under the lighting. However, that was nothing compared to her glistening blue eyes that swept the room with wonder.

I was just going to watch her.
This wasn't part of the plan.

I wasn't even supposed to be here, but I couldn't help myself. I see her take that strawberry between her luscious lips, and it might just be the sexiest thing I've ever witnessed. I sip my drink, trying to quell the heat inside of me. Jax might have been obsessed with her, but I can't deny her pull on me. I watch as she turns and catches me staring, her eyes locked. The room fades away momentarily, and it's just the two of us. Or maybe that's just how it feels.

I make my way over to her, determined to introduce myself. As I get closer, I can feel my heart pounding. Unlike me, I'm usually in control, but something about her throws me off balance.

Jax isn't too pleased to see me, and I would be lying if that didn't give me some sort of self-gratification. The smirk pulls at my mouth at his annoyance at my presence. It seems my little brother has already claimed the beauty standing before me.

The way she stares at me starts a war within my body. Every glance with those pooling eyes of blue that rakes across my face has me thinking what her eyes would look like when she's stuffed full with my cock inside her. Shit, I'm getting hard just thinking about it.

The moment my lips hit her perfect skin, I finally feel like I've been touched by an angel. My brother looks at me like I'm the fucking devil, and one touch from the delicious beauty in front of me, oh, how I want to fucking sin.

We both stand there watching her walk away, "Ah, she's a beauty." I whisper.

"Elijah, seriously, what are you doing here?" He puts on his best fake smile as she turns and looks back at us.

"I already told you..."

"Bollocks, you hate these functions; that's why you leave me to do it." My brow raises, "What was it you said?" He presses a finger to his chin, "Oh yeah, that you'd rather cut out your own heart than listen to the rich pompous assholes discuss whose dick was biggest." A loud laugh crawls out of the pits of my stomach, but he still doesn't look impressed.

"Well, was I wrong?"

"I guess not." He mutters.

"She's quite...enchanting.

"You just met her."

"What can I say? I like what I see." He rolls his eyes.

"She's not like one of your toys, Elijah."

"I'm positively offended, brother."

"I'm being serious...she's well...she's different."

"Careful, Jax, anyone would think you have already fallen for her." He lowers his head, "fuck, Jax, Luca will have a fucking field day with this shit."

"Tell me something I don't know." I hear him mutter.

"Does she know?" He remains silent, "Jax, does she know?"

"No, I thought I would leave that as a surprise." He smirks.

"And if she runs like the rest of them?"

"Then I will fucking bring her back." He growls.

"Jax..."

"We are not doing this right now." He turns and walks away from me, "Try to stay out of trouble."

"Would you expect anything else?" I called, and I think I heard the slight sound of a snicker.

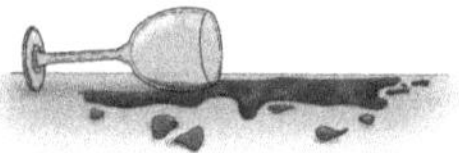

He hasn't been gone long, but I would recognise that walk anywhere. He looks like he's about to murder someone; it can't be me because, true to my word, I have just been observing the crowd. These functions were as dull as watching paint dry. Bored to tears.

"Who crawled up your ass?"

"Don't tempt me, Elijah." He warns.

"Listen, I did what you asked..."

"Why would you assume it was about you? Guilty about something?"

"You know, you're distrust of me is getting fucking tedious."

"It's not you." He gasps.

"Well, don't leave me hanging."

"Oak Haven." Once the words fall out of his mouth, my back stiffens, and my blood runs cold. Nothing could shake me, but the mention of that fucking house does it every time. "She wants me to buy that fucking house." He yells.

"Does she?"

"Know?" I nod, "Of course not; she thinks it's haunt-ed."

"Well, she's not wrong," I mutter.

"Look..."

"I don't want a pep-talk, Elijah; I just yelled at her for something she knows nothing about; I just want to drink." I nod, "Alone."

Usually, I would push my brother, but I could sense the urgency in his body. If he needed to be alone, then that's what I would give him. I couldn't blame him; the mere mention of that house sent shivers down my spine.

We should have burnt that house down years ago with that bastard in it, but Luca said it wouldn't solve anything. It would have freed us all; we would forever be locked in this prison while it stood. I never under-stood it, but Luca's word was final and to hell with the rest of us.

I'm sure there was a reason. Luca was built on con-trol. It seemed like a raging obsession like he needed it to survive, and he must have control of steel to still allow that bastard to breathe and stay in that house of horrors. I shake my head.

It does no good dwelling on the things we can not change.

I'm just going to take a walk around before I leave. I'm not much of a drinker and can't fake a conversation for these walking contradictions. That's when I spotted her. She looks pensive as she twirls that strawberry around the glass. Sitting alone. Something so beautiful should never be alone.

She is less receptive towards my charms than she was earlier. In fact, she barely acknowledges my existence when I sit down. I can't stop watching her; I'm absolutely captivated by her beauty, even though she does look like someone has just ripped out her heart. Of course, I know who. Jax is an idiot. Never could control his fucking temper.

The silence is deafening. Leaning across the table, I gently touched her arm, but I wasn't expecting her to tip the entire glass contents on my lap. I'm just trying to grab her attention and, hopefully, bring back that sunny disposition I was so intrigued by when I first met her.

Fucking perfect.

Then she does something surprising in her haste; she's on her knees before me. Christ, does she know how fucking beautiful she looks right now. She's stroking my leg, and it's not only my temperature that rises.

"You know, darling, if you wanted my cock...all you had to do was ask." A smirk plays on my lips, and she looks absolutely horrified. I regret the words as soon as they leave my mouth.

"What..." I hear her gasp, and what I wouldn't give to listen to her gasping around my cock right now. Her mouth gapes open, "But I don't...I mean....it was an accident."

"And yet you're still stroking me," I cock a brow; she moves away like she's just realised what she's done to me.

The moment she leaves, I'm once again alone. I fight with myself not to go to her room because, god damn, I fucking want her. Jax wouldn't go back until he knew she was asleep. He would spend the evening drowning in his own little pity party.

I didn't want to scare her away. Well, not yet, anyway. I probably should have checked on Jax before I left, but that conversation wouldn't be one I wanted to have...not with him in his state. So, against my better judgement, I tear myself away from the hotel.

She would see me again soon, and it might just be sooner than planned because, in one night, that little vixen had me feeling things I hadn't felt for a long time.

The way she eye fucked me had me wanting to bend her perfect body across my fucking knee.

Jax was right; she wasn't like the others.

She was a fucking surprise.

The tension in my body hasn't left since London.

I almost lost her...almost.

The mention of that damn house had rage pouring from my veins; why would she be interested in that house. Good investment? I almost want to laugh; nothing good came of that property, but of course, it wasn't the house that was the issue but the people that inhabited it.

I wanted Cara nowhere near that house or the owner. I should have ended his miserable existence years ago, but there was no turning back once I did that. A horrific family secret and a reputation we had worked too hard to build, it wasn't worth it; Luca was right.

Damn, Elijah just had to introduce himself. If I wasn't wound up about that house. It was he who rubbed me the wrong way. He only came to the function to see her, impatient as always, and it didn't pass my notice how she looked at him.

Hadn't I seen her repeatedly look at me that very same way, but she wasn't ready? Or maybe that was just me; I wasn't prepared. Not yet, anyway.

I have spent the last hour staring at the screen on my desk, and I just can't fucking concentrate. The numbers just jumble across the screen, darting in every direction. I pinch the bridge of my nose.

Working has been my life, but I don't want to be here today; I want to be out there, smiling and laughing with her friends.

I glance at her before I walk by, and it pisses me off that she doesn't even acknowledge I exist. She didn't even acknowledge my existence when she walked into the building. She resumed her position at her desk and smiled while she chatted happily with the other girls.

I have been sitting here trying to wrack my brain that after everything we had experienced together in London, she could just go back to acting like I was just her grumpy boss who she didn't need or want to interact with.

Sarah, send Cara to my office now. I command before taking my finger off the button.

I'm tense. I need to calm down, but I'm wired tight. I wait forever to hear that knock on my door, and I don't like waiting. It wasn't working if I tried to act indifferent; I thrashed open the door, glaring at her.

"Jax, you wanted to see me?" She gasps.

I don't even respond to her stupid question. Why else would she be outside my office if I hadn't wanted her here? Grabbing her wrist, I pull her into my office, slamming the door behind her and pushing her body into the door.

"Jax..."

"Why have you been avoiding me?" I accuse.

"I haven't."

"No?" I smirk, "Business as usual then, Cara?"

"I don't know what you want from me."

"I want..." shit, I'm at a loss for words. "I want you not to pretend that this," I move my fingers between us both, "means nothing."

"Jax, we are at work."

"Oh, this little act is for everyone else, is it, kitten?"

"I don't want this to be...complicated." She gasps.

"I don't either, kitten, but...."

"Is there something you need?" Her eyes fall to the floor; she won't even look at me.

Did I want something from her? I curiously look over her face; a slight blush paints her cheeks. "Do I make you nervous, kitten?" I feel her body stiffen.

"Please, Jax,"

"Oh, kitten, I do love it when you beg."

"Well, if you don't need anything," She turns her body away from mine, placing my hand across her waist and spinning her into my body. She's trapped against my body, her breathing erratic, her eyes slowly move up my body until they finally settle on mine, and she takes my breath away.

Now, kitten," I pull her body across mine towards the desk, gently pushing her against it, "why would you assume," my lips graze across her neck. I feel her body relax, "that I don't need anything." I whisper into her skin.

"What do you need?" She gasps.

What did I need? What a curious question, her here, calming the storm within my soul. That's all I needed, just her.

"You...," my teeth pull at her ear, and a sharp gasp falls from her lips, "on your knees, like a good fucking girl."

Walking away from her, I settle into my chair. It's risky because she could bolt out of this office anytime. I'm just looking at her back; her long, dark hair falls in waves as she moves her head. I've never been unsure about anything, but Cara makes me question everything.

I open the belt wrapped around my trousers; I know she hears the buckle as it opens. Her body moves, and I hear her sigh. Turning, she looks at me at last. "Jax," She utters, "isn't this...."

"Unprofessional." a smirk teases the side of my mouth, and she finally does it; she finally smiles, and warmth instantly pierces my heart as I see that smile seep into her dancing blue pools of mischief.

I watch as she slowly walks towards me. Her long, luscious legs tense with every movement her body makes; the way her hips sway in that tight black dress has me biting my lip. The only sound I hear is the click-clack of her heeled black shoes as she approaches me.

The moment she stood before me, I couldn't help myself. My hands glide up her thighs, and she's already gasping, but I want to see her on her knees with her plump lips wrapped firmly around my cock. "On your knees." I feel her body shudder beneath my words.

"What if someone comes in?" She whispers.

"Then, I will have to be very fucking quiet." I grin. Doesn't she know by now that I don't care who knows? She's mine.

I watch as she crawls between my legs, and oh fuck, she looks that fucking pretty on her knees. I want to fucking bend her over my desk. She's positioned herself between my legs, with her eyes raised, looking into mine, and then she does something entirely unexpected. She opens her mouth wide and sticks out her tongue like she's waiting for my cock to be slotted into the hot, sweet depths of her mouth.

Slowly the zip comes down, and she still sits there with her mouth wide and her tongue sticking out, awaiting my cock. I've never been so fucking hard in my life, she's everything I have dreamed of, and the way her eyes never leave mine suddenly makes me feel naked. The raw emotion pours from her, and it feels something close to what I imagine love feels like.

Finally taking down my trousers, my cock pops out, and she pouts, lifting her chin with my fingertips. Confusion pierces my body. "What's up, kitten?"

"I hoped I could feel you getting hard in my mouth." She meekly speaks.

"Ah, sorry, kitten, you're just so damn sexy; I think I'm permanently hard when you're around." That gets me a cheeky grin. Before her tongue flicks out against the base of my cock and I can't help the groan that falls from my lips.

She slides that long pink tongue from the base of my cock to the tip, and I think I'm almost losing my goddamn mind. "Ah, don't tease me, kitten." A slight smile appears on her lips before her tongue starts circling the tip of my head, driving sharp gasps to thrust out of my throat.

She wrapped her lips around my cock while smiling; she was trying to kill me; I was sure of it. Her tongue massages my length, and the rest of the world falls away. It's just me and her. Her lips clamp down hard, and the tip of her tongue pushes against my tip while she swallows my cock, gagging and forcing her mouth to the end. "Oh, fuck, kitten," I gasp while my cock pulses in the deep confines of her mouth.

Her hand massages my balls, and a finger enters my ass. My wide eyes are fixed on her, and she just smirks with a mouthful of my cock, pressing her finger inside of me like she is pushing a button. The pleasure attacks my body, and the groans from my throat collapse around our bodies.

"Oh fuck, kitten, your such a good little cock sucker," I gasp while pushing her head further onto my cock. I enjoy the ripples of pleasure that pump through my body as I listen to her choke.

Her finger moves faster and faster inside me, her head bobbing up and down maniacally, awaiting the stream of desire to pour into her mouth. My legs shake at the explosive onslaught of her mouth. "That's a good girl..." I cry out, "Swallow it all for me," I gasp as I finally release thick hit strands of cum deep into her glorious mouth.

She finally releases my cock from the vice around her mouth, and I watch as she gulps down every last drop with a smile on her flushed pretty face. My hand caresses her face by pushing my trousers back up and fixing my belt. "God, Cara, you're a fucking angel."

The door bursts open, and a smiling Elijah just strolls in like he hadn't interrupted a perfect moment.

"As always, impeccable timing."

"Ah, you know me, I'm nothing if not punctual."

"You? Punctual." I sneer; Elijah was anything but, although recently, he seemed to be just there at the right moment. A coincidence? I think not.

"Hello again, darling." He peers over the desk.

I'm unsure how she will react, but even Cara can surprise me. She teases her fingers across her lips, letting her tongue trail her bottom lip and slightly biting down with a smile on her face.

"Well, I should be getting back to work." She blushes while standing and straightening her dress before she turns and walks out the door. Not saying another word to either of us.

"Do you have to do that?"

"Do what?" He asks while taking a seat in the chair opposite my desk.

"You know what."

"Well, I had the decency to wait until you finished. You have to give me credit for that." He winks.

"Jesus Christ, Elijah, were you out there the entire time?"

"Not the entire time." He smirks.

"What are you doing here?"

"Oh, I just thought I would drop by and see how my brother is. Can't a brother drop in anymore?"

"A brother can, you don't."

"I'm offended."

"I'm sure you are. Now, what do you want?"

"I want to know when you are going to tell her."

"Soon."

"Jax..."

"I will tell her soon."

"The longer you leave it, the worse it will be."

"I just...I need more time."

"Well, it's your funeral, little brother."

It was indeed.

I groan at the little voice of reason that has just vacated my office. Elijah was right.

The longer I let it go on, the harder it would be. I just wanted to hold onto what we had right now because I wasn't sure if Cara would even stick around when I gave her my proposition.

I hoped and prayed that she would because every moment I was with her, I was never more confident that I was falling. I was falling hard, but I couldn't blame her if she ran. Dragging her into my world was fucked up. Who could blame her if she ran?

But god damn it, I hoped she didn't.

The girls haven't stopped hounding me since we arrived back from London, and each time they question me, I'm sure they can see the dishonesty on my face. I knew they would all have questions, but I didn't think they would interrogate me to this degree.

"Cara," Samantha wails. As I look across the women staring at me, awaiting a response, I suddenly wish I was anywhere but here. "We need details; you can't go away for three days and have no insanely ridiculous stories to tell."

"Yeah, we want to know." Essie glares at me.

"Well, the hotel was beautiful."

"Yes, darling, we may work in property, but we don't really care about the structure of buildings." Sophie smiles while studying her candy pink stiletto nails.

"I'm setting the scene." I laugh. "Jax was…" I had to be careful how I word this because I'm supposed to hate him, but every time I think of Jax, I have flashbacks of how his body felt against mine.

"Jax was what?" Essie grits out. The tone in her voice didn't go unnoticed. I wasn't sure what her problem with me was, but since I had returned, she had looked at me like I was something she had stepped in.

"As dull as ever; honestly, if it wasn't for the dreamy associate, I'm not sure I would have anything to tell you."

"Dreamy associate?" Samantha's eyes widen.

I retell the girls about my run-in with Elijah, and just mentioning his name turns my blood hot. They eagerly listen to the embarrassing tale of what happened at that table when we were alone in the ballroom.

"Oh, he sounds Absolutely dreamy." Samantha swoons.

Dreamy was one word for him.

"You must tell us what he looks like." Sophie squeals.

"Well…" His scent attacks my senses first, dark and seductive with a hint of evergreen forest.

"Hello again, darling." His sultry voice hits my body.

"Elijah," I breathe.

"We have to stop meeting like this….people will talk." He smirks. His lips gently graze my cheek, and a sharp gasp falls from my throat, "You look delicious on your knees, darling." He whispers so only I can hear. "Until next time, darling." He smiles, and his amber eyes swirl with gold, hitting my body in places and sending heat to crawl between the crevice between my thighs.

"Okay…who…the…hell…is that?" Samantha shrieks.

"That's Elijah."

"And where did we meet this delicious specimen?" My cheeks grow hotter.

"He's the dreamy associate." I giggle.

"Oh girl, if you don't want that man, I would be willing to mount that beast of a man." Sophie winks.

"I'm not sure your husband would approve." I laugh.

"Oh, I don't know…he might be up for sharing." She winks.

"Oh, I think you are perfect for each other." Essie beams.

"You do, uh." Samantha raises a curious brow, "That means there is no competition for Jax."

"Samantha," I raise my voice louder than necessary. "Besides, I have no interest in Jax." I lie.

"Yes, well, I can't chat with you a lot all day; some of us have work to do." Essie gets up and saunters back to her desk.

"Ooooh, touchy, touchy." Sophie drawls, "What crawled up her ass." I shake my head because I don't want to get involved in her one-woman show of hating anyone she thinks has a chance with Jax.

"Are you coming tonight?" Samantha asks.

"Sorry, hun, I'm still jet-lagged. I'm just going to catch up on some much-needed sleep." I lie once more. Samantha pouts, "Next time, I promise."

"Cara, client on line one," Essie calls; I nod while picking up the receiver and pressing one.

"Cara Roberts, how may I assist you."

"Miss Roberts, I'm so happy you agreed to take my call."

"How may I help you?"

"A little bird told me you were interested in Oak Haven." The silence ensues, and my stomach drops.

"I'm sorry, mister...."

"You can call me Caleb." It was a little strange but okay; this wasn't the usual way a businessman introduced himself on a first-name basis.

"I'm not sure where you heard that..."

"Oh, you'd be surprised at what I know."

"In any case, I'm afraid I will have to refuse your offer."

"You haven't heard my offer...yet," I hear the laughter in his voice.

"I'm sorry, but I can't help you."

"I tend to disagree; you are the perfect person to help me with my endeavour."

"Caleb..."

"Ah, we've been introduced; I will see you soon." The line goes dead, and I just stare at the receiver.

The way this man spoke sent chills down my spine. I wasn't sure why, but his last words seemed like a threat. Who was he, and how did he know I had even contemplated trying to land that property? I wanted to tell Jax, but what was the point in poking the bear? I had dealt with it, hadn't I? Even though his empty threat still sounded, I wouldn't see that man.

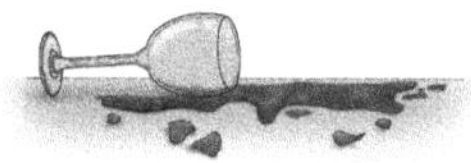

The drive over to Jax's house was long and albeit slightly painful. We have barely said two words to each other since we left the office, and to think I sacrificed a night out with the girls for a dreary drive with my grumpy boss with nothing but awkward silences.

"You know, you can drop me home if...."

"Why would I want to do that?" He smirks.

"You seem..."

"Tense?" He asks me.

"Yeah, you could say that."

"I don't often bring people home; it's a new concept for me, kitten."

"Well," I twirl a strand of my hair around my finger, "I don't often go home with anyone, so I guess we are in the same sinking ship."

"You are an odd girl, do you know that." He smiles.

"Yes, you might have said that...once or twice." I gaze out at the blanket of darkness, with only the road illuminated by the car's lights. "How far is your humble abode anyway." He lets out a sneer.

Pulling up to the big iron-clad gates, my eyes widen. I thought my apartment was beautiful, overlooking the city. Still, I had never imagined that away from the city could be so picturesque. I knew it would be impressive when I envisioned where Jax lived, but I had stumbled into another world. It quickly made me realise just how different our worlds were.

"Does it get your approval, Miss Roberts?" He grins.

"This is...wow, I can't believe you live here...alone."

"Uh, huh." He mumbles.

"You do live...alone, right?"

"Not exactly, kitten."

"Not hiding a wife in there, are you?" I nervously laugh at my joke, secretly hoping it isn't true, but stranger things have happened, like...me going home with my boss.

"No, wife, kitten, I promise." He smiles as he pulls up to the exquisite Victorian house before us.

I waited for Lurch to open the doors as we descended the cream-stone steps. I stood like a statue awaiting the greeting, but none came.

"What are you doing?"

"Don't you have a butler?"

"A butler?" He laughs, shaking his head, "No butler, kitten, come on." He grabs my hand, dragging me through the entrance. And there may be no butler, but this house was the kind of house you dreamt of living in as a child.

We have only entered the entrance of his house, and I'm already taken away. I look around. The architecture is breathtaking; to the right, cream-marbled stone steps crawl up to the next floor in a swirling effect, and tall chandeliers hang from the ceiling, boasting a stream of beautiful light.

"Are you going to stand there all night?" Jax asks me with a smirk.

"I'm sorry..." I blush, "your home is beautiful.

"My home is your home."

I'm sure that's what people said to be polite, but what a thought. No, I was getting carried away again. Whenever he spoke to me, an odd idea would enter my head. Besides, didn't he already share his home?

"I'm not sure whoever you live with would be impressed if I invaded their home."

"Trust me, kitten, they would be delighted." He whispers in my ear.

"Who do you live with, Jax?"

"Are you hungry?" I shake my head, "well, I am," he growls while pulling me through a range of walkways until we stumble into what he calls a kitchen.

"Wow, this is beautiful," I gasped, "you must spend all your time here."

"Do I look like I spend all my time in here," he smirks, "besides, River is the chef...." He leans close, wrapping his arms around my waist and carrying me into the open space, "he doesn't like people in his kitchen...." My bottom is planted firmly on the black marbled counter, "But I won't tell if you don't." He whispers.

"Who is River?"

"He's my brother, kitten."

"You have a brother..."

"Hmmm, now about satisfying my impending hunger." His lips press against my neck.

"I told you... I'm not hungry." I gasp as I feel his hands crawl up my thighs, sending shivers shooting through my body.

"Who said it was you that would be eating?" He raises a brow while he manoeuvres my underwear from my body, opening my legs wide with his hands and planting my feet on the edge of the counter. "Mmmmm, delicious." He murmurs.

"What if your friends come home?" I suddenly felt naked and vulnerable beneath Jax's steely gaze. My pleas go unheard; he just gives me a sneer before his head disappears between my legs.

The kisses crawl up my thighs, and I think I've died and gone to heaven. The shivers climb up my thighs as his lips graze my bare skin, sending shivers to crawl up my spine.

His lips clamp hard around my clit, and my hands tumble into his hair, feeling the soft strands through my fingertips. "Oh god, Jax," I call out. His tongue encircles me, and I nearly lose my goddamn mind pushing his head deeper into my dripping pussy.

His tongue slides down my lips, lapping up the wetness I can feel; his tongue feels like silk against my bare aching pussy, and the cries fall out of my mouth. Still, once his tongue enters me, my back arches, and the pleasure quickly moves through my body. "Oh god, oh god, yes, just...like...that," I scream into the open space.

Jax massages my pussy like he's starved for it encircling me with his delectable tongue. Every pulse of his tongue burns my body hotter. I can no longer call out words; I'm just an incoherent, sweaty mess. My head falls back, and I can feel the sweat drip down my spine. I'm so close to releasing all that passion into his mouth when I come back up, and my eyes fall on those amber eyes swirling with gold and mischief.

He's stood by the door frame leaning into it with one leg crossed over the other, his arms folded and the biggest smirk I've ever seen, just watching as I'm spread wide, screaming from the pleasure. I want to take my eyes off his, but I'm entranced by how he watches me.

His tongue flicks harder and faster, pushing me over the edge. My hands claw at his head; the pleasure is rushing through me in waves, but I still can't peel my eyes away from the visitor who watches from the doorway.

His hands grip my hips hard as he drives his tongue further into my pussy; staring into Elijah's eyes, I watch him stroke his tongue across his plump fucking lips, and I completely lose it. "Oh my god," I scream while looking at Elijah. A rush of pleasure gathers inside me, pushing harder and harder until I explode into smithereens. Screaming my pleasure into Jax's mouth while I look at Elijah, a blush crawls from my chest to my face.

"Elijah," I finally breathe out.

Jax pops his head up, "Kitten?"

"Elijah is here." I breathlessly gasp.

"Of course he is," Jax smirks with a roll of his eyes. "I thought you were out tonight?"

"And miss this little show; I'm glad I came home early." He smiles.

"I bet you are."

"I enjoyed the show you put on for me, darling." He winks. My mouth gaped open as I watched him turn away from the doorway he had taken such pleasure in leaning against.

"Come on, kitten." Jax holds me by the waist, lifting me from the counter and planting my feet on the ground.

"I'm confused, Jax; that's the associate from London."

Jax ignores me, and it really irks me that since I had walked through those doors, every question I had asked him he'd skirted over or chose not to answer at all, we walked into another grand room where the uninvited guest was perched on an armchair with a glass of scotch in his hand in front of a roaring fire.

My head was swimming with confusion and questions, and he hadn't answered. I fling my hand away from his, "kitten,"

"What's going on, Jax?"

"Nothing." He innocently answers.

"You," I gaze at Elijah, "you're not just a business associate, are you?"

"No, darling." He smiles while taking a gulp of the brown liquid.

"Who are you?"

"Look, Cara, we don't need to do this right now." Jax interrupts.

"I wasn't speaking to you," I glare at him, "you had plenty of opportunities to tell me who he was." Jax sighs, but I know he's not answering me, so I gaze back at Elijah, "Who are you?"

"I'm Elijah Kane."

"As in…" I can't find the words to utter.

"As in," he smirks, enjoying my inner turmoil. "I'm his brother." He smiles like it is an everyday occurrence.

His words hang around us all, and it feels like I have been punched in the stomach. Not only had I been spread across Jax's kitchen while he ate my pussy, but I had looked into his brother's eyes as I screamed my release into Jax's mouth.

It was bad enough thinking he was just an ordinary associate, but it was even worse that it was his brother. What kind of fucked up arrangement did they have here? My mouth gapes open, but no words come out.

"Yes, as fun as this is, I'm beat; I'm off to bed," Elijah announces while draining the last drops of liquid from his glass. "Good luck, Jax." He smirks while walking towards us.

"Asshole," Jax mutters.

"Me?" He looks amused but acts like he's offended, "I told you that you should have told her." He moves closer, and I can smell his intoxicating evergreen scent; he smells like the forest, and I breathe in his scent as he comes closer.

His lips graze against my cheek, and a sigh falls from my lips, "Don't be too hard on him. He's an idiot." I smile, "Good night, darling," He whispers against my skin before walking away.

"Why didn't you tell me?"

"I just...Cara, I don't have an excuse; he wasn't supposed to be in London, and I guess...." He runs his fingers through his hair, "I guess I just wanted to keep you to myself...for a little while at least."

"Keep me to yourself?"

"I think you've had enough surprises for one night." He smiles, "How about that drink."

Yeah, how about that drink.

This house was like a maze; it was so easy to get lost. I just want to lie down; when Elijah had shown up at the home, confusion had pierced my body.

Weren't they just colleagues?

Although Jax wasn't a social butterfly, he knew how to play the part.

But I was wrong, so fucking wrong.

The man who had burned desire through my core with only one look wasn't just a colleague. No, it was his brother.

Perfect, Cara, just perfect.

Now, I was wandering around his house, looking for an escape. I could have left, but I didn't want to be rude. Neither of them had done anything. It wasn't their fault my hormones couldn't keep it together for one night.

Elijah had disappeared once the bombshell had been dropped, but didn't Jax already say he had a brother? How many brothers did he have, exactly? I shake my head. I probably didn't want the answer to that question.

Elijah was his brother. I couldn't believe it, not because he hadn't announced he was his brother but because his brother did things to my body with one look. His brother had made me cum hard with his seductive stare, and the tingles of excitement ran across my body just thinking about it.

Opening the door to a room, I allow my body to collapse against the door. Sighing my relief into the empty space at finally being alone. I hear the sound of breathing. This wasn't an empty room; I should probably leave, but curiosity got the better of me.

Slowly, I walk towards the wooden oak four-poster bed and admire the intricate swirly details cut into the wood. With only a tiny stream of light coming from the large bay windows, I walk closer to the bed, and a gasp gets caught in my throat.

He's breathtaking. My eyes crawl across his body. His chest rises and falls with every breath, and tribal tattoos creep around his muscular, tanned chest. My eyes lower to his ripped and toned abs, and my mouth is suddenly dry. I can see the faint V-line of muscle, but the thin white sheet covers the rest of his delicious body.

"Go on then, kitten." I shiver when I hear Jax's decadent voice in my ear. "I wonder what naughty little thoughts are around your pretty head." I shake my head, "Kitten, you surely know how this works by now."

"I don't," I whisper.

"If you want one, brother..." his hands crawl around my body, teasing my nipples under the thin dress draped across my body, "You get them all." I gasp.

"I...can't...Jax." I gasp once more.

"It's entirely up to you, kitten," his hands move down my body, slipping his fingers across my bare pussy. I finally let out a long, slow moan, "You want him. Why deny your own desires," his finger enters me, and my head falls onto his shoulder. "It's human nature, baby, give in to your desires, crawl onto that bed and finally taste what you've been lusting for…" his hands move up my body, removing the dress from it. "Since London."

He goes back into the shadows, I spin around, but I can't see him anywhere.

"Jax?" I whisper into the room, "Jax I whisper again, no response. That bastard stole my clothes and slunk away like a sinful ninja.

I could just leave.

Deny my feelings for Elijah and go back home.

It was much easier than standing naked in front of the most beautiful man I had ever seen, watching him sleep.

Was Jax right? That I should…no, I couldn't do that. Could I? He stirs, and it's a stark realisation that pretty soon, sleeping beauty will wake from his slumber, and I will be stood before him naked. Staring at him like a pervert in a white van.

Stay or go.

Stay or go.

My thoughts are manic.

What's a girl to do?

Well, I'm already naked. I'm just going to lay next to him. The bed is big enough for him not to notice that I have invaded his space. I won't stay long, just long enough to satisfy the curiosity that is running through my veins.

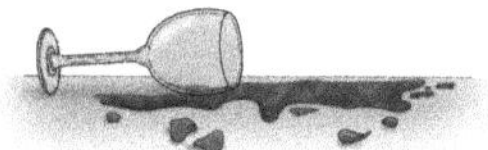

I crawl onto the bed, hoping he doesn't suddenly wake up and see the strange girl he has been flirting with suddenly leaning over him with her tits bouncing all over the place. I wish Jax hadn't tempted me with his very delicious brother because his scent attacks my body once I crawl near him. I suddenly wondered if he would taste as dangerous as he smelled.

He smells intoxicating. His scent makes me dizzy. I'm so close to him now, watching his chest rise and fall. I can feel the heat emitting from my body. I scoot closer. I'm just going to stay for a moment. I lay my head on his broad shoulder, my hair strewn across his body, my fingers trail a line across his tattoo, swirling and feeling the heat from his skin. His hand clasps across mine, and I gasp.

"How long have you been awake?" I blush even though he can't see the heat stinging my face.

"A while. Made a bet with myself that you'd leave, but look at you surprising me." His decadent voice whispers.

"Well…" my fingers trail his chest, "Jax stole my clothes, so I didn't know what to do."

"He did, huh?" A chuckle falls from his lips, and his hands move around my body, pulling me closer.

"How many of you are there?" I ask.

"Well, to my knowledge, only one of me exists." He sneers. I gently slap his chest.

"No, how many brothers do you have."

"Oh, feeling a little out of your element there, darling."

"I…I don't usually do this."

"Do what?"

"Well, anything."

"You are a beautiful woman, Cara. I'm sure any man would be lucky to spend even one night with you."

"I'm not too sure about that."

"Who hurt you?" I'm unsure if it was his question or if I had been playing pretend with Jax for a while now, but I can't stop the tears that silently fell down my face and landed in a puddle on his chest. "I'm sorry…I…got…you…wet." I sniffle.

"I tell you what, I will make a deal with you."

"A deal?" I push my head up to finally look at him and see that cheeky grin on his face.

"You tell me what haunts you that makes you cry in the middle of the night, and I will tell you about my brothers, deal?"

"Wouldn't you rather fuck me, Elijah?"

"Sure, darling, but there is plenty of time for that. If you're going to be our girl, that doesn't just mean we fuck you when we want. If we are doing this, we are doing this properly." My eyes widened. I had never even grasped what Jax meant when he said when you get one brother, you get them all.

I was curious how many brothers there were and what the other Kane brothers were like, but was it worth the most tragic story of my life? I wasn't even sure I could utter those words, let alone tell someone I barely knew what had almost broken me.

"It doesn't feel like a fair trade," I whisper.

"Well, that's because you haven't met the bear yet." He winks.

"The bear?"

"See, you're curious now, darling."

"I wouldn't know where to start."

"The greatest stories ever told all have a beginning. How about starting there?"

"Will I have to repeat this to each brother?" I screw up my nose at the thought of replicating my sadness multiple times.

"That's entirely up to you, darling, but I want to hear your story. I know it's a sensitive subject, but you are too beautiful to allow anyone to make you cry."

"You are very charming, Elijah. Has anyone ever told you that?" I smile.

"I have my moments."

I'm unsure how to word how I feel about Carter King or the torturous years I endured under his control. How do you explain that someone who you thought would keep you safe was the very thing that could ultimately kill you?

"Carter was my boyfriend...a while ago," I feel Elijah stroke my cheek with his thumb, and my eyes flutter close momentarily. "Carter...was...perfect in the be-ginning."

"Aren't they all?" He smiles.

"I wouldn't know, before Jax...there was Carter."

"And before Carter?" I shake my head, "You truly are special, aren't you, darling?"

"I'm just...cautious." He nods, "Carter was very con-trolling and..." A lump forms in my throat, and my lip quivers.

"It's okay, darling, you don't have to do this."

"I want to," I whisper.

"Carter...was abusive and controlling. I wasn't allowed to do anything if he didn't break my bones and my heart...then it was my mind that he broke." A sob crawls from my throat. "You don't hurt those you say you love." A tear falls down my face, "that's not love. Maybe love is just a myth like a unicorn."

"You know we won't let anyone hurt you again, don't you, darling?"

"You can't promise that," I whisper.

"Darling, if you're our girl, I don't think you understand exactly what we would do to protect you and ensure you always feel safe...always."

"You keep saying if?"

"Well, yes, darling, we are not going to force you into this...relationship, but if you start this with us, we will never let you go." He growls.

It was tempting. I mean, the promise of the Kane brothers elicited excitement through my body. Still, if I was going to even contemplate this madness, it wouldn't be for protection. I had learned to protect myself a long time ago. If Carter had taught me anything, he had taught me how to survive.

I don't notice the silence that ensues. I had endured so many more horrors at the hands of Carter that I could have told him, but what would that solve? He wanted to know what haunted me. Carter King haunted me. He may not be able to hurt me anymore, but he still haunted my memories.

"Your turn." I finally smile, hoping to change the channel of my depressing existence.

"What you went through..."

"I survived."

"Cara..."

"Elijah, I've told you more than I've told anyone. I don't want to keep dragging up the worst time. I don't know why I cried. I guess... I'm just overwhelmed with everything."

"You mean me?"

"You, Jax, this whole situation. I told you..."

"You don't usually do this." He smiles.

"You're stalling." I accuse.

"Me," He points at his delicious chest, which salivates me at the mouth. "Would I do such a thing, darling?" He smiles.

"Your brothers can't be that bad." I'm half hoping that is the case.

"Ah, that depends on your perception."

I snuggle into his chest, allowing warmth to fill me up as he embraces my body. "So, tell me about your brothers."

"Well, you've met Jax already. There is River. He is our little chef. We have a chain of restaurants, and River oversees and ensures everything moves smoothly with those. Nobody is allowed to cook in this house when River is home."

"When will he be back?"

"He should be back next week, darling."

"Well, that doesn't sound too scary." I breathe a sigh of relief.

"Oh, River is too gentle for his own good. Now, Luca, he's a different story."

"What's his story?"

"Luca is," he takes a breath, "complicated."

"That doesn't sound good, what does he do?"

"Luca, he...collects things."

"Like antiques?"

"Not exactly."

"So, there are four of you?"

"Yes, that's it." He smiles.

That's it. His statement is that four men weren't a large fleet. He acted like it was normal and I should just be accepting that there were four men. It was bad enough trying to wrap my head around the fact that there was Elijah and Jax, but four. I wasn't sure I could deal with four of them.

"That's a lot." I finally gasped.

"I wouldn't worry, darling. It's more like three."

"But you said…"

"Luca won't entertain the idea. Jax should tell him before he comes home, but he won't."

"When is he coming back?"

"Luca, who knows, would live in the wilderness if he could."

"Three is still…"

"Jax is right. This is entirely up to you. I know it's overwhelming."

"That's an understatement," I mutter.

"Hey," he pushes my face up with his fingertips underneath my chin until my eyes finally meet his. "Right now, it's you, just you and me. Nobody else. Don't worry about anything. Just lay with me. Sleep." He lays our bodies back on the bed, holding me close while slowly playing with my hair. "You're going to need it." He whispers into my hair.

I wasn't sure why I told Elijah more than I had told anyone, even Jax. There was just something about him that made me want to be so completely open and raw.

I wanted him to see me. I wanted him to see all of me. I wanted to give a tiny part of myself that nobody had, just like I had given to Jax.

It made no sense to me because I didn't know either of them, not really and after years of blending into the shadows, never wanting to be seen. I wanted them to see me. I didn't want to hide myself from either of them. I just wanted to matter.

To know that I existed.

To belong.

Somewhere in between a tragic tale of trauma, I wanted to be seen.

I didn't want to exist anymore.

I wanted the impossible.

I wanted to—thrive.

In a cold, harsh world, to be seen by someone who would appreciate the parts you had freely given. To be accepted with all your flaws and broken pieces. Was there anything more perfect than just being seen?

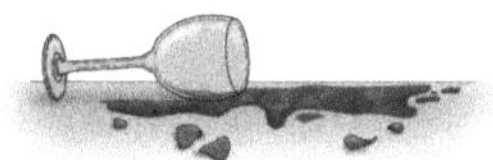

An aching in my chest awakens my sleeping body. As my eyes flutter open, I feel positively alive. That was the best sleep that I had experienced in years. I try to pull my arms to wipe the rest from my eyes, but I can't move. Panic settles in my body, and I push my head up to see my arms restrained above my head, chained to a metal bar that is fixed onto the wall.

WHAT THE FUCK.

I try to pull my arms once more, but all it does is strain the muscle in my chest and burn my wrists from friction against the cold steel that currently binds my body in place.

"Welcome back, sleeping beauty. I thought I would have to start the party without you." Elijah winks.

"Elijah, hilarious. Now let me go."

"Now, why would I want to do that, darling?"

"This is not normal human behaviour. People don't tie up other people while they are sleeping. Pretty sure that's classed as kidnapping." He smirks but never wavers in his stance. Not once.

"Kidnapping?" He cocks a brow, "I'm pretty sure you snuck into my bed in the middle of the night."

"Elijah, this is beastly. You can't just tie people up."

"Hmmm, beastly. I like it." He bites his lip and lets his eyes travel across my bound body.

"Elijah…" I plead with him.

"Why would you complain when you haven't experienced what I have planned?"

"I didn't.agree.to.this."

"You heard Jax, you want one brother, you get them all." He winks.

"Elijah, I'm not sure what weird shit you're into," I try to pull my arms once more. "But I am not going to just let you…"

He crawls across my body, leaving shivers as his body moves against mine. His hot breath on my skin causes my temperature to rise. "Oh yes, you are, darling, and you were going to fucking enjoy every orgasm I gave you, but…" His finger slides down my neck ever so slowly, "for doubting my intentions," His hands move across my heaving breasts in circles, causing gasps to fall from my lips. "Maybe you shouldn't get a release at all."

"Elijah," I moan out his name.

His finger and thumb grip the nub of my nipple, adding pressure and pulling my back arches, and a moan crawls from my throat. "But that doesn't mean I won't still play with you…repeatedly…bring you to the fucking edge…with no release…you don't get to cum…until you start acting like a good fucking girl."

"You wouldn't..."

"Hmmm, let's see." His tongue moves across my lips. It's like electricity. The moment his tongue hits my skin, electricity moves down to the crevice between my thighs, and I'm moaning with desire. "See how easy that was, darling; you'll be so much fun to play with."

He's nestled between my legs, spread wide on a midnight iron spreader bar. The twinges in my pussy pulse at been spread so wide. I have an aching in the crevice between my legs that won't stop. He's on his knees, just allowing his eyes to fall across my body, licking his lips when they fall back on my spread pussy.

"Do you know how beautiful you look? Spread wide for me...like this." His teeth clamp down on his lip while he looks at me hungrily.

"Elijah," I gasp.

"I wonder how good you will be for me, darling."

His tongue slivers out, trailing a snail trail of his saliva down my neck. My body shivers in response to the touch, "Oh god, so good." I cry out. A smirk appears on his lips as his tongue trails back up my neck. Gasps push through my mouth, "Please...Elijah," I cry out.

"Do you know what I do, darling?"

My eyes widen, "what you do?" I shake my head because he has failed to mention what he did for work.

"I collect." His lips brush against mine. The slight teasing has my body going into a frenzy of desire.

"Like Luca?" I gasp.

"Not quite, darling. Luca hunts people. I just chase them." His lips crash against mine, his tongue hits mine, and my back arches as he pushes his lips harder against mine. A mix of saliva and desire has me gasping into his mouth. "I can be very..." his tongue slides down my body, "persuasive..." I can feel the hot wetness of his tongue as he travels across my stomach; looking up at me, he grins, "And if that doesn't work...there are other ways to get what I want."

His lips hit my thighs, and I nearly explode, "Oh god, Elijah...please...I will be good." I beg.

A stinging hits my body as his hand came down hard across my exposed pussy. I don't even have time to react. My body is still trying to comprehend what has just happened. Once more, he brings his hand down, hitting my pussy hard, and a loud scream falls from my lips. He never lets up. All I can hear is the slapping of my skin as he repeatedly beats my dripping pussy with his hand.

The stinging is replaced by pleasure, and my body tingles with desire as his hand again comes down hard across my pussy, "Please, please fuck me." I beg. A knowing smirk appears on his face, and I'm the only one shocked by the dirty words that tumble out of my mouth.

His hand moves roughly across my sore pussy. The sting crawls up my body with every graze of his rough hands, crawling across my body, his fingers dancing between my soaking pussy lips. "Look how wet you are for me. You are a good fucking girl, after all." He breathes into my ear.

"Oh, god," I cry out.

"Does it turn you on when I talk to you like...this." His fingers still dancing across my sore pussy.

"Yes," I breathe out.

"Look at you. Even your pussy is blushing for me. Are you sore, baby?"

"Yes," I breathe out once more.

"Oh baby, you don't look nearly sore enough." He whispers before moving away from my body.

I'm unsure if I have thoughts in my head any longer. All I can think of is the searing heat of stinging that pumps in the crevice between my thighs. The silence is unnerving, and I wonder what he will do next. When he's going to do it? The not knowing is pure torture, but mixed with the mounting desire, excitement travels the course of my body.

That is until I see him standing there with a thick, long rope that entwines in an intricate swirling motion with thick tassels falling from the end. My eyes widen in disbelief. "What is that?" I utter.

"This?" He holds the black leather strange tool in his hand, "Oh, this is just a flogger, darling."

"And what do you plan on doing with such a contraption?" I knew the answer, but I had to ask him anyway.

I had hoped it would stall him because I wasn't sure my poor pussy could take another beating, definitely not one that looked like it could rip me in two. I would have rather felt his hand again than have that anywhere near me.

He never answers me or gives me a warning as he lashes it against my pussy. A piercing scream falls from my body. The stinging from his hand was nothing compared to the searing heat I felt from his scary friend.

Once more, he raises his hand, bringing the flogger down hard against my pussy, my arms thrash in the restraints, but this time, a loud moan falls from my lips. The heat burns, but the desire hits a height I've never experienced.

The flogger repeatedly hits my pussy, one lash after another. The pleasure courses through my body, moans dripping from my lips as fast as my juice drips from my pussy. Once more, he brings it down hard against my clit, and tears crawl down my face as I cry out, and a gush of desire coats his body as I finally release.

"Oh baby, didn't I say you couldn't cum until you were a good girl." The look of disappointment on his face renders me confused. I want to respond, but I can only pant and look up at him with a flushed face. "Look at the mess you've made," he smiles.

"Elijah," I finally pant.

He slides his hand up and down his thick, long cock, and I salivate at the mouth. Watching his wide hand grip his cock as he rolls it up and down. My lips are encased tightly as I bite down on them, and a small whimper comes from them. "Is this what you want?" I nod, "But baby, I thought you were sore." He mocks me.

"I am," I croak out.

He positions his cock across my soaked pussy. I hold my breath, awaiting the searing pain I know will accompany me once he enters me. Still, instead, he slides his cock up and down my pussy lips moving faster and faster. My body shakes with every move-ment of his cock against my sensitive pussy.

"Oh, fuck," I cry out.

"If you insist." He smiles before ramming his cock deep inside of me. The way he fills me up instantly causes a stiffness in my veins. My breath catches in my throat. He raises his body, holding onto my wrists and starts thrusting gently at first, "God, Cara, you feel...fuck," he gasps.

The spasms of pain hit me, but with every thrust, the pleasure again overtook me. I can feel him stretching me wide, the never-ending pleasure pushed through my body, "Oh, Elijah, you feel so good.... don't stop... don't stop." I scream.

That's when he brings a knife into my view. I was so consumed with how he made my body feel that I hadn't noticed until the steel glinted under the room's low lights. I want to cry out that I don't want to die today, not like this. My body shudders, but with every thrust of my hips, I can only manage to moan my pleasure into the room.

"Do you know the most exciting thing that can happen to your body is fear," he breathes into my skin, "Tell me, darling, are you scared?" I nod, "Because I've been dying to taste you since I met you." He rasps.

The blade grazes my neck, slowly crawling down my body. I shudder beneath the thrusting and coldness against my skin. "There is nothing quite like..." the knife travels across my chest and quickly nips my skin. I feel the open wound almost instantly. "Adrenalised blood." He gasps.

His head dips, and I feel his mouth come down hard across the stinging open wound he had just created. A sigh falls from his lips as he laps up my spilt blood. Thrusting his hips harder, his cock penetrates me more roughly. My body jerks as I scream out with euphoric pleasure.

"Look how much your body enjoys being pushed past its limits," he breathes, again nicking my skin. This time, he smeared my blood across my chest, creating a heart shape, the blood that covered my chest. "One day, I might let you cut a heart into my chest," he rasps.

"Oh god, oh god," I scream as his thrust becomes more manic in a mix of blood, want and passion. He tips me over the edge, high climbs through my body that I'm not sure I will ever come down from.

"That's it, darling, cum for me." He growls.

The way my body responds to him as I cry out all my release into the night, a tumbling pleasure erupts from my core. Crashing over my body like a tumbling ocean. The stream of desire pours out of me, covering his cock.

"Oh, fuck," He screams out, and I feel a gush of his own mounting pleasure thrust deep inside of me, filling me up and bloating my stomach with his hot seed.

It takes a while before I get my breath back in my body. Looking down, I see the dried evidence of my blood that sits in a heart on my chest, and scary as it was, it was the most erotic act I had ever experienced.

"Elijah?"

"Yes, darling." He raises his head, and his eyes bore into mine.

"You and your brothers are going to ruin me, aren't you?"

"We will completely break you, darling," he smiles, "but don't worry, we'll put you back together." He winks.

I didn't doubt his words. Nothing seemed simple with the Kane brothers, and I had no doubt that he wouldn't break me. The only thing that concerned me was how badly I yearned to be broken.

I had been broken before, but nobody fixed my broken pieces. I hadn't been put back together. Some parts were shattered. Some were lost. My missing pieces were what haunted me.

Maybe they would put me back together, but they'd already given to me. They'd have to put me back together differently because of what I had already experienced from Jax and Elijah. I wasn't sure if I could ever be put back the same.

He was wrong.

You couldn't ruin something that was already broken.

I didn't want to fall, not again. But my heart had a long rest.

I couldn't hide from my feelings forever.

Maybe this wouldn't be the most incredible love story ever told, but perhaps I would find my heart again.

The day I met River is the day I think I fell in love.

He was just so bloody cute and sweet, the way Jax had spoken about him. He was the one I was most worried about meeting, but Elijah had said the bear from the wilderness was the one I should be worried about, not baby cakes.

I wasn't sure why they named him the bear, but I assumed it was because he was grizzly. He was the oldest of the Kane brothers, and I would be lying if I didn't say Luca Kane didn't intrigue me.

I had been here three months, and the bear hadn't returned. When I asked what kind of work he did, I was unsure if I was ready for that conversation.

Elijah had said he collected things. That is a massive understatement. He hunted things, not collected them. People, to be exact. These were not very nice people, so that was to be excused. It sounded horrific. How would you even get into that line of work?

Yes, as much as Luca intrigued me, he also sounded terrifying. He was a walking red flag, and I wasn't sure if red was my colour.

My first thought when Jax had brought me home and confessed that they liked to share was this was madness. Every girl's dream, I would imagine. Four sexy men who wanted to possess, own and protect you, but the panic set in as soon as I had realised who Elijah was.

When River came home, I had already been playing with his two brothers for a week, and making that decision wasn't even that hard. They were so different, yet they had both completely consumed me. I had thought it would be harder than it was, but in the short time I had with them both, we had become like a little family.

When River came home, I knew what I was expecting. He was the final brother because, by Elijah's admission, the bear wouldn't entertain the idea of me, but maybe we could be friends. I would hate to think I was the cause of anyone's anger.

Maybe Luca would warm to me just as I had his three brothers. It wasn't a crazy thought; if someone told me this was what I would be doing months ago, I would have laughed at them. It wasn't even a possibility, but here I was, living my best life with three men who had quickly crawled their way into my life.

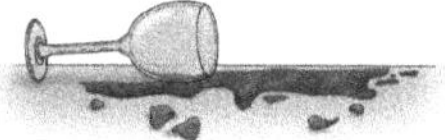

I'm sitting in the kitchen watching River as he mixes some concoction in a bowl. He's as charming and good-looking as his brothers but has the most amber eyes I've ever seen.

The different swirls of brown as the light hits them are almost enchanting. His short blond hair is styled to the side, and every so often, he raises his head and gives me a smile that lights up his whole face.

"What are you making today?" I ask.

"Cupcakes." He smiles.

"Cupcakes at ten in the morning?"

"You haven't lived until you've had dessert for breakfast." He winks.

"Can I help?"

"Sure, doll, you can tell me your favourite colour."

"I don't think anyone has ever asked me that before."

"Well?"

"Amethyst." I smile.

"Pretty, just like you. Then Amethyst cupcakes you will have."

"I'm not sure that's what I meant by helping, though."

"Were the rules of this kitchen not explained?" He cocks a brow.

"Nobody is allowed to cook in here when River is home." I put on my best Jax mocking voice.

"Hey, I don't sound like that." I hear Jax scold me.

"Well, you weren't supposed to hear that," I mumble.

"Good morning, trouble." Jax pulls me into his body. His lips crush against mine, and the swimming desire immediately leaves me breathless. I'm gasping into his mouth.

His hands crawl down my body, resting just under my ass. He lifts me up and puts me on the kitchen counter, allowing his tongue to trail desire down my neck.

"Hey, not while I'm cooking." River scolds him.

"I'm just getting her warmed up for you, buddy." He winks.

His fingers expertly crawl down my body, unbuttoning the black cotton dress that is draped across my body. Jax made it a rule that I wore no underwear because it wouldn't stay on for long. His hands expertly massage my breasts, and I'm gasping from the shocks of pleasure that pierce my body.

"How am I supposed to concentrate on this with you doing that to her?"

"I'd think it would inspire you to get a move on."

Jax lays my body flat, and I look up and see the desire swirling in River's amber eyes. I feel Jax's lips slowly kiss down my body. Gasps of pleasure fall from my lips.

"Here, taste." River shoves his fingers in my mouth, and I slowly suck the frosting from his fingers, listening to the short gasps that fall from his lips. I'm excited at what my mouth does to his body in moments.

River towers across my body while the sensation of Jax's mouth reaches my inner thighs. Taking a plastic spatula, River smears Amethyst-coloured frosting across my nipples, smearing them until the pointed nubs are covered.

His body arches across mine as his head comes down, flicking his tongue out and sucking the stiff peak into his mouth. I cry my desire into the room, reaching back and gripping his shirt as the pleasure thrashes through my body.

"How does it taste?" Jax asks.

"Delicious," River responds.

I feel Jax slide his fingers deep inside me; my back arches while River teases my nipples with his tongue. "Oh god, oh god, oh god," I cry, feeling Jax twirl his fingers deep inside my dripping pussy.

Jax ejects his fingers and stands, holding his hand towards his brother, "Here, I'm sure you'll find this appetising." My eyes widened; surely, he wouldn't do what I thought he would.

River grabs his hand, plunging Jax's fingers into his mouth. Tasting me on him. I watch as he licks off every drop. Moans crawl out of my body, and a burning feeling of desire hits me as I watch the most erotic act I've ever witnessed.

"You are right; she's fucking delectable." He smirks, "Although I wonder what she would taste like frosted up." He winks.

"I thought we were having cupcakes." I moan out at the ongoing desire that currently hits my body.

"You are the cupcake." River whispers before pressing his lips towards mine and allowing me to taste myself on his lips.

River walks around the counter, standing by Jax and passing the bowl to Jax. I watch as he smears frosting across my aching pussy. My back arches at the cold sensation that travels through my body. "So sensitive, kitten." Jax smiles, continuing to smear my pussy with frosting until I'm covered.

I feel River slide his tongue across the frosting, driving his tongue hard up my soaking folds. "Oh god," I cry, digging my hands into my hair. The pulsing pleasure tips me over the edge.

Then something surprising happens. Jax bends my legs onto the counter, opening me up and holding my thighs tightly. River allows his dexterous tongue to roam across my pussy, hitting every sweet spot. The moans crawl out of me in a manic thrust of lustful desire. His tongue hits my ass.

That's not where his tongue needs to be, but why does it feel so damn good? Every time his tongue flicks across my ass, my body jolts, and surprisingly, the moans slip from my lips. He enters me, and the gasps erupt from my body, causing my pussy to drip.

"Ah, you're well-lubricated now."

"For what?" Neither of them responds to me; they just share a knowing smirk.

"All fours, kitten." Jax rasps in my ear.

He sounds desperate.

They both look positively delicious.

They look at me with sweet, dark desire laced in their eyes, and how they watch me causes my body to shake recklessly.

Spinning my body around, I get into position on all fours just like I've been asked and flatten my palms against the cold counter, instantly sending shivers up my spine.

I hear the faint shuffling of clothes removed, and my excitement peaks. A hand caresses my ass gently, rubbing in small circles.

The tender touch has me letting out a comforted sigh. "I'm more of an ass man," I hear River whisper, "and I fucking love your ass, so fucking sweet." He gasps.

I feel his cock line up against my ass, and panic shatters my body. His hands firmly grip my hips, tilting my body slightly into an upright position. Jax's eyes fall across mine, and his thumb encircles my cheek, "relax, kitten," I shake my head, "I promise we would never do anything to hurt you." I scowl at his words, "Do you trust me?" I nod, "then, relax."

But I couldn't.

No matter how often he told me I should, I couldn't relax. The impending feat of a cock pressing against my ass had my body going into shock. I had never had anything near my ass, let alone had a thick cock shoved into my tiny virgin asshole.

He presses his cock harder against the hole that should never have anything enter it, and once again, my body stiffens. Comes close, his hand falls across my aching pussy, and the way he rubs my wet pussy lips has me arching my back, pushing further into River's cock. "That's right, kitten, you're so fucking wet." He gasps.

His fingers plummet deep into my pussy, curling deep within the hot sticky wetness of my centre. Pushing my body further into the edge. "Oh god, please don't stop," I beg. I see Jax nod and feel River push the tip into my tight hole. My body shakes and stops, allowing me to get used to the thick cock now inhabiting my ass.

"I'm going to push a little further," I hear him gasp into my ear.

I want to respond, but Jax twirls his fingers deep inside me, and I lose all thought.

The fact that River is slowly pushing his cock through absconds my notice; all I can do is cry out the never-ending pleasure that runs through my body with every thrust of Jax's fingers. One more thrust and a scream emits from my throat as I feel River fill me up.

He slowly thrust, and the pain shooting through my body moments ago quickly turned to pleasure. It rushes through me like a lightning bolt. Rendering me, unable to cry out words, just incoherently screaming with every thrust.

"God, you're such a good....girl." He gasps. "Your so...fucking...tight...fuck, Cara, fuuck." He growls.

Jax ejects his fingers from my dripping pussy and starts working his fingers across my clit; once again, my back arches pulling River deep within my ass. The erotic explosions hit my body in an all-consuming way.

"Oh god, oh god... I'm going to..." I scream out.

Jax positions a champagne glass beneath my dripping pussy, but I'm too far gone to question his motives. River grips my hips and thrashes his cock deep within my hole, crying out how I'm such a good girl for taking his cock so well.

The pleasure runs through me; my body feels hotter than the sun. One more thrust and I come undone. Releasing all that built-up desire with an explosive rush, pouring out of my pussy like a waterfall.

The screams crawl out of my mouth, and my body shakes with the release of desire that crawled out of my body like a demon.

River thrusts once more, gasping in my ear and feeling his hot cum splash inside my ass, filling me up and ejecting all his desire for me. I gasped, feeling euphoric at being ripped open by the Kane brothers once more.

Jax lifts the glass positioned beneath my pussy and brings the glass to my lips, "Drink." He commands. I look at him with confusion, "Drink, kitten, taste how fucking good you taste."

I open my mouth, and Jax tips the glass, allowing my juices to slide down my throat. Gulping down every drop they had caused to drop out of my pussy.

"Good girl," Jax utters before smashing his lips against mine and flicking his tongue against my lips, "Mmmm, delicious." He rasps before releasing me.

River grips my neck, pulling my head back to meet his, and his lips crash against mine, his tongue flicking against mine in desperate need. "You were so good, baby; you taste so fucking sweet." He smiles as he finally releases me.

He finally released my body from the hold his cock had on my body. My body falls forward, and the pants still fall from my lips. A throbbing in my ass emits, but the underlying release makes me suddenly smile out of nowhere.

"How was that?" River asks.

"It was...it was wonderful." I pant.

I don't hear the rest of the conversation; I'm in constant euphoric bliss.

I have experienced more with the Kane brothers than I had experienced in my entire life, and the stark realisation hits me.

They were going to ruin me, and god damn it, I was going to let them.

I have been here for months, and still no sign of the fourth. I knew he wouldn't entertain me, but I was curious when the bear would rear its ugly head. His brothers would barely divulge any information about him. All I was told was he was complicated.

What did that even mean?

A train wreck was complicated. A natural disaster was complicated. This entire arrangement we had going on was complicated, but the mysterious Luca, what made him so complicated?

Another mystery I suppose I wouldn't uncover, just like that house I was never allowed to speak of, lest they all look at me like I had invited a demon into their home. I shudder at the memory. I made a point to just let any thoughts of that house die because it seemed like it wasn't welcome in this house anyway.

I had never regretted entering this dynamic with the Kane brothers; every moment was perfect. Until Mother Nature decided to rear her ugly head and attack my body. It felt like my ovaries were being battered by a hacksaw.

The pain travels through my abdomen at an alarming rate. I suddenly wish I was at home...alone, where I could bleed to death on the bathroom floor and pity myself for all the woes of being a woman.

But I couldn't do that.

I was here. I was having a terrible time pretending I was fine in their house. It was almost embarrassing to pretend that the sharp pains that jolted my body didn't exist.

They knew something was wrong. They repeatedly asked me if I was okay, and my answer was always the same. "I'm fine," That sentence could be summed up in many contexts. How often had a woman said she was fine but was anything but?

I'm curled up on the sofa, lying on Jax's shoulder and listening to his heartbeat. I glance around at them, and they all have the same look. A look of uncertainty and worry. I'm unsure what they had to worry about; their body wasn't trying to kill them alarmingly, causing them to cry in agony.

"Why do you keep looking at me like that?" I finally gasped.

"You don't seem yourself, kitten, and you seem unwilling to let us in on what is happening in that pretty little head of yours." Jax sighs.

"I told you..."

"You're fine." River and Elijah recite in unison.

Jax tips my chin until my eyes finally meet his, "Don't lie to me; I know when something is bothering you. You're our girl; we would do anything for you."

"I know," I whisper, tears in my eyes.

"What's bothering you, princess?"

"It's embarrassing," I whisper.

"Okay, now you have to tell us." Elijah winks and ignores the scowl I direct at him.

"It's gross." I sigh.

"Princess, there is nothing, and I mean...nothing. That you could say that we would think was gross." Jax smiles.

"See? That's what I mean; you don't think anything is wrong with me." I sigh, getting frustrated with him. With them all.

"What?" River stands with his hands on his hips and races towards us, "you," his fingers tease my cheek, "are perfect." He slams his lips against mine in a rush of desire until my soft moans fall into his mouth.

I can feel my pussy clenching and the fresh flow seeping out, and now I'm groaning in annoyance.

"God damn it, River, now look what you've done."

He looks around at his brothers, who shake their heads with confused looks pasted on their faces. "What did I do?" He asks.

"It doesn't matter." I grit out.

"Cara, I have been very patient with you, and you play the brat very well..." Jax sternly grits out.

"Brat?" My mouth opens in surprise, but I don't wait for him to continue what he probably would regret saying.

I quickly move away from him. The pain pierces my gut, and I hold in the sharp gasp that threatens to come out. Finally getting the energy to stand, I feel his hands crawl around my waist and pull my body onto his lap. "Please, let me go," I beg.

"Now, why would I want to do that, my bratty little princess." He whispers into my neck, sending electricity shocks to crawl up and down my spine.

His lips hit my neck, and I'm unsure if it's my predicament I won't speak of, but the desire runs through my body hard and fast. "Oh god," I gasp out. "Please..." His tongue hits my ear, pulling my body against his. I lean into his delicate touch, "Please, Jax, we can't...." I cry out.

"No?" His fingers dance across my swollen, aching breasts, and the slightest touch against my hard nipples has me screaming into the room. "Fuck, kitten, you're so fucking sensitive," he gasps.

His hands crawl down my body, and my heart races with panic. "No, we can't," I scream, but it doesn't deter his movements across my body. His fingers are dancing close to the apex between my thighs, and I silently curse his actions that don't seem to be ceasing. "Fuck, Jax, I'm on my period." I finally utter.

His fingers immediately stop in their tracks, and I feel confused. I was horny with the dwindling desire coursing through my body, but I also felt utterly gross and in pain.

It was a strange situation that I had found myself in. The other months when Mother Nature had reared her ugly head here had been a breeze, but this month was painful and arduous.

"I see," His words fall into my ear, "Why didn't you just say that?"

"I...I don't know, you are men and..."

"Princess, we want to take care of you; how can we do that if you won't let us."

"You don't want anything to do with this; it's disgusting."

"I don't find your little fertile body disgusting, do you?" He asks his brothers, and of course, they agree with him.

I feel my body lifted, and I instantly wrap my arms around his neck. "Jax, what are you doing? I just said..."

"Bath?" Elijah asks.

"Bath." Jax agrees.

"Jax, you don't need to do this." I try to protest.

"Now, kitten, didn't I say we wanted to look after you?" I nod with tears welling in my eyes, "then that's what we are going to do."

The scent of rose and lavender fills the bathroom when we enter. Jax refused to put me down, "princesses don't walk when they can be carried," he had whispered in my ear.

The feminist in me wanted to protest, but the young girl who had dreamed of something so chivalrous growing up had wanted to experience the notion that good men still did exist.

My eyes widen as I look at the oversized bath brimming with pretty pink bubbles bubbling on the top of the water. Little candles are placed across the bath's rim, and blood-red rose petals paint a path to the tub.

"You...did this...for me?" River and Elijah stand there with their sleeves rolled up, allowing the muscles to pop beneath their shirts. The tightly fitted trousers cling to their muscular frame with wet patches in different places. They beam at me in response.

Jax finally puts me on the ground, and as my feet hit the cold, marbled stone floor, a shiver runs through my body. "Arms up," he commands.

"You know, Jax, I am capable of undressing myself."

His fingers tease my belly beneath my white shirt, "Sure, kitten, but why would you want to? Arms up."

He gently slides his hands up my body, teases the shirt over my head, and throws it to the ground. His fingers fumble with the button of my stone-wash jeans, and I hear the zip come down. His lips find mine, sliding his tongue across my lips, parting my mouth with his; I get lost in swimming desire when his lips press hard against mine. "Jax," I breathe into his mouth.

He crawls down my body, releasing me from the clothing that had felt like the only source of protection from the crime scene in my pants. Lifting my body, he lays me across the chaise lounge near the bath.

Bringing his hand around the band of my granny knickers, he slides them off quickly, and the uncomfortable feeling I previously had is now back. He crawls up my body, unclasping the bra from my breasts; a gasp falls from my lips as he lightly grazes my nipples with his fingertips.

"You know what's good for cramps?"

"Chocolate?" I offer.

"Orgasms." He whispers in my ear.

My legs are parted, held open wide by River and Jax, "This would never survive." I utter at the cream chaise lounge I'm currently laid upon.

"We can always buy a new one," Jax whispers.

I feel his tongue come across my hardened nipple, and a sharp gasp leaves my throat. River teases the other nipple into his mouth, and the pleasure rushes through my body. Their tongues simultaneously massage my nipples, and all thoughts of why I had been unwilling leave my head. I can only imagine how good their smooth tongues feel against my raw, exposed nipples.

"Oh god, oh god, don't stop, don't stop." I cry out, feeling my pussy pulse with desire from every stroke of their tongue.

Looking down, Elijah kneels between my thighs, and a wicked grin spreads across his face, "I have been dying to taste you, darling. Just. Like. This." He rasps with excitement.

His teeth come down against the string of the tampon, and his tongue slivers out, hitting my ass as he clamps down on that string, and as surprised as I am, I can't help thinking how sexy he looks between my legs.

"Oh fuck," I cry out as Jax and River continue to tease my nipples.

Elijah pulls the string and waves the silk fabric under my nose, "Does this remind you of anything?"

"It's... it's...," I murmur with absolute perplexity.

"It's definitely not the cause of your embarrassment, surely, darling," he says tauntingly, sliding his tongue out. He laps up the blood from the used tampon, "fucking delicious. I'm going to fucking devour your pretty little pussy, darling."

He smiles while his fingers dance down my body to my wet pussy. I'm unsure if his comment should make me mortified or turned on.

"This is what makes you feel so uncomfortable?" Jax whispers, "You think us men are so disgusted that we won't want you because you are on your period?"

I nod, feeling like the biggest fool because he had summed up my thoughts.

"I love this icky feeling," Elijah whispers, tongue dancing across my thigh, "it makes me want to feel all of you."

"Oh, please, please, please," I cry out.

Their hands slide up my body in sync as they reach my nipples. Their hands teased my body in ways I thought were only reserved for dreams. River's hand slides across my belly to my pussy, "so wet, so fucking wet," he rasps. Elijah slides a finger up my pussy, and I instantly clench in response to the intense feeling.

"Fuck, you are so tight, baby," Elijah rasps as Jax and River continue to tease my nipples and my body.

"Fuck, I want you, kitten," Jax whispers.

"Let me have the honour, mother fucker," Elijah growls aggressively, and Jax agrees.

Elijah spreads my legs wide and slides the head of his cock against my wet pussy. My body screams in anticipation, but his head stays pressed against where I want him. "Please, please, please." I cry out.

"Tell me who you belong to." He orders.

I look into his eyes, "uhm," I murmur.

"Jax, River, or me?"

I look from Jax to River, "Jax, River, you."

"Who?" He growls.

"Jax, River, and you," I murmur louder.

"I want you to look at me when you say it," Elijah demands.

Looking at him as he teases my pussy with his head, I murmur, "Jax, River and you."

"Close, but not quite," Elijah demands one more time.

"Jax, River and you," I say urgently.

"Say my name."

"Elijah?"

He slaps me across the face, causing me to cry out. "Say my name," he orders again. His eyes flash with the hunger of anger and frustrated desire.

"Elijah?"

"You have to mean it," Jax says.

Their eyes lock, and he slams into me as my eyes roll into my head. The pain is intense, and I try to catch my breath when I feel him pull out, "no, please," I beg.

Jax looks at me, "You can do it.

"Jax, River, and you...Elijah." I say louder.

"Louder." He orders.

"Jax, River, and you...Elijah." I murmur.

"Louder," he demands.

"Jax, River, and you...Elijah."

Jax pulls him from my body, and I whimper at the loss of his cock. "Enough, it's enough; you have to take her. She can't take anymore," Jax says as he strokes his cock.

As Elijah looks at me, his eyes flash with something I am unsure of as his hands slide over my body. Their eyes lock, and they pull me down the length of the chaise lounge past them, where they lay me out.

I lie prone, and Elijah slides his hands beneath my waist and ankles. Opening my legs wide, I can feel his fingertips glide over my ass, and he lifts me slightly. I lay there breathless, not knowing what to expect, but when I felt the wet tip of his tongue slide across my ass and down my slit, I screamed in shock.

Jax kneels in front of me and takes my face into his hands. "This is what's going to happen right now." He whispers, "You'll allow River and Elijah to take care of your aches and pains; nothing will be forced upon you.

Then, when you're ready, and your body is prepared, you will allow me the honour of taking you."

"But I want you now, Jax," I whimper as Elijah teases my ass, his tongue swirling around my tight hole.

"This isn't about what you want," Elijah growls as his tongue flicks against my ass.

"It's about what's best for you," Jax whispers.

"Fuck." I cry out as Elijah's tongue slides into my ass, and I feel a finger slide inside my pussy. I'm overwhelmed with the sensations as Elijah's tongue teases my ass, and his finger curls inside my pussy and presses against my g-spot. I start to writhe as the sensations build, and I'm unsure if I can take much more.

"You look so sexy like this," Jax whispers.

Looking up, River and Elijah are standing beside Jax, and River is stroking his cock. The other two are standing beside me, their eyes locked on my body. Elijah spreads my ass open, revealing my puckered hole, and licks his lips off my juices. "You're definitely our princess." He murmurs before his tongue licks me.

I try to moan, but he presses his thumbs against my tight hole, and I cry. "Eli," Jax growls. He pulls back and looks at me as I gasp for air.

"You're so tight, princess. You need to relax." Elijah whispers against my ass before he blows against it, "Just relax, baby," he says again before he blows against me gently, "Relax and enjoy it."

"I...oh...oh...oh," I repeatedly murmur as his tongue swirls and flicks against my ass and his finger flicks against my clit. I feel another finger slide inside my wet pussy, and I cry out.

Jax's finger slides across my pussy, "so wet, so tight," he rasps.

"Oh, please, please, I need to cum," I cry.

"No, you need to cum with us," Jax whispers as I feel another finger slide inside me.

"Oh, oh, oh," I cry out as I feel all three of their fingers curling into me. "Oh, God, oh, God, oh, God," I cry as my orgasm consumes my body. Their fingers curl inside me, and I feel a third finger slide inside. My breathing is heavy and laboured as I scream out in pleasure. When they pull out of me, I feel empty and frustrated.

I hear a click, and I tell myself to relax as they spread my body and slip leather cuffs around my ankles and thighs. "Relax, princess," Jax whispers behind me. I cry out as my knees are pulled back to my chest and my wrists are pulled over my head.

"Oh, God," I cry as they open my legs.

"Let's see how many times we can make you cum, princess," Elijah whispers as he traces his finger along my slit.

"Oh, God," I murmur again as they stroke my body.

"Jax, use your mouth, please." I mewl.

"What do you want," he growls.

"You," I murmur.

"What do you want?" He repeats. "Tell me what you want." He demands.

"I want you. I want you between my legs. I want you to use your mouth on me, I want you to eat me, I want you to eat my pussy, I want you to fuck me...please...fuck me." I beg.

"That's it," Jax purrs against my skin as I feel his tongue slide over my clit, "that's exactly what I wanted to hear."

"Oh, God," I murmur as his tongue slides through my slit.

"You taste so good, princess," he growls as he laps at my clit before he slides his tongue through my lips. I cry out in pleasure as he flicks against my clit.

"Oh, God," I cry as his tongue flutters over my clit, and I feel his fingers slide through my wetness. His tongue swirls around my clit, and I cry out in pleasure.

Jax's fingers slide through my pussy, "So wet, kitten, so fucking wet."

"Oh, fuck," I cry out as I feel his fingers curl inside me.

"Oh, fuck," I murmur as his fingers curl inside me and find my G-spot. His tongue swirls over my clit, and his fingers press against my G-spot. "Jax," I whimper as my eyes roll into my head.

"That's it, kitten, cum for me."

Feeling his fingers slide inside of me, I scream out in pleasure as I feel his fingers curl inside of my pussy and his tongue swirl against my clit. When he pulls back, I cry out in frustration.

Feeling his cock slide between my lips and back and forth before he growls, "You're so fucking tight." He holds my hip with his free hand as he slowly pushes his cock inside my tight slit just an inch before he pulls back again. "You're so fucking tight and so wet." Again and again, he slides his cock in and out of me.

"Oh, God," I murmur as I feel his cock slide through my slit. My eyes lock on his, and his eyes lock on mine. I throw my head back against the cushions. When he pulls back, I cry out in frustration. I feel his cock press against my tight hole before he holds my hip and pushes deep inside me.

"Oh, God," I murmur as he slides his cock in and out of me.

River kneels beside me, and a warm towel rubs against my skin. I turn my head to the side and reach for him. "Please," I murmur. He gives me a wink before he wraps an arm around my waist, letting the towel fall to the side, and then he settles against the side of the couch beside me. I turn my head, and my eyes lock before he leans close to my ear.

He growls, "You're so sexy like this." Then he bites down on my earlobe and takes my nipple into his mouth.

"Oh, God," I cry as Jax slides deeper inside me.

"You're such a fucking good girl," Jax hisses as he keeps his hips pressed against my ass and his cock buried deep inside me. He slides his hands up my skin and cups my breasts as he pulls back until he's almost out of me. "I love how tight you are, I love how you grip my cock, I love how you feel inside of me." He whispers as he pulls back until he's almost out of me.

"I love how you're so fucking tight; nothing better than feeling your pussy gripping my cock, kitten, nothing." He pulls back until he's out of me, and I moan in frustration. The hand on my hip pulls my leg back until my knee is pressed against my chest. I groan when his cock slides back inside of me.

"Oh, fuck," I murmur as his cock slides through my slit. He grunts before he pulls back until he's most of the way out of me again. "I'm close." He whispers as he slides back inside of me.

"Oh, God," I murmur as his cock slides through my wetness. Reaching up and running my fingers through his hair, "That's it, fuck me," I whisper.

"You like this, do you?" Jax whispers as he slides back inside me.

"Yes," I whisper as he presses his cock deeper inside me, "I like this, I like you, I like all of you," I murmur, and I feel my eyes rolling into my head.

"I like you too, kitten; I fucking love you." He whispers back as he pulls back and slams his hips against my ass.

"Oh, God," I cry as the hand on my hip pushes my leg back further.

Jax slides his hand into my hair and pulls my head back. "I love you, princess," he whispers against my ear as his hips slam against my ass. The hand on my hip moves down and over my pussy before he presses against my clit. "I'll never get enough of you." He says against my skin as he rubs my clit.

"Oh, God," I murmur over and over again. "Fuck me, Jax, fuck me harder, fuck me deeper, I want you to fuck me harder, I want you to fuck me deeper, fuck me harder, baby, fuck me harder...harder...." I murmur my words as I feel his cock slide over my G-spot.

"Oh, God," I whimper as he leans forward and traces his tongue over my ear.

"You're close, kitten; I can feel it; I can feel your pussy gripping my cock." He whispers in my ear. "Cum for me, princess." He whispers, and I moan.

"Oh, God," I cry as I tense my body. It's like I'm vibrating from the inside out. River's tongue and fingers are swirling against my nipples as Jax keeps his cock deep inside me. He moans against my skin as he licks my neck.

"Oh, God," I whimper as my body tense. "I'm going to cum, Jax, I'm going to cum." I murmur.

"Cum for me, princess, please do it." He whispers in my ear, and I cry out in pleasure.

"Oh, God," I cry out. Then my pussy tightens around Jax's cock, and I feel myself cumming as Jax's hips slam against my ass.

"Oh, fuck," Jax hisses as he presses into me, "fuck, you feel so good, kitten."

"Oh, fuck," Jax hisses as his fingers tighten in my hair.

"Oh, God," I murmur as my body relaxes and my eyes roll into my head. I feel Jax's hands move from my hips to my waist, and he pulls me onto the couch. He leans over me, his hands on either side of my head.

He whispers, "You're so fucking beautiful, kitten." Then he presses his lips against mine. Wrapping my arms around his neck and holding him against me. He growls against my lips before he slides his tongue into my mouth. His cock is still buried deep inside me as he pulls back and stares down at me.

"You're such a fucking good girl, kitten." He whispers before he lowers his lips to my neck and trails them over my skin. I feel myself growing tense as he pushes his hips forward. River crawls onto the couch behind me, and I feel his cock slide between my legs, pressing against my pussy. I murmur against Jax's lips before I lick them.

"Yes," I murmur as his hips push forward.

I wrap my arms around his neck and hold him against me. He growls against my lips before he slides his tongue into my mouth. His cock is still buried deep inside me as he pulls back and stares down at me.

"Yes," I murmur as his hips push forward.

"Let him fuck you; let him stretch out that little ass." He whispers.

"Okay," I murmur.

Jax leans back, and River pushes his cock against my ass. I bite my lip and whimper as I feel my body tense. "Relax, kitten, relax. It's just River, baby." Jax whispers as he runs his fingers over my cheek. "Relax, kitten."

Then River pushes against me, and I take a deep breath. "Oh, fuck," I cry out as he moves forward.

"Fuck, that's it, relax, kitten, relax for me, let him in, give me that tight little ass," Jax whispers as he runs his fingers through my hair.

Then River pushes forward, and I whimper as my body tenses. "Relax, kitten," Jax whispers as he leans forward and licks my lips. "Relax, kitten."

"Oh, God," I whimper as I feel River's cock slide inside me.

"Fuck her," Jax says, and River pushes forward.

"Oh, God," I cry as I stretch around him.

"Fuck her, fuck her harder," Jax whispers against my lips.

River pumps his hips forward, and I yelp.

"That's it, kitten; you like that, don't you?" Jax whispers in my ear.

I swallow and nod.

"Oh, God," I cry as River slams his hips against my ass.

"She likes that, Jax; she likes it hard," River says, and Jax growls behind me.

"Turn around and suck your ass off his cock, kitten," Jax whispers.

I move and kneel between River's legs. I blush as I wrap my lips around his cock and lean forward. I moan against his cock as I feel his hand slide into my hair.

"That's it, kitten, that's it, suck that ass off his cock." Jax whispers.

Moaning against River's cock, and suddenly my body tenses.

"Oh, fuck," Jax groans, "she's going to cum."

Blushing as River grips my hair and pulls the head of his cock from my lips. He strokes his cock, and I watch. I feel my body tremble, and I look up at him, and he grins. Then I feel my pussy contract against nothing, and I moan. "Oh, God," I murmur against River's thigh as I feel my hair pulled back.

River's hands slide up my thighs, and I feel him pull me against his body, whimpering against his skin and feeling his cock slide between my legs. Feeling Jax's fingers against my pussy, he slides one inside me.

Moaning against River's skin and feeling his cock pressing against my back door. He leans forward and runs his lips across my back.

"You're going to take both of us, princess; you're going to take my cock in that pretty little pussy and Jax's cock up your ass," River says as I feel Jax's fingers slide out of me.

Moaning still against River's skin as Jax slides his fingers between my cheeks, and I feel him press against my used ass.

"Relax, kitten," Jax whispers in my ear.

I take a deep breath, and Jax pushes against me, whimpering against River's skin as I feel my body tremble. "Relax, kitten, relax." I hear Jax whisper behind me.

Taking a deep breath as Jax pushes against me. I whimper as I feel my body tense up. Biting my lip and whining as I feel Jax's cock slide inside me.

"Relax, kitten, just relax for me," Jax whispers in my ear, and I nod as I feel River's cock slide between my legs, pressing against my pussy. I take a deep breath, and Jax pushes forward.

Feeling River's cock pressing against my pussy, I moan against his skin.

"That's it, kitten; you love that, don't you?" Jax whispers in my ear.

I nod as I feel River's cock sliding between my legs.

"That's it, kitten; you love to be stretched open, don't you?" Jax whispers in my ear.

I nod again.

"She loves it, she loves that big cock in her little pussy, and she loves that cock in her tight little ass," River says as he grips my waist.

I whimper against River's skin, and I feel my pussy contract.

"Oh, God." I whimper, and River grins against my skin.

"Fuck her, Jax, fuck her," River says as he slaps my ass and Jax growls.

"Oh, God, you're so fucking tight," Jax growls against my ear. "Oh, fuck, kitten, you feel so fucking good," Jax says.

I whimper against River's skin as Jax slides deeper into me.

"That's it, kitten; you love having both of us filling you up, don't you?" Jax whispers.

I nod against River's skin as Jax slides deeper with every stroke.

"Oh, fuck," I moan as I feel my body start to tense.

"Oh, fuck, she's going to cum again," Jax whispers.

I moan against River's skin as I feel my body tremble. "Oh, fuck." I sigh as I feel Jax slide deeper and deeper.

I feel my body shudder, moaning my excitement into the room.

"Oh, fuck, I'm going to cum, you little fucking slut; I'm going to cum in your tight little ass," Jax growls against my ear as I feel his cock spasm.

I moan as I feel him filling me up, and I pant as my body presses against him. "Oh, fuck, oh, fuck." I moan against River's skin.

"Oh, fuck, I'm going to cum, darling; I'm going to cum in your pussy." River moans and I feel him grip my waist. I whimper as my body shudders, moaning again as I feel my pussy twitch around him.

River grunts, and I moan as I feel his cock spasm, he leans forward, and I turn around and presses my lips against his. He groans as I feel Jax slide out of me.

"Oh, God," I whimper as I feel Jax's cock slide from my ass.

"Relax, kitten. I'm not done with you yet." Jax says, and I blush.

Turning around and gripping the back of the couch, I feel Jax spread my cheeks. "Oh, God," I moan as I feel Jax press against me.

"Oh, fuck," Jax groans as he slides inside me, gasping and moaning against the couch as I feel my body tremble.

"Oh, fuck, kitten, you grip my cock so fucking nicely." Jax moans as he grips my waist. "Oh, fuck," Jax groans as he slides deeper into me.

"Oh, God," I moan.

"Fuck, kitten, you're going to cum again," Jax whispers, and I cry out as my body tenses.

"Oh, fuck," I moan against the couch as my body trembles. Moaning against the sofa as Jax slides deeper into me. My eyes roll into the back of my head as I feel my pussy contract around his cock.

"Oh, fuck, kitten, how are you so fucking tight? You're so fucking hot." Jax whispers in my ear.

Panting against the couch as I feel my body continue to tremble. I open my eyes, and I look at Elijah. He has a grin as he stands up and kisses me.

"How are you feeling, princess?" River whispers.

"I am feeling better now," I whisper, and River smiles.

"You're so fucking sexy, kitten," Jax whispers, and I blush.

I look down, and I see Jax leaning against my back. I moan as his cock pulses inside me.

"Oh, God, Jax, you're still hard." I moan as I feel my body start to tremble. "Oh, God, Oh, God, Oh, God." I groan over and over again as I feel my body shudder. "Oh, fuck," I moan as I feel Jax slide out of me.

I whimper and feel him kiss my back before he steps away from me. I lean against the couch, and I feel him lean back against the couch next to me.

River stands up and leans against the back of the couch, brushing my hair from my neck.

Elijah leans down and kisses my shoulder, and I moan into River's mouth as I feel his arm slide over my waist.

I push back against him, open my eyes and look at him.

I wrap my arms around him, and I giggle when he moans.

"Hey, what are you doing?" River says.

I giggle, turn around, and press my lips against his before wrapping my arms around his neck.

"I want to take a bath with you," I whisper in his ear.

"That sounds like a good idea." He whispers.

Elijah stands up and slides out of the couch. He holds his hand out to me, and I smile before I slide off the couch and take his hand.

He wraps his arm around my waist and pulls me close to him as he leads me towards the bath.

River turns on the jets in the bathtub, and I smile when I see him.

I walk over to the counter, bend over and grip it. I moan when I feel Elijah's tongue slide over my pussy.

I moan and pant when I feel him slide two fingers inside me.

He pushes his fingers deeper, and I whimper when I feel him brush against my G-spot.

He groans as he tastes me, and I moan as his fingers move deeper. He groans, and I sigh when I feel him lean forward and I feel him lick my clit.

"Oh, God," I moan as his fingers slide deeper.

I whimper and moan as his fingers slide in and out of me.

He pushes his fingers deeper, and I gasp as he pushes them deeper.

"Oh, God," I moan as he pushes his fingers deeper inside me.

My body shudders, and I moan as my pussy twitches around his fingers.

"Oh, fuck, princess," He moans as he feels my pussy twitch around his fingers.

I look over my shoulder, and I smile as I see River.

He has a grin on his face, and he leans over and kisses me before he stands up on his tip toes and kisses me again. He pushes me forward and runs his tongue down my back.

I giggle, and I lean back against him.

I feel Jax run his fingers up my thigh, and I glance over at him.

He grins, pushes himself off the couch, and walks to me.

He wraps his hand around my throat and pulls me up against him.

He pushes me forward until my back is pressed against River's chest. He wraps his other hand around my throat and slides his fingers through my hair. "Oh, God, kitten," He whispers. "Oh, fuck, you feel so fucking good." He whispers as he thrusts his cock into me. "Fuck, you're so tight, kitten." He moans.

"Jax, Jax, Jax," I moan. "Yes, Oh, God, yes." I moan.

I feel River groan into my ear as he thrusts into me.

"Oh, God, kitten," Jax moans.

I wrap my arms around Jax's neck and lean back into River's chest. "Oh, fuck, you're so fucking wet, princess." Jax moans.

"Fuck, damn, princess, you're so fucking hot." River moans.

I'm panting, and my body is trembling as I feel my orgasm start to build in my body. "Oh, God, I'm going to cum." I moan.

"Oh, fuck, princess, cum for me." Jax moans. "Oh, fuck, princess, cum all over me." Jax moans.

"Oh, God." I moan as my eyes roll to the back of my head. I whimper and moan as I feel my orgasm build and then explode.

"Oh, fuck, kitten." Jax moans.

I gasp, and I moan as I feel him slide his cock out of me. I lean back against him, and I push back against him. He wraps his arms around me, and he thrusts into me over and over again. "Oh, fuck, kitten," He moans.

Jax picks me up and places me into the bathtub. Elijah and River follow him, and River sits beside me. Jax and Elijah sit on either side of me, and I smile as the water slides over my body.

Jax leans forward and brushes his lips against mine. Elijah leans forward, kisses and nips at my neck, and I moan. River leans forward, and he touches his lips against mine. Jax kisses and licks my neck and my shoulder, and I sigh.

I feel Elijah pull away from me, and I whimper in protest. He kisses my shoulder, and I smile as he pushes me forward. I moan as Jax wraps his arms around me and pulls me back against his chest. He wraps his arms around me and pushes my head back against his shoulder. River kneels before me, and I smile as he places his hands on my knees. He pulls my legs apart and runs his tongue between my legs. I moan, and I tilt my head back against Jax's shoulder. He moves his hands up to my waist, and he slides his hands down my thighs.

I whimper in pleasure and feel him run his fingers over my pussy. I whimper in satisfaction as he pushes his fingers inside me. Elijah pushes his fingers back into me, and I moan.

He brushes my hair out of my face, and he leans forward. He touches his lips against mine and slides his tongue into my mouth. "Oh, God, darling." He moans, and he pulls away from me.

"Oh, God, Elijah." I moan.

I look over my shoulder, and I smile as I see River. He has a grin on his face, and he leans over and kisses me before he stands up on his tip toes and kisses me again. He pushes me forward and runs his tongue down my back.

I giggle, and I lean back against him.

"Oh, fuck, princess, you're so fucking good." River moans.

"Oh, God, River," I moan.

I tilt my head against his shoulder and moan as he pushes his fingers back into me. I moan and run my tongue over his fingers before I wrap my fingers around them.

"Oh, God, Elijah," I moan.

He wraps his arms around me and buries his face into my neck. I moan as I feel his lips and teeth against my neck. "Oh, fuck, darling, you make me so fucking hard," He sighs.

I moan as I feel him bite down on the side of my neck, and I sigh as I feel him suck on my neck. "Oh, fuck, darling, you're so fucking sexy with your lips wrapped around my fingers." He moans.

"Oh, fuck, darling, you're so fucking sexy," He moans, and I open my mouth to him to the point that he slides his fingers out of my mouth. He pulls his fingers out of my mouth and kisses me before pushing me forward slightly.

I moan as I feel Jax pull away from me.

I lean forward and place my hands on the bathtub's edge.

"Oh, fuck, kitten, I've been dreaming about this moment for so fucking long." He moans. "Oh, fuck, kitten," Jax moans and I moan as I feel him spread my cheeks. I sigh as I feel him slide his tongue between my cheeks. He moans as he runs his tongue over my opening.

I take his fingers into my mouth and run my tongue over them before I wrap my fingers around them. He moans as he pushes his fingers into my mouth, and I wrap my lips around them. "Oh, kitten," He sighs.

I run my tongue over my fingers, and I wrap my fingers around them, and he pulls them out of my mouth. He leans forward and kisses the back of my neck before he pulls away from me.

I collapse from exhaustion and euphoric ecstasy in the warm, bubbling water and lay back against Elijah's body. Feeling him soap my hair, I sigh with satisfaction as he massages my hair, and little happy sighs fall from my lips.

I feel their hands everywhere. Every slight movement causes my body to shudder in erotic bliss. The way Elijah massages my head has me groaning with pleasure, Jax and River soap my body and all I can think is: this day just can't get any better.

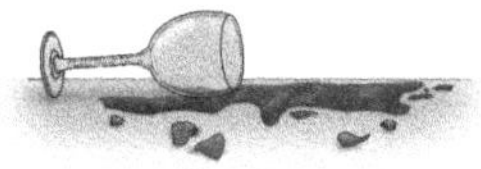

Walking into the room I had been carried out of before, I was given the most orgasms anyone had received in the history of the world.

Honestly, I was waiting to be headlined with an award for receiving that many orgasms in such a short space of time. I was unsure how I had any bodily fluids left, but they were right: orgasms were great for cramps.

My eyes widen at the scene in front of me. There was an array of snacks on the table, and the room that looked built for a showroom was now a cosy ambience.

The roaring fire blows heat to every corner of the room, and the cushions on the sofa have been arranged like they had been building a bed fort and the vast television screen was switched on.

I hadn't seen them switch that thing on since I had arrived.

"What's all this?" I point to the scene in front of me.

"This is your pamper princess day." Elijah smiles.

"Pamper Princess Day? Did you just make that up?"

"Maybe," he smirks. "Come on, princess, come sit." He pats the space on the sofa between himself and Jax. River is seated on the floor, kneeling where they want me to sit.

Sitting down next to Jax and Elijah, I'm oddly suspicious of their intentions. It was just a period. It wasn't the end of the world. Jax places his arm around my shoulders and pulls my body into his, and I can't help the comforting sigh that falls from my lips.

"Now, this is what is going to happen, kitten," my body freezes excitedly. "You are going to let us take care of you." He whispers into my hair.

"I don't deserve any of this," I utter barely a whisper.

"Look at me," he sternly commands, moving my head towards his, but my eyes remain looking down. "I said...look at me," his fingers tip my chin until my eyes slowly raise until I meet his.

The intense feeling washes over my body as his gaze penetrates my soul. A slight blush crawls up my face, "You deserve so much more. I want to give you the fucking world, Cara, don't you see how special you are?"

I shake my head because I'm not special; I'm no different than anyone else, but he's making me believe I am the way he's looking at me right now. His grey eyes' intensity and raw emotion knocks me back, and I'm at a loss for words.

"It's okay if you don't believe it, baby. I will believe it for both of us until you realise how much you affect everyone around you purely by being you. I will believe it for the both of us." Before crushing his lips against mine, he whispers, "Now turn around." I squint at him, "trust me." He whispers.

Turning with my back against Jax, I wait for what I was supposed to trust him with. The minutes seem to go by, and nothing happens. Even though I know I can't handle it anymore, the Kane brothers, a sliver of excitement, crawls up my spine.

I feel his hands run through my hair, and a little girlish laugh falls from my lips. Gently, his fingers tangle in my hair before I feel the stiff brush gently moving through my damp hair.

"What are you doing?" I ask incredulously.

"I would think that would be obvious, kitten." He whispers near my ear.

"Jax," I moan.

"You agreed to let us take care of you."

I spin my head around, giving him a slight smirk, "Actually, I think you told me that's what was happening."

"Your right. Now turn around and let me finish." Pouting my lips in defiance and slowly turning my head, I once again feel the brush gently moving through my hair, and a small smile appears on my lips.

Those deep amber eyes that swirl with gold specks look upon me with mischief, and suddenly, I feel all girlish. The smile that had appeared on my lips seemingly grows wider. "Something amusing, darling?"

"No," I smile even wider.

"Hands." He holds his large palm out towards me, and I look at it like a foreign object I've never seen before. I hear a huff pass his lips before he pulls my hands towards his.

"Elijah," I wail.

I see the slightest smile hit the corners of his mouth, "Pamper Princess Day, remember?" He cocks a brow.

He starts by slavering some cream-based solution on my hand and gently messaging my skin. The soft sighs leave my mouth. If they wanted to pamper me, who was I to argue?

I had thought the princess treatment was over until I felt River massaging my feet; he looked up at me with so much care in his eyes and smiled a smile that instantly melted my heart.

With my hair now braided and my nails painted in my favourite colour. I look down at the shimmering purple hues as the light hits my nails and smile.

"Pretty," I utter.

"Not as pretty as you." Elijah smiles while moving his thumb in circles across my hand.

"How did I get so lucky?" I utter.

"That is exactly what I ask myself daily," Jax whispers into my hair.

"I don't deserve you. I don't deserve any of you." I croak, trying my hardest to hold back the tears that threaten to fall.

"No, princess, you deserve so much more." Jax leaves a soft kiss on my head.

The pamper session from Jax, River and Elijah relaxed me. My eyes feel heavy, and my heart feels full. I had never imagined I would find any man who had treated me the way they had, let alone found three.

"Come on now, lay down." Jax pats his lap for me to lay my head on.

"Honestly, Jax, you've already done so much."

"You need rest, kitten. Now lay back and relax."

Who was I to argue? Laying my head across his lap, River slides my legs across Elijah's knee and sits with my feet raised onto his lap. I feel Jax run his fingers through my hair, and my eyelids grow heavier with each slow movement I feel at my head.

"Now sleep, kitten." He whispers before leaning down and pressing a feather-light kiss on my head.

My eyes are moments away from fluttering shut; the relaxation overcomes my body, and I can feel my body slipping into sleep as my eyes threaten to close. A yawn falls from my throat, "Here with you. With all of you, it is my favourite place to be." I whisper.

"Mine too," I hear him whisper back before my eyes finally give way, and I allow sleep to consume me.

Still, with a smile, I finally felt what I had been missing.

I finally feel...happy.

Another fucking girl.

How many times had they tried this? It was tortur-ous. She's laid across them like she owns the place. Like she owns them. She may have twisted them around her little manicured finger with her magic pussy, but she wouldn't be getting a welcome party from me.

I haven't been home for a while, so she probably has been here longer than me, but business called. Hunting that last guy was a ride. I felt at home in the wilderness, but my wayward brothers got into trouble if I stayed away too long. I had been hoping to relax once I returned, and what did I find? Their next little project.

"Luca, your back," River announces excitedly. He was the only one who ever got excited that I had returned home. I swear the boy thought I would abscond from society and live amongst the bears. Now, that wasn't a bad idea. "This is Cara." He winks.

Already smitten, I see.

I see Jax whisper something in her ear, but I'm too far away to hear the details. A small smile appears on her lips, and now she's walking towards me. Long legs stride towards me, her hips swaying with every step. That long, shiny dark hair sways across her body, and those big, bright blue eyes tempted me to fall in line like my brothers had.

"Welcome home, Luca." She smiles and moves her head close to mine, but I slide out. The confusion creases across her eyes. My gaze moves across my body, and within moments, my hand is wrapped around her throat, pushing her against the wall. I want to see fear in her eyes like they all have, but she smirks and bites her lip, once again tempting me.

"Luca…" Jax starts, glaring back at my brother. He smirks, and whatever words he is about to say die on his lips.

"I'm not fooled by a pretty face," She smiles.

"So you think I'm pretty." She smirks. My grip around her throat tightens. She's gasping for breath, and her wavering confidence slowly diminishes.

"You are just a toy. A toy they like to play with, and once they get bored, they will find a new toy to play with." The corners of my mouth upturned, but I couldn't get over the sadness that crossed her eyes. Finally releasing her neck and stepping away, "Enjoy your toy boys." I call before turning away.

"Luca…" Jax calls, but I know what he wants, and I'm not in the mood to play, "Luca, you just got home."

"You should have told me." I grit back.

"I thought you'd be happy."

"That you found a new toy?" I raise a brow, "highlight of my fucking day." I turn and stomp away from my moronic brothers. Always thinking with their dicks and who would have to pick them all up when she got cold feet and left? Me, that's who.

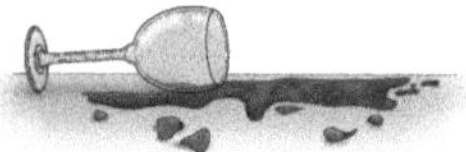

The memories come back.

My heart is pounding, and the adrenaline rush courses through my body. I've tracked him to the forest. A stream of water crawls across the moss-grown rocks, and birds sing in the overgrown trees. It is an ideal location to lay low; nobody would ever suspect you'd come here, but they didn't call me the tracker for nothing.

He could run, but he couldn't hide.

I hear the crunch of leaves as I race through the forest, the sun hitting my skin with every step. He has nowhere left to go. He can't outrun me. He knows he can't. The smirk crawls upon my face with victory as I reach him.

"You should have killed me when you got the chan ce.." His evil sneer mocks me.

I wake up in a cold sweat. The words repeat in my head. I should have done, but I thought he could redeem himself. It was one thing to take a life but to take your own blood that will haunt you forever, even if the evil incarnate is the very thing you should kill.

I wasn't always this cold, or maybe I was. It's been that long; I just don't remember anymore. We didn't exactly have a conventional upbringing, nor did we have the same mother, just a bastard who enjoyed impregnating slaves. I don't think I ever met my mother. She was just a little toy he liked to play with.

Shit, aren't they the exact words I told her about my brothers.

They weren't like him.

I had made damn sure they had some semblance of an everyday life, but what was normal anyway?

Deep down, I know we were all fucked up, hiding in the shadows of our own darkness, and they had brought an innocent into the fold. Of course, I wasn't going to be happy. Jax knew I wouldn't be happy, but the selfish bastard invited her into this house and their lives anyway.

They would ruin her, take every shed of her humanity and destroy it, or she would destroy them. Either way, her being here was a thorn in my side.

What did they need a woman for?

We had been doing fine without her for all these years. She had to go. I couldn't have her here. If she stayed, I knew I would end up ringing her skinny little neck. Imagine her mocking me. She had a nerve. The muscles in my jaw tighten, flipping the covers away. I pull on some grey sweats and make my way to the kitchen. It's always quiet at this time of day. Everyone is asleep, just as I like it.

Peering into the kitchen, I stop. Surprisingly, I'm not alone. Everyone isn't asleep, it seems. She's stood in a silver negligee that barely covers her pert ass, swinging her hips as she does something at the stove.

"What are you doing?" I scream louder than I intended.

Shit, I was losing control.

She turns and smiles, "Oh, hey Luca, making pancakes. Would you like some?" Even the sound of my name on her lips grates on me.

"No, and don't fucking say my name."

"What would you like me to call you then?"

"I wouldn't, don't speak to me." She shrugs and returns to the stove, again shaking her hips. It had to be illegal to have hips like hers. Every slight movement causes my cock to throb.

I run my fingers through my hair but can't tear my eyes away from her body. Every movement causes my brain to go haywire. I'm losing fucking control, I never lose control, but as I watch her, she's slowly driving me mad.

I stride towards her because I can't think. The temptation of her body burns through my veins. She turns the stove off and crashes into my body. Her eyes search mine, and a blush creeps up her face. "Sorry I didn't see you there. I will be out of your way if you just give me a moment."

"Do you always make food this early?" I grit out. I hate small talk, but I'm trying to exhibit some control.

"Well, when you want something, you should take it." She smirks, wrong answer.

Grabbing her by the hips, she felt fucking sinful, and I immediately hate myself. She's looking at me with want, but I don't want her to look that way. Pushing her against the counter, my body crashes against hers, and she gasps.

"I fucking hate you." I spit at her, and her eyes swim with sadness. Turning her body away from mine, I bend her over the counter, her bare ass is pushed out, and suddenly my throat feels dry. My fingers slide into her dripping cunt, and she cries out. My cock is throbbing with need.

"Luca... you don't need to do it like this." She utters.

"Why would you think I would want to look at you," I whisper, "just because I despise you doesn't mean I won't still fuck you."

"You...despise me." She sobs.

"Good little toys don't fucking speak."

"I'm...not...a...," My cock is pressing against her centre, pushing through a gasp that leaves my throat, "Oh fuck," she cries out. Slamming my cock deep inside her, I feel her pussy grip me like a vice. "Luca...I..." Her words die on her lips and are replaced with erotic moans that fill the kitchen.

Finally, I can enjoy the tightness of her sweet pussy as I pulse deep inside her. "Luca...you don't have to do it...like this." She gasps once more. The more she spoke, the harder it would be.

My hand grips her neck, squeezing her tiny neck and pushing the pleasure through my body. Her pussy tightens even harder around my cock, and I'm about to explode. Her sharp gasps are the only noises she makes.

My hips thrust against her body, pushing my cock further into her right dripping hole. "Fuck, you...have...the...tightest...pussy." I gasp, finally enjoying her tight little cunt. "Toys...don't...speak," I pant.

My other hand grips her hip. I want to climb inside of her fucking body. Bury myself within the restraints of her wonderful essence and sink into the pleasure that runs through my veins.

I can hear sobbing while she gasps, "Almost...there...little...toy," I cry. Her body shakes beneath mine in an explosive array of pleasure. My cock mounts her at an exceptional speed. Pushing her body further onto the counter, my cock shudders as I finally cry out all my anger and feel the thick strands of my cum fill her up.

I move away from her and make myself decent. She slowly gets up, pulling that tiny negligee back over that fucking ass that teased me into fucking oblivion. She turns and glares at me, her cold blue stare burning with hatred.

Good, I wanted her to hate me.

She stalks towards me and raises her hand to my face. I catch her dainty little hand in mine in mid-air. "That is not a very smart idea."

"Don't...ever...do...that...again." She breathlessly scolds.

"Don't pretend you didn't enjoy that...toy."

"Luca..."

"What did I tell you about my name on your lips?"

"You are the most infuriating man I've ever met."

"The most infuriating man you've ever met...yet," I smirk.

"You're not as tough as you make out." She smirks.

"Oh, I know, little toy, I'm much worse."

"You tell yourself that," She moves her body against mine, and I stiffen at her feel against me. Her furious eyes blaze heat beneath my skin. "You hate me?" I watch her waiting for the punchline, "And yet you couldn't wait to fuck me." I swallow down a gulp.

"That's what you do with toys," her head moves close to mine, and I can smell the sweet feminine scent of jasmine that pours from her skin. "You fuck them," I whisper.

Her hand moves up my chest and falls into my hair. Her fingers expertly tease my strands, leaving tingles wherever she touches me. "You couldn't look at me while you fucked me." She whispers, her head moving closer to mine. Her tongue flicks out, grazing my lips, and I can't help the growl that falls from my throat. Her teeth clamp against my lips, biting until she breaks the skin. Moaning her sweet cries into my mouth.

"Such a brave little toy." I gasp.

Her tongue crawls out again, sliding across my lips and begging to be let into my mouth. "A toy you want to play with," She breathes against my lips before turning and walking away from me.

"Cara," I call, and she turns her head and smirks in my direction.

"So, he does know my name." She mutters before disappearing from my sight.

Shit, she was going to drive me crazy.

I couldn't get sucked into her. I just couldn't. I had to keep my distance, no matter how tempting she might be.

Everything I've ever loved left me. Why would she be any different?

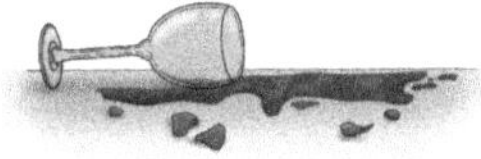

"Luca, there you are." Jax happily calls.

"Where else would I be?"

"Still as sour as ever, some things never change."

"I just saw Cara. She looks pleased with herself." He winks while patting me on the back.

"That's what you wanted to discuss: the little toy you brought back home. Remind me not to go away for so long next time. Who knows what rabid strays you will bring back." I spit back at him.

"Cara is not..." His brow creases with worry, "that's not what I wanted to talk about."

"No?"

"We need to talk about Oak Haven."

"Think I would rather hear you waffle on about your toy." I drawl while walking away from him.

I throw myself into the armchair and watch the sparks from the newly lit fire, and the smell of smoke fills my nostrils. This was always my favourite room. Wall-to-wall bookcases that housed various books, the walls were decorated blood red, which always brought back fond memories when I would come back after a hunt.

"Luca, don't walk away from me." I groan. Once again, my peace had been interrupted.

"The conversation had ended."

"No, it hadn't," he growls, "as usual, you walked away because the conversation made you uncomfortable."

"Everything you do makes me uncomfortable, Jax," I smirk.

"We need to talk about it."

"No, we don't. Oak Haven is in the past."

"It's not in the fucking past," he yells, "it's like a great fucking black cloud that follows us everywhere and unlike you, we can't all bury our head in the fucking sand and hope it goes away."

I wish I could scream back and tell him that he was wrong. I still had nightmares about that house. Everything about that house was tainted. I swear, late at night, I could still hear the faint screams of women who used to crawl through the walls. I shudder to think about the horrors that actually went on in those rooms.

"We already discussed this. We can't take our own blood."

"I know," he mutters.

"He stays in his lane, and we just have to...live with the consequences of his actions."

"Except the vermin has resurfaced."

"Why would he? After all this time."

"I don't know. I was hoping you could find out." He looks at me with pleading eyes, begging me to end the torment we had all suffered at the hands of the sick bastard who inhabited Oak Haven.

"Fine, but until I know more. You do nothing. Do you understand?"

"Fine, but you know it's only a matter of time. He's been living on borrowed time for far too long."

"I know," I mutter, half to him and half to myself.

I knew he wanted it over. I knew they all wanted it over. They thought they would finally be free once the evil was gone. Everything they deemed dark would suddenly appear light once he was gone.

But that's the thing about darkness: once it touches you and has its dark talons wrapped around you. It's hard to break free of the choke hold it has around your heart.

Every bone in my body was stiff. The rage that courses through my veins is something I just can't shake. I'm annoyed that he's back. I'm annoyed that now I have to dig into that damn horror house, but most of all, I'm annoyed at how quickly the toy has clawed her way beneath my skin.

Imagine her acting smug because she had given me a one-liner and strutted off like she had won something. Jax should have never brought her here, but what annoyed me the most wasn't even her presence or how easy it was for her to fall into our lives as if she'd always been there.

I hide in the library, allowing the impending doom to travel around my body. Letting it fester like a parasite that had embedded its way into my skin. Allowing the darkness to once again take control of me. Occasionally, I hear the faint sounds of her laughter coming from the next room. It's like an angel has pushed its way into our lives, letting cracks of light where there was only dark.

Before I knew it, night had fallen, and silence had inhabited the house. I hear nothing but the sound of my own shallow breathing. I tip back another scotch before descending the stairs. I might as well go to bed, be haunted by my mind once more.

I'm standing outside my door, but I don't go further. I'm battling with myself. I'm not sure what this feeling is, but I can't get her fucking ass off of my mind. How she stood up to me is not a feeling I'm used to. Looking at her, you'd think butter wouldn't melt in that dirty little mouth, but then she challenged me and every fibre in my body wanted to just let go.

She's probably with one of my brothers tonight.

I knew which room Jax would give her. It was the most feminine room in the house. Made especially for a girl he deemed acceptable for us all, he had never used it.

It wouldn't hurt to just...check in on her.

Shit, I sound like I care, but I don't.

I walk inside and open the door to the room I shouldn't even be standing at. She's on her side in a silk black negligee this time. Somehow, it looked even sexier than the one I had seen her in this morning.

Okay, I've checked on her.

I should leave now.

So why are my feet walking towards the bed and not back out the door? I don't even close the door. The crack of light allows me to see her beautiful face. Her plump lips are sealed, and her chest rises and falls with every breath. The way her ass pushes out in the fetal position has my cock throbbing.

Removing my pants, I quietly climb behind her. If she wakes up now, I will have no excuse for climbing into her bed. But she doesn't even move. I can hear her heavy breathing, and I want to listen to her panting while she squeezes my cock with that tight pussy.

Embedding myself within her walls while she sleeps sends shooting pains of desire to crawl up my spine. The thought of fucking her without her knowing makes my cock throb harder.

A sharp gasp leaves my throat from taking her without her knowledge. Knowing she's filled full of my hot cum with no understanding of how it got there is pushing me closer towards the edge.

I trail a line across her body, feeling the soft silk against my rough hands. If she wakes now, I'm not sure if I could leave. Resting my body close to hers, I hear a sigh fall from her lips. I'm enveloped in the warmth of her body and the sweet scent that pours from her veins.

God, why does she affect me like this?

My hand slides under the curve of her delectable ass. I had never thought an ass could illicit such feelings inside my body, but hers does it every time. My fingers dip into her tight cunt, while my thumb encircles her clit.

I listen to her breathing get faster, but she remains motionless. Feeling her coat my fingers with her juices, my breathing becomes rapid with every pulse her pussy makes around my fingers.

Positioning my cock at her centre. I'm so fucking eager to enter her. I don't think I've ever been this excited in my life. Thrusting my body hard into her, I feel her pussy grip me, and it feels so fucking good.

I wanted to take her slow and savour every sensation that would shoot through my body, but I was so fucking hungry for her I couldn't help myself.

She finally stirs as I rock my hips against her ass, feeling the mounting pleasure as I push my cock into the hilt.

"Fuck," I breathe into her hair.

Her head moves, and I know it won't be long until she realises I've stuffed her full with my cock. Her body is enjoying every fucking sensation I'm giving her while she's unaware, sleeping soundly at my side.

Fuck it, I want her to wake up.

I want to hear her fucking screaming.

Pushing harder and faster into her dripping cunt, my hand slides around, squeezing her voluptuous breast, taking them out from the tiny little silk negligee she had wrapped around her body. They fill my large hands. Twisting her nipples, I finally hear her cry out.

Her body stiffens. I can feel the panic set into her body with how tightly her pussy grips my cock. Thrusting deeper inside of her, I'm in fucking heaven. Her body makes mine come alive. Her moans grow louder with every thrust.

"What...are...you...doing?" Her erotic moans cry out to me.

"I had to have you, little toy."

"Luca," She cries out, and I don't even give a fuck that once again, my name falls out of her mouth. I want her to scream my name while she collapses around my cock. "Oh god, Luca," She calls.

My hand moves up her throat, but I don't want to hurt her this time. This time I want to possess her fucking body like she's possessed my mind. My hand wraps around her throat, pushing her body further into mine.

I'm so fucking deep, she's clenching around my cock. Strangling the life out of me. The moans fall out of my mouth. "You're such...a...good...fucking...girl." I breathlessly cry.

"Luca," She screams as her body shatters beneath mine, squirting all her desire, coating my cock and adding pressure to my cock before the rush of desire courses through my body in an explosive wave.

My mouth finds her shoulder, and biting down hard, I cry out all the pleasure that's been building. Pumping thick strands of hot cum deep inside her tight, wet, dripping cunt.

Collapsing at the side of her, I finally release her throat but don't move. I'm a breathless, sweaty mess. Her breathing matches my own. I don't even want to take my cock from her pussy. It feels so warm nested inside of her.

"It's nice to see you too," her breathless whisper calls out. "I guess you're going to run again?" She asks.

What a curious question.

"Not this time. I'm just going to stay a while." I wrap my arms around her body, pulling her closer to my chest. The warmth of her body sends heat to my chest. I know this is dangerous, that having her so close will be my undoing, but for tonight, I would make an exception.

I finally release her pussy from my cock. And that gives her the opportunity I hadn't anticipated. She turns in my arms, nestling her body close to mine. Her fingers trail a line across my chest and leave tingles in their wake.

"Did I say you could move?" I scolded her.

"No," she smiles. "Just like I didn't say you could fuck me while I slept." I scoff at her remark. Like I needed permission.

Her fingers trail my neck, reaching up to my face. She tips her head and gazes into my eyes, and that's when I realise why I don't want to look at her. She sees every dark part of my soul and accepts me anyway. And that fucking terrifies me. "You have pretty eyes," she sleepily replies, kissing my chest softly.

"Go to sleep now, or I will leave."

"Fuck and run," she smiles, "I wouldn't expect any-thing less."

"Then stop asking for more."

"I haven't said anything." she innocently gasps.

"You don't have to." She gives me a knowing smile before she lays her head on my chest and lets her eyes drift off to sleep.

The only sound I can hear is her shallow breaths. Her warm breath hits my skin with every breath. I look down and watch her sleep. She is beautiful when she's awake, but while she's asleep, something stirs inside of me.

She's almost ethereal. I must keep reminding myself that she's real because she feels like a dream.

Her dark hair falls across my body, and the warmth of her skin against mine creates a sense of calmness in my body that I didn't think was possible. This moment was the happiest I had ever been, and that thought alone made me want to run. Run far away from the little vixen, making me feel things I had no business feeling.

But I don't.

I stay there, wrapped in her warm embrace. Remembering her face and body just like this. Enjoying the euphoric feeling that had taken over my body. I could have let her go and slipped back to my room, but I didn't want to. I wanted to stay here, cocooned in her sweet embrace.

"Good night, little toy," I whisper into her hair, leaving her a soft kiss on her head that I hoped she wouldn't remember.

"We have a surprise for you," Jax announces.

"You do?" I smile widely.

"We sure do, darling." Elijah interrupts.

"We thought we couldn't keep you locked up here as our little...plaything forever." River winks, "Although that does sound more fun." I let out a little giggle. "So, we are having a fun day out."

"We are," my eyes widen. "All of us?"

"Sure thing, darling," Elijah smiles.

"Why don't you go get ready?" Jax offers.

"You don't need to tell me twice." I excitedly squeal.

Quickly pecking all three of them on the cheek, I walk out of the room with a spring in my step.

I'm nearly skipping out of the room, excited that they are taking me on some adventure. I wasn't ever one for surprises, but their admission of a secret date fluttered my chest. I don't see him. I just feel him as I crash into his hard body. Slowly raising my eyes to meet his, the coldness in his stare stops me in my tracks. "Luca," I gasp, "Did you hear..."

"I did." He coldly states. His arms are wrapped around my waist, and the heat burns through my body. One touch from him, and I'm breathless.

"You can let me go now," I whisper.

"I'm afraid I can't do that."

"How am I supposed to get ready if you don't let me go." I give him a knowing smirk.

"You're not." He growls.

"Don't do this again," I mutter.

I feel him push my body against the wall. His body pressed even more into mine. I know what he's do-ing. He always does this when a conversation of me leaving the house is brought up. He uses his body to render me compliant, but that didn't work today.

"I said no." He growls once more.

"I don't care what you said. God damn it, Luca, I'm not your fucking prisoner. You can't keep me here forever."

"You go out." He states.

"I go to work with Jax. I come home with Jax. That's it, Luca. I'm going...with or without your consent, but I'm going." I'm trembling; the way he looks at me makes me want to slink back, but I know if I do that, he will win.

His thumb trails my lip, and I quiver beneath his touch. I know he can feel what he does to my body. His mouth upturns in a smile as he gently moves his fingers across my lips. "Open wide, little toy."

"Luca," I gasp.

"Open wide. I won't ask you a third time."

God, I'm dripping just from his forceful request. I slowly open my mouth. "wider." He commands.

Once more, I open my mouth for him, feeling him slide his fingers into my mouth. My mouth closes around his fingers, and I lace my tongue up and around them. Suckling and moaning while I massage his fingers with my mouth. "Good...girl," he gasps.

Once he ejects his fingers from my mouth, I'm soaking. Looking at him with all the desire he had forced to crawl through my body. "This changes nothing. I'm still going."

"God damn it, Cara." He screams at me while hitting the wall at the side of my head. My eyes widen at his sudden outburst. His hand falls into my hair, dragging my head back, tugging at my hair. "Why do you have to be so difficult, little toy." He whispers.

Looking into his emerald eyes, I'm taken aback. They look stone cold, but the creases by his eyes show something else...uncertainty. "I'm not going to run away, you know." I mock.

"Cara...I," his hand crawls to my face, his thumb caressing my cheek, "fuck, I'm just trying to keep you safe." He finally utters. He's back to his stone-cold stare, "I hate that you make me like this." He speaks more to himself than me.

"You want to keep me safe?" I ask, dumbfounded that the same man who can't bare to look at me while he fucks me wants to keep me safe.

"Yes," he whispers while pressing his forehead against mine. "That's all I want. You safe."

"Then come with us." He shakes his head, "What better way to protect me from...what are you protecting me from again?"

"Everything." He growls possessively.

"Wow, Luca, I didn't know you cared," I smirk.

"Don't lie, it doesn't become you."

"So you'll come?" I excitedly ask.

His hand is back nestled around my face, stroking me and causing a warmness in my belly. I really treasured these intimate moments with Luca because while they were fleeting when they happened, it felt like my body exploded from the inside out.

"You haven't left me much choice, have you?" Jumping up and down with glee, I squeal with delight. "Keep that up, and we will all stay home." I smiled because I knew an empty threat when I heard it.

Moving away from his body, it felt like I actually had room to breathe. He took up a lot of space when he was near me, and my thoughts would get lost in his magnetic gaze.

Sliding back around the door, I poke my head in to see Jax, Elijah and River happily talking away.

I felt Luca thread his fingers through mine, and though he couldn't see it, the widest smile appeared on my face. "Hey, guess what?" They all look up at me, awaiting my confession. "Luca is coming," I shout while still smiling.

"How did you manage that?" Jax laughs.

"Magic," I whisper back.

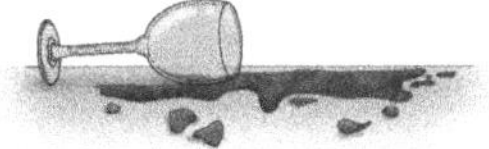

"Why are you wearing a dress?" Luca looks me up and down with a look of confusion.

"It's warm. What else would I wear?"

"Something that isn't..."

"Isn't what?" I place my arms across my chest, awaiting his usual insult.

"Short," I hear a sigh pass his lips. I look down at my dress, "and it's...white, Jesus Christ." He pinches the bridge of his nose like my outfit offends him.

"Luca,"

"Come on, before I change my mind."

"Aren't we waiting for the others?"

"No, it seems you are riding with me...with that on." He scowls at me while passing me a white helmet.

"Well, at least it matches my outfit," I smirk.

He doesn't look amused. I move closer to his body, sinking my nails into his broad shoulders. My eyes roam across the muscles that are popping beneath his black t-shirt. My head moves closer. "What are you doing?" He frowns.

"Well, I was going to give you a kiss..."

"A kiss," he shakes his head and gives me a horrified look. My head moves closer until he stalls my body by placing his hands firmly on my shoulders, "No, Cara, I don't kiss."

"Ever?" I ask, dumbfounded.

"No." His answer is curt.

"You'll fuck me, but you won't kiss me." I scowl at him. He doesn't respond, "A kiss is innocent, and sex is.."

The realisation that he will never kiss me turns a knot in my stomach; I'm not even sure why I care, but the fact he won't let me kiss his lips, not even once, horrifies me.

"Innocent?" He knits his brows together, "Baby, nothing is innocent about you." His hands fall across my waist, picking my body up and crashing it against his.

The butterflies flit in my belly as his eyes roam across my face.

"Luca, I don't understand,"

"He places my bottom on the waiting motorbike and leans across my body, allowing his dark musky scent to invade my space, "any man can fuck you, Cara;

sometimes it means something but most of the time it doesn't."

"Thanks for the sex ed class." I spit back at him.

"Sex at most times is meaningless. It means nothing to many men," his nose brushes against my cheek, and the tingles of excitement pierce my body. "But a kiss...a kiss is more intimate. You are saying something that words can't express. The only time a man should kiss a woman," his hot breath fans my face, "is if he truly means it."

"So, you'll never kiss me?" He scowls, "Sex with me is meaningless," I breathe exasperated.

"I never said that." He whispers, "But no, little toy, I won't kiss you." His hand makes a tight fist into my hair, pulling my head back and making me stare into his enchanting eyes, "until I mean it."

The thoughts swirl around my head like a moving vortex, but Luca had that effect on me since I had met him. I didn't understand him at all. He confused me but also intrigued me at the same time. He was so different from his brothers. It felt like I had to beg for his attention because I desperately wanted it.

I sit behind him with my arms around his waist as he rides off at high speed. The wind flowing through my hair, finally feel free. Birds must feel like this when they spread their wings and soar high into the sky.

No problems.

No worries.

Just free.

That's what Luca was like. He was like an injured bird who just needed to fly. I wish I could bring him the peace I knew he deserved, but that's the funny thing about peace. Nobody can give you what you have to give yourself.

I expect a quiet picnic in the afternoon sun when we arrive at Central Park, but nothing like this. Central Park has been turned into a carnival, and my eyes instantly light up as I take in my surroundings.

"There are rules." Luca growls.

"Rules to a carnival? Says who?"

"Me," he growls.

Best humour the bear with a sore head, lest he throw an epic hissy fit and march us all home because I dare challenge him. "Okay, go on, hit me with it."

"What, no smart remark."

"Honestly, Luca, what's the point? It's always your way or no way."

"I'm glad you're finally catching on, little toy." I roll my eyes and pout at him, "Oh, don't pout. When you leave, you will be free to do as you wish again."

"Leave? Why would I leave?"

"Because, little princess, men like us don't get the girl in the end." He whispers while running his fingers across my neck, allowing sharp gasps to fall from my throat.

"I'm not leaving, Luca. I'm afraid you are stuck with me." My arms wrap around his neck, and he looks at me uncertainly.

"You can't do that." He scowls.

"Do what?"

"Make promises you can't keep."

"Luca, I promise, I'm not going anywhere," I state more firmly this time and watch as his eyes soften.

"We'll see, little toy." He whispers before releasing my arms from his neck. "Rules, you don't leave my sight. I want you to have fun today, but I also want you to be safe. If anyone, and I mean anyone, makes you feel uncomfortable, you tell me, and I will make them wish that hell was their final resting place." His eyes darken.

"God, Luca, wouldn't want to get on your bad side."

"No, you wouldn't, princess. Lucky for you, you're growing on me."

"Growing on you? Like mould?"

"Something like that." He chuckles while threading his fingers through mine and walking through the park to meet his brothers, waiting by the candy floss stand.

"Hey, princess," River beams at me as we finally reach them. "We were beginning to think you two got lost." He winks.

"No, Luca was reciting the rules of the carnival." I roll my eyes.

"There are rules to a carnival?" Elijah side eyes Luca.

"See, that's what I said." I gloat.

"There are rules for you." Luca rasps.

"Okay, enough of that, candy floss?" Jax offers.

I rub my hands together, my mouth watering at the sight of all the pretty colours that will melt on my tongue. "Oooh, don't mind if I do."

Picking apart the bubblegum pink candy floss and letting it melt on my tongue is something I hadn't experienced since I was a child. Small, satisfied moans fall from my throat each time an explosion of flavours erupts inside my mouth.

"How does she make eating candy floss look sexy?" River gasps.

Looking across at them, they each stare at me with an intensity that burns desire to my core. My legs wobble, and my body shudders as slivers of excitement crawl up my spine.

"Stop looking at me like that." I blush at their intense stare.

"Like what, darling?" Elijah smirks.

"Like you want to do something we would probably get arrested for."

"Now, wouldn't that be a fun story to tell?" River winks.

"As fun as that sounds, I don't think orange is my colour."

They all laugh except Luca, who looks like a big lump of stone. I couldn't understand why he would agree to come out if he didn't want to be here. He just stood within a safe distance, watching but never participating.

After a few goes on the Ferris wheel with each of them, I was all ridden out. Skipping over to the burger stand to replenish the excitement that had washed across my body, I crash into a rigid body.

Looking up, piercing blue eyes stare back at me, "Sorry, I wasn't looking where I was going."

"Like an excited little bird, flapping her wings." he smiles.

"Something like that." I blush.

"Well, off you go, little bird, soar."

Walking away from him, I looked back, but the strange man I had collided with had already disappeared.

"Who was that?" I hear a deep, angry voice behind me. The hairs on my neck prickle with the intensity of his accusation.

Spinning around, I see Luca staring at me like I had grown an extra head. "I don't know,"

"Cara," he scolds.

"I don't know, Luca. I accidentally bumped into him in my excitement to get some food."

"What did he say to you?"

"Something about soaring like a bird, I'm not sure."

His stare doesn't leave my body, and I'm oddly feeling uncomfortable from the fiery anger that seems to be emitting from his body.

"Do you want some food?" I offer.

"No, I'm not hungry."

"Fine," I stomp towards the burger stand and wait patiently for my burger. Luca is never far behind me.

"Hey, princess, when you've eaten, we must go." River apologetically sighs.

"Let me guess, Luca."

"Yeah, I'm not sure what happened, but he's in a thunderous mood."

"Does there have to be a reason? It's Luca." I roll my eyes.

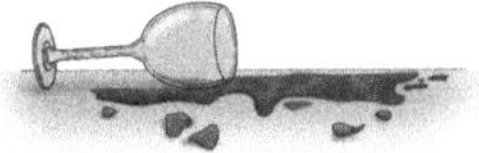

The ride back to the house was silent and uncomfortable. The ease in which I had felt across his body was now gone. The tension in his body pulses beneath my fingertips, and as I walk through the door, I'm met with silence.

In his rage of coming home, he beat the others here, which was fantastic because now I was stuck with the grump with ten different personalities. Still, today, this one wasn't much fun.

I'm walking to my room because I can't be bothered playing this game with him today. He ruined a perfect day out, and for what? I wasn't asking, so I guess I would never know.

I enter the room and try to shut the door, but he blocks it with his hand, still giving me his death stare. I gasp.

"What, Luca?"

"Strip," He growls.

The words poured over me in moments; that was not what I expected him to say, but I shouldn't be surprised. Luca was unpredictable at best but looked like a crazed beast right now.

"Luca, have I done something wrong?"

"No, now strip." He commands more forcefully.

He looks at me with coldness as I slowly undress, his eyes never leaving mine. I know he must see the look of confusion, but his face is like stone, never giving away even a little sliver of emotion.

The only emotion I get from him is a nod of approval when I'm standing before him naked and exposed, but nothing more, not even the gasp of desire he usually can't contain when his eyes roam across my body.

"On the bed," he commands.

"Luca, are you sure I haven't upset you?"

"On the bed, Cara," He rasps out.

Slowly turning and moving to the bed, a small idea pops into my head. If he wanted to be difficult...well, I was going to have some fun with it. Stretching my body out like a cat and pushing my ass out as far as it will go with my back arched, I climb seductively onto the bed.

I don't think my movements have done anything but entertain myself for a moment. Then I hear a sharp gasp leave his throat, and my efforts are rewarded with a beaming smile that I would never show him.

I feel his hand slide up the curve of my ass, and I try my best to stay still until he allows me to move. It's the way Luca liked it, and if I was honest, the anticipation of trying not to move when he touched me always sent a current of desire to travel through my body.

He doesn't speak; he just rests his warm, rough hand at the base of my back, and I can feel the trickle of desire between my thighs. I hear the belt and have an odd recollection of what Jax did, but I wasn't sure Luca would do the same.

The belt comes down hard against my raw naked ass, and I yelp at the sudden slash of the belt as it connects with my skin. Once more, he slashes the belt against my ass, allowing a piercing scream to trickle from my throat. The heat from my ass burns through my flesh at the sudden impact from his belt, and I whimper at the after-effects of the pain that pumps at an unnatural speed.

I feel his body clamber onto the bed behind me, his legs resting at the side of mine. I don't even have a chance to allow the searing heat of pain that dissipate before I feel his hard cock pressing at my centre.

In one swift movement, he spears his stiff cock into my dripping, aching pussy, and this time, the scream that falls out of my mouth is one of pleasure, not pain.

His hand grips my throat tightly, pulling my body towards his until I feel my back against his chest. The beating of my heart races when I feel his cock push deeper inside me.

"Luca," I gasp.

"Little toy, did I say you could speak?" He grunts.

"Luca," I scream, feeling his hips move slowly, pushing as far into my pussy as he can go, my head resting on his should. My eyes lose focus while he has my throat in a vice around his large hands.

"Luca, I gasp. "I'm sorry if I did something wrong," I gasp, tears welling in my eyes.

"Now, little toy, why would I touch you...like this...if you did something wrong."

The pleasure continues to hit my body in waves, and I feel an odd sense of peace as his last words hit me.

"You're mine, do you understand?"

I try to grunt that I agree, but my words get caught in my throat.

His body moves harder against mine, and the pulsing of his hard cock as he fills my pussy drives me over the edge. Gasps and moans fill the room as he slowly moves inside of me.

"You're mine," he grunts once more. "Nobody gets to look at you that way. Who do you belong to, little toy?"

"You," I finally manage to gasp out.

His cock penetrates me faster and faster. I can feel my legs buckling as an explosion of pleasure quickly enters my body. Every sensation from his cock renders my body entirely under his control.

"Say it, say you're mine." He growls.

"Oh fuck," I cry out.

"Say it, tell me you're mine." He growls once more.

"I'm yours, Luca, oh fuck, god...you...feel...oh...my...god," I scream against his body.

"That's right baby...this ass," he pushes his body further into mine, and the onslaught of his cock has my pussy clenching around him. "This pussy," one more thrust of his hips and my pussy clenches around him, releasing all my desire around his cock. "It's all mine."

He screams out as I feel his hot cum splash against my walls.

I collapse against his body in a sweaty, gasping mess with a smile on my face. Luca wasn't annoyed at me; he was upset that someone had dared to look at me with desire in their eyes, and that kind of possessiveness made me smile.

The fact that he cared that much was progress.

"You're mine," he whispers in my ear. "I would kill for you, you know, little toy." A sliver of chills crawls up my spine. "One day, I'm sure that's just what I will do; touching what's mine is a sure way to die." He whispers.

His words should terrify me.

They should make me want to run after the horrendous scars Carter left on my soul. I should be terrified, but it wasn't like that with Luca. No, he didn't terrify me. It was the opposite.

He made me feel...well, safe.

We collapse onto the bed, and I feel him pull my body into his chest, finally letting me gaze into his emerald eyes. Sex with Luca was never permitted to be intimate; it was just sex, but the moments after... they were the kind of intimate that would ruin you for anyone else.

He looks down at me with uncertainty; his eyes are soft but hold something deeper, some secret that he won't tell me. His eyes fall across my face, and I see them flutter close. I think he must have fallen asleep until I hear his deep voice in my ear.

"Promise you won't go away," he utters barely a whisper.

"I promise,"

His eyes finally open, and he looks down at me with sadness, "I really wish that was true, little toy."

"It is true," I gasp.

I'm unsure what to do to prove to him that I'm not going anywhere. He doesn't seem like he believes me anyway. Then it hits me: Luca has been unpredictable because he's waiting for the day when I disappear from his life. When I disappear from all of their lives.

"I don't think," my words get caught in my throat while he looks at me intently, "You know how happy you make me."

"Me?" He knits his brows together, "I don't make anyone happy."

"Tell that to my warm heart whenever I see you then, Luca, because I don't think it got the message." His eyes widen, and I'm just waiting for him to bolt out of the room, but he doesn't. He stays.

"Is that your way of saying you are staying?" He smirks.

"I'm not going anywhere," I whisper while nestling my face deeper into his warm chest and inhaling the intoxicating scent of his body. "I promise," I whisper into his skin once more.

Part IV

Walking Away Is Easy, Right?

Most girls dream of a love
that time will stand still for.
I never expected to fall for one man
let alone four.
You can have it all.
That's what we tell ourselves,
That we can have it all.
Then, life intervenes and shows us
that maybe, just maybe,
We can't have it all and what we
thought was our happy ending
was a road we would have to walk,
Alone.

Goodbyes are never easy. If anyone knows that, it's me.

There was so much I wanted to say to each of them. I had thought about sitting down and writing them a letter, but what would I say when I thought about it?

I'm sorry for leaving.

My relationship with each of them was unique, but it wasn't expected or natural. It was greedy.

Most women couldn't hold down one man and me? I had four.

I knew it was a cowardly way to do it, but I just couldn't face any of them, least of all Jax. None of them would understand. They had placed me so far on their pedestal that I was never coming down.

Luca would hate me the most. I would have just proved him right. I really thought we had reached not really a truce but a level where he didn't look at me like he hated me, even if he did repeat it every single time he fucked me.

It would only hurt more the longer I stayed, so it was best I just left and forgot about all of them. Okay, forget because the Kane brothers were pretty unforgettable.

UNKNOWN:
'You did the right thing,'
'I'm glad that you came to your senses,'
'before you made me do something I didn't want.'
'This is nothing personal, Cara,'
'You've just been given a lifeline,'
'Use it wisely.'

I can feel the colour draining from my face as I glance at the text that has reminded me exactly why I had to walk away from the only man who had brought me happiness.

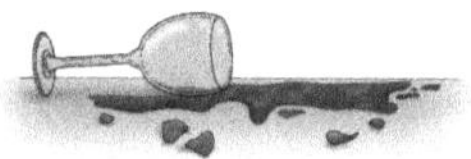

THREE WEEKS AGO

The day Luca had fought so hard to keep me in the house was the day I should have listened, but I didn't. I wanted some semblance of normality, not that there was anything normal about our arrangement.

Still, I wanted to feel like we were like other couples who did things other than have explosive sex.

Luca was possessive.

I knew that.

After Carter, you would think it would terrify me to be possessed by another man, but it was strange.

It didn't.

Carter wanted to control me, but Luca, I think, was just terrified he would lose me.

That kind of possessiveness had excitement crawling through my veins.

That day had led to the horror that was delivered every day.

I should have heeded the first warning, but I was being selfish. I wanted to be selfish. I didn't want to leave Jax or his brothers. The stark realisation was that I may not be left with any other choice.

At first, it came in the form of an email.

UNKNOWN:

What have you been up to?

I didn't realise what a bad girl you were until...you started playing with your boss.

Tell me, Cara, do you have a death wish?

The little bird catches the worm.

Keep playing with things you shouldn't, and you may just...find yourself

In trouble.

I stared at the screen in disbelief.

My heart was pounding.

I could feel the perspiration slip down my spine as the words on the screen jumped out at me.

There was a beating feeling hitting my head.

"Hey," I feel a hand slide onto my shoulder. Quickly tapping the evil words off my screen, I jump up. Clutching at my heart and look into Sarah's eyes. "Are you okay?" She asks with concern in her eyes.

"I'm fine." I shakily respond.

"You don't look fine, girl. You're as white as a sheet. I'm going to go get Jax."

"No." I scream, "I mean, I'm fine. No need to alert Jax to my jumpiness."

"Are you sure?" I nod because I wasn't.

I wasn't sure at all.

The fear still attacked my body in waves, but I couldn't tell Jax.

I could just see it now.

Luca would go on a manhunt, and I would be put on lockdown.

No, this was fine. I was going to be fine, I tried to reassure myself.

"I'm fine, Sarah. Sorry for scaring you. What can I do for you?" I give her the best smile I can muster beneath my trembling body.

"I just wanted to check up on you. We haven't seen you on a night out for ages."

"Oh...I've been...busy." I blush.

"We know." She whispers.

"You do?"

I wasn't sure how she could possibly know. I hadn't told a soul. We had been extra careful around the office. Because I always used to work late, going home with Jax undetected was easier. We had been so careful, but not careful enough, it seemed.

"Essie saw you in Central Park," a wide smile appears on her face, "and let me tell you. She was not happy." She laughs.

"She saw me and Jax?"

"Oh, she saw all five of you. Livid she was that you were with all of them." She smirks, "Oh, you know what was strange though?"

"What's that?" This entire conversation was bloody strange.

"Did you know Jax had brothers before…you know." She winks. I shake my head, "No, neither did we, but Essie did."

"How is that possible?"

"I don't know, I told you strange. You know where I am if you need a break from the beasts." She winks once more before walking away with the sound of her laughter following her back to her desk.

Sarah leaves me with more questions; nobody really knew Essie. She had just come here and quickly slipped into our lives as if she had always been there. For a girl so timid, she hadn't been shy about making herself part of our group, but I had never questioned it until today.

I wasn't sure about anything anymore.

I was confused about my feelings for Jax, River, Elijah and Luca. I wasn't sure what it was, but it wasn't love. It couldn't be that. Fondness, maybe, but not love.

With the impending threat that seemed to see me, I couldn't see it, stalking in the shadows. I was oddly aware that I was running out of time. I was running out of time with all of them. The realisation that I would have to let them go hits me in the chest with a pain I've never felt before.

The sadness crawls across my body, and I slide into a dark, murky sea of misery. It crawled across my body in waves because I didn't want to go. I didn't want to leave. Hadn't I promised Luca I wouldn't leave, and now, I had no choice.

One more night.

I would have one more night with them, then leave their lives, and we would all be safe. Nobody would get hurt, and the men who had brought me so much joy would find a new toy.

Luca was right from day one.

This was only meant to be temporary.

So why did it hurt so much?

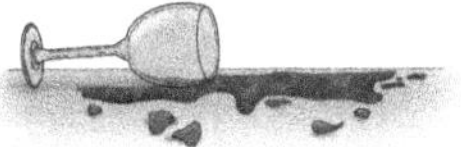

"Kitten, are you okay." I stop pushing the food around my plate and see their concerned looks as all four seem to have been watching me push it around it.

"I'm fine," I lie.

"Is there something wrong with your food?" River asks.

"No, it's perfect as always," I smile.

"Perfect?" Jax cocks a brow, "But you haven't touched it."

"I guess," I look down at the steak and vegetables in its delicious marinated sauce, and he's right. "I'm not that hungry," I utter.

"Is it your period again?" Elijah whispers, and I can feel a small slip of a smile pulling at my mouth.

"No, but I sure would like to revisit that day." I wink.

"What day?" Luca asks.

"Oh, you didn't tell him?" I smirk. "It was before you came home; let's just say your brothers...took very good care of me," I smile.

"Yeah, we did, baby." River excitedly shouts across the table.

"And that's what you want?" Luca asks.

What a curious question. No, I just wanted to tell them what was happening so I didn't have to leave them. What I wanted was not to be terrorised by an invisible threat. I wanted to return to when we were all happy, without the looming danger threatening me.

But we never really get what we want.

So, for tonight, I would put on a brave face and let them all enjoy me because, by sunrise, I wouldn't be here. I had chosen today because it was the start of the weekend, and the working week was over. It was easier to leave as they all slept.

I knew it was cowardly, but I also knew they would never let me leave without good cause, and I couldn't drag them into whatever I had following me in the dark.

So, I pretended I was okay for one last night and nodded with a beaming smile.

The excitement pierces my body, which is a welcome feeling from the terror that had shrouded it. Yes, this was a perfect way to say goodbye. Jax stares at his phone as it rings, and the rest hold a serious expression.

"Well, are you going to answer that?" I hear Luca huff.

"Of course, kitten, don't go anywhere. I will be right back." He winks as he walks out of the dining room.

"Where would I go?" I nervously chuckle.

"You might run away." Elijah winks. I can feel the colour draining from my face instantly, and he must have noticed because he reaches over and strokes his thumb across my hand. "Hey, I was joking, darling."

"I knew that," I knit my brows together and hope that the lie I told has fooled them. It seems to have worked until my eyes finally meet Luca's, and it's an expression I've seen before, full of mistrust.

"Hey, kitten." Jax stormed back into the room. "We are going to have to take a rain check," he solemnly speaks.

"Oh?"

"Unfortunately, my brothers and I," he looks at each of them. "Have something important that needs dealing with."

"Right now?" Elijah huffs.

"Right now." Jax sighs.

I watch as they all quickly peck my cheek and run out of the room on their very important business, whatever that may be. Would they have been so quick to rush out had they known this would be our last night together?

I clasp my hands under my chin, looking down at the table and sigh. It was for the best. What would I achieve by giving them one last night before I snuck out of their lives? Nothing, I would just leave them confused. It wasn't even a goodbye. It was me not wanting to let go but knowing I had to.

"Now you can explain what's going on." His deep, dominant voice travels across the room.

"Didn't you leave?" My eyes widen, and my mouth gapes open like it's catching flies.

"Now, why would you think I would leave you alone?"

"Luca, I'm not a child. I don't need you to stay home and babysit." I spit at him while pushing my chair back, hearing the legs scrape across the hardwood flooring and racing towards the door.

He catches my wrist in his large hand and spins my body against his. My body crashes against his hard body, and the tremors crawl up my legs within moments.

Slowly, my eyes travel up his body until they meet his eyes. Once again, fierce anger lay dormant within his emerald pools that captivated me.

My back is pushed against the wall encased by his body. The gasps fall quietly from my mouth, and he hasn't touched me yet. "Where do you think you're going, little toy?" He breathes into my ear.

"I was…" His fingers slide down my body, parting my legs. I gasped at the close contact of his grip on my thighs, "I was…" I pant, and his hand glides ever so slowly up my inner thighs moving closer and closer to my now dripping pussy, "I was…" I try to speak again. His fingers hit my pussy, and I melt into his touch, "Oh god, Luca." I cry out.

"Yes, little toy," he smirks, "you were?" He cocks a brow.

His fingers entered me, and any words I wanted to speak died on my tongue. I can only submit to how his fingers move inside me, causing an explosion of desire inside my brain.

"I love how your body reacts to me, little toy. How you fucking melt against my touch. Do you know how fucking crazy you make me?" He growls.

"Luca, please…" I beg.

"Ah, look at you begging, like a good little toy," his fingers push further inside me, and my body instantly sets alight. A fire rages within me, and I can only cry out.

I desperately want to hold onto this man for dear life. I want to bathe in his exotic scent and drown in the darkness that consumes him. I want to hold on and never let go.

Out of all of the Kane brothers, Luca affects me the most. I'm unsure if it's his unwillingness to give me what I want or because he gives me what I want, even if I didn't know that's what I wanted to begin with.

His fingers fall from my needy pussy, and I whimper at the sudden empty feeling. I need this man to fill me up, to take away every thought I have. I just need him to consume me and set my body ablaze in the only way he knows how.

His hand clasps inside mine, and he pulls me towards the door. Panic sets in. Does he know what I have planned? But how could he? He's still moving towards the door, but it's dark out; there is no other reason for us to go out there. I knew he suspected something was off, but maybe I was just being paranoid.

"Luca, where are we going?" I ask with panic thumping in my chest.

"We are going for a ride." He whispers into my hair.

"Now?"

"Sure, you never ridden under the stars before? It can be quite...the experience."

We ride through the night with only the headlights on the motorcycle and stars that light the sky as our guiding light. My hands clasp tightly around his waist, and I just want to stay here, in this moment.

The bike finally comes to a standstill, and as I look around at my surroundings, Rockaway Beach sits before us. The water slowly moves in waves, like a black lagoon dancing beneath the moonlit stars.

"I didn't realise you were so...romantic." I gasp.

"I'm not."

"Luca,"

"Don't ruin it by opening your pretty little mouth."

Luca exits the bike, and I'm about to do the same until he gives me a stern look, "Don't move, stay." He orders.

I watch as he removes his clothes. My mouth is watering just watching this beast of a man standing before me with muscles bulging from every part of his delectable body. His hard cock bobs up and down, and I gasp with mesmerising desire.

The moonlight hits his skin, and he takes my breath away.

All I can think is: my god, he's beautiful.

"Are we going skinny dipping?" I quiz.

"Not exactly." He smirks.

Climbing back onto the bike, I let slip a slight smirk. As sexy as he looked, a naked beast rising back onto the bike seemed to stir something inside of me that amused me.

"Something funny, little toy?"

"You, you're funny." I giggle.

"Is that so?" He gives me a look of mischief. "Then, I will expect you to laugh through this entire show."

"Show?" My eyes widen, and my smile quickly fades.

His hands move across my body, quickly removing my clothes. I had hoped he would have struggled, considering he was too stubborn to allow me to move. Still, he was adept at removing my clothes in even the most awkward places.

His hands slide up my thighs, and I fight the urge not to cry out from the slight touch of his skin against mine. "I don't hear you laughing." He mocks while spreading my legs wide and looking down at me with hunger in his eyes.

He pushes my body across the bike, and my back falls into an arch almost immediately. "That's a good girl, just how I like you." He presses his nose to my pussy, and I hear him inhale. "Fuck, you're fucking intoxicating." He breathes out.

"Tell me, little toy, is it funny yet?" His tongue slithers out and glides up my wet pussy lips, causing my body to squirm and shudder beneath his touch. "I don't hear you laughing." He mocks again before driving his tongue into the slit between my pussy lips.

My hands crash into his hair, tugging and pulling with desperation. "Oh god, please Luca, fuck, please…" I beg.

He continues to tease me, sliding his tongue up and down my soaking pussy lips, which causes a fiery desire to move through my body at an exceptional speed. My body squirms beneath his touch, and screams of pleasure fill the dark night air.

"So fucking good, you're so fucking good for me." He breathes out.

His head rises, and his hands rest under my ass, lifting me. My body crashes against him, his lips find my neck, and for a moment, he just pants into my skin.

"You taste so fucking…good." His tongue teases my neck, "but I really need to fuck that tight little pussy of yours, fuck, Cara, you drive me fucking crazy." He gasps.

I feel my body has been lowered onto his hard throbbing cock, and a gasp crawls out as the tip of his cock enters me. "Oh, fuck," he rasps into my skin.

"Be a good girl for me and show me just how desperately you need my cock,"

"Luca," I cry out.

His hand flattens against my back, pushing his cock further into my dripping cunt, and the gasps of desire just fall out of my mouth; looking into his eyes, I slowly move my hips. Listening to the sharp gasps of approval that emit from his throat.

"Fuck, that's good...that's my good girl," He whispered into my skin.

My hips rock faster, and I feel his hand tightly grip my thigh, his breathing as erratic as mine. "Oh god, Luca, oh god," I scream at the pulsing pleasure I feel from his cock that fills me up.

"That's good," he rasps, gripping my ass and thrashing my body hard against his cock that fills my little pussy, stretching me out. "Fuck, you grip...me...so fucking...good, baby, oh fuck," I hear him growl.

He grips my wrists, pulling them behind my body, and the fear ignites in my eyes. He can see the sudden change, but the sick bastard enjoys it. My back arches, and once again, my body betrays me.

I can feel the pulsing of my dripping cunt as it wraps tightly around his cock. The sharp gasps of approval from his lips tell me he's enjoying this. His hand comes down across my pussy, and I shudder beneath his touch, feeling him slide two fingers inside my pussy, stretching me even wider around his cock.

"You love it when I stretch you, don't you, little toy?" I mumble my approval with sharp gasps. "Can you feel how much your sweet little cunt enjoys being filled, fuck, your little cunt feels so good, baby?"

"Luca, oh...Luca, fuck." I finally gasped.

His fingers move inside me against his cock. My hips grind harder and faster, chasing the release building deep inside my body. Screams fill the air with my gasps of pleasure.

"Come on, baby, fuck me like you're starved for it. Fuck me faster, little toy, like my cock is the only thing...keeping you fucking alive," he pants.

His other hand tangles within my hair, pulling my head back to look into his dangerous eyes that are wild with desire. Faster and faster, my hips rock, and my eyes slowly lower.

I feel a sharp pull on my head as my head is once again raised until I'm looking into his eyes again.

"Oh no, baby," he pants. "You look at me when I fuck you, I want to see all of you…just…like…this." He thrusts deeper inside me, and the screams rip from my throat. "You show me…exactly…how much you want this."

"Luca, oh fuck," I cry out.

His body crashes against mine, and I'm unsure where I end, and he begins. We are locked as one, riding the wave of explosive pleasure that moves faster than lightning.

"Fuuuuck," I hear him growl. "You feel…so…fucking …good..baby," the pressure mounts and the pleasure builds inside me. I'm unsure if I have any breath left in my body to cry out my screams of desire. "That's my….fucking….good girl," he pants.

His eyes burn through mine with an intense need. "Now, fucking cum."

My body shakes when those words leave his lips, and an explosion erupts. Something so intense couldn't be honest. My body feverishly shakes as I spray all my desire around his thick cock and fingers filling me.

My body still shakes from my release, but he isn't nearly done; he pumps harder and faster, chasing his own release, but he's just not there yet. I can already feel the build-up of a second orgasm moving through my body.

"Please cum, please fill me up," I beg him.

"Fuck, baby..." he rasps.

"I need to feel your hot cum fill me up, please, Luca," I cry out.

"Oh shit," he cries out.

I feel his cock jerk deep within my pulsing pussy, and the hot remnants of his desire finally splash inside me. The crawling desire finally reaches its peak, and I feel my pussy tighten around him as I once again shudder with desire and cry out, "I'm cumming, I'm cumming,"

Collapsing against his body in a hot, sweaty mess, I'm breathless and lay in his arms. The after-effects of Luca stained my soul forever, and without knowing what was happening, my body shudders, and I feel a silent tear slide down my face.

Out of all of them, I would miss him the most, and that thought alone made my heart heavy with despair.

I didn't want to leave.

But what choice did I have?

At least when he was gone, I would always have tonight.

I will never forget us, just like this.

That was better than nothing.
At least I had tonight.

"Where is she?"

"Who?" Sarah's eyes twinkle with mischief.

"Sarah, I don't pay you to be smart."

"No? You also don't pay me for information." A slip of a smirk forms on her dark, plump lips.

"Did you find her?" Elijah comes racing behind me.

"Oh, sweet Jesus, there's two of you." Sarah gasps.

I glare at Sarah; I know she knows more than she's letting on, but I fear how Luca would react if I didn't find Cara. It hadn't escaped my notice how close they had become over the last few weeks, and that surprised me more than anyone because Luca didn't ever get attached to anyone, least of all a woman.

"Sarah.." I pinch the bridge of my nose. "I just…I want to know she's safe." I finally utter.

"You know it crushed her leaving you." She finally speaks. "She…"

"What?"

"She feels more than I think she would care to tell you. Well, any of you."

"Sarah, please tell me where she is."

"Tell me why she left you first."

Shit, if I knew that, we wouldn't be having this conversation right now. We should have never left, but when we came back, she was wrapped in the arms of Luca, looking deliciously naked and content.

"I don't know," I mutter.

"She didn't tell you?" She gasps. The shock was clearly evident on her face.

"Clearly not." I was losing patience with this conversation and annoyed that Sarah knew something I didn't. "Sarah," I growl.

"I don't really know anything, Jax. All I know is she showed up at my house last night unannounced. Of course, I let her in. All she did was cry the whole night.

I've never seen anyone's heart physically break before, but I witnessed something like it."

"Cara is at your house?" Elijah interrupts. She shakes her head. "Well, where is she then?" He grits.

"Cara had some bad news regarding her mother," She looks down at her hands. "Cara has gone." She mutters.

"What do you mean she's gone?"

"She went home, Jax, she's gone."

"Great, she's gone to her apartment. We will just..." Elijah happily makes plans.

"No, she went home," Sarah emphasises the word 'home' and it finally clicks. Cara is no longer in New York. She's gone. "I was hoping you'd come to find me," Sarah whispers. I look down at her water-filled eyes. "Nobody should be alone when they lose someone." I nodded because I knew exactly what message she was trying to relay.

"Lose someone?" Elijah mutters, "Who did she lose?"

I shake my head at him, "You know, for someone so bright, you sure do say some stupid shit."

I knew where she was.

That was more than I had this morning.

Arriving back at the house, everything was quiet until it wasn't. River races outside with a look on his face that I don't think I've seen in years.

"Shit, where have you been?" He screams at me.

"We went to find out where Cara went."

"Great, where is she?" He smiles, looking hopeful.

"Well, she's just in my pocket. Just wait there, buddy. Let me fish her out." Elijah mocks.

"Oh, you make jokes all you want, but you haven't spent the morning with the fucking psycho."

"I'm so glad you've given Luca back his title." I roll my eyes. "What's he done now?"

"Why don't you enter the psyche ward and see for yourself?"

"Well, this should be fun." Elijah rubs his hands together and smirks at us both.

"Can you try to act like a normal human for once?" I scolded him.

"Normal? Us? Come on, Jax, why mess with a good thing." His hearty laugh sounds as he strides towards the front door.

I needed to prepare for what I walked in on. The house had been trashed. You would have thought we had been burgled by how the furniture was thrown at the walls. Glass paved the floors. It was just a mass of destruction.

Was that blood? Shit, who's blood-painted my fucking walls.

"I told you it was bad." River gasps.

"Where is he?" I grit.

"Oh, the Hulk decided he needed a break from breaking shit. He's in the library...drinking before he chooses another room to destroy."

"Drinking..but... it's...you know what," I put my hands up. "Never mind."

"He won't speak to you. He just grunts and flies into a rage." River warns.

"Yeah, we'll see about that." I turn to go face my brother, and slowly turning back, I look at River. "This is because Cara left?"

He shrugs, "What else would it be?"

I knew that's what it was. I couldn't understand why she would leave. Shit, I knew something was wrong last night when we left, but we didn't have a choice. Oak Haven had become a thorn in my side, and with a string of girls going missing, I knew who was behind it.

I had begged Luca to come with us, but he had refused, stating that Cara shouldn't be alone. I should have seen how quickly he had bonded with her then, but I was too wrapped up in the shit show we had let unfold to see it.

None of us had seen it because Luca was the one who wouldn't entertain her in the beginning, so how did he become the one who fell hardest for her?

I wanted to race in there and show the big giant some tough love. Maybe it show him that he couldn't fly into a rage when things didn't go his way, but it was strange. I hear my feet tap against the floor as I reach the library, and I'm unprepared for what I witness.

There, he is slumped into the leather armchair next to the roaring fire with nothing but the sound of crackling from the fire. The fire illuminated his face, and it looked nothing like it did yesterday. Dark circles form under his eyes, and pain slices through his soul. His hands are bloody and bruised, and he holds an empty glass with only the tiny remnants of the whiskey that he's clearly thrown down his throat.

Over the years, I had seen Luca in many states but never to this extent. He looked like a ghost of his former self, which only seemed fitting because he seemed haunted by the loss of Cara.

"I found her," I call into the room before approaching him.

"I don't care." He spits back at me.

"The house tells a different story." I raise a brow while edging closer to my broken brother. "Luca,"

"I don't need a lecture, I know I fucked up." He lowers his head, "I will pay for the damage I caused."

"That's not what I was going to say,"

"Just go, Jax." He sighs in defeat.

"Did you not hear me? I said I found her."

"I heard you." He mutters while walking towards the fireplace and slamming the glass down on the marble top.

"We are going to get her." There is nothing but silence. I wasn't sure what I expected, but it wasn't this. "Luca, she will want you there…" I'm staring into his back that's slumped over the fireplace.

"Why would she want any of us there," he finally turns, glaring at me. "She left. Let her go. She made her choice." He spits out.

"She had to leave." I finally gasped.

"Had to leave," a sinister chuckle passes his lips, "had to leave...she fucking promised." He screams into the air while picking up that Glass and throwing it at the wall. The loud crash echoes around the room as it falls to the ground and shatters into pieces.

"What did she promise?" I ask, completely dumbfounded that they seemed to have a secret to which the rest of us weren't party. I try to appear indifferent, but I can't help the little sliver of jealousy that slips up my spine.

"It doesn't matter," he mutters, falling back into his chair.

"Luca," I touch his shoulder, and he drags his body away from my touch.

"Don't touch me. Just leave. Go on, go chase her. Be disappointed." He mocks.

"She needs us," I utter barely a whisper.

I hoped I would appeal to his better nature, but my common sense told me that he didn't have a better nature right now. The sliver of humanity she had lit inside his soul had all but gone when she had

I was wasting time here. What I should have been doing was boarding a plane so that we could stand by her side. So that she didn't need to be alone while she was grieving, but I couldn't go, not without Luca.

A sinister chuckle passes his lips once more, and the way he stands from the chair sends a cold chill across my soul. Standing tall, the fiery anger is laced within his eyes.

"You know, you keep saying what she needs. Always the same fucking story with you, Jax."

"What's that supposed to fucking mean?"

"I said this would happen. I said she would leave, but you just had to throw her into our lives, didn't you? I didn't fucking want this." He screams. "I didn't want any of this." He whispers.

"Oh, this is my fucking fault?" I ask him dumbfounded.

"Oh, of course not, Jax, you're the perfect brother. I wouldn't dream of blaming you for anything. Little Jax who always has everyone's best interest at heart...until he doesn't." He mocks.

"Look, I know you're hurt.."

"Hurt? I'm not fucking hurt. I'm disappointed. I'm pissed off, and I'm fucking wondering why you still give a shit that the girl you decided to invite into our lives that came in like a fucking tornado is worth travelling to some back shit little town to be once again...rejected. You want to be disappointed. Then go. I'm not fucking chasing after a fucking liar." He spits.

"Fine. Be a stubborn bastard. We will leave without you." I finally admit defeat. Luca wasn't coming, and I had to face up to the fact that his ego would once again be his undoing.

"Your funeral, little brother." He utters before sitting back down and crossing one leg across the other.

His words hit me like an ice pick has entered my heart, and he doesn't even realise how true his words are.

"It's not my funeral we are going to. It's Cara's mother." I finally sigh. "So, you can come with us and be there for the woman you love or stay here with your little pity party. It's entirely up to you."

"Love? But I don't." He shakes his head as if he's mulling over my words. "I can't...I don't." He repeats into the air.

"Sure, you don't big guy." I finally smirk before walking away, leaving him with his thoughts and secretly hoping he would come to his senses before we had to go.

The destruction of Luca follows me through the house, and I groan. Doesn't love her? Yeah, try telling that to the fucking house that had felt his rage from her leaving. He was delusional if he thought this was an act of disappointment. This was an act of pain, passion and loss.

"So, is he coming?" Elijah asks as I enter the kitchen.

"Who knows." I shrug. "He's stopped breaking shit, though, so that's something."

"Plane tickets are booked." River smiles. "Do you think she will be happy to see us?"

"I don't know," I answer honestly because I didn't know anything.

"What if she doesn't want us there?" River looks worried, but he just said what we were all thinking.

"Then we will leave. We are going there to support her, so she knows that even though she couldn't tell us. We are there for her; if she doesn't need that, we will leave. Sarah was right; nobody should have to go through that alone." I finally utter.

"She won't be alone. And we won't be leaving...without her." I hear a deep voice behind me, and quickly turning my head, I see Luca standing in the doorway with his packed bags.

"No, she won't." I smile.

Goodbyes are a strange thing.

My mother and I didn't really have a strong rela-tionship. It was estranged, especially after Carter. She blamed me. Said that I should have just lived with it, that women had been doing the same thing for centuries, and they survived.

Now, I was all alone, and the likelihood of getting married at my age was slim.

She couldn't grasp that Carter would ever hurt any-one, least of all me, because he was such a sweet boy.

I had contemplated her words. She actually convinced me that I was the problem. That I was ungrateful. I should have been grateful for every horror I had endured under his influence, and I almost went back...almost.

I didn't want to get married. I didn't want to be beholden to a man because I felt I had no choice. I didn't want to sit there when I was old and wish I had done my life differently. I just didn't want to live with regrets, but I knew if I had stayed with Carter, old age would have never come because, eventually, he would have killed me.

I told Sarah I couldn't look after her because it was too hard, but that wasn't it. I didn't want to look after her. I didn't want to put my life on hold for a woman who couldn't help her only daughter through the hardest time.

I felt guilty and selfish, but I would have resented her if I had stayed with her. I already felt a separation in our relationship. I just didn't want to resent her. It was the only way I could still hold loving feelings for a mother who had given me none.

I wish that I could turn back the clock. Spend more time with her. Try to repair a relationship that she had broken with her biased morals. But that's the thing about time. It goes by so fast, and it's the only thing we can never get back. Once it's gone, it's gone.

As I sit and listen to the priest say his lovely words about what a kind and gentle person my mother is, I wonder who the person he speaks of is. She wasn't evil by any measure. She lacked empathy and human compassion for anyone who didn't fit her ideals.

Looking around, the chairs are filled with all the people that had known her over the years. There isn't a dry eye here, well, except mine. I feel sad, sad that I would never see her again. Sad that I would never speak to her again. The pain in my chest tells me the sadness moves across my body in waves, yet I still can't cry for her.

I don't even hear the words that the priest speaks anymore. His lips are moving, but I hear nothing. The only thing I hear is static noise, like a rampant buzzing sound that has crawled through my senses.

The buzzing becomes louder. I'm not sure a bee hasn't crept into my ear and is now looking for residence in my brain. The pounding in my head beats like the sound of a drum.

"Are you okay, dear?" I hear the faint, soothing voice beside me.

Looking to the side, I see an elderly lady with pale blue eyes that remind me of kindness. Curly silver hair and deep-set lines show her age, but looking past her age, you could see she was beautiful in her youth. A kind, tight-lip smile appears on her face.

Did I know this kind elderly lady? I wasn't sure, but the buzzing in my head slowly dissipated. I'm thankful to the stranger beside me for helping lift the fog clouding my brain.

"I'm fine." I finally answer.

"I'm Mavis," she smiles once more. "I used to play bridge with your mother at the community centre long ago."

"Oh," I smile, "that's nice."

"Such a sad way to go." She mutters.

"There are worse ways to leave this earth." I cut out. Her face drops to the fall at my response. "Sorry, that was rude."

"No matter, dear." She pats my hand. "We all deal with grief differently."

I'm unsure why, but her last words piss me off. Was she implying I wasn't grieving because I hadn't cried? Shit, I hadn't cried in over 10 years, but that didn't mean I had no feelings, did it? I was still numb. That was a feeling...sort of.

The service moves slower than an old lady walking down the street. It's painful sitting here, knowing everyone here thinks I'm a monster because my eyes don't leak for a woman who would have rather seen me dead than single.

What did they know anyway? They played games with her. They should have tried living with her. Then, we would see how many of them cried. I could feel the bitterness of bile rising up my throat. Threatening to crawl out like I was an extra from the exorcist.

Deal with grief differently. Her words swim around my head. Was there a rule book of what you were supposed to do? Was I doing it all wrong? I didn't know. I needed to get out of here.

It felt like I couldn't breathe, which made no sense because I was already outside. I had the perfect oxygen source, surrounded by trees, yet it felt like I had been suffocated.

"Where are you going, dear?" I haven't even left my seat, and the nosy stranger who deemed my grief inadequate is interrogating me now for wanting to leave.

"I need some air." I finally choke out.

She smiles, "Well, there is plenty right here."

"If you'll excuse me," I snap at her.

My legs shake beneath me. Threatening to fall, but I wasn't giving Mavis the satisfaction of seeing me crumble to the ground. I'm sure that would please her to see some semblance of a broken daughter at her mother's funeral.

Standing tall with legs that still shake like jelly. I look at the casket my mother lay within, beautiful rosewood with blood-red roses sitting atop. She would be proud, only the best for mother.

I closed my eyes and said a silent goodbye because it was silly to sit at a grave and weep or, in my case, force myself to cry. She was gone. She couldn't hear me. Who was I talking to? The wind that currently thrashed its way through my hair.

Funerals weren't supposed to be happy, but I had never been to one as silent and depressing as this one. I had often thought about my own funeral over the years, and this is not what I would want.

Weren't we supposed to celebrate their life? Not mourn their passing.

I wouldn't want this.

I would like people to be happy and smiling.

Remembering me as I was in their lives.

Not sitting there in doom and gloom.

Maybe Mavis was right; my grieving method differed, but what was the alternative? I sank into a deep, dark depression that I couldn't claw my way out of for an estranged woman I called mother.

I feel the first droplets of rain splash against my face as I turn away from the casket. Perfect, of course, it would rain. Even the universe could cry, so why couldn't I? I shake my head as I slowly and wobbly walk away from the woman I didn't even know.

I hadn't lost anything today, or had I? I had always hoped there was a possibility of repairing our relationship. But it was too late now. She was gone. Maybe I couldn't cry because all I felt was regret.

Regret that I hadn't tried hard enough. Regret that I had let my feelings drive a rift between us both. Regret that I hadn't been there for her in her final days. That was a feeling. I hadn't cried but felt regret. Regret that now it was too late to fix anything.

Time really was priceless.

It is the one thing we all take for granted and the one thing we can never get back.

Time is a funny thing.

Just passing us by.

We can't taste, feel, or touch it, but we feel its departure once it passes us by.

Yes, time was funny, and hers had run out.

I wondered if we knew that time was fleeting, would we do things differently, or would we move through life exactly as we always have, never noticing that time, in the end, is not on our side?

My legs shake as I walk down the stone pathway.

My head once again becomes foggy.

The weakness is overtaking my body.

I hadn't eaten, maybe that's what was wrong. It felt like I was in a swirling vortex, trapped.

I see shadowy figures in the distance.

Maybe I was hallucinating, like when you're starved of water in the Sahara desert.

My throat feels dry, and my head pounds like someone is beating on a drum.

I need to sit down, but I can't go back. I can only go forward.

The problem is, I'm unsure if I will even make it one more step before I collapse to the ground in a heap of what Mavis would assume was grief.

The shadowy figures stand in the distance, their muffled voices calling me, but I don't hear a word.

The blood rushes to my head, and a clear mist covers my eyes.

It's inevitable.

I'm going down.

Chapter Twenty-Four

Uninvited Party

Cara

I can feel the blood rushing to my head. It crawls around my body at lightning speed.

I can hear the mumbles of my name being called, but I can't differentiate the voice.

My legs shake, and a sudden weakness overcomes my body.

The scene in front of me is spinning. I can see the faint shape of someone rushing forward, but my vision is so blurred that I'm unsure who.

I crash against a rigid body, and I can feel my body being lifted from the ground. My head hits against a chest.

My eyes want to close.

My body is exhausted.

I raise my eyes and see the swirling emerald eyes bore into mine with concern.

"Luca," I breathe out.

He takes a moment to assess if I'm okay before his look of concern turns to a glimpse of fiery anger. The only words I hear pass his lips, "You promised."

"I'm sorry," I utter as fresh tears fall.

He looks down at me with that same anger.

That same passion I had seen when we first met, but this time, there was no look of hate, just anger that burned within his eyes.

It felt like my soul was burning beneath his penetrative gaze. "You promised," he repeats once more before his head crashes against mine. His lips brush against mine slowly, his hand cupping my face. The heat of his kiss burns a fire through my body. His lips mashed against mine harder and faster in a burning, yearning passion of desire and need.

The moans fall from my lips and get lost in his mouth.

"I thought you didn't kiss?" I breathlessly whisper.

"I don't kiss unless I mean it. Don't ever fucking do that again." He scolds.

"Do what?"

"Leave," I hear him utter before he gently presses his nose against mine, driving me insane with the light graze against my nose.

"I thought," tears crawl down my face, and my heart hurts. "I thought it would be best." I choke out.

His fingers brush away the tears from my face, and the pad of his thumb moves in circles as he caresses my face. "Cara, when you left, a piece of me died that day. Don't ever think your absence wasn't felt. Your leaving was not the best. It was the most horrific thing that could have happened. You left a hole in my heart." He looks back at his brothers. "In all our hearts," his lips pressed against my head, "I said we don't get the girl, but I had you. I fucking had you, and I won't lose you. Men like us may not get the girl or even deserve her, but god damn it, do I want her." He whispers.

"Are you trying to make me cry," I sob as fresh tears crawl down my face.

"No, little princess, I'm trying to say..." he stalls, just looking down at me. "I'm here. We are all here. We came here for you."

"All...of...you." I choke back a sob.

"All of us." Jax, River and Elijah respond in unison.

"Hey, kitten." Jax smiles, "Now, how did you crawl into the monster's heart." He winks.

My eyes widen, and I look up at Luca, monster? He wasn't a monster. I'm just looking at him in shock. "Luca isn't a monster." I finally gasp and see something I haven't seen before: Luca's lips upturn in a slight smile, which takes my breath away.

"Anyway, it's not Luca that's the monster here." I gasp.

"Oh yeah, who is it then?" Elijah mocks.

"It's me," I utter.

"You take that back right now." River demands. I shake my head. "Princess, didn't I tell you before? You're perfect."

"I'm perfect. I couldn't even cry for my own mother. I'm a monster." I finally gasped.

"Now, that's not true. You cried." Elijah smirks.

I feel breathless.

What was I supposed to say to that?

That my eyes were dry until they showed up. What was the point? I could do no wrong in their eyes.

I want them to drop that pedestal they had put me on because I didn't deserve it.

But they are all looking at me like they are waiting for me to agree. The pressure mounts. Luca looks down at me with that deep, penetrative gaze, and the shivers climb through my body.

Suddenly, he makes me feel raw, exposed and unsure of everything. With just one look, I'm drowning.

"I..." he smiles. Shit, I broke first. "I cried when I saw you," I whisper.

"Of course you did, baby."

He looks like the cat that got the cream, and I'm instantly regretting the words that spilt out of my mouth.

"At least you didn't trash an entire house." Elijah laughs. The glare that Luca gives him would turn anyone to stone. I'm pretty sure he would have done it if he could have killed his brother with that look.

"You trashed the house?" I look up at him, but he won't even look at me. "Why?" I utter. He still won't look at me. Reaching my hand and teasing my fingers against his face, I hear a slight moan crawl from his throat. "Luca?"

"Because, little princess." He finally looks down at me with those piercing emerald eyes that could set the world on fire at any moment. "You left. You left me, and then," he sighs, "nothing made sense; when you left, you took the life right out of my life. Don't ever do that again. Don't ever take the light from my life." He whispers.

"I...I didn't think..."

"No, neither did I, but my once sunny life was grey once you were gone. I don't want to live in the dark anymore. I don't want to live an existence without you in it."

"Luca," I gasp and feel fresh tears spill down my face.

"I never wanted anything. I was content living my existence....until I met you. I can't go back, princess. I won't live a life with you gone."

"But, you don't like me." I gasp.

"Now, what gave you that idea." He smiles while pressing his nose against mine and his forehead against mine.

It was strange; this one seemed to mean much more out of all my tender moments with them. His skin against mine, how his breath fanned my face and breathed new life into it. It was barely anything, and yet it was everything.

Every moment with Luca tipped new life inside of me, and the moment the tip of his nose touched mine, a warmth spread to my chest, and I finally knew what it felt like to come home.

Each of them had given me something I never even knew I needed. They had given me so much love and tenderness. They had given me something I didn't even know I needed or wanted.

I thought home was a place, but it wasn't a place built from bricks.

This was home right now.

With the love in their eyes, looking down at me.

Luca pressed his soft skin against mine.

That was home.

So, maybe home wasn't a place at all.

Perhaps home was this moment, right now.

A feeling, a spark, something that set your world on fire and gave you peace.

That was home.

"Where would you like us to take you?" Luca breathes against my skin.

I instantly know the answer, and with a smile, I can feel appearing on my lips as I look into his eyes, I know exactly where I want to go.

"Home," I smile. "I want us all to go home."

Elijah wasn't joking when he said Luca had trashed the house.

It looked like I had just entered a warzone. Luca didn't put me down until we were back at the house, like a caveman protecting his property.

Walking through the house that once held so much happiness, I was astounded at what I saw. Glass paved the way. Everything was destroyed, and my eyes widened as I stood in the entryway. Disbelief pierces my body.

"Why does it look like you went to war?" I gasp.

"Come on, kitten, it doesn't look that bad." Jax smiles.

"Not that bad?" My eyes scanned the area. It looked like a warzone.

"Luca will fix it," Jax whispers, and I feel his arms come around my body; everything disappears instantly.

"He did this because of me?" I gasp.

I feel his arms tighten across my body, holding onto me like I may disappear at any moment. "He did this because he's a lunatic," Jax utters.

"Asshole." I hear Luca grit out.

"I didn't want...any of this."

"Kitten, this is not your fault." Jax tries to reassure me but fails miserably.

"This is all my fault," I lower my head in disbelief. "I thought...you would all just forget about me, you know, find a new girl and—."

My body is instantly spun around until I'm facing Jax. That's the one thing I didn't want to do. I didn't want to face him. I didn't want him to see the tears that threatened to fall again.

"Now, kitten," he tips my chin with his finger gently and raises my head until my eyes finally meet his. "How could we possibly forget you?"

I just look at him. I want to say something, but as I open my mouth, no sound comes out. All I can do is stare at his stupid, beautiful face with my mouth gaping open.

"Kitten, we could never forget you. You're our girl. What did I tell you in London?"

I try to rack my brain, but my thoughts are muddy and black; Jax had said many things in London, and I was supposed to remember something so specific. He's looking at me with hope; he's hoping I remember, but I don't, not right now.

"I told you that if you stayed, I wouldn't let you just walk away. I meant it."

"I thought," shit, what did I think? "I thought you were trying to charm me." I finally croak out.

His head moves closer to mine. I can feel his warm breath kiss my skin, and it feels like warmth rushing through my body. "I meant it." He says once more. "Kitten, I won't let you just walk away. You're our girl." He smiles while brushing the pad of his thumb against my cheek.

Then I did something I had been avoiding since they crashed my mother's funeral. I let go. Closing my eyes, I give in to his touch. Feeling the shockwaves of warmth travel through my body, I don't think; I just feel the tenderness and love that Jax showers me with and finally feel like I'm home.

"You're our girl." He whispers.

"I'm your girl," I utter, and for the first time today, I truly mean the words that spill from my lips. I'm there, girl. I had been there, girl, since I came here. I just couldn't admit it because admitting that I actually cared for them was far more terrifying than the reason I left them.

"There is, however, a consequence for your actions." He sternly states.

"A consequence?"

"Yes, you left without saying goodbye, without ending what we have."

"I couldn't say goodbye." I croak out, feeling the first tear slip down my cheek. "It was too hard, I didn't know how."

"Well, kitten, that just means you didn't want to leave, did you?" I shake my head. "Then why did you?"

"I—." I couldn't tell him. I wanted to say it to him. I tried to tell them all. I wanted to end the ordeal, but as I opened my mouth, I couldn't find the words to explain that leaving was out of my control. That was never a choice I would ever make.

"I don't know," I finally say.

"You don't know why you left?" Elijah mocks.

"That's not good enough," Luca growls while racing forward, gripping my hand in his and pulling my body hard against his. "No, little toy, that's not nearly fucking good enough."

What was I supposed to say? That I was risking all of our lives just by being here. I couldn't leave them now, even if I wanted to. That the psychopath that had threatened my existence would be back because, one way or another, the psychopath would know.

They would see that I broke my word and came back.

I no longer cared what the mysterious person behind the hate mail did to me because I was no longer afraid. I wanted to be here with all of them, even if that meant putting myself in danger.

I'm a coward.

I say nothing.

I wasn't sure Luca wanted excuses.

Within moments, his lips crash against mine, and a feeling of euphoria instantly overtakes me. One light brush of his lips against mine, and I'm lost. Taken over by the desire that swims through my veins.

"No, that response is a fucking insult." He whispers in my ear, his lips moving down my neck, and shivers from his touch burn my body with heat.

"Luca," I gasp. Shit, I was panting, and he had barely touched me.

His fingers grip the black dress that clings to my body, and the buttons pop open within moments. "Fuck, Luca, you don't need to act like an animal." I regret the words as soon as they leave my mouth.

His deep gaze renders me still, "An animal?" He raises a curious brow, "Oh, little toy, you will be so fun to play with."

"Luca—." I try to protest, but he puts a finger to my lips.

The dress is ripped from my body, and I await my consequence. The anticipation is almost killing me. Every second feels like a lifetime.

"Is my consequence that you're planning on boring me to death." I roll my eyes.

My body is instantly thrown to the ground, and Luca slithers across me like a snake ensnaring its next meal. Caught in a trap with no way of getting out. His hands grip my throat, and his silky voice penetrates my ear.

"Oh, little toy, that little mouth of yours will be the death of you." My body shudders as the threat of his words hits me.

"What's wrong? Nothing to say? Or did I bore you to death?" His words slither around me.

I blink rapidly and stare at the intense gaze of his eyes that renders my body still. I suppose I could fight, maybe struggle, but the sick bastard would probably enjoy that, so I do nothing. Just lay there beneath him, still.

"That's a shame you can't speak, little toy, but there are other ways." My brows raise, and a curious smirk falls across my face. "I'm going to eat your fucking pussy until you pass out." I shake my head, "I'm going to fuck you over and over again, each orgasm more intense than the last," His fingers crawl down my body, parting my legs. "This little body is mine, and when I'm done with you, you'll give me it freely."

"No, Luca," I finally croak out.

"What did you say?"

"I said no, fuck your games, fuck your consequences and—." His fingers slam into my pussy, my body betrays me. Fuck. The moment he enters me, the pleasure climbs through me, and my body tingles with desire.

"Oh, this isn't a punishment princess,"

"But Jax said—."

"There were consequences, yes,"

"If it isn't a punishment, then what is it?"

"It's a funishment," he smirks.

"What the fuck is a funishment?" I ask.

"Oh, you'll see." Jax laughs.

His hands crawl over my body, leaving moans from my throat with every teasing touch; his hands slide down my body, teasing the apex between my thighs. I'm dripping at the thought of having him touch me, but his hands move back up my body anytime he gets close.

The desperation crawls through me with fierce want and need. I need him to touch me almost more than breathe air. Once more, Luca's hands fall across my belly, slowly touching my thighs. His thumb brushes across my soaking pussy that tingles with desire, but once again, he moves away from the spot I desperately need him to touch.

"Please," I beg.

His smirk tells me he isn't going to give me what I so desperately need. "Please, Luca, please touch me."

"But I am touching you," he smirks, "here," his hands move across my waist, "and here," his lips tease my neck, and when I feel his hot wet tongue nuzzled against my skin, bursts of moans fall out of my body.

"Luca, please," I beg once more.

His hands move between my legs, light strokes across my aching pussy, but it's not enough. The desire moves through me in waves. I need him inside of me to fill me, but he's just taunting me.

"Please, I need you." I pant.

A growl falls in my ear, and I can feel the sticky wetness coat my thighs, "look how wet you are for me, such a desperate, needy little puppy." His fingers move across my soaked pussy lips, and I cry out from each light stroke. "I fucking love how wet you get for me." He rasps.

His fingers finally dip into my pussy, and an explosion of desire runs through my body. My back arches, and I melt into his touch; looking into his eyes, I can see hunger and a hint of mischief. That's when I realised my torment was far from over.

His fingers fall out of my aching pussy, and I groan disappointedly.

"What's up, little toy," I pout. "You didn't think you would be given your release so easily, did you?" I nod. "After the fucking stunt you pulled, oh, you are in for a long night."

"Luca," I gasp.

"Keep begging, it does give me pleasure," he cocks a brow while moving his lips close to my ear, "But it won't help you." He whispers.

His lips fall down my body slowly, grazing his teeth across my skin. Moans fall from my body, but the teasing from his mouth continues. Gasps crawl through my body with every light touch until his lips finally find my pussy, widening my legs as he grips my thighs. His tongue gently glides up and down my soaking pussy lips, causing my body to shudder.

"God, you taste fucking sinful." He gasps.

The gasps from my body cause his tongue to hit me harder repeatedly. My head is swimming with desire, and I can feel the build of desire crawling through my body until, once more, he stops again. Looking at me with a wicked smirk.

"Luca," I cry, "please don't torment me. I need..." I gasp.

His hands move up and down my thighs, causing shivers and slight moans. "Yes, what do you need?" He raises a brow.

"I need to cum." I scream out.

"Oh, I do like my little toy desperate. Look how desperate you are. I bet you can think of nothing else."

His tongue crawls up my inner thighs, "just nothing but chasing that release." His tongue moves faster and faster, edging closer to my aching pussy. "Will he give me it, or won't he?" His tongue slivers up my soaking pussy lips, and as soon as his tongue connects, my body cries out with desire.

How long will he torment me for?

"Please, Luca, I need you," I beg.

"Did you need me when you left?"

"Yes," I croak out barely a whisper.

He stops, and I'm unsure what he's thinking right at that moment. A crease crosses his brow as he looks down at me, and for a split second, I'm so sure my torment is over until I see that wicked grin playing on my lips.

"I'm sorry, little toy," His lips hit my ear as his fingers run up and down my aching pussy, moving faster and faster as loud moans fall from my lips until he stops again. "But I just don't believe you."

"Luca, please, I never wanted to leave, not any of you," I plead.

"And yet you did." He spits back at me.

"I'm sorry, but you have to believe me. I didn't, especially not you." I gasp.

"Now, little toy, why would you think that would work?"

"What?" I ask with surprise, clearly evident on my face.

"Acting like I mean something to you won't work."

"But, but you do." I feel a tear drop down my face as the words struggle to crawl from the lump in my throat.

"Careful now, Princess, the beast is hungry."

"Luca, you are not a beast." I softly speak.

"No?" His brow raises in a cheeky move before he lets slip a smirk. "Oh, Princess, when I've finished with you, you'll wish those little words never left that pretty little mouth of yours."

He never says another word as his body slivers down mine; the anticipation of what will happen next causes fear and excitement to hit my body wave after wave.

His light touches that graze my thighs cause an aching between my thighs, and I can already feel the wetness dripping between my legs. God! I had never been this desperate in all my life. Heat pierced my body instantly.

"Looking a bit flushed there, darling," Elijah sneers.

Looking up, I see him towering above me and peering down at me with a mischievous smirk, clearly enjoying my obvious torment. I'm about to say something when the hot, sweet desire pierces my body from Luca's tongue, hitting my clit.

"Oh fuck," I cry out.

His tongue massages my wetness, sliding up and down my aching pussy. My body thrashes as I feel the desire quickly move through me at an alarming speed.

"Oh god, oh god, oh god, fuck, just. Like.that," I scream.

His lips clamp down across my clit, sucking me into oblivion. The screams fall from my body on loud bursts as my body shudders from the intense climax of my desire as it drips down my thighs in a rush of sweet release.

My body relaxes instantly at the release I desperately need, but it seems my torture is not over.

Luca never comes up for air when I feel his tongue enter me. The pulsing of his tongue deep inside my dripping pussy instantly pushes me over the edge.

I'm panting, chasing my release once more.

"Go on, kitten, cum for us." Jax rasps in my ear.

"No," I gasp, "I won't,"

"You won't?" River smiles. Ah, but sweetheart, you look so close already."

"I'm not," I whisper.

"No? Then I guess Luca has lost his touch."

I instantly cry out as I feel Luca push his tongue deeper, twisting and massaging my depths, pulsing pleasure crashing through my body in a mass of feelings I never thought possible.

"Oh fuck, Luca, Luca, Luca..." I scream as the gush of my own desire climbs out of me.

"I thought you said you wouldn't cum?" River mocks.

"Now, do it again," Elijah commands.

"No," I pant. "I've had enough."

"Oh, darling, we are just getting started "Elijah laughs.

The threat of his words spills over my body, but I never get a chance to react to them because, within moments, Luca's Seductive kisses land between my thighs once more. My back arches with a heightened sensitivity that pushes through my body the moment his lips connect with my skin.

The prickles of excitement pierce my body with every light graze of his lips against my skin.

"Luca, Luca, oh god!" I scream. "Please, please," I beg.

"Oh, you want more?" Elijah smirks.

His tongue hits my aching pussy, and the pleasure climbs me again. "Yes, yes, oh god, yes." My hands fall onto my head as my body burns with heat.

"Look at you, darling, so desperate and needy when not five minutes ago you claimed you wouldn't cum for us." My eyes widen as I look up at him, "Now, be a good girl and cum for us."

"Please, oh god," I scream in response to feeling his tongue swirl deep inside me. The mounting pleasure hits my body, pulsing faster and faster.

"Cum for me, now." He whispers into my ear, and an explosion of desire pounds my body in a shudder of pleasure. "Good Girl." He smiles while stroking my hair.

I just lay there in a sweaty mess as I see them all looking down at me. Usually, this would be where I would feel the heat sting my face, and I would rush to cover my face with my hands, but not this time.

This time, I am just basking in the glow of the many orgasms I've received and allowing their hungry gazes to wash across my body because I see them just like this. The need, the want, the hunger in their eyes. All of it. All of it was for me.

I was theirs, and they were mine.

So, instead of hiding.

I lay there, and I finally let go.

I close my eyes, and I smile.

"Oh, kitten, that's exactly what we want." My eyes shoot open, and I see Jax. "We want you smiling, but this is far from over, sweetheart." A blush creeps up my face. "Although that helps," he whispers, "do you know how fucking hard it makes me when you blush for me like that."

His fingers tease my hair ever so gently, "You're such a good girl," he smiles as his lips find mine and drown out any words I would speak.

For one day, I could forget. One day, I could pretend that we were all normal and happy. I could give myself and them one day.

So, for today, I was free. There was no threat, just me and my guys enjoying each other. For one day, we were all free, happy with not a care in the world and with that one simple thought, I exhaled and allowed the freedom and pleasure to drown me in erotic bliss because, for one day, I was there.

Wholly and utterly devoted to them.

I watch as they all start removing their clothes, and my eyes widen with surprise. All of them. I can't think. It looks like a sausage party, and if I wasn't like a bitch on heat right now, my brain might have connected the dots.

But it didn't.

Not until it was too late, and by then, any thoughts I had in my head had all but evaporated.

My arms are lifted, and my body is pulled as I crash on top of Luca, "Hello," I smile as I feel the heat of his skin against mine, not even questioning his motives.

"Well, don't just lay there," I look at him with confusion. "Do I have to spell it out for you?" My eyes widen because clearly he did.

I feel his warm, large hands grip my waist as my body is raised into the air and within moments, I'm impaled on his large, hardened cock. The screams from my body encircle our bodies as I feel him slam deep inside me in an effortless motion.

"God, little toy, so fucking wet," he gasps, "so fucking tight."

My hips automatically grind against his, and the pleasure crawls through me instantly. His hands crawl up my body slowly and wrap around my throat. He pulls my body closer to his, and I feel him penetrate me deeper.

"Now, little toy, I love you." He states, and my eyes widen in shock; my heart bursts when those words fall from his lips. "It might not seem like it, but I do, but right now, I really need to have you. I need to have you all."

"I don't understand," I utter barely a whisper.

"This might hurt, baby, but remember we love you."

"Hurt?"

"We need to claim you. We need to claim this little body, you belong to us, and we need to claim every fucking part of you."

I wasn't sure if I was excited or terrified. The fact he had just declared his love for me with the same sentence of 'this might hurt' had me thinking it was the latter because why would they hurt me if they loved me?

His hands move down my body, landing on the curve of my ass; my ass is raised in the air, still stuffed full of his cock, and my chest is pressed against his.

"Luca," I breathe into his chest.

"Yes, baby?"

"This is a strange position." He doesn't respond. He smirks while gently thrusting and hearing the pants fall from my lips.

"Hello darling," I hear Elijah's sultry whisper in my ear, his hands slowly gliding up my waist.

My body freezes momentarily, but I've done this with them. I can handle taking him in my ass at the same time. I will just need to adjust. My body relaxes until he presses his hard cock against my already-filled pussy.

"Elijah," I gasp. "It's impossible."

"Oh, I promise you, darling, it's possible." He grunts as he presses harder against my filled pussy. "It's happening." He gasps into my back.

The pressure causes my body to stiffen. My brain circuits, I couldn't possibly, I could barely fit one in there, and he was currently trying to force another. Panic hits my body wave after wave.

"Elijah, I—." A sharp, piercing scream crawls from my body as I feel him slowly enter me, stretching me wider than I've ever been. The pangs of pain hit me instantly.

"Oh fuck, you feel so good, darling."

"I can't...I can't." I cry out. "It's too much, it's too much." I sob as tears crawl down my face, aching in my groin, hitting new heights.

They don't move; they just lay deep inside me, two cocks neatly breaking me in two. Allowing the tears to stream down my face, nobody says anything as I'm sandwiched between their cocks.

"Okay, darling, you can slowly move now," Elijah whispers into my back.

"No, no, no, I can't." I cry.

"You can do it, darling." His hand strokes my hair and leaves feather-light kisses down my spine. "We would never do anything to hurt you. Now move."

My hips slowly encircle their body, and sharp twinges hit my body. "I can't, I can't do it." I cry out.

"Slowly, move slowly." He whispers into my back.

Once again, I try to move my body. It feels like I can't breathe. I feel full and stretched out. I can feel the pulsing from their cocks as I slowly move, and a strange tingling shoots through my body. At last, I felt something other than pain. Surprisingly, a small moan falls from my lips.

"Such a good little fuck toy, you're doing so good, baby." Luca coos at me.

His words of admiration hit my body instantly, and my movements were more vigorous. The crawling pleasure shocks me as I scream my pleasure into the room. The stretching, the aching, the pleasure. I feel euphoric, and now my hips automatically move at a speed I'm used to.

I can hear their grunts of approval, and the fact that I'm pleasuring both of them at once, just like this, makes me feel sexy and empowered.

"Oh god, you both feel so fucking good." I cry out.

"Oh fuck, darling, don't stop. Keep fucking doing that." Elijah gasps.

The pleasure is intense, I can feel my pussy tightening around them both, and I know I won't last much longer before I collapse around their thick cocks. That's when I feel something pressing against my ass.

My body stills, and once again, panic hits me.

"Don't stop, fuck, don't stop." Luca cries out. "I'm so close. So fucking close."

"But—."

"Don't stop, kitten." I hear Jax's sultry voice in my ear.

The pressure against my ass gets more intense, but my body is failing me. I'm moving against them harder and faster. I'm just trying to chase the release that's building inside me.

My body once again stills as I feel Jax enter my body. It feels intense. My body is lighter, my head spins, and I'm not sure how I've managed to have three cocks penetrate my body without passing out.

"So fucking good, kitten, so fucking good." He rasps.

My body continues to move, and as I feel Jax spear himself deep inside my ass, the dizzying feeling reaches new heights. My body feels like it will explode from the heat that burns within.

The screams crawl out of my throat. Loud and shattering. I can barely contain them; repeatedly, they get stuck, and it feels like I'm gasping for air. The aching in my throat continues, and I think I'm screaming out until the crawling pleasure again hits my body in waves.

"Hello, Princess." River smiles down at me.

I barely acknowledge his presence and think I have nothing left to give. They have completely filled me and consumed me. I don't think I'm awake, not in the true sense. It's like I've floated up and out of my body, and the only thing I can think of to feel is the passion that flows through my veins.

He caresses my face as I feel the head of his cock slowly glides past my lips, stopping any screams that want to fall out. All I can do is moan around his cock as it gradually feeds into my mouth.

"That's a good girl." He gasps. "Who's my pretty Princess." He gasps as I allow my tongue to encircle his cock that fills my mouth. I feel his cock push deeper, allowing the saliva to run down my face as I make gagging noises around his cock. "Such a good fucking cock sucker." He moans.

My pussy clenches with each gag around River's cock. The crawling pleasure hits me; their moans push me over the edge, and I can feel the pleasure rising to new heights. I want to scream out how good they are making me feel, but all I can do is whimper onto River's cock.

My body rocks against them, and the pulsing of their cocks around my body causes an explosive desire to flow through me, pulsing around them tightly. I can hear their cries of desire.

"That's it, baby, cum for us." Luca cries out.

A gush of desire falls from my body as I moan harder and faster against River's cock that I can feel pumping against my lips. The moment my body shakes with desire, I feel all of them fill me up like a cum dump. Gasping at my release, I just bathe in erotic bliss.

"Such a good girl." River smiles as he finally releases my mouth from his cock.

"Now, you're ours." Luca smiles up at me.

"Yours," I smile back.

I wasn't sure what that word even meant until now. He had said it repeatedly since we had met, and I never knew the meaning. It was only a few words but held such a hidden, possessive meaning.

When someone declares you belong to them, in the real world, it doesn't usually mean forever, but with the Kane brothers, I had no illusions. This was never a punishment. This was about claiming what was theirs, and they had just claimed every inch of me.

I was theirs, and they were mine.

It was supposed to be simple.

My brothers had gone, and all I had to do was look after our little Princess. She had been difficult when we brought her back home, but Luca had said that even though she wouldn't admit it, her mental state was not the same, and the only way we could help her was by being there for her.

Whatever she needed.

We just needed to be there.

So, that was my job, watching Cara while they were gone. Right?

Wrong.

I should have said no, yes, that's what I should have done, but when she looked up at me with those shining ocean-blue eyes, I was lost.

"Please, River." She pleads.

"Luca would kill me."

"I won't tell if you don't." She winks.

"I don't think that will matter, princess."

"Please," she pouts while fluttering her elongated lashes in my direction.

"Oh, don't give me that look, princess."

"Please, River, I'm going crazy in here."

"I don't know…" I mutter, slowly losing the battle of telling her no.

"What is the worst that could happen? I will be with you." She links her arm through mine, "You'll look after me, won't you." She sweetly smiles.

"Of course I will, Princess. I will always look after you."

"So, we can go out tonight?"

"You stay with me at all times—."

"Yes, yes, yes." She interrupts, jumping up and down excitedly.

"I wasn't finished, princess."

"I'm just…excited." She squeals while jumping in my arms. Her warmth instantly envelopes me, and I softly kiss her silky hair.

"I know, Princess. Why don't you go get ready."

"Really? We can really go?"

"Hey, have I ever said anything that wasn't true?" She shakes her head. "Go on, then, princess."

She seems unsure, but why wouldn't she? Luca hadn't allowed her to go anywhere, not since that phone call that had collided all our worlds. We knew it was coming but didn't think it would come so soon.

I should be with my brothers, but someone had to look after her, even more so now that he had resurfaced. Luca's rules were clear: we don't leave the house, and Cara should always be watched.

Well, technically, Cara would be watched. I wouldn't let her out of sight, but I was breaking his most important rule: don't leave the house. He had been very specific about that one, elongating each syllable to ensure he got his point across.

Maybe Cara was right.

What was the worst that could happen?

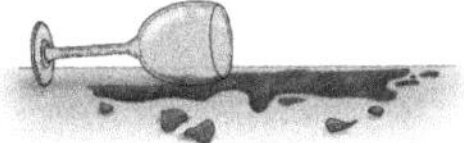

She glides down the stairs like an angel. Cara had enchanted me from the moment I had set eyes on her. Still, watching her like this, my heart instantly burst inside my chest with love and admiration for the woman who had stolen our hearts. Even Luca, I didn't think he could love anything, but she had enchanted each of us, and I was in awe.

Her long dark hair falls down her body in waves, her glistening blue eyes look back at me, and I see the brightest smile painted on those plump red lips. If I had ever wanted to envision true beauty, it still wouldn't come close to Cara.

My eyes scan her body; those long, toned legs have me throbbing. Shit, her legs were something I had always desired about her, but that was nothing compared to her delectable ass. I slide my tongue across my lips. I don't even care that I'm salivating at the mouth. The red dress that clings to her body does nothing for my current raging party in my pants.

"Will I do?" She asks while smiling sweetly.

"You'll more than do, Princess. I'm rethinking my decision."

"Of going out?" Her face drops to the floor, and that once bright smile slowly slips from her pretty face.

"Yes, I would much rather ravage you, darling," I smirk while pulling her into my arms. "Although I did promise," I whisper into her hair. "Guess I will have to wait to devour you, my sinful little kitten."

"River," I hear her gasp.

"Keep panting like a desperate little kitten, and I will not be responsible for you not leaving this house."

"I guess," she looks up at me, "you approve." She smirks.

"I guess I do." I smile back.

The ride over to **THE MOONLIGHT CLUB** was arduous. Usually, Cara and I would bounce off each other with banter galore, but as we sit in the sleek black car, there is nothing but silence.

"Are you okay, princess?" Her large eyes look into mine, but they give nothing away. There is nothing but a vacant look.

"I'm fine." She smiles.

She was not okay. Anytime a woman said she was fine, it was the complete opposite. I wasn't sure why she was so excited to leave because she looked like she had been led to her death right now.

"We can go back if you like, princess?"

It feels like I wait an eternity for a response before a sigh finally passes her lips, "why would I want to go back?"

"You just... don't look like you want to be here."

"I'm just excited."

"If you want to leave and go back, just say the word." I place my hand across hers and find a semblance of the girl I had met before life had broken her beautiful little spirit.

"I don't want to go back." She protests. "We can't go back anyway, no matter how much we may want to. We can only accept our fate and go forward." She sighs.

"Cara—."

"I'm fine, River; honestly, let's enjoy our freedom while it lasts." She smiles.

Her responses were becoming stranger by the second. A crease crosses my brow; I should have stuck to my first answer when she had begged to be taken out. I should have, but it was too late now, and I had a limited window to get her back before Luca came home and noticed that we were gone.

The car pulls up, and the line is longer than my arm to get in. A groan leaves my throat as I exit the vehicle. She doesn't move; she's always been so independent and would never let anyone open a door for her. As I walk around to her door, she still hasn't moved; pulling it open and holding my hand out, she finally takes it and stands before me.

"You know, princess, that I'm here for you." A smile falls across her lips, "You are the most important thing to all of us, and we just want you to be happy."

"I know," she sighs.

"You just—." My hand curls around her waist, pulling her body closer to mine, "She doesn't seem happy anymore. Is there anything I can do to rectify that?" I'm desperate; I know I sound desperate, but I can't lose her. Not again.

Her eyes flutter as she finally looks up at me with wonder, eyes deeper than the ocean, and I feel like I'm drowning in her swirling pools of blue.

"You and your brothers are perfect." She whispers, "I'm very happy." She smiles.

"Princess—."

Her hands flatten against my chest, and she looks into my eyes, "I'm very happy with you; there is nothing you can do that you haven't already." Her smile grew, unaware she was melting my fucking heart with one look.

Her hands crawl down my body, and I swear my heart reaches up my body and beats within my throat. It barely feels like I'm breathing. Her dainty little hand finds mine, and I can feel the warmth of her skin as she threads her slim fingers through mine.

"Shall we go inside now, River?" She smiles.

"Okay, princess." I smiled because she was my weakness, and one soft look and bright smile from Cara wiped away any doubt and problem I ever had. Like an angel that washed away my worries, her light melted my heart.

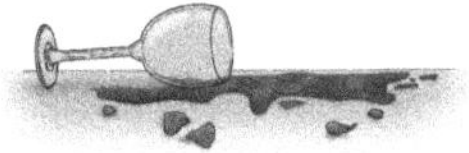

The moment we enter the bar, the ambience completely changes her mood, and it's like a semblance of the Cara I knew and loved. Her eyes light up as soon as we set foot through the doors.

The lights hit her skin in the darkened room, and I'm not sure I've seen anything more beautiful. The room is full of bodies, and a sliver of panic hits my spine.

This was supposed to be a quiet night out to see her smile.

Still, I had seriously miscalculated the popularity of this bar.

I clearly didn't get out much—so shoot me.

Luca probably would if he ever found out I had brought her when we were on high alert at the monster who roamed in the night, and that was more terrifying than what they had gone to hunt down.

I tell myself we are just staying for one drink, but as I move her through the room, I know that's a lie.

She perches on the black stool, and I notice that the bartender's eyes wander across her tiny little body. She doesn't see, of course. He's practically drooling. His hands move closer to hers, and my heart races.

My eyes watch as his slimy hands move closer.

Once more, I tell myself.

My arm moves across her waist as a warning: she's mine. I feel like an asshole, but the closer his hands get towards my girl, the faster the rage crawls through my body.

Count.

When I get ten, we leave.

One.

He smiles at her.

Two.

His eyes roam down her body.

Three.

His slimy fingers tap the bar.

Four.

His tongue moves across his lips, and he's practically salivating at the mouth.

Five.

He clears his throat. Yes, he was breathing; I was counting it. God! The longer I waited, the faster I felt like ripping his head off his fucking shoulders.

Six.

His body moves closer to hers, leaning across the bar. A growl escapes my throat; I'm losing control.

Seven.

His fingers edge closer to hers.

Eight.

His hand touches her dainty little perfect hand, and I don't even think before I grab his skinny wrist.

Her eyes search mine, and I'm not sure if she can see how badly I've been trying to control myself, but as she explores my face, confusion is laced across it.

"River, are you okay?" She finally asks.

"Fine," I grit back.

My grip tightens on his wrist. It would be easy to drag his body across this bar and end his miserable little life. He's looking at me with uncertainty; my grip tightens, and that's when I see it.

The fear.

"Let go." He grits out.

"Now, why would I want to do that." I can feel his pulse quicken.

"If you don't let go, you'll be sorry, and when they cart off your body, I will take that sexy little thing and do what I fucking want to her."

The pulsing rage courses through my body; I don't see anything. I see her taking a sip of a drink I didn't even know she had. When did she get a drink? Everything is muddled; the only thing I can see is the mist of red covering my eyes.

His body moves like it weighs nothing; one pull of his arm, and he's levitated across the bar, his scrawny neck beneath my hands. I can hear his laboured breathing, his eyes darting to see if he will be rescued.

They'd never get to him on time.

My fist connects with his face, and all I can hear is the high-pitched scream that crawls from his throat. Thick crimson blood drips from his nose. He's a bleeder.

Gripping his throat tighter, I can hear him wheezing. It would be so easy to snap his fucking neck, get my girl and leave.

"Tell me again what you're going to do to her." He shakes his head. "Really, I wanna hear how you're going to do what you fucking want." His eyes are bulging, and his face is changing shade; he's moments away from unconsciousness.

I release my grip on his neck and watch as he coughs and breathes in the air I had previously restricted. He looks at me with dead eyes but still says nothing.

In one swift movement, I hurtle his body across the bar, and he crashes into the ground in a heap. The commotion has garnered attention. God knows how they heard with the God-awful music they have pounding in the background.

Looking to the side of me, I know she won't be happy. I promised her a fun night, and this is what she's got, but panic gripped a tight hold across my heart as I searched for where she had been sitting. I no longer care about the broken man on the ground.

My brain can't process what is happening; sweat pierces my spine, and creeping coldness crawls across my body.

She was gone.

Fuck.

Part V

Drag Me To Hell

He's not who I thought he was.
He wraps you into a false sense of
security,
Before taking what he wants.
He thinks he owns me.
That he's created this place of
paradise,
But he doesn't see,
That while he's in heaven,
I'm in hell.

My eyes try to open, but the pain in my head renders them shut. I'm unsure where I am or why I can't remember how I got here.

The only thing I can sense about this place is the thick, moist scent that attacks my senses. I try to pull at my arms, suspended and raised in the air.

Tugging doesn't help; once again, I find myself restrained. The feeling is all too familiar.

Elijah? No, Elijah likes to see the surprise on my face before he blissfully torments my body; only he knows how.

Luca? It could be Luca. It was part of some sick kidnapping fantasy, but this was going far, even by Luca's standards.

"Luca," I call out into the room.

"Luca," I call once more.

"Guess again." A thick, deep voice calls out to me.

So, I wasn't alone, but I didn't recognise the voice.

"Who's there?"

"Open your eyes, princess; I have been dying to meet you."

"I...I can't." I shakily answer.

"Maybe this will inspire you to open your curious eyes."

I feel a hand slide down my body; the scent of dark musk and dampness fills the air. His hand travels across my exposed belly, and his fingers shoot to the crevice between my legs.

Was I naked? I didn't feel him tugging at any clothes; wouldn't I feel cold? But I didn't...I felt nothing.

"I bet you're probably wondering if I've fucked you yet." He whispers while his fingers dance near my exposed pussy. "Even unconscious, your body wanted it..." he breathes into my ear, "but conscious, I get to hear you..." his fingers slam into my pussy. All I can manage to do is cry out, "Scream."

"You're not Luca," I sob.

"No, Cara, I'm the thing that gives Luca nightmares...I wonder, little lamb, if I will be the source of yours too."

"Please...let me go." I sob.

"I'm afraid I can't do that...you didn't listen, and now you mine. I won't ever let you go."

Didn't listen? What was he talking about? We had never met. Or had we? I wasn't sure. I wasn't sure about anything anymore. I wasn't even sure any of this was real. It must be a nightmare; I wasn't usually this manic. Yes, that was it. This was a bad dream, and I will wake up any moment...now.

"Wake up, wake up, wake up," I repeat repeatedly.

"You're not asleep, Cara; if you'd just heeded my warning, you might not be here right now."

"Your warning?"

"Yes, little lamb, I wrote to you regularly; surely you haven't forgotten."

"That was you." I gasp. "But I did, I did leave...I left them all."

"You went back." He screams.

"They weren't going to let me go." I sob.

"Yes, we have that in common."

I don't want to look at him. I don't want to open my eyes. I want to wake up from this nightmare but realise I'm not dreaming; this is happening. I'm not with Jax, Elijah, River or Luca. I'm in danger, and if I don't look at my captor, how will I ever assist myself?

"Why don't I remember how I got here?" I force my eyes to open, but other than a flutter, they still stay closed.

"Ah, that would be the forget-me pill slipped into your drink." I can feel the smile in his words.

"You drugged me." I shriek.

"Me? No, I would never do such a thing... hasn't anyone warned you about the dangers of going out alone...Who knows what would have happened if I hadn't been there."

"I didn't go out drinking; I don't know what you are talking about."

"I must say I thought you'd have got Jax or Elijah, hell, even Luca to act as your bodyguard, but River," he sneers. "That boy was far too easy to manipulate...it wasn't even a challenge." He whispers.

"Wait. River was there?"

"Hello?"

Nothing but silence fills the air, but he hasn't gone. I can still feel his presence hovering around my body. I had hoped to stall whatever sinister plans he had concocted. I half wished I had remained unconscious; then, I would still be oblivious to what was happening.

Ignorance was bliss; I wish I could return to ignorance.

I can hear the jangling of a belt, but I dare not think why I would be hearing that sound. The moment it crashes to the ground, my body stiffens. His hands come around my body, and I'm helpless to fight it. I can feel his hand gripping my ass, my body is raised, and I don't want to open my eyes anymore. I'm numb; all I can do is sob as the tears crawl down my face.

I want it to end, but he hasn't even started yet.

He's gripping my body that tight; I'm encased in a vice. I feel him enter me with force, and a loud, piercing scream crawls out of my throat, and finally, my eyes shoot open.

"That's right, little lamb, scream for me." His hoarse voice sounds in my ear.

"Oh god, oh god," I cry, "please help me." The tears tumble down my face in a waterfall of sadness that encases my body.

"God can't help you here, little lamb; you're in my fucking world...the moment you entered my doll house, you became my little doll, the only god here...is me...so cry out for me, little lamb."

Looking into his eyes while he thrusts his body hard against mine, I'm met with a cold, soulless stare.

I had never imagined what I thought true evil was until I looked into his haunting eyes. His stormy eyes of glacial blue are deeper than the ocean, but as I look upon them, there is nothing, no emotion, as he takes from me.

Just dead and soulless.

Nothing.

"Now, cry for me, little lamb," he breathes into my skin.

Scars adorn his body, but his face is perfect and sculpted with stubble lightly dusting his jaw, tanned and emotionless. The high cheekbones and plump pink lips compliment his hauntingly beautiful face per-fectly. I can feel the curve of his toned physique as he bangs his hard body into mine.

His hands wrap around my ass, forcing my legs around his waist. I try to move them, but his grip on my body forces me to relent to him. He thrusts his body hard against mine, and his cock roughly penetrates me repeatedly. The screams from my mouth and the sobbing do nothing but drive his moans into my ear.

"See...how your body wants this...wants me." He gasps.

"No, no.." His cock moves harder and faster deep inside my dripping hole. The pleasure courses through my body. My legs are shaking with every thrust of his cock. "Oh god, oh god, oh god," I erotically moan.

"Fuck, Cara, you...feel...so...fucking...good." I hear his rasps in my ear.

"Please...oh god," I cry out. "Please... don't...do...this," my moans ring out in the air.

"You're going to cum for me, little lamb." I shake my head, "Are you going to do it naturally or forced?"

"It's all forced." I meekly whisper.

"As you wish," A sly smile appears on his lips as his hand travels down my body, pushing his cock further inside of me; I can't stop the panting that comes from my mouth. I'm panting like a dog, begging for a treat.

His cock fills me up. Pushing my body further into the release he's so desperate to get from me.

I try to squeeze my muscles from exploding all over his cock, but my body cries out for the release he's pushing me towards. His hand comes across my clit, and I know I'm moments away from exploding. The screams that fall from my lips tell me I'm moments away from release.

"You will fucking cum for me, little lamb." He repeats as he roughly pushes his fingers across my clit and thrusts his cock harder inside my soaking pussy. "You're so fucking wet for me. Cum for me, little lamb." He pants.

Harder and harder, his fingers move across my clit until a loud, piercing scream shoots from my body. My head thrashes back, my fingernails digging into the palms of my hand.

A gush of liquid pours out of me in one big explosive release.

I can feel his body shudder beneath mine, pushing harder and harder, "Oh. You. Fucking. Slut. Oh. Fuck." He screams, his body shakes, and I feel him fill me up with his hot cum with every jerk of his cock. "You are the best fucking doll I've ever had." He pants. Lifting his head to look at me, "You might just be my favourite."

Those words are more devastating to me than this entire act.

He would never let me go if he thought I was his favourite.

Nobody knew I was here. I was stuck here as his slave where he could do what he wanted to me, and once again...I was numb.

"Think about me, little lamb, all fucking night long."

His body is still inside me, and I struggle to get him to release me; his arms are like iron bars. His body is shaking with every breath. The lustful look in his eyes is replaced with a look of pure hatred.

"You will never get away from me, little lamb."

My eyes stand wide open.

The sense of loss has left me swallowing my sobs.

My body is quivering with the memories of what happened to me, and I am shaking with the fear of what I still had to face.

The dark room creeps in around me, and the eerie noise of the wind outside has me huddled up on the floor. The constant drip, drip, drip of the rain running down the windows has me wondering if I'll ever leave this place alive.

I close my eyes and see my mother, who looks like she hasn't slept in days, staring at me with a pleading look. She looks half-crazed; her eyes are red and puffy from crying.

"Cara, darling, how are you?" She asks with a soft whisper.

"I'm fine, Mom," I whisper back to her, "I'm not missing any limbs if that's what you're asking."

Her body visibly sags with relief.

"When will you be home?" She asks, "Everyone is worried about you, sweetheart."

"I'm not coming home, Mom," I whisper back at her, "I can't leave him."

She shakes her head, "You're coming home."

I hear her voice as the silent tears fall down my face. Her voice was a reminder of the insanity that wracked my brain.

She was dead, and I could never commit to cry for her, but now, here alone in this evil place, I could cry for her.

The distant noises outside were terrifying, and they weren't calming down like they had in the past. The darkness surrounding me was almost suffocating, and the muffled moans and screams of the other girls in this house echoed in my head.

I thought I heard the devil's voice, but sadly, it was too late to run.

The only way out was to be his.

I knew my mother would have never wanted me to be in this place with the devil. I knew there had to be a way out of this. I just had to find it.

I looked down at the chains' links wrapped around my wrists and then at my ankle. The metal was cold against my skin, and I noticed the chain was silver.

To my surprise, it wasn't the standard cold metal. As soon as I touched it, I felt a prickle run up my arm. I pulled my hand away, but it didn't go away.

I lifted my hands to my face and saw the silver chain glowing. It was a shiny metallic glow.

It was beautiful, and it was warm.

I ran my hand along the chain, and I could feel the heat radiate from it. I looked down at the silver chain around my wrists.

They were glowing, too. I could feel the heat from the chains, and I could feel my body produce sweat.

I tried to break from the chains, but they were glowing so hot now that I could feel my skin begin to burn.

The pain that radiated from my skin was too much.

I was burning from the inside out.

I couldn't stand it any longer.

I fell to my knees, and I screamed for my life.

I felt as though I was going to burst into flames.

My body shook with the pain.

I was crying so loud my lungs hurt.

I looked up at the ceiling, and everything went dark.

I had fallen to the ground, and everything went very silent except for my blood rushing in my ears.

I couldn't breathe.

My hands were shaking with the pain.

I was cold, and I could feel my body begin to give way to the pain. I was shaking apart with the pain. I couldn't stand it.

I felt my chest tighten, and I could feel my lungs filling with air. I tried to take a breath, but my lungs wouldn't fill.

The pressure in my chest was too much, and I felt my body seize up.

I was gasping for air that wasn't there.

My body was beginning to give way to the pain.

I was beginning to feel my heart beat faster and faster.

My chest was burning.

My lungs felt as though they were going to burst inside of me.

All I could feel was the hot warmth of the burning chains.

I could feel my skin melting off, and then I felt the skin melt off the rest of my body. I felt the flesh melt right off the bone. I could feel my bones and my organs begin to burn. It was too much to bear, and I knew I would die.

I would die while chained to the floor, and it was my own fault.

I felt my body scream from within me, and my heart slowed down.

It was going to be over soon. I could feel the heat from the burning of my body begin to fade. I could feel the pain dissipate, and then it was just a memory of what once was.

I could feel my blood begin to flow again through my veins. I could feel my heart beating again. It was so loud I could hear it beating against the floor beneath me.

I could feel the panic running through my body, my eyes shot open, and I felt freezing cold water hitting my body.

"You're not dying on me so soon, little lamb." His cold stare pierces my soul. "We are not nearly done playing."

Death would have been preferable.

I wanted to die; why couldn't he have left me to slip away into nothingness? Tears crawl down my face, and pain hits my chest, and without knowing it, I utter a word that seems to offend him. "Luca," I cry out in this dark, desolate place.

So, I was the monster.

That's what they told me, but I couldn't see it. Dolls were there to be played with. If they didn't want it, they wouldn't get wet. That's what my father had said. They wanted it; they just liked to refuse their natural desires.

Maybe Luca was right; perhaps he was crazy.

Or maybe I was; I just didn't know anymore.

I walked across the creaking dark wooden floors; I wasn't sure how this house was still standing. It was like me, broken, but it still worked. It had fixed all its broken pieces and put them together differently. It had been reborn, just like me.

Coming back here had breathed new life into me. Here I was somebody; here I was a god. Nobody could stop what was coming. My wrath would burn them all, and they would finally know what it felt like to live in hell.

I would never have taken her; it was more of a threat initially. The thrill of seeing the fear lace across her face made me so fucking hard. Watching her had become something of a rush. I could see why they were taken with her, and it was only a matter of time before they lost her.

That would be my revenge.

She surprised me.

Jax had found her; hadn't it all started with him? I thought taking her away from Jax would tear her walls down, but it didn't. It wasn't Jax that she cried out for in the middle of the night...it was Luca.

That was interesting to me.

I knew she played with all of them, but I was so sure that the one she favoured the most was golden balls; it turns out she preferred the beast from the wilderness the most. The one who couldn't quite manage to end my minor operation.

This thought excited me more.

Hadn't Luca wrestled with his demons, me being the operable demon he couldn't erase? He came close…once, yet he just couldn't manage to do it. It was so easy. We had stood face to face, breathless, with not a soul in sight. Nothing but our breaths echo around the trees.

I was so sure that this was it. This was the moment that he would finally snap and end my life.

I wasn't afraid of dying. Oh no, quite the opposite. I welcomed death. I was the monster in their eyes; what kind of monster feared dying? Death was easy; it was living that was hard.

Life and death are two sides of the same coin. You would never know which one you favoured more. I wasn't afraid of death because I had died long ago. The moment I was reborn, a shift in my reality occurred.

Most people live as if they are already dead. Just moving through life, one depressive day at a time. Never moving forward, just doing the same fucking thing day in and day out. That's what they call living? Well, I would rather be dead. Yes, death didn't scare me.

I welcomed it.

I waited for it, but it never came.

After the great chase from the beast, he glared at me with contempt, sighed and told me to go. Was he letting me go? Free? To do as I pleased. Can't say I wasn't disappointed. After all the build-up....it was such a letdown.

That moment right then, I would make him wish he had taken my life because I think with a smirk, I had just taken the most precious thing that meant something to him, and this time, he would have to try to kill me to get it back.

Try? I laugh maniacally; there is only one winner here: me. It was always me.

"Talking to yourself again?" I smile as I hear the clack of her patent blood-red shoes hit the floor as she enters the room. "People will think you're mad if you keep that up."

"Now, doll, why would you assume I give a fuck what people think."

"I don't," She whispers as she chambers onto my lap.

"Silly little doll." Her hips grind against my groin, pressing harder into my growing cock. I know she can feel my excitement, but I'm not nearly excited enough to give her what she wants.

"Oh," she grunts, "You want to play games, do you?" She grabs my face with both hands and kisses me. It's hard, punishing. She bites down on my lip, and I can taste the tangy blood on my tongue.

I loved how her lips moved from my mouth to my cheek, tasting me.

Her eyes, they look at me so possessively, so willing to give her what she wants and so fucking desperate for me to give her everything she needs.

She stops kissing me, her eyes are burning with lust, and then she jumps off me. "Go play with your dolls. I'm bored with you." She skips out of the room, and I hear her heels clack on the wood.

She would never get what she wanted, but I kept her entertained.

I walk behind her, and my hand grasps her shoulder; she is taking it to the next level. She was becoming just like me. She was becoming a monster.

"I'm not a doll," she reminds me; she glares at me. "I'm not just here to play with."

"Oh, I know," I snicker. "You're here to fuck." I push her back onto the cold wooden floor and pin her arms above her head. "You're here to be my fuck doll." I kiss her neck, sucking and biting hard enough to leave a mark.

"You don't have to be a doll to fuck," she gasps, "you just need to fuck."

"Oh, doll," I smirk. "You're going to fucking pay for that."

I rip open the buttons on her blouse, exposing her white lace bra. God, how I fucking love white lace. It just makes me want to fucking rip it off.

I push the material down the side of her body. I can feel her skin on my fingertips as I draw my hands down her arms; she's perfect. My hands stop, holding onto her wrists. I look at her, see the lust in her eyes and feel her pulse quicken under my touch.

"You want this; you've always wanted this. We both know you'll never be satisfied with the fucking fairy-tales." I push her arms above her head and pin them there, keeping my weight from crushing her.

"I want you to fuck me," she whispers lustfully. "I want you to fuck me like a doll, and I want you to fuck me like the monster you think I am." Her hips move against me, pressing her pelvis up to mine, grinding on my bulge.

"You're getting to be a real fucking pain in the ass," I growl into her ear. "You're not going to get what you want, doll."

I know it drives her fucking crazy when I call her that. I know it reminds her of him. I know it pushes her over the edge.

I reach up to her wrists and push them onto the floor above her head.

I run my hands down her body, feeling her skin beneath my fingertips.

I gripped her tightly, letting my hands travel down her hips. "You're nothing but a fucking doll to me," I hiss, and I instantly push my knee between her legs and press against her hard. She moans; her sound is like a fucking drug to me. "That's it, doll," I smirk. "Scream for me. Let me hear how you moan."

I let my fingers knead into her flesh, feeling her shaking beneath me. "Let me hear how you fucking moan."

"Fucking let me hear you, doll." I grind my knee against her pussy.

"Oh, Jesus," she moans, "I want you. I need to feel you inside of me."

"I don't give a fuck what you want," I snarl at her. She was getting me all worked up, and I was so turned on. I lean in and kiss her. She kisses me back, and she moves her mouth lightly against mine. I bite on her bottom lip, and she moans loudly.

She had no idea what she had gotten herself into. She had no idea that she had just fucked with the wrong person.

"Fuck, that feels good."

"Mmm, you like that?" I bite down harder, and she moans in pleasure. "Hmm, good little doll."

I let go of her wrists, and she wrapped both arms around my neck, pulling me closer to her. My fingers push inside her panties. She was so fucking wet. "Does that feel good, doll? Hmm?"

"Fuck, I need you...I need you inside of me."

"Oh," I laugh. "You do, do you?" I rip the panties from her body, toss them over my shoulder, and thrust my fingers inside her hard.

"Yes!" She moans. "Oh, please," she begs. "Fuck me," she begs. "Fuck me."

"That's right." I bite her neck, not hard enough to leave a mark. The sound she makes when I bite down on her skin drives me wild. "Scream for me." I thrust my fingers inside of her harder. "Scream for me." She moans loudly. Her heels move up and down on the floor, straining against my hold.

"I'm going to cum."

"Not yet," I groan. I hadn't finished playing with her yet. I run my hands up and down her body. Her tits look fucking good. It makes me want to fuck her until she's screaming.

"Don't stop," she moans. "Please." I bite down on her neck. "Yes, oh, yes, yes, yes." I can feel her clenching around my fingers. "Oh."

I pull my fingers out of her pussy, and I look at her. She's covered in a sheen of sweat. Her chest is heaving up and down. Her legs are spread open. I've left finger marks on her hips, and I've torn one of her fucking stockings. Even in her dishevelled state, she's never looked more beautiful.

"Go to the fucking door and close it," I order her. She doesn't ask questions. She doesn't argue; she just gets up and walks to the door. "Good little doll," I whisper as I watch her.

The door closes with a loud click. I can hear her breathing hard, her chest heaving up and down. She's biting her bottom lip. She's waiting for me.

"You ready for me, doll?" I ask her as I stand up and unzip my pants. "You ready for me to fuck you like the little slut you are?" I drop my pants to the floor and step out of them; I will show her what fucking happens when she pushes me too far.

I unbutton my shirt slowly and let it fall to the floor; I watch her flinch when she sees the tattoos on my chest. I kneel in front of her and bite the inside of her thigh. "You like that?" I growl at her. "You like that?"

She doesn't move, and she doesn't say a single word. She just stands there patiently. I can see her holding her breath. I can see her eyes watching me.

"Hmm?" I bite down. I can taste her pussy on my tongue. She tastes fucking good. "I said," I bit her again. "Do you like that?"

She doesn't move. She doesn't say a single fucking word.

I run my tongue up her inner thigh. She shifts her hips, and I bite down harder; she's not going any-where; I make sure of that. I taste her again. I let my tongue drag up further and further. Her legs widen, and I pull her to the sofa's edge. "I can smell how wet you are," I tell her.

She makes a sound; it's a whimper. I can feel her shaking. I run my tongue along her pussy lips. "I can taste how fucking good you are." I drag my tongue up to her clit, and I run it over and over it.

I can hear her heartbeat. It's beating so fast. I look up at her; her eyes are begging me. She's begging me to make her cum.

"Is that what you want?" I ask her. "Is that what you're begging me for?" I flick her clit with my tongue.

"Hmm?" I flick her again. "Because if you are, you'll have to beg a lot fucking louder than that."

"Oh, God," she moans, "please,"

"Please, what, doll?" I flick her clit a few more times. "Please, make me cum." I hold out my tongue and slowly drag it up to her clit. Her hips jerk towards my mouth. I leave a trail of her juices on her stomach and lick her clean. I grab her thigh and squeeze it.

I'm drunk with power. She was listening to me; she was fucking listening to me. I drag my tongue up to her pussy again, and I flick her clit with it. "Please."

I look up at her; she's fucking begging me for it. Her pussy is soaked. I can see the juices shining on her lips and smell her. Fuck, she smells good. I can see her tits bouncing in front of me. I can see her stomach muscles tensing and relaxing. I can see her hip swaying as I drag my tongue up to her clit again.

"Beg for me," I tell her, "I want to hear it."

"Please." She's begging me with her voice. I can hear the desperation in her voice. "Please, make me cum." I drag my tongue against her clit a few more times, enough to make her think that I'm going to let her cum.

"No," I say. I take my mouth away from her pussy.

"Please, I need to cum."

"You think I'm going to make it that fucking easy?" I growl at her. "You think I'm going to let you cum that fucking easy?"

She doesn't move. She's waiting for me. She's waiting for me to tell her what to do; she's waiting for me to tell her how to make me.

"No," I tell her. "I'm not going to let you cum."

"Please," she begs.

"No," I tell her. "Not until you beg for it."

"I'll do anything," she says. "Please."

"Beg for it," I tell her as I look at her. "I want to hear you beg for it."

"Please let me cum," she says. "I need to cum. Please, I need to cum."

"That's better," I tell her. I run my tongue along her clit. It's so fucking hard. She's practically thrashing around in front of me. Her chest is heaving, and her heart is beating.

"Please," she begs. "I need to cum."

"Fuck," I whisper as I look at her. "You need to cum, huh?" I look down at her pussy. It's so fucking wet. I can see the juices shining on her lips. I can see the juices glistening on her skin. Fuck, I want to taste her.

I grab her thighs, and I pull her towards me. I spread her legs open further, pushing her knees to her chest.

I crawl on top of her, and I stare at her. I grab her hands, and I wrap her arms around my back. She digs her nails into my shoulders.

"Please," she begs. "I need to cum."

"Beg for it," I growl at her. "I want to hear you beg for it."

"Please," she moans. "Please let me cum."

"That's right," I tell her. "That's what I want to fucking hear." I drag my tongue along her pussy lips. "I want to fucking hear you beg for it. You need it so fucking bad, don't you, doll? Beg me for it."

"Please, I need to cum," she moans.

"No," I tell her. I pull my mouth away from her. "Not good enough," I tell her. I take my phone out of my pocket and take a picture of her. I take a photo of her with her arms wrapped around me, her mouth open and panting.

"I want you to tell me differently," I tell her. "I want you to tell me how fucking bad you need it. I want to hear you say it. Open your eyes," I tell her. "Open your eyes and tell me how fucking bad you need it."

She opens her eyes, and she looks at me. Her eyes are glassy, and she's shaking. "I'm going to make you beg for it," I tell her. "I will make you say how fucking bad you need it. I will make you say what you really want, over and over and fucking over again. I will keep doing this until you beg for it," I tell her. "I'm going to keep fucking torturing you until you beg for it and can't take it anymore."

"I'll beg for it," she tells me. I run my tongue along her pussy. "I'll beg for it. Please, I'll do anything. Just let me cum."

"No," I tell her as I pull away from her. "I'm not going to let you cum until you beg me for it," I tell her. "I'm going to make you beg me for it repeatedly."

"I'll do anything," she tells me. "I'll do anything you want. Just let me cum."

"Anything?" I ask her as I look up at her. I grab her arms, and I pull them behind her back. I hold them there with one hand while I grab her other arm and pull it behind her. I tie her wrists together, and I spread her arms apart.

I grab her hip with my other hand and pull her towards me. I stare at her as I run my tongue along her clit. "Anything?" I ask her again.

"Yes," she moans. "Please." I run my tongue up and down her pussy, and I can feel her hips jerking towards me. I grab her hips with both of my hands, and I slam my tongue inside of her. "Yes, anything," she moans. "Please."

"Sit up," I tell her. I grab the back of her neck and pull her to a sitting position. I'm still behind her. I'm still holding onto her arms. "What do you want?" I ask her.

"I want you to let me cum," she tells me. "I want you to fucking let me cum."

"That's not what I mean," I tell her. "What do you want?"

"I want to suck your cock," she tells me. "I want to suck you."

"Answer my question," I tell her. "What do you want?"

"You know what I want," she says. "I want you to fuck me, I want you to tear into me, I want you to fuck me hard."

"Goddamn it," I tell her. "Say it."

"I want to fuck you," she moans.

"Again," I tell her.

"I want to fuck you," she says again. "I want you to fuck me."

"That's a good girl," I tell her. I grab a handful of her hair and pull her head back. I trace her throat with my tongue. "Open your mouth," I tell her.

"Anything," she moans. "I'll do anything." I pull her head back further, and I slam my cock into her mouth.

She wraps her lips around me, and I feel her tongue moving against me. I pull my cock out, and I slap it against her lips. I can tell she wants more. "Please," she begs.

"Anything?" I ask her.

"I'll do anything," she moans.

"Beg me," I tell her. "Beg me to let you cum. Beg me to fuck you. Beg me to fuck you harder than you've ever been fucked."

"I'll do anything," she moans. "Anything you want me to. Please, let me cum, please just let me cum. Please, please, please just let me cum."

"Now, ask me to fuck you," I tell her. "Ask me to fuck you hard."

"Please, please fuck me," she begs. "Fuck me, please." I grab her hips, and I lift her up. I grab her ass with my hands, and I slam her down onto my hard cock. I grab her hips, and I slam her down onto me again. I can feel her ass slapping against my hips as I slam her onto my cock.

"Harder," she begs. "Fuck me harder." She reaches back and grabs onto my shoulders. She pulls herself up higher, and I can feel myself hitting deeper.

"I want my hands," she says to me.

"No," I tell her. "You said you'd do anything. This is one of the things you wanted," I tell her. "You're going to do it like this. You're going to let me fuck you like this."

I put my hands on her hips, and I move her up and down my cock. I feel her squeezing her muscles, her pussy is contracting, and she's fucking squeezing my cock. She's squeezing it and drawing as much of it inside of her as she can. She's fucking trying to milk my cock, and I can feel her pussy grabbing me.

"Cum for me," I tell her. "Cum for me right now."

I feel her pussy start to shake. I feel her tighten around me, and then she's pulsing, and I can feel her body shaking. She's so fucking tight, squeezing me, and her pussy is throbbing, and she's cumming. I feel her body shaking as she cums around me, and I feel her pussy squeezing the cum out of me.

It feels like she's fucking sucking my cum out of me. My cock is pulsing, and I'm filling her. It feels like she's sucking me dry. I can feel my cock throbbing, and I can feel my cum filling her. She's squeezing me and milking me and drawing my cum out of me.

"Fuck," I moan as I start to cum. "Fuck, fuck, fuck, fuck, fuck." I fill her, and my cock is pulsing. I feel her milking me, and I feel her pussy pulling more of my cum out of me. I keep filling her. I can feel my juices dripping out of her pussy and down the crack of her ass.

"Fuck," she moans. "Fuck, fuck." I pull my cock out of her, watching as some of my cum drips out of her pussy. It runs down her lips and down the crack of her ass. I grab her ass with both of my hands, and I spread her cheeks. I lean forward, and I lick her. I run my tongue up and down her pussy, and I taste my own cum. I can feel her pussy contracting more. I can feel her pussy squeezing my tongue.

"Fuck," I moan as I taste my cum for the first time.

I pull my tongue out of her and start to stand up. I grab her by the neck and pull her to her feet. I grab her by the hips and turn her around so she's facing me. I slide my hand down her stomach, and I hold onto her pussy.

"I'm not finished with you," I tell her. "I'm fucking not finished with you." I move to the couch, and I drop her down onto it. I spread her legs open wide, and I slide in between them.

"I'm fucking not done with you yet," I tell her. She spreads her legs wider, and I grab her hips and pull myself closer. I grab my cock, and I slide it into her.

I watch as she takes me inside of her. I watch as she takes every inch of me inside of her.

I watch as her pussy stretches around me. I watch as she takes more and more of me inside of her.

"Ah, fuck," I moan as I slide into her. "Fuck, fuck, fuck, fuck." I grab her hips, and I pull her towards me. I grab her ass with both of my hands, and I pull her towards me again. I slam myself into her. It feels so fucking good to be inside of her. It feels so fucking good to have her around me. I pull her towards me, and I slam into her again.

"That's right," she moans. "Fuck me. Fuck me like you mean it. I want it hard, and I want it deep."

I slam into her again. She spreads her legs wide open, and I slam into her. I reach up with one hand, and I grab onto her hair. I pull her head back, and once again, I swallow her moans with my mouth. I kiss her, and I run my tongue along her lips.

I kiss her as I slam into her again and again. Fuck she feels so good. I can feel her pussy squeezing my cock. I can feel my cock pulsing inside of her. Whenever I start to pull my cock out, I feel her pussy grab me. I feel her pussy trying to grip me and keep me inside her. I slam back into her, and I can feel her pussy grabbing and sucking at me.

"That's right," she tells me. "Fuck my pussy. Fuck my fucking pussy."

I slam into her, and I can feel her ass moving. I grab onto the back of her knees and spread them wider. I grab her ass with both of my hands, and I pull her down onto me. She moans into my mouth, and I can feel her pussy contracting around me again. Fuck, the feeling of her pussy squeezing my cock turns me on. I feel her pussy grip me, and I slam into her again.

"Ah, fuck," I moan. "Fuck, baby."

I slam into her again, and I can feel her body shake. I can feel her pussy getting wetter and wetter. I can feel her pussy getting wetter and wetter until it's soaking the couch.

"Fuck, baby," I moan into her mouth. "Fuck, you're going to cum so hard for me."

I feel her pussy starting to pulse around me. She's fucking milking me, and her pussy is sucking the cum right out of me. Her pussy is squeezing me, and I can feel it getting wetter and wetter. I can feel her juices soaking the couch and running down her thighs. I can feel her juices drowning my cock. Fuck, her pussy is so fucking wet.

I pull my cock out of her, watching as my cum drips. I watch as her pussy pulses and her juices drip down the crack of her ass. Fuck, her pussy is so fucking wet. I grab her by the hips, and I pull her towards me.

I tilt her hips towards me and force myself inside her. I push her legs up towards her head, and I push myself inside of her. Her pussy is so fucking wet, and her juices are dripping down my cock. I grab her arms and pin her wrists down by her head. I hold her like that, and I slide my cock out of her, and then I slam right back into her.

I slam myself into her, and I can feel her pussy getting wetter and wetter. I can feel her pussy gripping me harder and harder.

I can feel her juices dripping down the crack of her ass and off her pussy. She's so fucking wet, and I can feel every inch of her around me.

I stand up, and I grab her by the hips. I flip her over on the couch, and she's on her back. She spreads her legs open wide, and I spread them wider. I grab my cock, and I force myself inside of her again and again.

I'm fucking her hard again, and I'm fucking her deep again. I slam into her, and she reaches up and pulls my head onto her breasts. My mouth comes down onto her nipple, and I start to suck. I suck on her nipple until it's hard in my mouth, then bite it. I grind it until her pussy is contracting around me even harder.

I watch as my cum pulls from her lips, and I wipe it across her lips. I wipe it across her cheeks, and I wipe it across her nose. I wipe it across her eyes, and she licks it all off. She takes all of my cum all over her face and swallows it all down. She takes my cum all over her face, and she takes it all.

"Fuck me again," she moans.

I grab the back of her knees and spread her legs apart. I grab her ass with both of my hands, and I grab her so fucking hard. I hold her so firmly that my fingers leave marks on her ass. I pull her towards me, and I force myself inside of her. I grab her by the hair and use my other hand to grab her throat. I use my hand to constrict her throat, and I start to choke her as I fuck her harder and harder.

I start to fuck her so hard that she starts to scream. I begin to fuck her so hard that she starts to cry, and her voice echoes through the house. I fuck her so hard that she screams so loud that the walls begin to shake. Fuck, her pussy feels so fucking wet. It feels so fucking damp, and I can feel myself throbbing inside her. I can feel my cock throbbing inside of her.

I'm fucking her hard, and I'm fucking her deep. I'm fucking her so hard that she starts to scream louder and louder.

I start to cum inside her, and I begin to cum so fucking hard.

I start to fucking cum so fucking hard. She starts to scream so fucking loud. I pull myself out of her, and I grab my cock. I jerk myself off, and cum drips out of her pussy.

She's still screaming, and I start to come so fucking hard. I begin to come so fucking hard that cum drips down my hand. I start to cum so fucking hard that cum drenches her pussy. Cum drips out of her pussy, and I use my hand to wipe it all over her pussy and her thighs, smearing it across her slender toned stomach.

"There, little doll, now you're my little cum slut."

I am unsure how long I have been here; I am only sure I'm alive...barely.

I had hoped they'd come and show up just like they always did, but my faith in being rescued quickly diminished as the days passed. They weren't coming to save me. I was all alone, but at least I was alive. For now...I was alive.

I feel the pain attack my ribs and rumbling in my belly. The bastard hadn't even bothered to feed me. What kind of kidnapper didn't feed his prisoners?

One that wanted you to die in complete misery, I was guessing, but I would rather be dead than feel the hunger pangs of intense pain that stabbed my body.

I didn't know who he was. I was sure everything would make sense once I looked at his face, but it didn't. All it had done was leave me with more questions than answers.

He hadn't come back. He had just left me here like a stray animal on the ground. I wasn't sure what was worse, the threat he would never let me go or the maddening silence.

I was choosing the latter because even though his presence terrified the shit out of me, the silence was much worse.

There was no light in here. It was dark. The darkness just encased me like my fate. I knew I wasn't going to make it out of there. I feared you would never leave alive once you entered this desolate place.

How did my fate bring me to this point?

I knew I was playing a dangerous game when I started my relationship with the Kane brothers. Still, I never in my wildest dreams could have predicted that a madman with a vendetta would hold me prisoner, with my only crime being that I had fallen in love with all four brothers.

Wasn't love supposed to set you free?

I had never felt more trapped before, but if I could go back, I wouldn't change a thing, not a damn thing. Even if I knew this was where I would end up, I would do it all again to have them love me the way they had. I had no regrets.

A life without love is no life at all. Even if all you have is fleeting heart-bursting moments, you've lived.

I hear the click-clack of shoes coming closer and closer. Hadn't I moments ago wished that I wasn't alone now that the silence was over? I prayed it would return because what was waiting for me on the other side of that door was far more terrifying.

The closer the sound gets, the more my heart thumps erratically.

So, this was it.

The moment I would endure more pain, or maybe he would finally release me from my prison and let me die. Someday, perhaps I would be free. That was my fate. I just wanted it to be over; why prolong what is?

The door swings open, and I don't even raise my head; I keep my eyes firmly on the ground, looking at my dirty knees and hands as I sit in a crumpled mess.

Closer and closer, I hear the clack of shoes as they enter the room, but still, I force myself to keep my eyes on the ground. The scent swarms me as soon as they enter, but it's different; it's not him.

It's feminine.

I breathe as I open my eyes and slowly raise my head to the figure standing before me. Red heels stand before me. My eyes move up her slender, toned legs encased in black fishnet tights, forcing my eyes further to see ripped, tight denim shorts that sit low on her tiny waist. A detailed snake tattoo curls around her stomach in luminescent greens and reds. Further up, my eyes move to see a tiny crop top that houses her voluptuous breast with the words 'baddie' written in bold red.

I'm unsure I want to come face-to-face with the woman who stands there because what woman would be involved in such a horrific project. That's what I was right: a pet project to the madman.

I couldn't sit idly by and let another human be tortured for some madman's sick, sadistic fantasy. Still, here she was, standing before me, not speaking, just allowing me to take her in and assess her with every slow movement my eyes made, edging closer and closer to her face.

My breathing was erratic; this was the moment. This moment right here, when I would come face to face with the woman that had disturbed my deep dive into the abyss of my own depression.

My eyes raise, and a gasp struggles to cram out of my throat.

No, it couldn't be.

But why?

Sure, she looked different, but it was definitely her; there was no mistaking those big almond eyes that right now shone with some sick satisfaction at my reaction. Her hair was no longer Brown, or maybe it never was.

She was blonde. Blonde. Her hair moved down her body in waves, light shimmering golden blonde hair with deep crimson tips. Her mouth curls into a smile, and I know she's not here to save me. She's part of the problem; once more, coldness creeps across my body.

"Essie," I finally gasped.

I can barely believe it, the poor Christian girl we had taken under our wing. Had invited into our circle and invited into our lives. The girl I had shown nothing but kindness to was an accomplice in my kidnapping, but why?

"Hello Cara, you doing okay?" She smirks.

Wow, the timid little thing I had grown to love was no longer here. I wasn't sure who stood before me, but it wasn't the same girl I had spent time with, worked with, and gave my attention to. I wasn't sure who she was, but she wasn't who I thought she was.

"This is because of Jax?" I am dumbfounded because what else could drive her to such extremities?

"Jax?" Her eyes widen, and a loud outburst of laughter travels through the room. "Oh, you actually think I have an interest in Jax?"

"Well, don't you?"

"No, you poor naive little thing, you were always my target. My interest, sweet little Cara, was always you."

"Me?" My eyes widen, "but why?"

"Oh, plenty of reasons." She looks down at her perfectly manicured nails, then raises her eyes to meet mine. "The sweetest one is, of course, revenge."

The way revenge slipped from her tongue had the fear curling inside me. "Revenge? But I've never done anything to you." I gasp.

She crouches down, pressing her hand against my throat, taking a knife from her inner thigh. I can feel the cold steel pressing against my windpipe. So, this was it. I would die here in this room and never know why.

"You took everything from me." She spits at me.

"I didn't do anything to you." I splutter out as I feel the blade dig deeper against my throat.

"Enough," the loud boom of his voice calls behind her.

Her eyes finally leave mine as she looks back at him, "Put the knife down. Did I give you permission to play with my toy? Let her fucking go." He screams.

"I want my vengeance," She screams back.

"You know that's not how this works,"

"I want—."

"Let her go."

I can feel her releasing my neck, and she finally moves the blade an inch away from my throat, "we will play again soon; this isn't over."

"Essie, but I never did anything to you." I plead.

"You took him away," she screams with tears falling down her face, "he loved me, me. Until he met you, and you destroyed him."

"Jax?"

"No, you fucking idiot. Carter." She breathes before walking away from me and leaving me with the other monster in the room.

Carter King.

The source of my nightmares.

They say you can't outrun your past because as fast as you run, it soon catches up with you. Carter King had inhabited my worst nightmares; now, through Essie, he was back. I would rather be dead than be reminded of the evil that had almost destroyed me. Yes, I would rather be dead.

"Oh, look at you, my poor little broken toy. That's my job." He sneers.

"Are you going to hurt me?" I sniffle as a fresh set of tears fall down my face.

"Oh, I sure do hope so."

"Can I ask you something before you do?"

"I don't really allow requests, not this early, but as you've already had a scare, I will allow it."

"Why does Essie want revenge?"

"You'll have to ask her that yourself."

"How does she know—Carter." I manage to choke out the words.

"And spoil the finale," He cocks a brow, "now where is the fun in that?"

Still no wiser. I didn't know her reasons or his. I was stuck in limbo forever, wondering why I was even here, tormented and locked up by the clinically insane.

"What about you?"

"What about me?"

"You knew Carter, too?"

"I never got the pleasure, which is a shame because he sounds like such fun."

"He wasn't fun." I snap.

"Yes, well, we never had the pleasure of meeting."

"Then what are your reasons?" I hear him push out a breath like this conversation was tiring for him, "Please," I plead. "I have to know why you brought me here."

"I suppose it wouldn't hurt." He laughs, "It's not like you're ever getting out alive." My eyes widened. I knew I wouldn't, but hearing those words crushed me. "I have to teach my brother a lesson," he smirks.

He walks towards me, his hand stroking my matted hair, "nothing could hurt him, you know," he whispers, "not a damn thing," his fingers tease the back of my neck, "I didn't think he even had a heart, until you."

His hands grip my neck forcefully, and a whimper crawls from my throat as my body is lifted from the ground until I'm facing him. "Luca found his heart, and then I ripped it away."

"Luca," I gasp, "you're there, brother." It wasn't really a question, more of a shocked response.

"Don't look so surprised; surely they mentioned me." He smiles, and I shake my head. "Oh, well, surprise, you've managed to fuck every single one of us." His tongue slivers out, coating my cheek.

"Please, let me go." I gasp.

"Then who would I play with." He smirks.

"The others that I hear screaming through the walls." I spit back. He doesn't even warn me before I feel the sting of his hand across my face.

"That smart mouth," His hand strokes my stinging cheek. "Will be the death of you."

He turns and walks away from me. I finally let out a breath. I welcomed solitude. I needed it. The silence had driven me mad, but I would rather lose my mind than be stuck in here with him and lose my soul.

I hear the clang of the door as it shuts, and my head and shoulders slump down with relief. My body is exhausted. The confessions given to me had nearly broken what was left of me, but by some miracle, I was still holding on.

A buzzing forms in my head, and my senses shut down. I can hear nothing. See nothing. Feel nothing. I'm numb. Had he finally done it? Had he finally broken me? That was the end goal, wasn't it? Would he kill me once he had completed his goal? Give my lifeless body to Luca to break him, too.

His fingers slam into my pussy, and I cry out.

"You didn't think I would leave without playing with you." He whispers into my back.

"Please," I plead.

"I do love it when a bitch begs," He gasps, "can you feel that little bird," He pressed himself against my ass. "Feel how excited you make me, and your fucking dripping for me." He gasps.

"I don't want this." I cry out as I feel his fingers move deeper inside me, my slush of juices coating his fingers, moving out of me much like my self-respect.

I think I've become numb. Numb to every pain he decides to inflict on me. Numb to the fate he handed me. Just numb. The whimpers crawl through my throat with every movement he makes inside of me.

"Cum for me, my little slut." I shake my head. "Your body wants this." He whispers, curling his fingers deep inside me, pushing ever so close to the edge. "Don't you feel that? That warm, tingling feeling spreads through your body. The neediness to just let go. That feeling to finally release all your sweet pussy juice over my fingers."

"Please," I cry out. "Please don't make me do it." The tears drip down my face, but the harder I cry, the harder his fingers move inside me.

"Oh, you are so close now. I can feel how close you are to releasing yourself all over my fingers; go on, Little Bird. Fucking cum." He growls in my ear.

I can feel myself tightening around his fingers; the pressure is almost too much. I don't want to satisfy him, but my body surrenders beneath his forceful touch. A piercing scream falls into the room, and I feel a gush of wetness fall down his hand and drip into my thighs.

Breathless, I stay there, just still, secretly hating him. I hate every moment that he takes from me. I hate that my body does exactly what it wants it to do. But most of all, I just hate that I exist. That I'm still here reliving every horrible ordeal he puts me through.

"I hate you." I finally manage to whisper.

"You might hate me, but your body loves me." He whispers back, teasing his tongue across my ear.

I want to argue with him. I tried to fight back but had no fight left, so I could only scowl at him and this desolate place. Not that he could see me because he was still pressed against my back.

I feel his fingers finally move out of me. Still, it's not relief because I'm just beginning to realise he will just keep taking from me, using me like a toy as much as it kept him entertained. When the entertainment was over, I would be no good to him, and that is when I would finally be free once I was too broken to play with.

He turns to face me, "See, didn't that feel good?" I shake my head. "I will be back, little bird." He moves his fingers into his mouth and makes a groaning noise. "You're a delicious little bird. Don't go anywhere now, will you." He smirks while leaving the room, slamming and locking the steel door.

I stand there staring at the door I will never walk through. The only thing stopping my freedom is a door I will never get to walk past. A door that keeps me holed up here as his personal sex slave. A door I have come to hate.

My body crumples to the ground in a heap; there is nothing but silence. I raise my head and scream until I can't scream anymore. Nobody can hear my cries, but the pain within my soul crawls out in a high-pitched, painful scream that seems to hit every wall in this dark place that has become my home.

I slam my hand down the cold stone floor, letting the tears fall freely down my face and whimpering as my hand hits something cold and hard. Taking it in my hand, I can feel the smoothness of the large stone in my palm and lifting my arm high in the air, I throw that damn stone at the wall as I once again scream my frustration into nothingness.

A loud shattering noise can be heard over my screams, which stops my outburst almost immediately. My eyes widen with surprise as I force myself to stand. Slowly walking towards the wall that had just disturbed my painful screaming, I see the shattered mirror.

Why hadn't I seen that earlier?

Large pieces of glass are scattered across the ground; kneeling down, I take one in my hand, feeling the sharp edge of the glass. I just stare at it as if I'm in a trance.

I could end my misery right now. That's what I wanted: to stop the pain and finish it on my terms, not when he got bored of playing with me. After all, I had experienced the one thing I thought I never would: I had experienced love and would love them until my dying breath.

This was my way out. I didn't see any other option. He would never let me go, and I couldn't stay here and endure much more of this. Essie was on the warpath, and I wasn't sure what her plans for me were. The only thing I knew for sure was one of them would kill me eventually, but not before they tortured me, and that wasn't something I could accept.

Sitting in a heap, I hold the glass between my fingers and say a silent farewell they would never hear. I hold the cold glass to my wrist and close my eyes.

Death was always imminent. I knew that this way, I could control how I would die; they couldn't take that from me. My death would be my choice, and like a bird, I could finally....fly.

The door crashes open, and my body is tackled to the ground. My wrist is repeatedly banged against the floor, and I cry as the pain hits my wrist. The clattering of glass can be heard as the shard of glass finally falls from my grip.

"You didn't think I would allow you to kill yourself?"

"But—how,"

"Oh, I see everything, little bird, and we are not nearly done playing; you will live to see another day. That I can promise you."

"But I don't want to live," I scream back at him.

His hand wraps around my throat like a snake coiling around its prey. This wasn't dominant and masterful. This was a threat that I had crossed the line. His grip tightens harder against my throat until I'm gasping for breath. It feels like the breath is leaving my body, and I'm moments away from passing out.

He moves my body upright while still gripping hold of my throat. "That's a shame, little bird because you don't die until I say you die. You don't eat, shit or sleep without my say-so. You belong to me, and you will only do what I want you to. Now stop acting like such a brat." His grip loosens on my throat. "And accept your fate." My eyes widen at his last words. "It will be much easier for you that way."

I hear the click-clack of heels, and a shiver of anger overcomes my body. I had nothing to lose, only my life, but I didn't care for that anymore. Her smug smile is pasted on her face as she looks at me. The sliver of victory almost pours from her veins.

I assess if I will make it out alive, my eyes darting to every corner of the drab room I've been stuck in for months. Without another thought, I lurch towards her, my nails digging into her arms. Looking at her face, she no longer looks smug; I think I see a sliver of fear, and now I'm feeling smug.

She rocks on her heels as I fight to take her down, my hand in her hair, gripping her tightly. A scream emits from her throat as I fight to pull her down to the ground.

"Aren't you going to help me?" She screams at him.

With a slight curve of his lips and his finger pressing against his chin, he nods, and I think this is it. I've really gone and done it now. "Why? I'm curious to see how this little show unfolds."

"You bastard." She screams back at him.

"Ah, what's wrong, Essie? Your little master not running to your aid." I mock, "See, even the hand that feeds you doesn't care about your evil, miserable little life."

"I'm not the prisoner here; you are." She sneers.

"Aren't you?" I raise a brow, "You're no different than I am; the only difference is you willingly let him fuck you, but that's hardly surprising. Who would want a desperate whore like you." I spit back at her. Gripping her hair tighter and pulling her head close to mine, "Only the fucking deranged wants to fuck you; no sane person would fucking touch you, you fucking vermin."

"I fucking hate you." She screams at me.

"I'm not fucking crazy about you either," I mutter as we crash.

As we roll around on the ground in a scuffle. I feel her nails dig into my neck; it must be deep as I feel the sharp sting, but it's strange; I don't feel pain. I'm completely numb to it. They could slice me right now, chop my body into little pieces, and I don't think I would even flutter an eyelid because it didn't matter what they did to me any longer. I had died the moment I stepped through that door.

You couldn't kill a ghost; the only thing you could do was release it.

She grabs my body, slamming it to the ground, and I wince at the force of the impact as my back is crushed against the concrete floor, and her body crashes against mine. Her hands are in my matted hair as she lifts my head from the ground before pounding it against the floor.

I want to struggle and hit back, but the surge of energy I had moments ago has all but disappeared. The buzzing in my head is the only thing I hear. It feels like a band is playing a symphony in my head.

I feel my body relax, but I'm not entirely sure why; my eyes flutter close, and I can hear their distant voices swarm around my body, but other than the constant pounding and buzzing, I hear nothing.

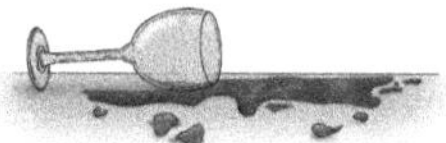

My eyes open, and darkness swarms me. I'm lying on the ground where she had left me. There was no light. There were no voices. There was just me in the dark. Alone, once more.

Was I dead?

Had they finally done it? Had they finally released the ghost?

I try to lift my head from the ground, and a sharp shooting pain moves through my skull, and all I feel is sadness, not because of the pain but because I am still here. I was still alive. I was still breathing. I was still trapped.

I can hear my shallow breaths, confirming that I am still here. The tears fall down my face; it's like the dam has broken, and I don't know how to stop it.

All I can think is: I don't want to be here anymore.

Even through every traumatic event I had been forced to live, I had never wished for death. Not once.

How broken do you have to be to wish you'd die because that's the only way you'd ever find peace?

Slowly, I lift my head. Once again, the pain travelled faster than lightening through my skull.

Okay, you can do this.

My head flops back down, and I sigh in frustration. If he had fed me, maybe I wouldn't feel as weak as I did. Or perhaps I shouldn't have attacked Essie; it wasn't my finest moment.

Just lift your head from the ground.

Once more, I squeeze my eyes and lift my head from the ground, trying to ignore the intense squeezing pain that feels like my skull is encased in a vice. I try to lift my body this time, and as I open my eyes, a sense of satisfaction overcomes me.

I did it. I'm sitting up.

Looking around the room, I'm entirely alone. You'd think I would appreciate the solitude, but I hate it. I hate the silence; it slowly wraps its talons around you, causing madness in your body that you fear will never leave.

Looking around the room, I sigh, still in the same drab room I hated. There were no windows, so I could never differentiate between day and night. It felt like it had been so long since I had felt the sun on my skin.

It's funny, isn't it? The things we take for granted. Like a slight breeze blowing through your hair. Watching the crisp leaves fall from the trees during fall. The sun hits your skin on a warm summer day. The decadent smell of coffee in the morning and wrapped in the arms of someone you love, feeling their heart beating next to yours.

The little things you think you won't miss are the same things you crave once they are gone. In the end, it is those small things that make life worth living. And amid darkness, when you're alone, you only have to remember the small things that gave you so much joy.

No use dwelling on the things we couldn't change.

I look around the room again, and I almost think my eyes are playing tricks on me. I squeeze them shut, thinking it's a mirage or maybe a concussion that has me seeing things, but as I slowly allow my eyes to open, to my surprise, the scene in front of me doesn't change.

I slowly allow my broken body to get up off the ground and take silent, quiet steps to the other side of the room, looking around in case it's some sick trick. Still, as I stand there motionless, nothing happens.

One step

Two steps

Final step

A crack of light shines through that steel door that has held me here prisoner, and finally, in the dark, I find something I hadn't seen in a long time.

I found hope.

I gently pull my fingers between the gaps and hear the door creaking as it slowly opens. I half expect him to be waiting on the other side of the door. Still, to my surprise, the long, dimly lit hallway is completely empty, devoid of human presence.

The joy pulses through my body in a mass of emotions; all I had to do was step onto the other side of this door and finally have what I was dreaming about. I would finally be free.

Taking in a deep breath and allowing it to fill my lungs, I finally breathe out and step one foot on the other side of the door. I expect an alarm to alert him of my escape, but again, there is silence. Taking my other foot, I'm finally on the other side of the door.

And finally, I can breathe.

I smile with only one little thought in my head.

Freedom.

My freedom is in my grasp.

I can almost taste it, but now I'm on the other side of that door; why does a crawling fear move up my spine? This is what I wanted: to be free. But a nibbling feeling claws at my mind.

It was too easy.

Way too easy.

He had left the door open. He knew I would wake up soon; like the idiot I am, I had done precisely what he knew I would do. I had run in my excitement without assessing the danger behind this door. I was about to fall into the trap.

But what if it was a trap?

What if this was my only chance at finding freedom? Would I crawl back into my hole if even more horrors awaited me? No, I couldn't go back even if I wanted to. I had to go forward and say I tried to leave once the opportunity arose.

A caged bird is a scary thing. When you're young, wild and free, you're not supposed to be trapped like an animal. The feral instinct will one day make you snap until you fly home.

Home. That was my new goal. I was going to fly home, and if I didn't, then I'd make damn sure I died trying.

My feet push down on the plush crimson carpet. I had expected the floor to be hard, glass scattered around, like this was some crack den, but the most horrifying part of this house was the room I had just left.

I wondered if anyone who came here had ever gotten this far. I didn't think so, hadn't he said everyone who arrives here never leaves. So, why had he left the door open? Maybe he felt bad for what happened there. Did monsters even have a soul? I guess I was about to find out.

The hallway seems to go on forever, and the only door I can see is the one I had just entered through. How strange that I was up here alone. Hadn't the screams haunted me in the night? But there couldn't have been screams if I was entirely alone.

Maybe it had finally happened.

Maybe I had gone mad.

There was no explanation except those screams for help were just voices in my head. I had thought he was the deranged one, but maybe it was just me.

"Oh, where does my birdy think she is going." His voice booms into the atmosphere, and fear pierces my spine.

Shit.

Of course, he knew I had left that room. Didn't he say he was always watching? I stop, not moving. Unable to regulate my breathing. The intelligent thing to do would be to walk back to that room and just take my punishment for leaving.

Even as I think I know, I do not intend to return to the damp, cold, depressing, desolate room. I would rather die than go back in there, and if I didn't find a way out, I feared that death was all that awaited me.

Why did I care?

Isn't that what I had wanted?

Isn't that what I had wished for, death to take me?

No, I would not die in that room where he had ripped out my soul and tarnished my positive mind and heart. He had already taken everything from me but wasn't killing me where he had broken my spirit.

He may have defiled my body and poisoned my mind, but he was not taking my life in a place that had left me with no hope.

If he wanted to kill me.

Well, he would have to catch me first.

I'm on edge. Every second I waste could be the second I get caught, but I don't know where I am or even where I'm going. The only thing I know for sure is that I must keep moving.

The lights flicker, and the fear rushes through me. I can't move; the fear renders me immobile. I'm just standing in the darkened corridor with the lights flickering on and off, erratic my breathing.

The silence surrounds me, and with every moment, I'm less and less confident that I can do this. After all, he had let me out. It was just another game, and I was standing in the gloomy, gothic-darkened corridor waiting for him to pop out and lead me screaming back to the room of horrors.

Finally, my feet cooperate and slowly start moving. I stop once more to look for what could be lurking in the shadows. Still, I hear nothing but my fast heartbeat that almost beats out of my chest and my erratic breathing that swallows my body with the fear I'm encased in.

"Little birdy," I hear him sing. "Little birdy, now where do you think you're going?" He kept repeating the exact words over and over again. "You can't escape because you don't really want to. You want to be here. With me. As my doll. Go back to your room, and we will forget this ever happened."

Go back to my room? Yes, that's what I should do. He was right; of course, he was right. I wouldn't be punished because I would be playing by his rules. I turn my head and look at the steel open door that I had slid through with excitement. Yes, I should pretend I was never close to escaping because I never was.

"Little Bird, so what's it going to be?"

I couldn't see him, but I could hear him. I knew he could see me; he could see me standing here, staring back at that door. I shook my head. I couldn't go back. I couldn't be trapped in there forever. I had to at least try to escape.

I needed to run.

I turn my body around, turning my back on that door I had looked upon with venomous rage for so long. With my head held high, I look back down that darkened corridor, no longer fearful of what might await me.

"Oh, little bird, what a surprise." You chose the hard way, but when I catch you, you're fucking mine, and this time it won't be so nice." I laugh into the air; his theatrics were almost comical.

Nice? Not a single moment here or with him had been nice. I had been living a nightmare I couldn't wake up from, nice? He had to joke, I think, as I started sprinting down the corridor.

I don't last long before I feel the pangs of pain shoot from my chest. God, being locked up here had made me so unfit I couldn't even run down a corridor without having the wind knocked from my body.

My legs are slowing, and I can feel them weakening. A dizziness overcomes my body at an alarming speed;

the thumping from my chest causes a panic to instant-ly rise.

My vision is blurred, everything looks wavy, and the corridor doubles. It is getting longer and longer the more I look at it. I need to find an exit if I can even see it.

"Oh, little bird, you seem to have some issues." He mocks.

"Fuck you," I scream back, hunched over as I try to refrain from what little breath I still have left in my weak body.

Picking back up speed, I run, and I run until I come to a standstill. I want to jump up and down because I thought I was trapped in some maddening maze with no end in sight, but there sits a crimson door with a gold handle.

Finally, I was going to get out of here.

"I wouldn't go in there if I was you,"

I would roll my eyes if I had the strength, but I didn't. I had nothing left to give. I was amazed I was even still standing. I'm sure I was only here in this moment, still pushing forward from sheer stubbornness to leave this hell hole.

My feet push forward, and I'm almost within reach of my exit. My hand pressed against the gold handle of the door. As I looked upon the door, it seemed oddly fitting that it would be red to represent all the innocent blood spilt for his entertainment.

"Little Bird, I'm telling you, you don't want to go there. Turn back now and go back to your room."

Pulling down the handle, I smirk. It felt good to disobey the madman. All I had done was play dead for him, allowed him to abuse and take everything good, and now it was my turn to say no. I only wished I dared to do it in that room, but it was better late than never.

"Little Bird, last chance." He hums.

"Fuck you,"

"Little Bird, you will not like what you find on the other side of that door."

"Well, it can't be any worse than stuck in that room with you."

Pulling down the handle, I swing open that door and step inside. My eyes widen as I scan the darkened room. There was nothing in here; silence fell around me, and that's when I saw it.

Six glowing red eyes were in the centre of the room.

Okay, I had definitely gone mad. Now, I was hallucinating. Deep, angry growls erupt from inside the room, and I don't even think as I turn around, racing towards the door, but I'm just not fast enough. It crashes shut with a loud bang.

"Now, little bird, didn't I tell you that you didn't want to enter this room."

The fear pierces through my body. Backing my body against the wall, I'm trapped like a rat. I have nowhere else to go. I should have listened and tried to look for another exit, but I hadn't; I had run to the first door I had seen.

Stupid Cara, very stupid.

The lights switch on, very nearly blinding me. Looking into the room where the demonic flashing red eyes had halted me, I suddenly wished I was back in the dark.

There they stand, looking angry that I've invaded their territory, with pointy ears and standing to attention like they want to pounce at the prey that has come into their domain. Silky black fur, baring their white sharp teeth with drool falling from their mouths. Three majestic black Dobermans stand before me.

"Beautiful beasts, aren't they." I hear his voice at the side of me.

I wasn't sure which part of the menacing beasts I was supposed to find beautiful because the way they were looking at me right now, they looked like their lunch had been handed to them.

"They don't bite unless they are instructed to." He whispers.

"Is that my fate? Being mauled and eaten by your rabid dogs." Once more, they growl.

"Tut, tut, don't be mean, little bird, they can hear you."

I look to my side to see the glee in his eyes. The bastard was enjoying tormenting me. This was just a game to him. You had to play by the rules if you were going to survive.

"I suppose," he steps towards me, his fingers lightly graze my face as he tucks a strand of my hair behind my ear. "You thought you'd finally escaped me."

"I don't like that room." I manage to strangle the words from my throat.

"Well, why didn't you say." He smirks, "Little bird, only good little dolls get rewards; tell me, have you been a good doll." I shake my head because I haven't played the game he wants me to play. "Are you going to be a good doll?" I nod, hoping my punishment won't be so severe.

His hands move up my body, and I stay still like a good doll. He smiles, satisfied that I'm not screaming and fighting to get away from him for once, even though his hands on my body make my skin crawl.

"You have to be punished, though, you know that."

I shake my head with tears in my eyes. "No, please, I will be good; I swear I will be good." I plead.

"I would really love to believe that," He rips the clothes from my body, and I shiver from the draft that flows around my body. "But I don't." He whispers into my ear.

My body is stretched by the bounds on my wrists and ankles. The pain slices through me like a knife. He's had me strung up in the air for hours while I hear the distant growls of his dogs that are hankering for a bite. Much to their annoyance, he keeps them well away from me.

"Are you ready for your punishment now, little bird?"

His words almost cut me open. "This isn't my punishment?" I ask in disbelief.

"No, little bird, I have something much more fun planned for you." I hang my head in defeat. "However, if you're a good little doll, as you suggested you would be, you'll get a reward."

"A reward? What kind of reward?"

"Be a good girl, and you'll find out."

This was fine. I could do this. All I had to do was submit my body to the monster, and my torture would end. Easy right? Wrong. I feel the first sting across my back, but I don't cry out.

"Good, you're doing good." He coos at me like you would a child.

Once more, I feel the tough leather hit my skin in the same place, but this time, I whimper as tears fall down my face. He never lets up; the burning heat from the pain is almost too much to bear. My skin feels raw and hot from the abuse he repeatedly makes on my back.

"You look so beautiful when you bleed for me." He pants.

"Bleed for you?" I gasp.

"Ah, I have to mark you my little doll; how else would everyone know who owns you." The tears crawled down my face; he would never let me leave. "Every part of you belongs to me, and now you have the marks to prove it."

I wanted to argue. I wanted to scream out in pain, but all that would come out of my throat were the little whimpers of sadness as the pain moved through my body.

"Such pretty little welts; your body is beautiful when it blushes."

His hands moved across the exposed wounds, and each time he grazed my wounds, a sharp gasp of pain would fall from my lips. This didn't deter him; it encouraged him to do it more.

"Don't you understand how beautiful you look, marked by my hands?" His fingers run through my hair, pulling my head back. "You make me shiver, baby."

"Caleb," I gasp. "If you're going to kill me, please just do it."

"Don't you see, little doll, I would follow you even in death." His hands move from my hair to my face. "How strange a little thing like you would make a monster like me—feel."

He pauses. I'm not sure I even want to hear the end of that sentence, but his last words just hang in the air, looming over both of us with threat and mischief.

"You're not going to kill me?" I ask with hope.

"Death is so final; we could do this dance in hell, but I'd much prefer to dance in the light." A crease forms across my brow. "Do you want to die?" I shake my head. "Then dance with me."

"Dance with you?"

"All you have to do is say yes."

"Like I have a choice." I scoff.

"You do have a choice. You've always had a choice. You can now choose to submit to me, dance with me, and become my perfect little doll."

"And if I say no?"

"I'm not entirely sure, little bird, but if you choose to dance with me today, all your pain will be over."

"You will let me go?"

A sneer falls from his lips. "Even in death, you won't be free from me. What makes you think I would willingly set you free?"

"But you said I had a choice," I whine.

"You do, but not to leave; you can never leave. You're Mine. You can choose to be with me without pain or torture. You can be free here, but I won't let you leave little bird.

My head falls because I finally realise that while I may not die, I'm stuck here with him. He was never going to let me go. My choice would only be to make me comfortable while I was under his control.

"So, what will it be, little bird." I raise my head and look at him. "Will you dance with me?"

What a curious question and one I had never thought I would ever get. I had thought only death waited for me. Everything he had done was leading us up to this point. Right to this moment. He could just take it, but I can finally see as I look at him. That was never what he wanted. He wanted me to willingly give him my submission because, without it, he's just a monster forcing it.

He was still a monster, but I was sure deep down in the black confines of his soul, there must lay a heart within there somewhere. Something that had driven this change, so I made a deal with the devil.

I was stuck in hell already; I might as well make my stay less miserable, and if you played the game, there was still hope that you'd fly home one day.

Sighing, I finally give in.

"Yes," I whisper. "I will dance with you."

In the beginning, this was my chance. My chance to exact revenge. Finally, I had her in my clutches and would end her miserable life. When Caleb met me, I was broken, a soulless girl with her heart ripped from her body, but that would all change.

It was simple, really.

I would get my revenge, and so would he. His brothers would be heartbroken, and I would finally get to watch her take her last breath just like I had to watch him take his.

She didn't know me.

Pretending to be her friend was much easier than I had anticipated. The stupid girl sure did trust easily; I thought there would be at least some suspicion, but she actually bought the whole sad little lost girl with no parents. A small chuckle falls from my lips.

The plan was simple, but he ruined it.

Once again, she had her claws into another man. Caleb was always a safe bet. He didn't feel anything for anyone, and then she came here and became his new favourite plaything. Well, I would just have to take that away from him, too, because I didn't work this hard to only get this far. She had to go, and if he couldn't do it, then I would.

She still had some fight; that was one thing I wasn't expecting. Anyone else would be broken, and parts of her were, but then there was a sliver of determination; I could see it in her eyes.

All I had to do was snuff out that hope.

It's a shame, really, another time, another life, we could have been great friends, but I would never get back what she had taken from me. It was unforgivable. She had to go.

I watch from the dark, peering into that room, and I hear her finally agree to submit to him, stupid, stupid girl. I hadn't expected her to agree so quickly; she had fought from day one and had fallen because he had expressed some emotion. Women were so fickle.

I was going to walk away because the fact she had crumbled so easily beneath his charms annoyed me. Caleb didn't have what his other brothers had, but he had that brooding bad-boy thing.

The way her body is bound looks deliciously painful. He keeps using the word dance, but we all know what that means. He circles her like a prey envelops its victim before it prepares to devour its next meal.

He touches her body, but what's curious is she doesn't resist. She's allowing him to touch her without complaint. His ego must be enjoying this, but as I look upon her face. I see it. That look of sheer disgust. She didn't want this. She didn't want him touching her.

She was merely playing the game.

Interesting.

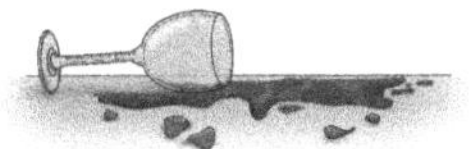

Walking into the dining room there, she sits. All clean and looking as perfect as she had looked when

I had first met her. Gone was the look of fear in her eyes. The matted hair and dirty skin, and she just sits there eating her meal, looking smug as fuck.

I instantly want to clamber across the table and stab my knife into her devious heart. Now, that would be a meal he wouldn't forget. She eats steak while her blood pools on the clean white linen tablecloth. Ah, delicious. But I don't. I stare daggers into her soul while my brain thinks of all the creative ways it wants to destroy her.

"Essie, so nice of you to join us today." She smiles sweetly while mocking my appearance.

"Yes, well, darling, your last meal is important. I wouldn't miss it for the world." I smirk.

"My last meal?" A crease of confusion crosses her face.

"Don't worry, doll; Essie is teasing you," Caleb reassures her.

"Oh, am I?" I raise a brow.

"Don't start your shit again." He grits back while stabbing his knife into the table, causing the plates to wobble.

"This wasn't part of the plan," I scream back.

"Yes, well, that's the thing about plans." He places his fork in his mouth, chewing on his steak with a mischievous smirk playing on his lips. "Plans change."

My hands bang on the table, and they look at me like I'm the insane one. Like he hadn't just flipped a switch overnight and decided to keep the vermin that only knew how to take.

"Let me tell you both a story," I smile. I hear Caleb grumble, "Oh, I'm sorry I'm disrupting this fucked up little get-together you've got going on here."

"I told you not to start your shit; you know I can throw you back where I found you." He grits at me.

Walking around the table, my nails graze the table-cloth slowly, and my lips' smirk makes them both silent. When I reach his body, I see him stiffen. "Oh darling, who says you found me," I whisper behind him while my nails graze his neck. "How cute that you think, still now," My hands reach for her knife, and I stab the knife into the table, just missing his fingers by an inch. "That you're the one in control."

"Essie, don't fucking test me."

"I wonder how fast you are?" I whisper again, "Would you be fast enough to save your little pet?" He looks at the vermin who's sat beside him. "Well, would you?" He nods, "are you willing to bet her life on it?"

"Essie,"

"It's simple; all you have to do is shut up, listen to what I say, and your pet can live another day."

"Fine." He grits back.

"Wow, that was way too easy." I mock, "Well, aren't you a lucky girl? It appears you've just tamed the devil."

Moving away from him, I see them both relax. "Wow, so tense; I won't hurt you." I smile, "Well, not yet, at least." Moving the chair, I can hear it scrape the dark wood flooring; it almost sounds like nails have been scraped down a blackboard.

Positioning the chair right in front of I clamber onto it backwards with my legs spread wide. "Let's play a game."

"A game?" She asks.

"Yes, a game." I smile. "You do like games, don't you, Cara." She just looks confused. "Well, you'll love this one."

"I don't think now is the right time." Caleb glares in my direction.

"Nonsense darling, now is the perfect time."

He looks uncomfortable, so he should because I had a surprise for both of them. I was just going to torture her and end her miserable life, but I thought, why stop with her when I can kill two birds with one stone?

"You know death is inevitable for you, don't you?" She shakes her head. "Come on, you are not stupid. You didn't expect me to let you live after what you did."

"What did I do?" She barely whispers.

It wasn't possible.

How could she not know what she had done? As I looked at her, there was nothing but confusion. She was a good actress, but she wasn't that good.

"How can you not remember Carter King?" I spit at her. "Was it that unmemorable for you, or have the Kane brothers completely wiped any semblance of a memory you may have had," I scream at her.

"This is not the time or the place," Caleb screams at me.

"I've waited long enough." I grit, "But don't worry, Caleb, you'll get yours." He looks at me like I'm a venomous snake. "What? You didn't seriously think you could break our deal and walk away, right?"

"You bitch." He spits at me while charging towards me.

"I would save that energy; you're going to need it," I smirk.

He races towards me with that knife. Silly little boy, I used to play with knives for fun. Did he really think that would make me fear him? His hand wraps around my throat, and I feel a sliver of coldness hit my face. "Go on then, make me bleed." I raise my brows with a smile on my face.

"What did you do?" He screams in my face.

"Me?" I smile, "what could I do?"

His grip on my throat tightens, and my face feels like a balloon about to pop at any moment. I can barely breathe, but that smile never falls from my lips. "What did you do?" He screams. A sputtering of incoherent words falls from my lips.

I hear the dogs barking; they sound positively annoyed.

Oh, this was delicious.

He lets go of my throat in his haste to find out my dastardly plan. I see a look on his face I have never seen before, one that he had portrayed on many others' faces but never his own. And here we were, at war; the only one who looked fearful was him.

Gasping and sputtering for breath, I fall to the ground and look up at him. "You didn't listen, so I took matters into my own hands." I smile. He looks at me curiously. "All the family back together at last." His face drops, "See, while you were busy entertaining that murderous bitch, I was busy talking to your brothers."

"You fucking bitch, do you know what you've done." The rage seeps through his veins with every word.

"Better run before they catch you." I wink while clambering to my feet and quickly grabbing his most prized possession.

"You don't need her."

"Oh, on the contrary, we have unfinished business." A loud laugh erupts from my throat. "Oh, funny coincidence, just as you and your brothers do."

"Essie,"

The sound of bangs erupts through the house.

"You're running out of time." I sing.

His eyes dart to every corner of the room. "I promise I will be back for you, little bird."

"No, you won't; don't make promises you can't keep." I smile back at him as I watch him race from the room.

Spinning her around to face me, I finally see the missing look. I finally see the look of terror, and the sliver of excitement crawls up my spine. "Finally, alone at last."

"Essie, you don't have to do this." She begs.

"No?" I raise a brow, "suppose I should just let the past lay in the past." She nods, "forget about what you took from me?"

"I didn't take anything from you."

"You know, I never got the chance to talk about it earlier. He does nothing but Yap, Yap, Yap. But now he's busy—."

"Why is he busy?" She utters.

"Oh, at a guess, I would say his brothers have come here for revenge."

"Revenge?" Her eyes widen.

"Yes, darling, there is nothing sweeter than revenge. Speaking of which—" studying my nails, I slowly let my eyes move up and down her body before we finally make eye contact. "You took my brother from me," I spit at her.

"Your brother?" Her eyes widen, "but I don't know your brother." She gasps.

"Oh, you did; you knew my brother very well."

"Who?"

"Carter King,"

She shakes her head, and I watch all the colour drain from her face. Her tiny little body slumps to the ground, and I see the first slip of tears falling down her face as she looks up at me in defeat.

Well, this was going to be fun.

Part IV

Goodbye Oak Haven

It started with Oak Haven but it
ended with them.
I thought I would die there.
Hey, maybe apart of me did.
Every family has secrets.
Theirs would be my undoing.

It had been months since Cara had been gone. It felt like my soul had been ripped from my body. This time, she hadn't left...she had been taken. For so long, I had blamed River for her kidnapping to the point they always kept him away from me.

Still, the stark realisation that dawned on me with every second she was gone was harrowing.

It wasn't River's fault the light had been taken from my life.

It was mine.

Caleb.

The source of my nightmares, the source of my pain for many years. The inner turmoil I had battled that had waged a war deep within my soul. I knew I should have killed him that day in the woods, but as I looked at him...I just couldn't bring myself to do it.

I had given him a lifeline, and he had exacted revenge by taking the only thing I had ever loved.

I prayed it wasn't him.

I wished with all my fucking might that it wasn't him, but deep down, I knew his hate for me ran too deep.

He took Cara.

"Are you ready?" Jax stands by the door with the tension seeping through his veins.

"No," I sigh, "but let's get our girl anyway."

"What if—." River's sullen face falls to the ground.

"She won't," Elijah interrupts, "he wants to hurt us; she will be fine." He utters.

"You really think so?" River smiles.

"Sure, buddy." He gives a half smile while I share a look with Jax that says: I'm not so sure.

Caleb was a psychopath, and he would have no issues with killing any woman, least of all one that meant so much to all of us. Caleb was too theatrical to do away with her; he would want to see the pain on our faces as he committed the deed, and that wasn't a reality that I would be party to.

You could cut the tension in the air with a knife, but none of us knew what we were walking into. Essie clearly had an end game, so when Jax answered that call, the only thoughts in my head were: why?

Every moment I let him breathe led us all up to this point. We would always end up here, and I would again face the difficult decision of ending my brother's life.

This time, it was different. What he had done. What he had taken from me, well, what he had taken from all of us. That was unforgivable. Caleb was always living on borrowed time, and his time had almost run out.

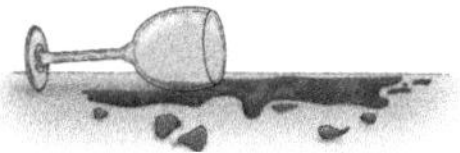

LUCA'S FLASHBACK

The screams rip through the house like the walls speak of the unspeakable pain. We had heard it for that long and were no longer fazed by the sound. It was like those nursery rhythms your mother sang to you as a child. Except these weren't sweet or comforting. They were just familiar. Something you got used to.

Walking through the house was like visiting a torture Palace. There were rooms our father forbade us from entering, and you obeyed him. That landed you one month in the cellar, stuck in the cold, dark basement with only the rats for company. It was worse hearing the squeaks through the deathly silence. It was enough to drive a grown man insane; to a child, it was absolutely horrifying, but our entire life was a horror story, so why would this phase any of us?

Caleb wasn't like the rest of us. He idolised our father. He thought the man was a genius. I often looked at him in disgust when he looked upon the man like he was some god. He wasn't. He was what you would envision pure evil to be. I was sure the man had to have been forged from the flames of hell because that's what this place was, like living in hell.

"I can't wait until I'm all grown," Caleb says as we move through the labyrinth of corridors. This house was like a fucking maze; it was easy to get lost.

"Oh yeah," I smirk. "So you can finally escape the madhouse."

He stops walking and stares at me like I have two heads. "Are you mad? Why would I leave? I can't wait to do all this myself." The look on his face is one of pride. "One day, all this will be ours."

"I don't want this." I gasp.

"More for me then, brother." He slaps me back before racing into the dining room to join my other brothers.

Yes, Caleb wasn't like the rest of us.

I had known this when I found him cutting up an innocent rabbit in the woods. When I asked why, he had merely looked at me and said: because I can.

That was the Kane motto taught to us by our bastard father.

Take what you want because you can. You're untouchable. The world owes you nothing, and it will give you nothing. You have to take everything you desire and own what you want. This world is not free, so you have to take what you desire.

Caleb thought he was a genius. I thought he was a nut job that needed to be locked up so he couldn't poison anyone again, but that never happened. He was free to just roam around like a hidden psychopath.

The rest of us just played ignorant, like we didn't know what happened here, but we did. We always knew. We heard the screams from the women. We heard them begging to go home, but they never did, and when one woman's screams went silent, it wasn't long before the next ones started.

It was like a vicious circle, but my only goal was to eventually leave this desolate place and get my brothers somewhere safe, away from him, so they could have a semblance of everyday life. Still, I feared it may be too late for Caleb.

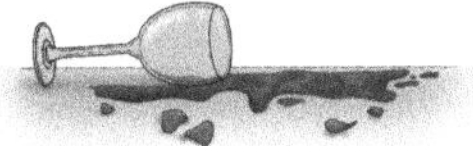

"Hey," I feel Jax place his hand on my shoulder; not even the comfort of the plane relaxes my body. "It's going to be okay,"

A sigh leaves my body. "You don't really believe that."

"I have to." He utters.

"This is my fault." I finally admit. He shakes his head. "Jax, I know you don't want to believe that, but I would have just had the courage to end this years ago; we wouldn't be here right now."

"We would."

"No, we wouldn't, just stop. Stop making excuses for me."

"Caleb wasn't the only one that Cara needed to fear."

"What?"

"Essie–."

"You mean that boring, plain Jane you had working for you?" He nods, "I don't understand."

"We all have a past, Luca, and eventually, no matter how hard you try. It just catches up on you."

"Essie helped him, didn't she?" I gasp.

"Yes, but we can't worry about that now." He lays back and closes his eyes, clearly done with this conversation and unwilling to divulge any more information, but would it really help to know anyway? I didn't think so.

I couldn't understand why she didn't come to me. Why she didn't come to any of us? She let her past swallow her whole until she drowned in times past. We could have helped her, kept her safe, but she had kept this deep, dark secret to herself, and that's when I realised that's what I had also done.

The ghosts of our past had eaten us all until nothing was left. I had never seen her drowning because I was too busy to keep my head above water.

If we had communicated better, maybe we wouldn't be here now. There was no point thinking of what might have happened if we had done something differently because we hadn't. That was a sure way to drive yourself mad.

The only thing I had was now.

I just wanted to find her and bring her home, but I knew what needed to be done before that could happen.

Caleb had to join our father.

I looked around at my brothers, and in all the time we had been together, this was the longest we had probably been silent. Each of us is just tormented by our thoughts. It wasn't just how we would find her or how different she may appear. It was stepping foot back in that house.

When we left, we made a pact that we would never darken that door again, and we hadn't. If she wasn't there, you couldn't pay me to cross the threshold into hell, but he had something we wanted, and I would walk through flames to bring her back home.

I had never felt pain the way I had felt it when she disappeared from my life. I had never thought I could love anyone, but Cara took my heart, not just a piece of it but all of it, and when she left, it felt like I had died.

I was going to get my heart back.

I was going back for her.

The demons I battled no longer mattered because I could no longer see or hear them; the only thing I saw was her.

I just needed her safely back in my arms.

Nothing else mattered.

Just her.

Walking up to Oak Haven, fear grips a tight hold around my heart. The bile rises up my throat, and a sudden feeling of turning around and running in the opposite direction takes hold of me.

I don't want to be here.

I swore I would never come back.

It's strange because it looks exactly the same. After all these years, it hasn't changed. It just stands before us all. The nightmare we had avoided for all these years, and now we were back. We were back to face the hell we had run from.

The wrought iron gates stand six feet tall; looking at them sends a piercing shock through my system. The day I had walked through these with my brothers was the happiest day of my life, and now, I was about to walk back through them.

"Are you ready?" River asks.

"No," We speak in unison as we all stand with our hands in our pockets, just staring at those gates like they were the monsters we were afraid of, but it wasn't the gates that we feared; it was what was behind those gates.

"We have to go through them at some point." River sighs impatiently.

"We know," I utter, "just give me a moment."

"He's right, you know," Elijah interrupts. "Stalling the inevitable will change nothing, and the longer we stand here waiting—."

"I know," I grit back at them both. I knew only too well what he was referring to.

"Jax," Elijah pleads with me. "We have to go get her."

"I know," I whisper. "I just—"

"You need a moment." I nod, "Well, don't take too long, or I will just go in there alone...if I have to."

"Always was a stubborn bastard." I laugh.

"Hey, that's why you love me."

I shake my head, "No, I love you despite that."

I look over at Luca; he has said nothing. He holds the same expression we all hold, and I knew this must be harder for him. He had seen so much more than we had. Heard so much more. He experienced so much more and was back to the place that had almost destroyed him.

"How you doing?" I ask.

"Oh, I'm just great." He mutters.

"Luca,"

"When we get in there..." He never looks at me once, "he's mine." He growls.

"Luca, you don't have to do this alone."

"Caleb is my problem. Yes, I do."

"Hey, we're brothers, aren't we." River pats him on the back. "We do this together."

"Because we are brothers, I must do this alone." He sighs, "Just get her out of there, and I will do the rest."

I never understood his need to protect, but I don't think I ever really understood Luca. Not really. Everything he did, he did with good reason. Maybe I wasn't supposed to understand him, but I don't think he understood us.

"You are not doing this alone." I finally speak.

"Jax, I don't want to argue."

"It's not an argument, Luca; you are not doing this alone."

I half expect him to argue, but he says nothing more, and that's when I realise just how beaten down he was. He didn't even have the energy to fight with me. I don't think any of us did.

"Ah, fuck this." I hear Elijah curse as he pushes up the wrought iron gates. They screech as they move open. The gates might as well be an alarm to alert everyone inside that we've arrived.

"Did I say we were ready?"

"No," Elijah smirks. "You'll never be ready, and I'm not standing here freezing my bollocks off for one second longer, so let's move."

We finally walk through the gates of hell, and it's like I'm a little boy again. Afraid of the monsters in the walls. The shadows that would up on you in the dead of the night. The screams that would haunt your mind. Each step on a cracked, cobbled stone pathway causes a fiery panic in my chest.

All the green trees that used to surround the estate have all but gone. There is nothing left but death. Even the trees look lifeless and tortured. I didn't think it was possible that this place could look any creepier than it had, but as we walk towards the jet-black estate that looks like it's been bathed in soot, I stand corrected. I'm just waiting for the cross of death to surround us, but it doesn't happen.

The only thing that surrounds us all is the deathly silence that seems to swallow this place.

Silence.

That was one thing I had always wished for here, and now that we had it, I wasn't sure I wanted it. There was only one reason we would hear nothing.

He knew we were here.

I wasn't sure how we would gain entry into the estate.

Did we knock?

What was the etiquette for taking down your psycho brother and taking back the girl he had stolen from under your nose?

As soon as we reach the stone-cobbled steps, I see the large jet-black wrought iron door with the skull that looks at us menacingly. It was only a door knocker, but the bloody thing had given me nightmares as a child.

"Welcome back to hell." Elijah mocks.

We all just look at him. Once again, he had broken the silence with his sarcastic outburst. On any other day, we would have laughed, maybe joined in, but not today. Today was not the day to join in; today was, well, it felt like doomsday.

"So, how shall we do this?" I ask. "Shall we knock?"

Luca sneers at me. He races up the steps, holding his leg high, and brutally kicks in that door. Sawdust flies around, and a loud crash erupts around us.

"Knock?" He sneers, "Why would we knock?"

"Yes, why indeed." I roll my eyes, "when we can just kick down the door." I shake my head, "why didn't I think of that?"

"Exactly," River rubs his hands.

"This is going to be fun." Elijah smiles as he enters the hell house.

Fun? Oh yes, most people went dancing, to the movies or something to that effect, but us? Oh, it appeared we had fun by going to war. Who needed smiles and relaxation when blood, destruction and death were to be had?

I can hear the dogs before I even enter; if that door-shattering kick hasn't alerted him, those damn dogs have, but other than the angry growls that come from upstairs, I still hear nothing. Nothing but the sound of our footsteps as we walk into the estate.

I look at my brothers, and I smirk.

"Hey, honey, I'm home," I shout into the deserted, desolate house from hell.

The days leading up to this point had been harrowing. Bile rose up my throat every time he touched me, and it took every ounce of willpower to swallow it down. After everything, I was still here, and now I had to pretend that I enjoyed his touch. It had worked, I couldn't believe it had worked, but somebody was about to foil my plan, and she was pissed.

The moment those words fall from her vicious lips, my world collides. I had been haunted by the memory of Carter since the day I had finally been freed from

480

his control. Still, he had taken a permanent residence in my brain.

The ghosts of our past never leave us. We just get used to them taking up space within ourselves until we are finally ready to let them go.

No matter what I did, it seemed the ghosts of my past would never let me go.

My lips tremble as I look into her eyes, "Carter was your brother?"

"Yes, funny how small your world is, isn't it, Cara."

"Please let me go."

"Now, why would you think I want to do that." She walked towards me slowly but with conviction. "You see, I have wanted to meet you for a long time."

"Why?" I whisper.

"I wanted to meet the girl who decided she would take everything from me." I shake my head. "So you didn't murder my brother, then flit off into the sunset and restart your life somewhere new?"

"No, I didn't—I never touched him." I stutter.

"I never said you did." She smirks.

"You said—."

"That you murdered him?" I nod. "Well, yes, there are plenty of ways to kill someone. You may not have pulled the trigger, but you were the mastermind behind when that trigger got pulled."

"Please, Essie," I beg once more.

"Didn't my brother once beg you, and your actions caused his death? Why do you think I would show you kindness where you showed him none." She screams in my face.

"That's not true," I cry as tears fall. "If I hadn't left, he would have killed me."

"That's just not true." She shakes her head at me. "He loved you."

"He didn't know how to love anyone," I utter.

Her eyes blaze with fiery anger, and that's when I feel the first sting of her palm against my face. She doesn't stop the hits across my face until my head crashes against the wall, and my body slumps further into the ground.

She crouched down to look at me. "My brother died alone and in pain. You broke his heart and his spirit before he left this world. Everything you have endured here still won't make up for what you have taken from me."

"I'm sorry," I sob. "I didn't have a choice."

"Get up." She screams while taking a fist of my hair and dragging my body from the ground. My legs wobble as I'm placed back on my feet. "There is always a choice, Cara; you just chose wrong."

"He would have killed me," I scream.

"I wish he had; then, he would still be here at least."

"Essie, I'm sorry,"

"It's too late for that now."

"So, you're going to kill me?" I ask.

My body is thrown into the seat she was sitting on before Caleb raced from the room; the pain moves through my body at the brutal impact of being thrown so roughly.

"That was the plan, but like I told you earlier. Plans change. You get to live another day. For now." I look up at her, hoping she can see the thank you in my eyes. "Well, that is. If they find you on time."

"I don't understand."

"Don't worry. You will."

I can feel her tightly grab my arms behind my back. The tight roughness of the rope hits my skin as she binds my hands. "Why did you call them?" She pulls the ropes tighter, and a painful sigh crawls from my throat. "If you want me dead, why did you call them?"

She moves to face me, crouching down in front of me. She pushes my legs together, binding my feet like she had tied my hands. "Essie?" Once more, she pulls them tighter until the pain from my ankles shoots up my legs.

"I wanted Caleb dead more." She finally answers.

"Why?"

The rope is wrapped around my waist and bound to the back of the chair. She was meticulously mummifying my body to the chair. It made it impossible for anyone to free me from the binds she had encased me.

"I'm not sure." She smiles. "I watched him playing house with you this morning, and I thought today is a good day for you to die."

"Why didn't you just kill him yourself?"

"I could have."She studies her nails. "But I knew Luca would get more satisfaction committing the deed himself."

"Luca is here." I gasp.

"They all are."She smirks.

The stark realisation that they were here had hope bursting through my veins. I never thought I would see them again, but they were here under the same roof. They were here.

I'm about to smile, but the slight smile quickly fades when I see the red canister in her hands. "Essie, what are you doing?"

She flicks the can down, and I can smell the gas as soon as it hits the ground; it follows her around the room wherever she walks. "Essie, you don't have to do this." I plead.

She hums a strange song as she continues to pour gasoline over every corner of the room. The bitch was going to burn me alive. I didn't deserve this. I didn't deserve any of this. Tears fall down my face, and the hope I had moments ago soon slips away.

She's standing by the doorway with a smile on her face. "I said you'd live another day if they reach you in time. Not that I would make it easy for you."

"Help. Help. Help." I started screaming at the top of my lungs.

"Oh, darling, I would save your breath. You're going to need it." She smiles. I see the brilliant golden flame burst through the lighter as she presses her finger down and throws it to the ground.

I can see her silhouette and hear the faint clack of her heels as she walks away from me. The flames engulf the room, and heat spreads closer to my body.

I was close.

I was so close to leaving, but instead, I would burn in a place that had felt like hell.

How poetic, I think as I roll my eyes.

I feel the smoke fill my lungs before my eyes close, and finally, I give in to my fate.

Dying alone.

Just as he had.

When fates collide. That's where your story ends.

In tragedy.

As soon as we walk into this shit hole, I'm ready. I'm prepared for him, but he's nowhere in sight.

"Go find Cara," I instructed River and Elijah.

"She would want to see you," River argues.

"She will, but I must deal with this prick first." He just stands there looking at me. "Go now," I scream more forcefully. They both give me a nod and head down the corridor.

"Now what?" Jax asks.

"Oh, he's coming. Caleb likes to play games." I knew only too well the kind of games he liked to play. Hadn't we already played this one in the forest, but this time, he wouldn't be walking away.

The theatrical music starts playing, and it sounds like some ominous scene about to unfold at the opera. Caleb sure did know how to put on a show. I roll my eyes as I look up at the ceiling, trying to distinguish where the sound is coming from.

"Is he trying to serenade us?" Jax smirks.

"No," I grit back. "He's fucking playing with us."

We don't move. I know he's watching. If he learned anything from that bastard we called a father, it was that you should always play with your food before you eat it, and that's precisely what he was doing—playing with us.

"I don't want to fight." He calls out.

"You should have thought about that before you took her," I scream.

"Where is he?" Jax whispers in my ear.

"Oh, he's close brother. Don't be fooled."

"Luca, that's why you're here?" He asks.

"No, Caleb, I thought we could sit down and talk about old times. Of course, that's why I'm fucking here." He was starting to piss me off with his moronic questions.

"You're here to take her from me?" He asks sullenly.

"Is he joking right now?" Jax frowns.

That was the question of all questions. Was he joking? It didn't sound like a joke, yet he had said it with such sadness. He was a psycho, the exact image of our father in every way. He didn't feel. At least not in the true sense, and yet, I wasn't going to get sucked into his game. Not again.

I hear his footsteps before I even see him. We both stand there, just staring at him. I was correct; there was no look of hurt on his smug face. He didn't want a fight? Yeah, that would explain the bat he had wielding in his hands.

"I thought you didn't want a fight," I smirk.

He spins the bat in his hands, never taking his eyes off of us. "Oh, this old thing." He smiles. "This is just a protection clause."

"A protection clause?" Jax raises a brow.

"Well, by my calculations, there are two of you and only one of me." He looks around the area. "But there seems to be two missing; where are the other two." He waves the bat towards us.

"This isn't a family reunion, Caleb." I grit.

"Naughty, naughty. You didn't answer my question."

"River and Elijah wanted to sit this one out." Jax offers.

"Really?" His brows raise with accusation. "Elijah, the thrill seeker, wanted no part of my demise."

"That's right." Jax States.

"That would be more believable if I didn't have something you all wanted. They will have to walk through here with her, and I can promise you this. None of you will make it to that door. Alive."

He takes a step towards us. "Unless,"

"Unless what?" Jax asks.

"Unless you all leave right now."

"Great, we will just get Cara and go." Jax proudly announces.

"I said you could leave. I never said anything about my little doll going with you. She stays here."

Doll? I want to break his fucking neck. I can feel the tension ticking away in my jaw. Every moment I spend here looking at him, the rage seeps through me, and all I can think of is breaking his body and finally ending his tirade.

"Do we have a deal?" He smiles.

"No," I growl back. "No deal."

"Perfect," he smirks. "I was hoping you'd say that."

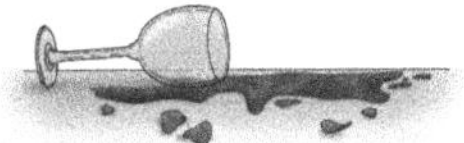

The sound of the dogs hit us. Of course, Caleb wouldn't fight fair and how poetic he had chosen the same breed our father had. If there was one thing I hated growing up here more than the bloody screams, it was the constant barking from the mutts day and night.

"Call off your mutts, Caleb."

"Afraid I can't do that." He smirks.

"Jax, you know what to do."

Caleb rubs his hands together. "Oh, this should be good. Jax going to play herd the dogs again." He calls out while rolling his eyes.

Jax takes off at a speed, the dogs following behind him. Opening the first door, the dog runs in, and Jax proudly comes out, closing the door and barricading the dog inside. It was our favourite game when we were kids, and Jax always won.

"One down, two to go," I smirk.

"Ah, yes, but then what will you do? You didn't think the dogs were a threat tactic, did you?"

"Everything is a threat tactic with you, Caleb."

"Oh, on the contrary, this is just entertainment before the main event." A small laugh falls from his lips.

Once again, Jax rounds the dogs up, taking them on a merry-go-round, dodging and sliding to confuse them about which way he will go next. He quickly opens another door, once again barricading the mutt in the room. Leaving it barking and scratching at the door, begging to be let out.

The last one.

When we came here, it was very calm. I knew it was too quiet. Caleb wasn't even threatening. His ease gave me a slick sliver of unease. He looked and acted too calm. When we walked through these doors. I wasn't sure what I expected, but it wasn't this theatrical show.

A patient Wolf is just an angry Wolf.

Waiting to take its first bite.

Don't be fooled by the calmness of an ocean's waters because, at any moment, it could rip through and destroy everything in sight.

I couldn't have predicted or prepared for what would happen next, but it seemed Jax had. I wasn't sure why he had gotten that last damn dog to chase him.

"It appears you are out of doors, but you knew that already," Caleb calls out to Jax.

"Who said I wanted a door." Jax mocks.

That dog is getting closer and closer, and the fear crawls up my spine. Jax crouches down, staring that dog in the eyes as it snarls with the venomous need to destroy its target in front of it.

"Jax," I shout.

"Not yet."

"Jax," I call once more.

"Nearly there." He smirks.

"As entertaining as this is. Bruiser will rip your head off once he gets close. I would start running if I were you." Caleb warns.

"Bruiser?" I roll my eyes. "Of course, you'd name your dog something as pretentious as Bruiser."

The dog edges closer and closer to Jax. The closer he gets, the harder my heart pounds inside my chest. A Sheen of sweat forms on my brow, but Jax stays still, never breaking eye contact with that mutt. Taunting it to go closer.

The dog pounds on top of Jax, its teeth merely inches from his neck as he wrestles that dog to the ground. Reaching down, I see the glistening blade he pulls from his foot. Shimmering in the dimly lit corridor.

The dog edges closer, and its snarly teeth finally bite down on his arm. Blood seeped from the white shirt covering his arms.

Jax barely cries out, and in one swift movement, he slices that blade across the dog's throat. A small whimper falls from its throat, and Jax throws the dog on the ground like it's made of nothing.

Then there is nothing.

Nothing but silence.

The dog lay motionless on the ground in a puddle of blood. The eyes were glassy, open and lifeless. No longer a threat. It is finally silent. The only noise that can be heard is Jax panting from his fight with the dog.

A moment passes when a loud roar comes from where Caleb is standing. His eyes blaze with fiery anger as he looks down at his beloved dog that Jax just obliterated. The calmness surrounding him is gone, and all that is left is the monster.

His movements are fast. The bat falls to the ground with a clash. His face twists as he reaches his hand behind until I'm staring into the barrel of the AK47 that he holds firmly in his hands.

"Where the fuck did he get that from?" Jax gasps.

"Fucked if I know," I mutter.

I thought the scariest threat he had was those damn dogs and that bat he'd wielded in his hands, but once again, he had fooled me. How had we not noticed the gun that lay beside his feet?

"Didn't anyone ever tell you, Caleb, you don't bring a gun to a knife fight?"

"You were the only one with a knife, jackass." He grits.

"You didn't really expect us to come here unarmed. You set three dogs on us when we arrived while swinging around a bat." Jax spits back.

"You killed my fucking dog." He screams like it's new news to us all.

"Yes, well, that's unfortunate—."

I hear the click as he readies the gun, quickly turning and pointing it straight at Jax. I can't even comprehend what's going to happen next. It takes a lot to take a life, but to take the life of your brother...you are never coming back from that.

"Put the gun down, Caleb." I try to reason with him. He doesn't even blink; it's like I haven't even said anything. He just looks through Jax like he is his mortal enemy.

"I said put the gun down," I scream.

"A life for a life." He utters before pulling the trigger.

Quickly jumping in front of Jax and shielding his body from the bullet flying towards us both. I see everything in slow motion, but I don't even think when I knock Jax behind me.

The bullet skirts faster towards me. Nobody says a word; the pain hits my body instantly, and I can feel the slick, warm liquid and smell the coppery scent of my own blood as it fills the air.

The only sound I hear is the loud crash of the bullet as it hits the ground.

My body shakes, and I fall to the ground.

"Luca," I hear Jax scream.

"Luca, don't you dare fucking die on me, you big psycho bastard."

My brother's arms spread warmly around me as I'm cocooned in his embrace.

"Stay with me. Don't go to sleep. Stay with me." He whispers, but I can only focus on the pain that runs through my body.

It always comes down to the love of a woman. Men have fought wars over women; if I had to do it all again, I would do nothing different. Meeting her gave me a new life. If I had to do it all again, I would change nothing.

You have to find the one worth suffering for. The one you would die for, and for her, I would die.

There is nothing but silence now.

My eyes gently close, and I feel nothing but peace.

The walk through the house was a solemn one. On edge, I'm unsure what I will find here. We each had our own thoughts about Oak Haven, but the same idea I knew we all had was we didn't want to be here.

My confidence was slipping with each step towards the rising smoke that seemed to bathe this side of the house in a fog of black smoke. I hear River coughing at the side of them, and then the smell of burning clouds my senses.

Shit.

"You said she would be okay." River gasps as we get closer to the heat surrounding us.

"We don't know that she's even in there."

"Don't be naive, Elijah, she's in there."

I put my hand on the door handle, and searing heat grazes my skin, forcing me to remove my hand from that handle. Placing my hand on the door's wood, I can feel the heat beneath my hand.

The door is old, it's probably been here since this goddamn house was built. Lifting my leg to the door, I thrust it, but it barely budged. Once more, I kick against the door and hear it rattle.

"Little help would be nice." I roll my eyes at my brother.

He buffs as he raises his leg and hits the door that doesn't seem to want to open. I press my foot against the door and join him. The loud crash of our feet banging against the door is the only sound I hear. Warmth hits my face.

"Keep going; it's weakening," I shout over the crashing of our feet against the door.

"This isn't working." River shouts back.

One more crash against the door, and it flies open. Heat attacks my face, and we both jump back. I expected to see the entire room engulfed in flames, but the fire had only hit one side. Thick black smoke swarms around the room like a demonic presence searching for a host.

"You were saying," I smirk.

My gloating party doesn't last long because I finally see her as my eyes scan the room. Bound to a chair in the middle of the room, slumped over with her eyes closed. She had lost weight and looked more fragile than I had seen her. As I peer at her, even like this, she takes my breath away.

Charging into the room, the heat rushes across me, but that doesn't deter me from racing towards her. The only thing that slows me down is the smoke that spirals around my body, gripping hold of me and trying to strangle any and all air I have left in my body.

We finally reach her in a coughing and sputtering mess. The smoke stings my eyes, and my vision is distorted, but once I touch her warm skin, I'm reminded of why I'm even here.

Nothing else matters. Just her.

"Darling," I call out to her, but she doesn't respond.

The pain instantly attacks my chest. We didn't come all this way to find her like this, not to find out we were too late. She had to pull through because I couldn't even think what would happen if she didn't.

River starts trying to unbind her feet while choking in the process. I've already released the rope from her tiny waist. Moving behind her, I fumble, trying to remove her bound hands. The roles were wrapped tight. The tension in my body crawls through me as I struggle to free her.

"Here," River throws a red and black pocket knife towards me; quickly reaching up, I catch it in my hands.

Flicking the blade open, the silver blade opens in all its glory; hacking at the binds, they start to loosen, but that wasn't what worried me. The binds that were taking too long to get through weren't concerning. That she had said nothing and hadn't moved once was concerning.

Finally, her hands are released, and I look at her bruised and sore wrists. The anger courses through me. Her marked little skin gives me hope. Pressing my thumbs against her wrist and slowly rubbing, hoping that the marks leave her skin, I feel it.

Thump, thump, thump.

The faint feeling of her heart slowly beating beneath my touch, and then, in the darkness, there was hope.

Picking her up, I hold her in my arms and race out of the room with River running closely behind me. We rush out of that relief that crosses my body as I feel the ship of air moves across my face. Finally, away from the heat, smoke-infested room that had moments ago clouded my thoughts.

Laying her flat on the ground, my mouth covers hers as I try to breathe new life into her. One breath. Two breaths. Three and pause. Nothing.

One breath.

Two breaths.

Three.

And pause.

"It's not working." River huffs.

"Thank you, Captain Obvious. Put your hands together and press her chest between my breaths, okay?" He just nods.

One breath.

Compressing her chest.

Wait.

Two breaths.

Compressing her chest.

Wait.

Three breaths.

He is about to press against her chest once more when I see something. A wheezing noise falls around us. "Wait." I hold my hands up and hear her coughing and sputtering. Quickly turning her into her side, I breathe a sigh of relief.

"Welcome back, darling," I whisper in her ear.

Her beautiful eyes shoot open, and it's the most beautiful thing I've seen in months. She just gapes at me like I'm not real. The glassy look in her eyes doesn't hold the happiness I thought I would see, there is just sadness, and it feels like I've been sucker punched straight to the heart.

"Am I dead?" She croaks. I shook my head, almost, but thankfully, I could say she was still there. "Elijah," She gasps as if she's finally seeing me for the first time.

"Hello, darling." I smile as if I'm also seeing her for the first time.

"Princess," River cries. "We thought we had lost you."

"Me too." She smiles, and I see a tiny little tear make its way out of the corner of her eye and fall down her blackened, soot-covered face. "You came back for me." She croaked out.

"Of course we did, darling; you are our girl." I reached out, stroking her face, and the coldness sweeping across my body disappeared.

Something as simple as her smile and warmth spreads to my heart.

Finally, I found you.

I'm pretty pleased with myself when I walk away, knowing that soon, the flames of retribution will swallow her, and I will finally get the Justice I deserve. That she will have paid for what she did to him.

Skipping up the stairs, I leave a trail of gasoline wherever I walk. The end had to go with a bang. We didn't have fireworks, but this would be a show none would forget—if they even lived to remember what happened here today.

The thought of them all burning filled me with glee. I would have spared Caleb; that boy had so much potential. We could have been good partners, but he had to ruin it. Fall for her like the rest of his idiotic brothers.

What did she have a magic pussy.

How disappointing.

As I walk from room to room, I hum, spreading the gasoline through this wretched house. I couldn't wait to watch it burn. I could almost smell the scent of burning flesh already as their bodies crumble with this house.

How delicious.

The strong scent of gasoline surrounds my body, and I just want to bathe in it. Is there anything sweeter? It smells like karma, and as the aroma hits my veins, the crawls of pleasure pulse through my body.

A gunshot can be heard.

Oh, how interesting.

My feet move faster to where I can hear the commotion; Caleb still holds the gun in his hands, and I would think he would slink back at having shot his brother, but he doesn't.

He seems annoyed; why?

I watch as Caleb stalks towards Luca, lying on the floor. He's not moving. A slip of smile crawls across my face.

It appears he's killed the giant beast. Huh, didn't think he had it in him. Good boy.

"You're going to pay for this." Jax stands, but Caleb doesn't seem to cower like I had expected him to. He smirks at his brother and raises his arm with the gun still in his hand. He harshly clips it against his head, and Jax falls like his brother.

Pushing my hands together, I start clapping. I see him stiffen, and he slowly turns, looking towards me as I beam down at him.

"Enjoying the show?" He smirks.

"Oh, it's more entertaining than that nauseating show you made me watch. I must say, Caleb, nothing surprises me, but you have."

"I'm so happy I have your approval." He raises a brow.

"Unfortunately, you seem to have miscalculated your victory, brother," Luca growls from behind him.

"You're alive," Caleb gasps.

I watch as the gun slips from his fingers, slowly crashing. The look on his face is sheer terror; slowly turning, he faces his brother. Neither one of them says anything. They look at each other, probably hedging bets on who will make the first move.

Well, this party just got slightly more exciting, and to think I was going to leave—I would have missed all this family drama, I think, with a smile.

"This ends now." Luca finally speaks.

Ah, I would have lost. I was so sure it would be Caleb who broke the silence.

"Ah, come on, Luca, you know, even if you, by some miracle, manage to kill me. It will never be over." He stares back at him. "I will always be with you." He smiles, tapping Luca's forehead. "Living rent-free, right here."

"You think you hold that much power. Caleb, you always were an egotistical fuck." Luca laughs.

Caleb circles his brother, not speaking, just smiling. Sauntering around his body, leaning down, I see his head dip against his ear. "If I don't haunt you. I will definitely haunt her." Luca tenses. "She was delicious, screamed for you. How disappointed she must have felt when she learned the amazing Luca wasn't coming to save her."

I watch the pain flash across Luca's face before it is replaced with searing anger. "Each time I fucked her. She begged. Begged for death, but I wanted her to feel the loss of never seeing—." His words get lost on his lips.

Luca has him by the throat as he slams his body into the wall. Gasping for breath, Caleb fights to be released from his brother's tight grip. Luca raises his body and slams him to the ground, quickly clambering on top of him.

"You know, Caleb, you always did talk too much." He grits as he forces open his mouth, gripping his wet, slimy tongue and taking a knife from the inside of his jacket. He flips it open, showing a sharp silver blade. In one swift movement, he slices the blade across his tongue.

He holds the tongue between his fingers and watches as the blood pools from his brother's mouth. He raises his head, looking up at me, and I slink back. The look in his eyes causes me to freeze in fear. He pushes that tongue back into his throat and wraps his hand across his mouth.

Caleb struggles to breathe; sharp gasps emit from his throat. Luca releases his hand, and he sharply gasps. "You didn't think your death would be so easy, did you?" Caleb looks through his brother. "I want to watch you fucking suffer, and then I want you to look into my eyes as you take your last breath, knowing I feel nothing. Your death will be my release."

"Don't you think this is a tad melodramatic?" I call down the stairs.

"Oh, don't worry, sweetheart, you are next." He growls back.

Next? Had he lost his goddamn mind? I wasn't next; if he thought I would be here long enough for him to submit me to the same fate as Caleb, he really hadn't been paying attention.

I wanted to retort with my usual sarcastic response, but how he looked at me led me to believe he wasn't bluffing, unlike Caleb. That he meant every word he said, which was even more reason for me to finish the job and get the fuck out of there.

I watch as his fist connects with Caleb's face. Blood just pools around his body; if it wasn't for the slow gasps he struggled to emit, I would think he was already dead. Still, he was just holding on, taking every ounce of pain that Luca bestowed.

His knife flashed wounds to his chest. The pain must have been torturous, but without his tongue, barely a sound passed his lips. That was unfortunate; I did love to hear them screaming.

The crimson blood covered his body, swirling around him on the floor like a piece of art yet to be displayed. Caleb looks up at his brother and smiles. Luca brings the knife to his throat and slices across his exposed neck. Finally, giving him the death he had always wanted.

I expected to see remorse across his face as he looked down at his brother, but nothing. Nothing but relief. I guess I wasn't the only one looking for vengeance and redemption. He had his peace, and it wouldn't be long before I got mine.

Slowly, I descend the staircase, hoping he is too enthralled with the spilt blood and the dead body he still sits upon to notice that I'm edging closer to him, but no such luck.

I walk past him, but I'm just not fast enough. His bloody hand is around my throat within moments. "Where is she?" He growls in my ear.

"Somewhere hot," I smirk.

"Don't play these games. I will have no trouble slicing this pretty little neck of yours. Now, where is she." He screams louder this time.

A scuffling can be heard, and a groan falls from my lips as I see two of them holding her up and walking towards us. Her head is dipped low, and I'm about to smile until I see her raise her head and smile.

God, why won't she just die?

He finally releases me. I was just a blip on his radar now. He had what he wanted in his sights. I was not even here, or I might not have been. He races towards her, and I want to throw up in my own mouth.

I don't hear what he says as he lifts her into his arms. Walking past them, none of them even notice me. I'm like a ghost just passing through. I shake my head.

What people do for love?

Moronic.

I'm close to the back of the house when I turn and look at them all fussing over the girl that they have murdered for. Jax finally groans and gets to his feet. Oh, how sweet, I roll my eyes.

I detest a happy ending.

"Hey, Luca, I told you she was somewhere hot," I smirk.

They all turn and look back at me as I hold the silver lighter in my palm, flicking it on and off, taunting them until I allow the blue flame to dance within my fingers. Throwing the lighter to the ground, I smile.

"Couples that burn together stay together." I smile.

The flames move across the house at a speed I had not predicted. The heat crawls across my body as I walk away, leaving them with only the sound of the laughter that rips from my throat.

Suppose they thought of me as mad.

Madness is subjective. Who is to say what is mad and what is normal? , For my madness could also be described as passion. That could be it. Nobody was mad; we had different passion strokes, and they could all burn in mine.

Walking out of the back door, I finally feel the breeze on my face. It whips at me, bringing me back to reality. The flames danced through every corner of the darkened house that housed many delicious horrors.

I wondered if anyone would remember the legacy that had stood here once. It was nothing but soot and ash. Probably not; legends aren't made. They are born. Out of the ashes rises something new.

Turning away from the flames of a legacy, I walk away. Knowing that even though I had not felt retribution today. One day, I would.

One day, she would pay.

One day, they all would.

But for now, a legacy was born.

Caleb may be gone, but the legacy he left behind would live on.

I never thought I would see them again.

When I sat in that chair, the flames slowly burned through the house's old wood that I couldn't escape. I had accepted my fate. It was what I had prayed for every night, and she was giving me what I had wanted all along, but it was funny; death was never what I had wanted.

It was the only way out.

Then they found me.

They had returned for me, and I could barely contain the warmth and love that spread through my chest, trying to burst open.

They had come back.

Then she reappeared, and all my hopes about leaving there alive with the only people I had ever loved were quickly dashed. I should feel warmth at being wrapped in Luca's embrace once more, but I feel nothing once I see her fling that lighter to the ground. Nothing but coldness as it creeps across my body.

I'm not even sure what's happening. My head can't process anything, and then I feel it. Something I haven't felt in a long time. Something I never thought I would feel again.

I feel free.

Luca hasn't put me down, and I don't complain. The wind whips across my face, a sign that I'm alive. That I made it. That I still exist.

That I'm still here.

He finally lets me down. Standing there, I feel him clasp his hand in mine, and it finally feels like I've come home. A sigh leaves my lips, and I feel warmth in my other hand. Looking up, I see Jax smile down at me. River and Elijah also give me a contented smile, but none of us says anything.

We just stand there and watch the fierce flames take the house and demolish everything inside it. The flames dance across the house as it slowly crumbles and falls into a blackened heap of soot and ash.

The nightmare may be over, and this house may no longer stand, but like all things, the memory of this house and the horrors it held for all of us would last a lifetime.

Freedom has a price to pay.

Nobody is ever free; we may escape the horrors that have inflicted our souls, but you are never free; some experiences stain your soul forever, and while the event may disappear, the memory never does.

This had been their horror. The pain they have lived with and even been subjected to. We shared a common horror and weren't leaving until it burned.

Night fell, and we stood there looking at the ash pile before us.

"Are you ready?" Jax asks.

Looking up at him with a confused look, "For what?" I whisper.

"To go home, kitten, unless you want us to take you to your apartment?"

"I—."

"We can never apologise enough for what happened to you here. We just want you to be happy."

"Then don't say silly things like do I want to go somewhere you won't be." His arms encircle me, and I melt into his touch, his lips pressing against my hair. "You don't know how happy that makes me."

"There is nowhere else I would rather be." I smile.

I didn't know what the future held. Still, as I walked away from the destroyed estate that had haunted all the Kane brothers, I knew that as long as I had them, the future no longer mattered because I was free. Now, a future was a possibility.

Home wasn't a place.

Home was this.

Home was with them.

Home was a feeling; I had found my home when they crashed into my life. They had shown me things I had never thought possible, and I wasn't letting that go for anything because when you find your heart, you hold onto it as tightly as you can.

So, maybe it wasn't a conventional relationship. Perhaps it wasn't what would be considered normal, but only when I lost it did I realise there was no place I would rather be on this earth.

That being with them, there was nothing I had ever wanted more.

I had nearly died for this feeling, and if I looked back through every traumatic event that led me back into their arms, I would do it all again if it meant I could be right here. In this moment with them because as they told me.

I was their girl.

And they were mine.

"Yes, let's go home."

I smile, secretly knowing I was already there.

HUNGRY FOR MORE?

**Before the Kane brothers there was Carter King
Pre-order the other lover
Only available at Amazon**

**Looking for something a little darker?
Well, you don't want to miss Capturing Ava
coming December 2023
Only available at Amazon**

About the Author

Calia Quinn is a romance writer from the united kingdom.

Calia's Debut resisting Jax is set to release October 2023

Calia creates stories with sassy heroines and morally grey men, with a mixture of steamy and humorous moments between her characters.

Calia has always had a love for the darkness.

In the dark, there is a beauty which is why the dark element in her tropes is present.

Calia's favourite romance has always been dark romance.

Who doesn't love a morally grey anti-hero?

When Calia is not writing, you will find her reading a mixture of tropes but almost always these involve romance because who doesn't love a happy ending?

You can find the author:

𝗮 amazon.co.uk/Calia-Quinn/e/B0BZ3YS1XN/ref=aufs_dp_fta_an_dsk

♪ tiktok.com/@caliaquinnauthor

𝐟 facebook.com/caliaquinn

instagram.com/caliaquinnauthor

g goodreads.com/author/show/29969021.Calia_Quinn

You can visit the author's website:

https://www.caliaquinn.com